£3·50

SUNSHINE
SOUP

NOURISHING THE GLOBAL SOUL

Jo Parfitt

To every Maya, Barb, Sue, Elske, Leila, Liv and, of course, Annie — you make my world go round.

Acknowledgements

So many people were more helpful than they realise in the writing of this book.

I give thanks to Annie Burgh and The Piglets (Lorna, Pippa, Janie, Diane, Mary-Jon, Debbie, Eileen, Jo and Jenny) who were there at the beginning of this book in 2007.

And to Apple Gidley, Christine Yates, Jae de Wylde and Laura Stephens who read the first complete manuscript and were both honest and gentle with me.

And to Mary Farmer, Asian expert, who helped me with the Thailand connection.

To Deborah Valentine, who devised the subtitle and my editor, Megan Kerr, who gave me a dose of my own medicine and was frighteningly, magnificently, frank. Thank you for insisting that I add the recipes, so desperate had I made you to get into the kitchen.

To my Hague Writers' Circle (Carolyn, Kathy, Fanny, Niamh, Paulina, Tracey, Eva, Melinda, Barbara, Julie, Cecilia and Kim) who have constantly cared enough to share their thoughts.

And to Niamh Ni Bhroin, Eva Lazlò-Herbert and Jae de Wylde (again) who read the version you now hold in your hands, 30,000 fewer words later – and thankfully, loved it!

Chapter one

The scrape of Rich's key turning in the front door echoed down the empty hallway. Maya sat in the bare kitchen on a plastic chair at the table that normally belonged in the garden. She set her mug of Merlot down in front of her and listened to the wrought iron latch clatter up then down. Then the familiar slide of his flight bag across the flagstones and into the place where the hall table used to be and the slop and tap of his shoes as he slipped them off, stepping first on one heel then the other. It would be the last time he would come in through that door.

'That's that then!' he said, first planting a kiss on his wife's cheek before lifting a chair out for himself and sinking into it.

'Okay?'

Rich ran his hands over his face and yawned. 'Fine. Fun. I think I'll enjoy flying her. Bit of a shame to be stuck in a simulator and missing the sunshine, but there'll be plenty more of that where we're going, eh?' He reached across the table to lay his hand on her arm. 'How was your last day?' Rich always asked how her day had been. It was one of the things she loved about him.

'I finally reached the end of the to-do list, put in a full day at work, drove the kids to my parents… '

Rich looked confused.

'They have no beds, remember?'

He nodded. Then he looked at her quizzically and Maya knew exactly what he was thinking.

'Jan lent us a lilo and a duvet.'

He relaxed.

'… and dropped the keys and the inventory off at the agents. So I think we're set,' she said, her voice flat.

'What's for supper? You okay?'

Maya suppressed the thought that perhaps, today of all days, he would not have expected her to cook. 'Jan's take-out of the week. My special squash goulash.' She paused to look at him. 'And am I okay?' She pushed her lips together thoughtfully. 'I'm not sure. Actually, now that the adrenalin's stopped, I think I may be having a bit of a wobble.' Voicing her thoughts made them real and a knot of sorrow rose in her throat. 'But hey, at least we have wine.' She forced a smile, poured a healthy slug of Merlot into a second mug.

'Cheers. To us. To our new life!' His chirpy voice echoed in the almost empty room. 'New?' He looked at his mug and turned it in his hand.

'Leaving present from Avril.'

'Ah.' He set his mug back on the table. 'Nice.'

'From that new pottery. They say Stamford on them.'

'I saw.'

Maya looked up into his eyes, knowing her own were growing glassy with tears.

'Look on the bright side. We are about to leave this doll-sized cottage and lack of summer, and swap it for glitz, glamour, streets paved with gold, and a big new four-wheel drive. I've been thinking about a Range Rover. What do you think?' His blue eyes were glittery and wide, like a child's.

'I love this cottage.' She leaned across the table to stroke the petals of the white rose she had picked from the garden and placed in a milk bottle. Their last milk bottle. The lump that was rising towards her throat caused her bottom lip to tremble. She closed her eyes and took a deep breath. Crying had not been on her list. She was happy to be moving. After all, it was her idea.

'I love it too. I'll miss it too.' He inched his plastic chair clumsily closer to hers, its weak feet dragging on the flagstones, and placed his arm round her shoulders where it rested against her neck. The bubble of emotion lurched in her chest. 'We can't pull out now. The container will have already left Harwich.'

Maya took a deep breath and steadied her voice. 'That isn't what I meant, silly.' She reached for the kitchen roll, tore off a square, and crushed it into her palm. 'It's just been a bit of a sad day. Let me tell you about it.' She looked up at him. 'Get it off my chest. Then I'll be back to normal. This is not a crisis!'

Rich poured them both more wine. 'I'm listening.' He still looked worried. Worried about her.

'I do want to go. Honest. I just don't like leaving. Today I had to say goodbye to Avril and Jan. They are not just my business partners, they're my soulmates. I'll miss them, that's all. Saying goodbye is shit, Rich. I won't know anyone in Dubai and I'm scared.' She put her hand over his to stop his fingers tapping the tabletop.

She looked at the windowsill where she had grown her herbs, at the solid wood shelves they had had made to fit, the old red Aga, squeezed into the space where the range had been, the practical yet outdated pantry. The Blu-tak marks on the back of the door where they had displayed Oliver and Matthew's paintings.

Rich eased his hand out from under hers then pushed his hair backwards over his crown, using both hands, one of the habits that had attracted her to him almost twenty years earlier. Now, his pale brown hair was greying above his ears.

'We can come back if it doesn't work out, eh? And hey, at least you don't have to wear a facemask in Dubai. And you can drive a car.'

All she wanted was for him to nod and agree with her rather than try to make her laugh. She scraped her hair into a ponytail then twisted it into a coil and held it close to her head for a moment before letting it fall.

'And you've got that cooking blog to do, haven't you? Seasons in the Sun, you're calling it, right? See, I was listening!' Rich continued, still trying to come up with solutions. 'That'll keep you in touch with Av and Jan. And you'll make new friends. If I know you, you'll be running some other deli in no time, getting involved. You can't help yourself.'

'You think so?' Maya stared out of the window, fixing her eyes on the soft golden stone that encircled the small courtyard.

'I'll be your friend. We're mates, aren't we? You, me, Oli, Matt. We are a team.'

Maya grinned. He was so right. She took the goulash out of the carrier bag and placed the take-out box in the microwave.

'Can I lay the table?' Rich looked around for plates and cutlery.

'We'll eat it out of the box.' She fished around in the plastic bag. 'Here, I got two plastic forks from work.' Maya took the bag and folded it over and over on itself until it became a small square.

'It's what you always wanted. What we wanted,' he said.

'And you're right. I will want a job. Once we're settled in.'

'Oh, you never know. You might develop a sunbathing habit, or an addiction to coffee mornings!'

'Oh, I don't think I'm cut out to be a lady of leisure,' she told the microwave, then turned back to the table and set down the box of goulash. Rick picked up his fork.

'Got any yoghurt?'

Maya raised her eyebrows. The fridge, in case he'd forgotten, was bare as a baby's bottom.

'D'you think they sell camels' yoghurt in Dubai?'

Maya chuckled. 'Well, if they do, you can be sure I'll write a recipe for it.'

'Early night?' Maya suggested. 'Taxi's for six, right?'

Rich rose from the table. 'I need a shower. We still have towels?'

'We do. Mum's fetching all the leftover stuff before the tenants come.'

'I'll go on up, then.'

Maya was alone in the kitchen.

'I'll just put this last milk bottle out.' She laid the rose down on the table, tipped the water down the sink and took her makeshift vase towards the front door.

She set the bottle on the stone pavement and turned the dial she kept beside it that told the milkman how many pints she wanted. Zero. Placing her flattened palm against the panelling on her front door, she stroked a split vein of paintwork with her fingers. No doubt the tenants would soon be nagging them to repaint it. She leaned her forehead against the glass in the window and caressed the mullion, noticing how broken her nails had become.

'I'm sorry,' she whispered. The pane was cool despite the late August sun. She'd never studied the butter-coloured stone that closely before. How porous it looked, pitted like skin.

Maya looked up the hill of St Peter's Street, where they'd lived since Rich left the RAF. Shoulder to shoulder, the stone cottages stood like jostling children in a school photograph, each sagging and crumpled, finding it impossible to stand up straight. She never tired of that view. It had been there for several hundred years and would still be there when they got back.

She shifted her gaze in the opposite direction, past Red Lion Square and in the direction of the delicatessen. Her delicatessen. She'd miss Seasons more than anything. Unlike this medieval town there was no way it would be the same when they returned, if they returned. Already, Jan had hired a lovely young Polish girl, called Danuta, to fill her place. Here, in Stamford, Maya was somebody. Seasons had become part of her, like an extra limb. Now that limb had been wrenched off. The hole she had left in Seasons would soon close up behind her, while Maya's wound would take longer to heal. Writing the blog had been Av's idea. Like Rich, she was one who always found a bright side.

Chapter two

Maya reached for Rich's hand and gripped it tightly, her heart and stomach lifting as the plane dipped and swung slightly to the right. She couldn't suppress a grin of triumph. He gave her knee a quick squeeze. Rich getting a job in Dubai had been her idea. She'd found the advert and pushed it under his nose just six months earlier and now here they were. She heard Oliver and Matthew both gasp as they looked out of the window.

'Cool!' gasped Matthew.

'Mega!' muttered Oliver.

As the wheels slapped down onto the tarmac, Rich clapped his hands together.

'We made it, guys!' he said, raising his hands towards his sons in a high-five salute.

'Well, duh!' said Matthew.

'No shit, Sherlock,' volleyed his older brother, desperate to outdo him.

While everyone else stood up to ping open the overhead lockers and grab their hand luggage Maya sat and gazed at the vast expanse of airport buildings and the constant traffic of planes, catering trucks, and forklifts.

Rich reached up for their bags and led the way. The boys slung their rucksacks onto their backs and shouldered their way down the aisle. Maya rose, pushed her book in her handbag, and joined them. Mother duck following her single-file brood. Rich turned back to check she was following.

'Okay?' he mouthed.

Maya nodded.

The plane was clamped to a spanking new tunnel, connecting them to a shiny white building filled with light and perfectly modulated air conditioning. Vast windows looked down on the departure shopping area, where people bought gold and dates and mobile phones, drank Costa coffee, sat on high stools at the bar. A pair of pretend palm trees thrust upwards towards a glass ceiling. Emirati women wore black robes while the men wore white. What should have been local colour was, instead, monochrome.

Rich steered one trolley while Oliver, naturally nominated second strongest by being the eldest son, awkwardly pushed another out of the arrivals hall. Two smoked glass doors slid aside to expose their first glimpse of what would become their home. Maya felt it first. Like a hot towel slapped in the face. The air was so thick you could feel your lungs contracting. It smelled of dry ice and body odour as a sea of greeters surged forwards expectantly then slumped back in disappointment each time the doors opened and then closed without releasing their loved ones.

'Look, there's Jim!' said Rick, waving towards a largish man with a shaved head, wearing a pink open-necked shirt and cream shorts that reached his calves.

'The man from Dad's new work who's come to pick us up,' explained Maya, relieved that everything was going according to plan. They had only been outside a minute or so, and it was almost sunset, but already sweat was funnelling down her back to below the waist of her jeans. Dubai and denim made a bad marriage. She shoved her sleeves up towards her elbows and blew a thin stream of cool air down the front of her shirt.

'Welcome to Dubai,' said Jim thrusting out his hand to each member of the family in turn. 'Good flight? My motor's over here. Follow me.'

'It's like being in an oven,' said Oliver.

'Steam room, more like,' grumbled Matthew. 'Only there you get to take your clothes off. Mum, will you take my jumper?'

'Can we have one of these?' asked Oliver from the back seat of the BMW X3 that still smelled of new leather. 'It's cool.'

'And expensive!' said Rich.

'Not too many notes, Rich, actually,' said Jim. 'You'd be surprised. It's my wife, Sue's, actually. I've got an old Porsche. Petrol's cheap as chips, you know, and cars are way cheaper than back in Blighty. I used to have a lucrative deal going with my brother; he's got a second-hand showroom down Basildon way. For years we had a new motor every year then shipped it back.' He paused and looked over his shoulder to where Maya sat between her boys.

'Is that legal?' asked Rich.

Jim sucked in his cheeks and made a hissing noise. 'Nope, the local boys have put the kybosh on that little game now. Too much red tape to make it worth my while. I'll fill you in over a swift one down the Red Lion another time if you like. Tell you how to find a good deal. Don't expect the wife wants you to spend all her shopping money on motors, does she?' He turned the key in the ignition and looked over his shoulder to wink at Maya.

She was a sucker for a Cockney accent; it reminded her of her ex-boyfriend, Mick, an irresistible 'bit of rough' who sold double-glazing. She wondered whether she would have ended up in Dubai if she'd married him.

Oliver slid his hand into the pocket of his shorts to pat his mobile phone. Jim kept up a running commentary about life in this burgeoning city. He told them about the 'bleedin' traffic', the clubs, the year-round barbecues, the camel races, the new metro they were building, the Formula One, the powerboats, and the best places to get fish and chips. When Maya could get a word in, she asked about the things that mattered to her, like opening hours, the postal service, and whether she could buy organic wholemeal flour. She also wanted to know the appropriate terms for all the clothes the locals wore, the masks, the robes, the headscarves. Jim answered patiently before turning to tell Rich where to buy London Pride beer and Stella Artois lager.

They were glad of Jim's air-conditioning as they settled back in their seats and watched the changing view of a city that looked like it never stopped moving. Clutches of camels grazed on the scrubland while cranes swung back and forth above their heads and skyscrapers grew ever closer to the clouds. Maya wondered where she might find this city's soul.

A few minutes later, they were in nose-to-tail traffic crawling towards what Jim called the 'old town' and they reached a wide river lined with rows of wooden sailing boats, three deep.

'This is the Creek,' explained Jim. 'Golf club at one end, old souk at the other. Them's the real Dubai. Which would you choose, Rich? Golf or shops?'

'Golf, every time!' said Rich.

'The club's a bit posh for the likes of me, but 'er indoors, my wife, Sue, had lessons here with an ex-pro.' He turned to Maya. 'You going to try your hand at golf, love?'

'I'm not exactly known for my sporting prowess, am I, guys? So Sue's sporty is she?'

'Well, she has to do something to keep her out of mischief. She played tennis for a bit, but I know you girls all prefer lunching and spending money.'

Maya wondered whether Sue had the potential to be her friend. Judging by what she knew already, she'd not be her type at all. Probably a salt-of-the-earth peroxide blonde with a lot of gold and an orange tan.

'How come you ended up flying planes, Jim?' She had been itching to know how someone with a voice like razor blades had made it to captain a plane when cut glass was expected over the tannoy.

'I'm not a pilot, darlin',' he said. 'Haitch Are. Human Resources, or human remains as we call it. Personnel it used to be. I'm the bloke who recruited your other 'alf. The mad bastard who decided to put him up in the Burj al Arab when he came on his look-see! Gotta tempt 'em in here somehow!' Dusk approached and when they stopped in traffic again Maya noticed the sound of the call to prayer that filled the air from all directions, which emanated from the minarets of the mosques all over the city. As the sun finally set and the sky turned royal blue, the onion-shaped domes of the mosques appeared beside the minarets, lit up in neon green, pink, and purple. Lights flickered on in the streets and the pole star shone out brightly.

'No moon tonight. Shame,' said Maya. 'I love seeing the moon and the stars out together.' Mick, her ex, used to come over all soppy at twilight. He'd tell her she was the sun and the moon and the stars. She'd been a sucker for starlight ever since.

'Any day now, love,' commented Jim. 'Then it will be Ramadan, you know? No eating on the streets for a whole month.'

'Oh gosh.'

'It don't affect us, really.'

'Will the shops be open?' Oliver asked. 'I need a local sim card for my phone.'

'Oliver!' growled Rich. 'Teenagers!'

'No worries, mate. Don't mind him. Shops always open round 'ere.'

'Do you have children, Jim?' asked Maya, curious to know a bit more about him.

'Two girls, sixth form in the UK. They were turning into expat brats here, with the maid picking up after them all day, so we wanted to give them a bit of a reality check before they head off to uni. Miss 'em like crazy. The wife too, but she's determined we done the right thing.'

'That must be very difficult,' said Maya, knowing how much Rich had hated boarding school and how adamant he was that their boys would never have to go.

Jim slowed down and waved off to the right. 'This 'ere's yer actual Jumeirah mosque,' he said. 'A beauty, isn't she? And there next door, is an old windtower house. See that chimney shaped job on top? That's yer actual windtower. They was the original air conditioning units, boys. Turned into a café now called The Orange Tree. My missus is always there with her mates having a chin wag. Great food, she says. Home-knitted, I call it. You know, muesli, smoothies and all that organic malarkey. You'd like that, Maya. Expect it'll will be your local soon enough.'

Rich turned round from the front seat to smile at Maya. 'There you go,' he said. 'What did I tell you?'

'Here we are, chaps. Home sweet home. Hotel sweet hotel, I mean!' Jim pulled up outside a grand hotel that had palm trees strung with spirals of white fairy lights in an apron of lawn in front. He pressed a button beneath the dashboard, the boot sprung open and within seconds their bags had been whisked inside by a porter.

'Ow!' shrieked Matthew, leaping out and turning to shut the car door. 'That door handle's boiling!'

'You'll get used to that, son!' laughed Jim. 'Use your fat arse like I do!' and he sashayed over to the driver's door and banged it shut with an exaggerated wiggle before handing the car keys over so the valet could park it.

Maya made a dash inside to the cool sanctuary of the lobby.

'Is it always this hot?' asked Oliver.

Maya looked at Rich. She shared her son's concern.

'It is August,' said Jim. 'It'll get better. You'll see.' Jim led them into the lobby where they all sat down on a clutch of white leather sofas and Rich handed their passports over to a smart oriental while another handed them glasses of freshly squeezed orange juice, their outsides cloudy with condensation.

'This is the life, eh?' said Rich, settling back into the sofa.

'Just 'til you can move into your villa, though, mate, don't go getting ideas!' Jim grinned.

'D'you think they have a games room?' Matthew asked.

'They've got the lot, matey. Squash, tennis, archery, pool. No danger of you getting bored.'

'Mum won't like that, will you, Mum?' said Oliver 'She doesn't like sport.'

Maya smiled apologetically and tried to keep her face bright.

'Tell you what Maya, give us your mobile number when you get one and I'll get Sue to give you a call. Then she can take you out to play?' He took a business card out of his wallet and handed it to her.

'Thanks, Jim.' She looked down at the embossed gold lettering on the card.

'Mum likes work more than play,' said Oliver thoughtfully. 'Don't you, Mum?'

'Blimey!' said Jim. 'That's a turn up! Well, you know what they say about all work and no play!'

'I'm not sure if I'm cut out for doing nothing all day. I like to be busy,' Maya explained.

'Oh, don't you worry about that. There's tons to keep you occupied. You could visit a different shopping mall every day of the week if you wanted to.'

'Right,' she said weakly.

' Well, I wish you luck, darlin'.'

'Are there many jobs out there, then?' she continued.

He stuck out his bottom lip and shrugged. 'Well, put it this way. It's not that there's a shortage of jobs, but the visa process can be a bit hairy. A few hoops to jump through. Know what I mean?'

'And Mum would be crap at that, wouldn't she, Matt?' joked Oliver.

'Take my advice, love, and bide your time. Take advantage of the coffee mornin's and clubs you ladies all love so much and ask around before jumpin' into anything. Okay?'

Chapter three

Depositing the boys at Emirates British School on their first day was weird. Maya followed the queue of four-wheel drives into the school car park, parked, and reached into the back for her handbag, where it lay on the cream leather seat of the Range Rover she was still unused to, when Matthew glared at her.

'You're not thinking of coming in with me, are you?' he said, grabbing his rucksack and opening the back door in one smooth move.

Maya looked at her youngest son. 'You sure?'

'I know where to go, Mum,' he said. 'I remember from when the deputy head showed us round last week. And there are signs everywhere.' He paused. 'I am twelve, you know. I can read.' He jumped down from the seat. 'Laters!'

'Make sure Dad gets them to come and set up broadband today, please,' asked Oliver through teeth that were almost bared.

'I'll ask him,' Maya replied. 'You know it's out of my hands. We're doing our best. I want the computer as much as you do. We have to wait for the company to sort it out.'

'Well just try, Mum. I need to get on Facebook.' He opened the car door and stepped out. 'Ouch! The handle's burning my skin off.'

'Bye!' she whispered. 'Bye, boys.'

And they were gone. She had not even turned the engine off. Maya sat for a while and watched her brave children disappear inside the glass atrium, shoulder to shoulder with dozens of other kids all wearing the same gray and white uniform. They could have been anywhere in the world. She'd made it. Here they were, several thousand miles from England, and proving they lived here for real by sending their children to school. She sat for a while, watching other children stepping down from other four-wheel-drives and peered into the driver's seats, at the other mothers. Even from here she could see that they all wore large fashionable sunglasses and that their hair was neatly coiffed.

She was alone for the first time since they arrived. And she'd done it. She'd negotiated the road works, the constant hooting of horns, an unnecessary number of traffic lights and roundabouts and found the school all on her own. For a moment she felt triumphant. Then her mood took an instant nosedive and she was filled with fear. She had to find her way back.

Silence and emptiness fell around her shoulders. Other mothers in the same position would have felt relief and freedom on this long awaited first day of a new school year. Maya watched the world outside her windscreen grow, becoming more alien and impenetrable as she shrank into anonymity. This was it then. The first real day of her new life.

The air conditioner hissed out at her, making the little blonde hairs on her forearms stand on end. Flicking on the indicator, she looked over her right shoulder and pulled away from the throng of slamming doors and brisk goodbyes towards her day. It was a little after seven in the morning and the hours stretched before her like rocks on a road less travelled. She'd need her wits about her for sure. And as with any unfamiliar path, she had no map, no idea how to get there nor what to expect when she arrived. The journey home was an ordeal in itself. God, they drove like loonies here.

Flicking on the radio, the cheery voice of the Dubai Eye morning DJ was no match for her mood. Too many words. Too many place names that meant nothing. She switched it off again, finding her thoughts provided more than enough chatter for her as she gingerly navigated the unfamiliar roads home.

It was a while until the sight of Park 'n' Shop loomed back into view and she could relax. In this direction, she easily found the exit she needed. Now she had to find her compound. Every side street looked the same, lined with dusty oleander and sandy verges. All the villas had the same pinkish stone, with similar cars parked under similar carports; every garden was planted just like its neighbour.

She drew into number 7 and yanked up the handbrake. A full stop to signal the end of having something to do and the beginning of, the beginning of, what? Letting the engine idle for a moment, she sat there staring at the wall in front of her. The last two weeks had been a whirl. Packing up the old life and unpacking it again here, piece by piece, paper by paper, all stuffed at random into brown cardboard boxes. Each one could have provided a home to a London tramp. They had filled eighty-six of them and had simply let the removal company cart the empties away.

Sorting out the school, the villa, the bank accounts, poring over maps, exploring a little in their new four-by-four had absorbed them totally. Rich and the boys had joined the sailing club and got themselves sorted out with kit and lessons. Maya had set to organising her kitchen, or to be more accurate, Maya and Annie had set to organising the kitchen. Annie was her newly acquired housemaid. Annie, who left her outdoor flip-flops, neatly paired beneath her neatly swept step. Annie, who would be there at the front door any moment, opening it to let her in. To welcome her home. Annie had come with the villa. The whole of Mimosa Gardens had belonged to Arabian Airlines for over ten years. Many of the housemaids had been lucky enough to pass from one family to the next, keeping their home and livelihood constant. Maya had not wanted to rock the boat. But she had not been at all sure about having a maid live in. It all felt very 'upstairs downstairs' to her. Annie had been less lucky to end up one of eight children to a poor craftsman in Karnataka, who succumbed to lung disease before his sons could earn a decent wage and support the family. And now Maya was in a position to make things better for Annie, whose husband had died of alcohol poisoning and, suddenly faced with the need to raise her daughter alone, had reluctantly placed Matilda in boarding school and come to Dubai. That had been fifteen years ago.

She dreaded the deafening silence she would face inside. Swallowing hard, she picked up her handbag from the rear leather seat and jumped down from the huge car and entered a villa that didn't feel like home. 'Hello, madam!' Annie called out brightly, as she held the door ajar. 'You have shopping?' She sounded hopeful.

'No, not yet, sorry Annie,' replied Maya, knocked off guard by having someone around who put helping her as her top priority. The supplies that had been in the house when they arrived were now depleted and they'd been eating out mostly. She'd not set foot in a supermarket yet. She paused in the marble hallway and looked up towards the kitchen, which lay, oddly, on the first floor. Would she go there, to the room in which she felt most at ease? Or would she find somewhere she could be alone? She deserved a sit down. A bit of me time.

'I'll just get myself a drink and sit and look at the garden for a moment,' she said. 'Okay?' as if she needed to ask permission. If she'd been back home she'd have sat outside on the patio, but it was 100 per cent humidity out there; she'd not last five minutes. 'I can do,' offered Annie. 'I make fresh juice?'

Now that was a good idea. 'Lovely!' Annie looked confused. 'Yes, Annie, yes please. Thank you,' she said, realising she was going to have to modify her language if she was to communicate with her and gave her biggest smile. Then she walked down the steps from the hall towards the French windows that overlooked their small garden, wondering how long she would need to take being waited on for granted.

Pulling a dining chair over to beside the window she watched green parrots flit in and out of the frilly tops of the palm trees, wishing she could eavesdrop on their twitter, but recognising there was no way she could turn off the air-conditioning and open the door to do so in this heat. Soon she heard the slop of Annie's indoor flip-flops moving closer.

'Just the job,' she said. 'I mean, thank you.'

Annie handed her a tall glass of bright orange juice, thick with condensation on the outside, and skirted with a square of kitchen roll to protect her mistress from the damp. She really thought of everything.

Maya took the glass.

Annie stood there.

'Thank you. This looks delicious.' She took a long sip.

Annie stood there. Maybe she was waiting for her next instructions?

'I don't need anything else, thank you.'

Annie stood there.

This was more difficult than she thought. Maya had no idea how to deal with a housemaid. What was she to do? She couldn't bring herself to say, 'That will be all,' or 'Run along,' or even 'You may return to your duties,' and so she focused again on her juice.

'Madam?'

Maya looked up. Maybe Annie wanted to talk to her. Was she supposed to suggest she pull up a chair and join her? Instead, she smiled and said 'Yes, Annie?'

'Oranges finished, madam.'

Thank you, God, thought Maya. This conversation I can handle.

'No problem. Just write it on the white board in the kitchen, will you?'

'No, madam,' she said.

Now this was getting confusing.

'Why not? I'm sorry, I don't understand.'

'I don't know writing English, madam. I am sorry. Not reading English.'

'No problem,' she said and at last Annie left her in peace. Getting used to having a housemaid was clearly going to be one of those boulders she would have to learn to cope with along the road.

From where she sat and swung and sipped her juice Maya felt less isolated; she could sense the life that surrounded her and could see the flash and splash of water spraying from the shared swimming pool that lay in the centre of their ring of villas.

Preschoolers enjoyed the cool part of the morning while their mothers sat and drank the coffee and juice their maids brought out to them. They were too far away for her to pick up snippets of their conversation, but close enough for her to realise that they were not speaking English. Whenever they stood up she could see that they were tall, lean, bronzed and wore designer bikinis. Several sported pretty tattoos. They all seemed to be much younger than Maya, natural and at home here.

Maya didn't feel she would fit in over there by the pool. Too old and old-fashioned, in her one-piece, one-colour swimsuit from M&S. Too pale, with untoned thighs that resembled cold porridge. Too nervous to take a step towards the edge of her comfort zone. It would take time to really belong.

She had belonged in Stamford. Her mind back-pedalled to her last day at the deli with Jan and Av. Jan, skinny-hipped and skinny-thighed, lived on a diet of black coffee and adrenalin. Avril was the opposite. Large chest, large behind, and a heart as big as a bucket. God, she missed her. And Seasons. The name had been Maya's idea of course. She was May and Jan and Av were January and April. She wondered if the customers ever got the joke.

Even on her last day, Avril had greeted her with her usual 'Hiya Maya'. She still thought it was funny after five years.

'Scuse the pong, I'm wrapping cheese. Just got a new lot in from Fen Farm. Be done in a mo'. Kettle's boiled,' Av had said.

Maya had smiled and laid her hand on Avril's shoulder as she squeezed past her partner's ample behind in the direction of the kitchen.

The kitchen in all its middle-aged glory hadn't a flat

flagstone to its name, all polished to a brassy sheen from years of feet walking back and forth. Taking two pottery mugs down from their hooks, Maya chose her favourite Italian coffee beans and ground them, sending a wave of aroma, thick and rich as treacle out to the shop where Avril wielded the cheese knife. A sob bubbled at the back of her throat and she took advantage of the grinder's racket to stifle the sound as she let it come. But once the tears started, she just couldn't stop. She grabbed a tea towel in which to bury her face. In seconds Avril was at her side, enveloping her in a wide, warm hug.

Maya flicked about aimlessly with the tea towel.

'It's okay. You can use it for a hanky just this once. I shan't tell Jan,' said Avril.

'I'm sorry.'

'Don't be. I understand.' Avril released her arms slightly and looked at her friend. 'Smile, Maya. You're about to have the adventure of a lifetime that others would give their right arm for.'

Maya sniffed and managed at last, to swallow her sobs. 'I know. I am happy, really I am. It's just today, everything's for the last time. Every smell is the last smell.'

'Don't tell me they don't have coffee over there?'

'Oh, not that. Well, not just that. Even this shop, it smells like a mouldy old cellar. They won't have mouldy old cellars in Dubai. There are no old buildings and no cold and damp weather.'

'You can't tell me you'll miss mould, cold, and damp?' Avril took over the coffee-making. 'Fetch us the milk, will you. This'll do you the power of good.'

'I can't help you in the shop today. I'm sorry. I just can't face seeing people. It'll only set me off again. I'm just about goodbyed out.' She hung her head. 'And it's not that I don't want to go. I do. But you know, it's that no-going-back moment when I suddenly wonder if we've done the right thing.'

'I know. Bit like that on my wedding day, and yours too, I'll bet. You stand there wearing a dress, that your dad had to remortgage for, in a church filled with flowers, and think hell, will I still fancy the pants off him next year, let alone when I'm ninety?'

Maya nodded.

'I understand. Don't worry about not helping in the shop. It's okay. I'll cope. They don't call me Spitfire for nothing. Anyway the capable Danuta is coming in later to learn the ropes. How about you do some stocktaking? That's bound to make sure you're glad to get out of here at closing time. I know how much you love having no one to talk to!'

Avril was always so cheerful. Always saw the bright side. 'You and Paul and the kids will come and stay, won't you?' Maya squeaked, tears threatening to resurface.

'Course. I'll email too. You can always count on a counter girl!' She took a sip of her coffee. 'And before you say you'll miss these mugs too, I went to the pottery and bought you four to take with you.' She lifted a plastic bag from where it had been sitting on a chair and pushed it onto the table. 'Here. Sorry, didn't have time to wrap them. I knew you'd miss the mugs you work with. So now you won't!'

'Thanks,' she replied weakly. 'You're better than Prozac, you are.'

By the time Jan arrived, laden with the ingredients for the lunch special, Maya was still buoyed up by Avril's mood medicine.

'What's the recipe today, Jan?' she asked, leaning her elbows forward onto the table and resting her chin in her hands.

'Vegetarian squash goulash and beet; goat's cheese and walnut salad with pine nuts; apple and tomato soup. Any good?' Jan replied. 'And I'll have a coffee if there's one left, please. Strong.' Jan plucked a pink elastic band with a large pair of orange bobbles on it off her wrist, crammed her long, skinny yellow hair into a pony tail, and grabbed her gingham pinny off the back of the door.

Poor Jan, her less-than-useless husband took her for granted and spent far too much time and money on improve-yourself seminars that had so far produced nothing but maxed-out credit cards. And Jan was like chewed string but knuckled down, put the kids first, the shop second, and herself way down the bottom of her list. Maya watched her put a slug of cold water into her coffee from the tap so she could down it in one. 'Ah! That's better. Tomorrow is D-day, eh? No second thoughts?'

'D for doom, dread or departure?'

'For Dubai.'

'Doh!' She might have known Jan would be expecting a straight answer.

'But, you want this, right? You do, don't you?' Jan tipped her head in concern. 'That's what attracted you to Rich in the first place, isn't it? The opportunity to travel?'

'Yeah, thanks for reminding me. The bloke I dumped for Rich was the absolute opposite. Mick, his name was. His idea of an adventure was to have a double portion of mushy peas with his fish and chips. But Rich and me, we wanted the same thing out of life. He'd always hoped for a stint in Germany when he was with the RAF.'

'I'd give my right arm for some sunshine and no money worries.' Jan patted Maya's hand to show that she really needed to be getting on. 'We'll still be here, keeping your seat warm.'

'Aren't you supposed to be in the stock room, madam?' called a voice from the shop. 'Thought you didn't want to talk to anyone. And shouldn't it be D for Dates? I think they have a few palm trees where you're headed.'

Lovely Avril. Dependable Jan. Would she ever find such incredible friends here?

Her juice finished, Maya stood up and took a deep breath. Small steps, Maya, she told herself, Today, she would drive to the supermarket Jim recommended. If she wanted to belong, she needed to do the right things.

Chapter four

The navy cut-off trousers, green polo shirt and brown deck shoes Maya had worn to take the boys to school no longer felt suitable, not even for a trip to the supermarket. She didn't want to be judged by the complete strangers who would push their laden trolleys past her down the aisles. Choosing the sundress she would usually have worn to go out to dinner with Rich and her white strappy sandals, she applied lipstick and mascara before taking another look at herself. It was a lovely dress, from the front, and fell in flattering folds to just below her knee, but when she stood sideways, no matter how hard she yanked her shoulders up and back and sucked in her tummy, she still looked pregnant. And her skin was undeniably the colour of lard. Was she showing too much cleavage for a Muslim country in the midst of its holy month? She fished the plain white short-sleeved jacket she normally saved for school speech days out of the wardrobe, and tried it on over the dress. She sighed. It would have to do. She was only going to the shop for heaven's sake and here she was as nervous as a twelve-year-old about to go to her first real party, with boys there.

Maya drove slowly, annoying the other drivers as she hugged the slow lane and the kerb all the way. She had the map Jim had drawn for her open on the seat beside her and looked at it nervously every few seconds – that is, when she wasn't checking the mirrors and the road signs. Frankly, it was worse than a driving test. At last she reached her goal, the green and yellow logo of the supermarket. Thank God there was plenty of parking, and decent sized spaces at that. This new car was a bit of a hulk and Maya wasn't confident about her spatial awareness. Gingerly, she pulled into one near the entrance, moved the gear stick to Park, and leaned back in her seat. Then she breathed out. She prised her shoulders out of the hunch they had maintained for fifteen minutes and felt the sweat run down her back like a skinny river, down between her shoulder blades and into the gap at the top of her knickers. She gathered her hair up in her fist and let the cool air-conditioning dry her out as best it could before she turned off the engine and hit the heat of the day in the short walk to the wide glass doors.

The lobby was cool and contained a cash machine, a drink dispenser and a vast noticeboard covered with posters, flyers, and cards. She would take a closer look at that on her way out; it would be good to find out what was going on around here and maybe find something to fill her days. Once she had become more confident on the roads.

Her spirits lifted when she realised no coin was needed to release her trolley. Maybe that was because there were no rivers to chuck them into here. As soon as her fingers closed over the green plastic handle and the wheels glided effortlessly across the sparkling white floor, she relaxed. This was okay. She knew how to do this. If anything, this would be fun.

Maya loved supermarkets, particularly foreign ones. As the child of a geography teacher, family holidays had always been self-catering, often camping and usually abroad because her father was passionate about travel. Her mother was a talented cook and came into her own when faced with nothing but a two-ring primus stove. Maya and her brother, Phin, would watch their parents just about clap their hands together in childish delight at the thought of shopping for food with labels that they couldn't read. They had become confident pointers and actors at market stalls. She and Phin, named after Phineas Fogg of course, still collapsed in fits of giggles when they recounted the story of her mother flapping her wings like a chicken at the butcher's stall and her father trying to do an impression of a mushroom at the grocer's so that they could eat coq au vin for supper. Roads, rooms filled with strangers, and having a live-in maid fazed Maya, but not supermarkets.

She took her time, poring over every shelf, lifting tins, studying labels. The vegetable section was impressive and had everything from papaya to strawberries. There was fresh fish and a decent-looking meat counter and she ran through her mental list of must-haves, checking that they could still get family staples such as Mini Shredded Wheats with raisins and Bonne Maman strawberry jam. The selection of breads would have satisfied the customers back at Seasons, though the cheese counter was not a patch on theirs and the Stilton looked smelly. With a range of spices and other exotic items, some of which she had never heard of, and many things that were cheaper than she was used to, Maya was suffused with a deep joy: in the kitchen, at least, she could be queen. Everything would be all right. Planning menus in her head, she danced round the shelves filling her trolley, her heart pounding once more this morning, only this time with true excitement.

The girl at the till worked steadily, moving each item over the scanner, smiling every time she heard a beep and keeping her eyes lowered. A single strand of hair escaped her black headscarf and she flushed slightly as she tucked it back out of sight. As the contents of her trolley slid down the ramp to the end of the cash desk, Maya watched a young man whom she guessed may have been Indian begin to pack her bags and reload them straight into a trolley. Trying to hide her surprise, she smiled at him. Was this how things were done?

'Hello, madam,' he said quickly and turned to focus on his task.

The till girl's dark eyes were beautifully lined with kohl. They lifted and met Maya's.

'Ninety-eight dirhams, please.'

'Sorry, I'm new,' Maya replied rather helplessly, fishing around in her purse. 'Not quite sure, which I need yet!' She smiled weakly and held out a red 100 dirham note.

'Red, like in hundred, okay? Then you will remember,' said the girl. Her dark eyes flashed.

'Oh, that's clever.'

After she paid, the bag-packer took the trolley by the handle and waited for her. Maya put out her hand to take it from him.

'Thank you so much,' she said, handing him a coin she hoped was adequate for his services.

'I take to car,' he said with a slight hint of authority.

Maya looked at him quizzically. 'No, honestly, it's fine,' she said, placing her hand on the trolley possessively.

'Is my job, madam,' he said, waiting patiently for her to remove her hand from the trolley and let him get on with it unobstructed.

Reaching into her bag for the keys, she clicked the car open in good time, so its lights flashed in greeting and showed him the way. Another button and the boot flew up and open, and he stacked the shopping neatly inside before disappearing. Someone to pack the shopping was something she could get used to. She hoped the frozen food would survive the heat for a few unairconditioned minutes while she returned to look at that noticeboard.

There was someone else in the lobby. A woman with a rather large behind clad in pale blue linen was bent over a bag filled with papers and was in the midst of a frantic rummage.

'Now where are you?' she muttered. 'Never are any darn pushpins on these boards. Reckon some folks make a hobby out of stealing 'em just so's to annoy others.' The woman gave in and tipped her bag out onto the floor in desperation. 'There you are, little fellers! Hiding!' She put a perfectly manicured hand to the small of her back and gave a slight groan as she creaked herself upright. A sheet of glossy dark hair with a beautiful grey streak at the front settled back into place around her face and Maya didn't want to stare.

Maya began to study a poster of a woman in a bellydancing costume. *Bellydancing* classes, it read. *Learn to love your curves.* Maybe it was time Maya tried something different? Out of the corner of her eye, she kept tabs on the other woman as she carefully unpinned about ten posters from the centre of the board and moved them to the edge, leaving space for her to place her own in prime position. Maya stifled a giggle. The cheek of it! Admirable though.

'A girl's gotta do, what a girl's gotta do, eh?' said the woman, grinning straight at her, showing off her perfect teeth.

'Absolutely!' Maya agreed, nodding furiously.

'Say, you're English!' she said, thrusting out her right hand. 'I'm Barbra Schneider, but everyone calls me Barb.' She laughed, though Maya was not sure there had been a joke.

'Maya Winter. Pleased to meet you,' said Maya, placing her palm against Barb's and feeling the strength of her fingers as she closed on them. 'Er, are you from America?' 'Sure am, Maya. And I'm pleased to meet you too, Maya. You're new, right?'

Maya smoothed down her skirt. 'Is it that obvious?'

'After twenty-five years being dragged kickin' and screamin' round the globe by my oil and gas man, I've got pretty good at spotting a rookie. Must be your pale skin just gave you away!' She looked Maya up and down then at her own bronzed legs. 'Mine are from a bottle!' She laughed again. 'I'm so pale that the sun is dazzled by the sight of my skin and just bounces right off 'em!'

'You're right, though. We are new. It's our second week. First time I've done a proper shop too.' On closer inspection it looked as if Barb's hair had been teased and lacquered into that perfect shape.

'Tough, ain't it? Finding the strength to do something you'd rightly find a piece o' pie back home?' Barb finished pinning up her posters. Maya lingered over the advert for the gym, even though she had no intention of going to one.

'You looking for something to do?' Barb asked, her voice softening. 'There sure is plenty to do in this place.'

'Well, yes, I was rather hoping to find something once we're all settled, you know. The kids started school today and...'

'I know, the husband's in the office, the maid's taken over and you're about to go out of your mind with a mix of boredom, loneliness, and missing your old buddies. Tell me about it!' Barb gave a snort of amusement and turned to face her.

'Well, it's not quite like that. I haven't had time to be bored. All that unpacking and getting familiar with the place, you know.'

Barb put her hand on Maya's shoulder and looked into her eyes. 'You'll be bored soon enough. This is my gazillionth posting and believe me, I know. That's why I keep busy. I've learned the tricks you see. It's the only thing that keeps me sane.' She smiled broadly and shook her head so that her perfect hair swung to left and right, caressing her jaw line, then picked up her bag and slung it over her shoulder. 'Say, who's your husband work for?'

'Arabian Airlines.'

'Mine's with Texas Oil. You said you had kids, right? Which school?'

'Emirates British School. They are fourteen and twelve.' She looked closer at Barb, noticing how her make-up had been so carefully applied that no cracks appeared, yet she had to be what, forty plus? Yes, she was definitely wearing foundation, even in this heat.

'Brandon, thirteen, American High. You live in Jumeirah 3, right? On the Mimosa compound with the others from AA.'

Maya's heart lifted. Maybe if Barb lived around here too, which followed if she was in this supermarket, she could be a friend? She might be big, bold, beautiful, and in-your-face, but in a way she reminded her of Avril. A positive thinker. She seemed genuinely friendly. 'You?'

'Nope, not from round here, I just travel all over the city putting up posters for folks. I'm downtown.' Barb shifted her bag higher on her shoulder, but Maya wasn't ready for her to leave right yet. This might be her only real conversation of the day and she wanted to make it last. She began looking at Barb's posters with new attention.

'You have quite a mix of stuff, here. Is this your job? You know, putting up posters for people?'

'Well, there's a question.' Barb lifted her bag off her shoulder and placed it on the floor.

Oh, good, thought Maya. *She's staying.*

'I guess you could say I do everything and nothing. I don't work for money, if that's what you're after. My career went down the chute decades ago and Bill, that's my husband, thinks a wife is for looking after financially, not sending out to work. But I am busy. Gotta be!' A smile stretched across her lips.

Maya waited for more explanation. 'A coffee morning, a book group, a photographer, a computer awareness course, Bible study meetings, and an afterschool baseball club. I'm sorry, I can't seem to find a common theme here.'

Barb was beaming now. 'I get involved. I help people. I like to promote things and I run a Coffee with a Twist club too. Without it I'd go round the twist! Ha!' There was that laugh again. She raised an elegant finger towards the poster for the coffee morning. 'We meet every coupl'a weeks. Have a little talk at each meeting – something to stop our brains turning to oatmeal – and raise money for charity. This year we are going to be supporting a local women's centre. Some expat women never really adjust to this charmed life, you know?'

'Really?'

'Afraid so, Maya. Not everyone finds a way to be happy and fulfilled – unlike busy old me!' Barb nonchalantly took the pins out of the poster for the bellydancing and used them for her own. 'The teacher of that class just left town,' she shrugged. 'Another best mate bites the dust. You have to learn to make friends fast here, I can tell you.'

Maya absorbed that comment for a moment.

'Say you come along to one of our Twist events sometime? It's a good place to start.' She tapped her poster. 'It is not nice being new-in-town, I know, I've been there more times than I have fingers. That way, I can introduce you to some of the others. Let me give you my card and a flyer.' She fished around in her bag, sticking her bum in the air again. 'Oh look what I found!' She handed Maya a pink card and a sheet about The Twist.

Maya thrust the flyer in her dress pocket and looked down at the card: *Professional Expat Wife, Barbra Schneider*.

'You have a great day now,' said Barb, and walked towards the doors, which slid open automatically to let her through.

The lobby felt cooler and emptier now and Maya had a last look at the board. There must be lots of wives here with time on their hands. Maya, though, was determined to keep her career alive. She hadn't spent five years running the deli to send her CV back to square one. Maya stuffed Barb's card into the pocket of her dress before patting her rounded hips. She would find something to do, but not until everyone in the family had found their feet and that included her.

Chapter five

With scarcely the need to wave a breezy 'hello there' to James, the guard at the gate to her compound, the barrier lifted like magic and Barb sailed through.

Here we go, she thought, swinging around into the carport that lay at the far end of the cul de sac in which they lived. The ground rose slightly as it reached villa 1123. Barb liked that. It made her feel that she could kind of 'preside' over the street. Not look down on them, oh no. Look out for them, that was more the thing. She was born to nurture, Barb. Destined to provide a welcome place for waifs, strays, and the new-in-town. Book club was at her place this month and after a quick scan of the sidewalk she could see that there was a good chance she was first, which was a relief. Could not stand lateness, though her hectic schedule meant that she was often obliged to be a little more than fashionably so. Of course, now that she had encouraged the neighbours to join the club, she guessed that may have meant that some of them could have beaten her to it. She switched off the engine and hopped out of the car, gathering up her purse from the front seat as she did so. Merry was already at the door, opening it for her.

'Hello, madam,' she said merrily. Merry was merry most of the time, which was fortunate really. It would have been cruel to have a name like that and then not live up to it. Irony wouldn't begin to describe it.

'Morning, Merry. Tea ready?'

'Yes, madam.'

'Girls here?'

'No, madam.'

Phew, that just gave her time to check her make-up and lay out some new flyers. Then she walked over to the dining table, laid with a fresh cloth in a rich burgundy, offsetting the Crown Derby bone china they had bought during their stint in London. She touched the cloth with her fingertips, then laid them on the large chrome coffee thermos, then its twin, containing hot water. A pitcher of juice, a bucket of ice, bottles of Masafi mineral water, two sparkling, two still, a dish of thinly sliced lemons, a box of assorted tea bags, a small pitcher of skim milk and another of cream, sugar, brown and white. She touched the table once more and turned to survey the room she knew to be an appropriate reflection of her life, her family, her experience. It saved having to answer too many questions. The china was a clear sign that they had lived in London, the rosewood dining set showed they had been to the Far East, the painted wooden cuckoo clock from Norway, Delft tiles from Holland. The Persian carpets were a clear indication that they had spent a good few years on an expatriate salary. It showed they had seen the world. Her eyes dropped to the photographs she kept on the top of the Thai sideboard. There she was, Bill at her side, beside the US Ambassador at a Christmas party. Bill shaking hands with a recent CEO of BP. Bill, Brandon and herself with Mickey Mouse. Brandon on a jet ski. Brandon on a sled led by huskies. Silver framed photographs placed in full view on the polished rosewood. She looked away and squared her shoulders. Her room spoke volumes. And if her guests cared to cast their eyes over the bookcase, filled with neat rows of books carefully ranged according to size and subject they would see a clear itinerary of the last twenty-five years on the spines of hardbacks. Their photograph albums too, had been carefully labelled and dated. Her collections were a credit to her. They proved who she was. And there, on the middle shelf, where they could clearly be spotted, the books on living abroad. *A Moveable Marriage, Dealing with the Dutch, How to Understand and Use a Norwegian, The Expert Expat.* She liked to think she had them all. A little book lay horizontally across this special shelf. It was where she noted any loans she had made, for though she liked to run a kind of informal lending library, she liked to get them back.

She looked down at the gold Rolex that Bill had bought her that Christmas and saw that it was time. Her guests would be there any moment so she moved over to the black leather chair she favoured, being, as it was, slightly higher than the couches her guests always seemed to prefer. For Barb, as she reminded herself, was rather short and did like to be able to watch over her girls and check they all had enough tea, candy, and sandwiches. She eased herself back into the cool leather and placed her arms on the armrests, pushing the back away from her just a little, so that her legs lifted from the floor and the footrest rose to catch her just behind the calves. Bliss, two minutes' peace. She closed her eyes.

'Hey Barb!' A hand touched her arm and Barb jolted upright, straightening the chair to vertical frighteningly fast.

'Gee, I'm sorry. Must have dropped off. Busy morning.' She beamed. It was Elske, the Dutch lady she had recently persuaded to come to a coffee, and now here she was at book club too. It was always so satisfying when someone came to appreciate the things Barb did for them. Elske's hair was looking nice today, too, if a little short, just the feminine side of mannish, though the highlights helped. The kind of hair you could wash in the shower and go straight out with, unlike hers, which took real effort with a hairdryer and some rollers to achieve that lift and shine.

'You have cut your hair, yes? I like the stripe.'

'Thanks,' said Barb, touching the streak fondly. 'Now which do you think might be the real colour – the grey or the brown?'

'Grey, probably,' said Elske, looking up at the room. 'You have a lovely house, Barb.' Her gaze flicked back and forth over the laden dining table, the sideboard, the occasional tables. 'So many things. You must have lived in many places.'

'Thank you, Elske. We have. Do help yourself to something to eat and drink and find a seat.' Merry could always be relied on to cater for book club beautifully. Barb had just left her a list that morning of the cake and cookies to buy and the sandwiches to make and there it was, all on the table. Merry was marvellous, but then, she had been well trained. After all these years, Barb knew how to get the best out of her staff, providing them with self-respect, new skills, and a decent pay check. There was no way a maid of hers would find it hard to get another job when they moved on.

Elske moved over to the table, her long legs and slim neck made her look like a baby giraffe looking around for good grazing. 'Did you make all this yourself?' she asked. Like most Dutch people, her English was perfect.

'No, you have to thank my Filipina right hand woman, Merry, for this. Try a brownie. They are Martha Stewart.' She watched Elske help herself to a cup of tea and place one single square of brownie in her saucer. Black tea. Only one cookie? That must be how she stayed so slender.

Barb got up to help herself to a Coke, filling the glass up with ice first, adding lemon. She needed another boost of caffeine after the morning she'd had. The doorbell rang and Barb turned away from the table, but didn't move towards the door. Merry would get it.

'Hello, Barb!'

'Hey Barb!'

'Afternoon, Barb!'

Here they came, their copies of *The Girls* clutched in one hand so that when they moved to give their hostess a hug, a handshake, or a kiss in greeting, depending on their nationality, they were hampered by only having one free hand.

Barb settled back in her chair, raising the footrest and lifting her glass to her lips. 'You go on and be sure to help yourselves, won't you,' she commanded as gently as she could from what Bill liked to refer to as her 'throne'.

Merry hovered in the doorway. Barb spotted her immediately. 'Thank you very much, Merry. This is wonderful.' She cleared her throat and called out to her visitors. 'Does everyone have all they need here?' and when no reply came, Merry slipped away.

'Well, I finished it and my painting. What did you think of it, Barb?' asked LaShell, running her fingers through the thick hair Barb envied. Maybe she should be blonde next time round?

'I am afraid I didn't have a painting to do and I still didn't quite finish the book.' Her laugh was filled with suitable self-deprecation. 'Again.'

'Too busy?' LaShell looked concerned. 'You do too much, Barb,' she said as murmurs of assent flowed round the room. But Barb just smiled at them all.

'That's me!' There were many things Barb would rather do than read a book, though she always made sure she bought three copies, largely to give away. To be honest, she had not even started to read this one. She always took the next book club read around with her in her purse in case she found someone to lend it to and if not, then at least it looked as if it had been read! Besides, she found it hard to focus on a whole book these days. Even those on her bookshelves were just for show.

'You should do something for yourself for once, take a class, come to Bums and Tums, learn something new?' LaShell continued, stirring her coffee round and round. The scrape of the spoon made Barb wince.

'Oh, I'm not sure. Lycra can be so unforgiving, can't it?' She laughed. They agreed. 'And it's so long since I went to school that they'd most likely make a dunce's hat just for me, probably put a big D on it!' Her shoulders rose and fell as she chuckled. 'Anyway, I do plenty of stuff for myself.' She fluttered her nails and turned her head so that her hair swung to left and right, sitting up straight as she did so and changing the subject. 'So, girls? What did you think of *The Girls*? Did you prefer Ruby or Rose?' To be fair, Barb did read some books. That one on how to pretend you had read a book when you hadn't had been a godsend.

'Naughty old Rose!' murmured Suchanatta, the Thai woman, married to the British HR guy at Arabian Airlines. Her skirt was frighteningly short again today, though she did have a pair of splendid legs. 'I don't know how she managed to have sex when she was attached to her sister. Do you? In the same room, maybe, but not the same bed!'

'Oh Sue!' exclaimed LaShell, clapping a hand to her mouth.

'Suchanatta!' chortled Barb. She liked to use people's real names. It showed respect and proved she had been paying attention.

'That must be a record!' laughed Megan, the New Yorker who had let her hair go completely grey and wore it in a sharp chin-length bob. 'We get onto sex in the first minute!'

'Sorry,' said Suchanatta, grinning. 'But I bet that's what you all wanted to talk about, eh?' She raised one elbow and winked at Barb.

Barb looked uncomfortable. She took another sip of her Coke. She bet Suchanatta and her sexy husband, Jim, had some fun in the bedroom. Lucky thing.

'Say, what did you think of the setting? What bearing did it have on the plot?' She thought it was her duty to get the discussion back on track.

This was just how she liked it. Being able to share her lovely home with a wonderful mix of interesting women who came from all over the world. Giving them all something to do and something to laugh about. Helping them all to make friends. Purpose and relationships, that's what mattered. If everyone else was happy that made her happy. When they left, their positive energy lifted the atmosphere of the house and made Barb's smile real for a while.

Elske was the last to leave. 'Thank you, Barb. I really enjoyed that,' she said, handing back the book she had borrowed.

'You're welcome, Elske. I am so glad you could make it. And that's so good of you to offer to host a meeting at your place. I was getting a bit stuck. People have a habit of letting me down at the last minute.' She smiled. 'Guess I'm just too darn nice to them when they drop me in it!' She gave a little growl to show, good-humouredly, that she may just turn nasty one of these days.

'Well, you may be disappointed. I'm not much of a cook and I don't have a maid to help. You'll get a pack of cookies from the supermarket.' Elske looked back at the table, where Merry was now clearing up. There wasn't much left.

'That's fine. There's no need. Anyway, you work, don't you?' She liked to show an interest in people and remember things about them.

Elske's face brightened. 'Yes, I do. I'm an artist.' She stood there coyly with her hands behind her back, like a child who has just told her parents she got came top in a math test.

'Gee! What kind of artist? Oils, watercolour, pencil?'

'Screenprinting. I make greeting cards, usually, and prints of course.'

'Interesting,' Barb said slowly, her mind working fast. 'Then maybe you should have a sales table at one of our Coffees with a Twist sometime.'

'Maybe.'

Elske rifled in her purse for something. 'Here!' She gave Barb a postcard showing four nativity-focused designs. 'This is what I do.'

'Neat! I love this one,' said Barb, pointing to one that showed a Mummy and Daddy camel with a baby camel in a manger and congratulating herself in advance for selling yet another table. 'I think you've sorted out this year's Christmas card problem for us all. Cool. Tell you what. Do you have more of these?'

Elske raised her eyebrows quizzically.

'You see, if you can give me a bunch of them, I can put them up on the noticeboards at the grocery stores and the schools when I do my weekly rounds. I can even put one of those fluorescent star-shaped stickers on the side, saying, "See me at The Twist." Oh, and the girls at Bible study will just love that one with the star.' Neat idea, Barb, advertising The Twist at the same time.

'That is very kind,' said Elske. 'You don't have to, though.' She raised her shoulders on their way to a shrug.

'Oh, I'd be happy to, Elske,' said Barb. 'Truly.' And she meant it. 'Would you do one teeny thing for me?'

'Of course I would!' Elske relaxed. People usually felt happier receiving favours when they could do one in exchange.

'There's a new family moved in near you. Husband works for AA like your Nico. British. Two boys. D'you know them?' Barb's back was to the front door. She knew that she needed Elske to do this for her before she would let her leave.

'Yes. They moved next door a few days ago. I must take her some flowers and say hello.'

'Next door, you say? What a coincidence! Maya Winter her name is, I met her at Spinneys this morning and she looked a little lost. I just thought maybe you could invite her to a book club or a Twist. Maybe even give her a ride? Would you?' Barb felt compelled to rescue that poor pale woman she had met this morning.

'Of course I will, Barb. No problem.'

Barb reached into her purse, where she had left it in the hallway, and fished out a flyer for the next book group. 'Give this to her too, will you? And don't forget to swing by and give me a bunch of your neat cards.' Barb moved away from the door.

'Bye bye Barb,' said Elske, putting out her hand to be shaken.

'Enjoy the rest of your day now,' said Barb with a broad smile on her lips.

The villa was now silent except for the clatter of crockery being stacked in the dishwasher. Barb looked at her watch. Good, it was almost time to fetch Brandon from school, then she'd take him to practice, then dinner, then Bill was off to watch a game and she had a committee meeting. A full agenda. Just the way she liked it.

Chapter six

As soon as Maya shouldered the front door of her villa open so that she could deposit the first of her shopping bags inside in the cool, Annie was down the stairs to greet her.

'I can do,' she said, twitching her head slightly as if disapproving that Maya had deigned to bring in the bags herself.

'Thank you, Annie.' Maya, desperate for a glass of water, climbed the stairs to the kitchen, feeling oddly bereft without her bags. When Annie deposited the first of the shopping bags on the kitchen floor, Maya stooped to begin unpacking.

'I can do,' repeated Annie with a loud tutting sound. Maya stepped backwards out of the kitchen, feeling both awkward and guilty. She could hardly stand there and watch her maid unpack, so she moved around to the sitting room and sank into her old faithful blue denim sofa. They had brought their furniture with them from England and now it looked parked rather than arranged here in this vast white space. The combination of white marble floors, white walls and white muslin curtains at the wide windows was unfortunate. The light was so bright it seemed to spotlight such an ill-fitting choice of furniture. It had looked fine in Stamford, against the stone walls of the sitting room, or the terracotta paint of the dining room. Now, their living area was more open-plan. If the kids had been smaller, they would have had great games chasing each other around and around, sliding on the slippery marble in their socks. She sat on the sofa facing a blank wall on the other side of which her new and unfamiliar maid unpacked her shopping, choosing places that were likely to make no sense but which Maya would not dare to alter. She itched to barge round the corner and take over. But instead she stared at the thick wall and listened to the crackle of bags, sliding drawers, and cupboards clicking shut, longing for it to end.

In the corner of the sitting room sat the last box, inside which lay her cookery books, still not unpacked. Their cottage had wide, deep shelves on either side of the inglenook that contained her adored Aga. And that was where she had kept her books. But the villa had no built in shelves at all so the books had to stay on the floor. Maya's thoughts went back to her shopping. She had been so inspired by the sight of fat bunches of deep green flat leafed parsley in the supermarket that she would make a lemony tabbouleh and use some of the fat tomatoes and baby cucumbers too. She would eat it for lunch, scooped up into curls of young Romaine lettuce.

It was not until she thought she heard the sound of Annie's flip-flops flapping away that she dared to venture back into the room that she longed to be hers.

Slipping off her shoes so that her heels would not make a noise on the floor, she sidled into the kitchen, closing the door behind her. Then she took the largest, lightest strides she could over to the door that led to the landing and closed that one too. She stifled a giggle. She felt like a schoolgirl on a sleepover tiptoeing to the kitchen with her friends for a midnight feast of such marvels as Dairylea cheese triangles and dry Weetabix spread with butter and jam. And here she was in broad daylight in her own house and feeling wicked and full of glee. Yes, that was it: 'glee' was the perfect word. A word that puffed up her chest and made her feel in the zone, drunk with happiness and anticipation.

She moved around the kitchen like a burglar, opening cupboards, removing knives and chopping boards from drawers, and wishing the fridge didn't hum quite so loudly in protest each time she closed the door. Boy, if Av and Jan could see her now, they'd have a fit. Normally her cooking left the whole place a bombsite, drawers gaping open like mouths, cupboards flapping and every chair covered in flour, even if she hadn't been using any. That was why Jan had become chief chef at Seasons, though Maya loved to do her bit, to create the recipes and to take over when Jan was ill or had a holiday. To her, cooking was both joyful and meditative. Time flew when she was in the kitchen. She never tired of making family meals; the fresher the ingredients, the more local, organic or in season the better. She loved to eat, which was probably why she had a bit of a paunch these days. And she didn't like to exercise. She hated being forced to watch herself wobble in unflattering wall-to-wall mirrors. Walking in the woods was more her thing. Gyms made her come out in a rash, even with an iPod to keep her going. She'd rather bop around the kitchen while she was cooking. Oh, for a bit of Radio 2. Her heart dipped. That woman had been right about missing things. She missed Radio 2. They often had it on in the shop. Maybe, when they got the Internet installed, she could listen to it on her computer? But for now, she wanted to feel good and cook, so she'd just have to sing. But what? That was it – inspired by the parsley she opened her mouth and began.

'Are you going to Scarborough Fair?
Parsley, sage, rosemary, and –'
The door clicked open.
'Madam?'

Maya couldn't bring herself to turn her whole body to face Annie, who she expected would be standing crestfallen in the doorway. 'Mmm?' she mumbled, trying not to be offensive, but not keen to look too happy either.

'I can help?'

Maya swallowed hard. This was her big chance to take control. Being in charge of the kitchen was what she wanted. It mattered. It bloody mattered. She laid down the knife, turned, and rested her back against the counter. Dropping her hands and placing them behind her back, she crossed her fingers tightly for luck. Then she tipped her head on one side and squeezed out the sweetest smile she could manage, just bordering on the sickly. 'Actually, er, um, would you mind, um, if I did it myself, today, just this once, er, Annie? Please?'

Annie nodded knowingly. 'No problem, madam. I do iron. You call me when finish and I clear up. Okay?'

Maya knew the sigh of relief that expelled itself from her lungs was a bit excessive, but she couldn't help herself and she had been holding her breath. She could have run across the room and kissed Annie for her magnanimity. Instead she just stood and grinned. Maybe this was going to be okay, after all. She could cook all she liked and not have to pack her own shopping at the supermarket, put it away when she got home or clean up her mess.

'Thank you, Annie. Thank you so much!' and when Annie had left the room, pointedly leaving the door open behind her, Maya punched the air with her fist. She'd clawed back some control at last.

Chapter seven

Easing her feet out of her red court shoes, Barb threw them out of her line of sight and flopped down onto her recliner.

What a day that had been. Successful though. Elske had called to report that she had persuaded Maya to go to The Twist, though she was too busy to go to them all herself what with all those cards to make for her sales table. All down to Barb, of course; she had pinned those adverts up in every grocery store in town. The Twist had signed up ten new girls and she'd persuaded Suchanatta to join the board to handle membership. Boy, that was a nasty job. All databases and administration. Being out there among real live folk was more Barb's scene. She hated being stuck at a lonely old desk. Jeez, she'd walked miles today. It was no surprise her feet hurt. She pulled one foot up onto her lap and began to massage it slowly. They really swelled up in this incredible heat. It was only just into October. Things wouldn't cool down for months yet. She took a neatly pressed white handkerchief out of her purse and moved it across her brow, before using it to mop her palms and discarding it. She leaned back, forcing her chair to move towards the horizontal and stretched out her arms and legs so that she looked just like the way Brandon would have drawn her when he was in kindergarten. Big fat tummy and stick legs.

Only her limbs were certainly not as skinny as they had been when he was still interested in drawing. She looked down at her arms. From this angle, they looked smooth and tanned from the shoulder right down to her wrist, where three matching gold bangles swung together.

Merry appeared in the doorway.

'Oh, hello,' said Barb. She didn't want a long conversation with Merry today. Her supply of helpful and supportive comments had just about run dry after the day she'd had.

'Can I get you a cold soda, madam?' asked Merry.

'Sure.' Barb racked her brains for something that might take a long time to make, though that was cruel. 'Ice tea would be lovely. Thanks.' And extracted her agenda from her purse. If she looked engrossed, maybe Merry would take that as a cue that she was too busy to talk. Besides, she needed to check she hadn't started double-booking herself again.

When she looked up, she saw the tall glass of ice tea before her, filled with six or seven cubes of ice and topped with a sprig of mint, just the way she liked it, placed on a circular glass drinks mat. Merry was nowhere to be seen. She relaxed.

She looked around the room at all her treasures. It had become her ritual. That and adding up the number of moves they had made. How many was it now? It was ridiculous that she could never remember how many off the top of her head. You'd have thought it would be ingrained – that, if you chopped her in half through the middle, she'd have rings like a tree, one for each move. Instead, she looked down at her waistline. She had added at least a pound of flesh per move. Fortunately, she knew how to dress well and cover up her bulges, cloaking them in well-cut shapes and fabric that would skim not cling.

First New Orleans, then Calgary, then Paris, Stavanger, then London, Bangkok, The Hague, Kuala Lumpur, Indonesia and now Dubai. That made ten, if you didn't count the first move from Amarillo to Houston. Hell, that counted. A move was a move, wasn't it? Eleven moves in twenty-five years meant she moved on average after little more than two years. Golly, was it really that often? She'd become a genius at grinning and bearing it. Guess it would soon be time to move on, then. She went back to the solemn business of counting. That made Dubai her eleventh move with Bill and fifth with Brandon. It would have been her fourth with Angelina. She couldn't help herself from glancing down at the low shelf that was deliberately not at eye level. It was the one she reserved for baby photographs. There, besides several of Brandon, stood the tiny heart-shaped frame that held a miniature photograph of a newborn. She looked so perfect. No one could have told she wasn't breathing. No one could have guessed it wasn't just another photo of Brandon. He was everywhere, just like in life, like his dad. He was a big active guy. His teeth so clean and straight and white, the braces had done wonders. Oh yes, she had lots to be thankful for. He was a great kid, lots of friends, always bringing them home for pizza and Coke after a game. Always the one to initiate a sleepover, a pool party, a barbecue. Took after her, of course. He certainly hadn't suffered socially from lack of a sibling. Then that photo of Bill and her on their wedding day given pride of place on top of the unit. There in a china mount decorated with pink roses. Smiling at each other, you could almost see the love between them, thick like honey. Bill's dark hair was glossy, he looked like a film star. Barb's hair was just the same colour and style as it was now, only now, of course, it had help.

Bill had always said it suited her. It was nice to keep at least one constant in her life. She had become accustomed to change and had built a hard protective shell over time, discovering that regular trips back to Texas and Skype conversations minimised homesickness. Back then she had loved Bill so much, for the way he had worked his way through college despite his trailer-park background and for his ambition and determination to rise above that bleak childhood with a single alcoholic mother. She basked in the fact that, having no family of his own, he had become the darling of her own. She was a typical hometown girl with a strong family who thanked the Lord before every meal. Bill was the absolute opposite. A bit of a rebel, in whom Barb found her first cause. He had bewitched her and loved everything about her. She would have been willing to do anything, to follow him anywhere. Her first love. She'd been a virgin when they married. Hell, at twenty-one she had hardly even touched alcohol. These days she had little time left for church, or so she told herself, when deep down she knew that Bill's tough start in life meant that he didn't think much of the power of God and chose, instead, the power of a regular salary. Over time, regular worship, like weekly meals with her parents and twin sister, had been just one more loss she kept to herself. She did manage to attend the Bible study group though, when she could. There she could be alone with her prayers and thoughts, though among other people. It was the only time she felt safe with silence.

She'd been bowled over by the just-graduated pizza delivery boy. He had been so grateful for the generous tips her father gave him and used the extra money to buy the smart suit that had found him a great job with an oil company. Bill loved the fact that Barb was pursuing a career of her own, as a nurse.

Once that ring was on her finger, she had shown her love for this big, strong, decent man by working extra hard on the house after her shifts to give him a real home. In the evenings, they would sit together on the swing seat on the porch, drinking home-made lemonade and listening to the cicadas. That had been her idyll. She had wanted nothing more.

Only, just as soon as she had gotten her little white clapboard house straight and finished painting its picket fence, Bill had burst into the kitchen where she was washing up after her encounter with the wrong end of the paintbrush.

'Hey, Barb, girl. You are never gonna believe this!' he carolled, picking her up by her tiny waist and spinning her round so that her hair flew.

'Careful, Bill,' she said. 'You'll get paint on your pants, I'm still cleaning up. Careful, it isn't dry yet.'

'I don't care about a bit of paint, darl'. We... ' He had stressed the word 'we' like he was bearing down on the word with all his weight, just like he did at night in the bedroom. And just like in the bedroom, what he said next squished all the goddamn air out of her in one fell swoop – 'We are off on an adventure. We are movin' to Houston.' The way those words ran together it sounded like he'd said 'TaYooston.' The power in the relationship shifted. Why hadn't she been consulted? Barb turned back to the sink and started running the faucet over her hands, lathering the backs of them rigorously with rough soap. 'Goodness!' she said. Then, taking a deep breath, like you have to when you start breathing again after a big shock, she added, 'Why?'

Bill was dancing around the kitchen. He grabbed a freshly baked cookie from the scrubbed tabletop and a glass from the cupboard before retreating to the refrigerator for milk. 'Exciting eh? Boy, Barbie, this is it. We are off! We've found the way out of sleepy old Amarillo! I'll be able to look after you properly. You can even quit nursing.'

Barb wiped her hands on the raggedy towel by the sink and sat down at the table. She needed to be sitting down. Her mind raced. She loved her work, looking after new mothers on the maternity ward. She'd just got the house so nice. Just planned a party for Mom's fiftieth. Organised a special day out with her sister, Angela.

'Sit down, Bill. You are making me dizzy dancing about like that. Come here and talk to me properly.' She patted the table with the flat of her hand, summoning him over like a teacher would call over a child to discuss his homework.

Bill placed his glass of milk down on the table so hard that it slopped over the edge. Barb jumped up to fetch a cloth and mopped at the spill, glad to be able to postpone the conversation slightly.

'Well, I was walking down the corridor and saw a sign up on the noticeboard that read, "Six month contract in Houston available for someone keen to get involved in oil field data acquisition. Will suit keen trainee or similar. No experience necessary." Anyway, I went straight to the guy in charge, had a quick interview, and got the job.'

'Golly,' Barb said again. They were going to have to move lock stock and barrel over to the other side of Texas to a place where she knew no one and would have to set up a new home all over again, only to have to move back again after six months. 'That's quite an opportunity for you,' she said. Just six months? Maybe she could stay behind? Maybe he could commute every week and come back at weekends?

'It's shift work, though,' he continued. 'Means I'll be four days on and four days off then four nights on and four days off. Think of all that free time I'll be able to spend with my beautiful new wife!' His eyes glittered at the prospect.

Shift work, maybe he could commute? She smiled and decided to look enthusiastic. It was only six months after all.

'That's great, honey,' she said. 'What does it mean for the future?' Maybe they'd soon return to Amarillo?

'That's the best part. They're going to train me up in an area that's needed the world over. Imagine that, Barb! We could get to Europe. Next time the fence needs painting, I'll be able to pay some other guy to do it for us! How about that?' He paused and took such a large bite out of his cookie that Barb marvelled he could open his mouth so wide without getting lockjaw. Money was important to Bill. She was not remotely motivated by the stuff. To him, a career meant money. To her, it meant doing something useful, making a difference. Bill had not thought to ask her how she felt about giving up her career. She swallowed down the unspoken words, not realising back then that this was to become quite a talent.

Barb took a long drink of her ice tea, ice tea that had been made by her maid, and recognised how far, literally, they had come since then. Of course, the six months had been extended and then the next 'opportunity' had been overseas. There had never been any question that Bill wouldn't accept a posting. Barb had no room to argue, her skills were pretty impossible to transfer, it had either been a question of getting local qualifications or learning a language or both. She'd let her licence slip. She was a good wife. Bill worked so hard, he deserved to have a peaceful home life. And so, one posting had become eleven and each time Bill had come home with a grin on his face about the next destination and its increasingly attractive benefits package, he climbed higher up the ladder. Now, he was way up in information management, working in some department that was known mostly by some acronym she could never remember. She'd learned to love the lifestyle. Well, maybe not 'love', exactly, but she did find some comfort in its familiarity and the people she met in what she knew was called the 'expat bubble'. A kind of ghetto in which they worked and played together. She knew how to handle it now. She hadn't lifted a paintbrush in twenty-five years. Bill had been right, he had always been able to afford to get some or other body in to fix stuff up. And if he had not picked up the check, the company had. Good old company. Had them all well and truly beholden to it. Like golden handcuffs. She replaced her drink on the coffee table and her gold bangles jangled against the rim. The inside of the diamond rings on her right hand chinked against the glass. What, honestly, did she have to complain about?

It was six o'clock. Bill was away on business, again, Kuwait, this time, she thought. Some conference. Mind you, when he was home, he wasn't exactly present, was he? Always at his laptop, or with his cell phone pressed to his ear, laughing and joking with the guy on the other end of the line. Barb saw that side of her husband when they were out in public, too. At home, just the two of them, he had become cold and distant. It was like living with a cardboard cutout. They hadn't had sex since Angelina, named for the aunt she would never meet. She imagined he grieved too, but he never said. Like her, he was good at charades.

Brandon was having dinner with a friend after the game and wouldn't be back for hours. When he was home, he was always glued to a screen of some kind, with a controller in his hand and a bowl of microwave popcorn on his lap. Barb had learned how to find the conversation and interaction she needed elsewhere. She had created a routine that thankfully left her so tired when she got home that she was almost glad of the silence. But, like a rubber boat with a leak, no sooner had she emptied her mind than it filled again. With thoughts she'd rather leave untouched. Thinking did her no good at all.

'Merry?' she called out.

Nothing. Good, she had gone back to her room. With no dinner to cook and no Brandon to sit for, she had left early. Barb was not going to be spied on. She drained her drink in one long gulp, sucking loudly to remove the last traces from between the ice cubes and padded to the kitchen in her bare feet. There, she re-filled her glass almost to the top with fresh ice, reached under the counter for the cookie tin and helped herself to a stack of rich, brown, cream-filled Oreo cookies. She didn't bother with a plate and returned to her recliner where she placed the cookies straight on the coffee table and then crossed over to the sterling silver tray where the bottles huddled, labels facing to the front, and poured Bacardi into her glass. Darn it, she had forgotten the Coke. Back on the recliner, she picked up the remote control for the TV in one hand and stuffed a cookie into her mouth with the other before reaching for her drink and settling down for the night. Luckily there was still plenty of Bacardi.

Chapter eight

To fill time she drove right to the other side of the city to the fish market, rather than buy it as part of her weekly supermarket shop. The fish came straight off the boat; so pink it looked like rare steak. Rich loved fish. Matthew hated bones, so tuna was ideal. On arriving home, Annie was on the front doorstep waiting for her as usual.

'Thanks Annie, but I could have managed it myself. It wasn't heavy,' she said climbing the stairs to the kitchen.

Annie shook her head and smiled. 'Boss home tonight?'

'Yes, he is. In time for dinner. I thought we would have tuna.'

'I can cook?' Annie wiped her hands on the tea towel she kept tucked into her skirt. 'I have nice recipe with chilli and little lime.'

'Well, actually, I quite wanted ...' but Maya stopped herself. 'Then I teach you English recipe too?' She found herself responding in the same sparse style, using limited pronouns and tenses. She thought that it might be easier for someone like Annie, who had only learned her English in later life, to understand. She recognised that speaking in this truncated way only perpetuated her maid's stilted language.

Annie lifted her heels slightly from the red flip-flops she wore every day. It was probably her version of a jump for joy.

'OK, Annie.' Maya walked over to the bookcase and took down a battered book that was starting to split at the seams. 'I am going to teach you about Delia Smith and her apple pie.'

'Madam,' said Annie, eyeing the book jacket, 'I not read English.'

'I will show you how to do it. Maybe you can take notes in, er, Hindi?'

'My language Konkani, madam, I not writing anything. No need. I keep in here.' She tapped the side of her head with her fingers.

Maya and Annie had both risen to the challenge. Teaching Annie how to use scales had been the highlight of her day. Maya had been incapable of opening a packet or jar without spilling some of its contents so Annie had followed her round the kitchen wielding a J Cloth. In the end Annie won and chilli and lime were added to the mix.

'You are good teacher, madam!' said Annie, happily peeling apples.

And now, with the supper sorted, she was poised to write her first post for the blog she had set up before leaving Stamford. She had called it Seasons in the Sun. Writing something that the whole world would see both excited and scared her, made her feel naked and exposed. But whenever Maya had an idea she liked to follow it through, so here she was embarking on yet another new adventure with no clue where it might actually take her.

Hello from Dubai.

She began

It has taken a whole month to get sorted but the Winter family is now fully installed in sunny Dubai. By 'fully' I mean that we have at last got broadband and I have taught myself how to blog. It seems fairly simple, so here goes.

From my window I can see a palm tree. It is not as tall as I would have expected and is bowed down under the weight of big fat bunches of yellow dates. I think they may be overripe. Did you know that dates are yellow or red when they are fresh? No, neither did I. Life here is full of surprises. It is safe, women can drive, and I don't have to swathe myself in black. We can drink alcohol and everyone speaks English. I can buy everything I can possibly want in the supermarkets and fresh and local ingredients in the markets. It is almost the end of the holy month of Ramadan and so, as the country prepares to celebrate; we too have reasons to be cheerful.

It is hot, more than 40 degrees centigrade mostly, and the humidity is rainforest heavy at times. Though things are starting to cool down now winter approaches.

I went to the fish market today. Or fish souk, as people call it here, and bought an entire yellow fin tuna, which the man cut and bagged for me to put in the freezer. It is so fresh you can eat it raw. I've experimented with a marinade that uses soy sauce, ginger and fresh lime (you can buy them all at Seasons of course). It is delicious with asparagus or French beans in a salad. So, here, below is the recipe and a photograph I took of it marinating. I'm not much of an expert with a camera, so bear with me.

That was it. She'd done her first blog. She wrote the recipe, checked it carefully for errors, inserted the digital photograph she'd taken of her own rendition of the dish, which she had now left in the fridge ready to cook for supper, and clicked the Publish button. Now all she had to do was wait and see. She turned off the computer and went downstairs.

Like the sofa, their old pine farmhouse dining table looked incongruous in such a bright, white, square room. It looked as if it had shrunk, marooned between the newly-shelved walls. Annie had laid the table at six, adding the white lace tablecloth to hide the green legs and thick top of the table beneath. There were even napkins, two wine glasses (one for her, one for Rich), and four water glasses (one for each of them). Maya slid aside one of the many French windows, shut it firmly behind her, and walked onto the balcony. It was odd having a first-floor sitting room, but, like many things about Dubai, she was getting used to it. She broke off a sprig of bright pink bougainvillea, leaning over the balustrade to reach it. Looking down its trunk for a moment, she saw how dry the flowerbeds were and marvelled that anything grew in such parched, pale soil. Just one stem would make the perfect centrepiece to Annie's table, particularly in that antique silver vase she had picked up on a trip to Sharjah souk with Barb. Maya was finding the heat a struggle, and it was taking her longer than she'd expected to find her way around. It was all part of culture shock, she knew. Barb had lent her a book all about it. The book had explained that this tiredness came about because all the new stuff she was having to learn to do was exhausting, like being back at school. She would have liked to be out there making friends already but hadn't the energy quite yet. Still she knew that the lethargy would pass and she'd soon be back to her normal self, getting out there and getting involved. At least writing the blog would give her days some structure and purpose. She was enjoying having time to experiment in the kitchen too. Back home, they had just about lived in the kitchen, sitting around this same table, clothless, of course. That room had been crammed from floor to ceiling, each wall lined with shelves that were higgledy-piggledy with books, games, and an assortment of what the boys called 'random stuff'. The kind of stuff she was always intending to tidy up, when she found a moment. Now she had too many 'moments'.

'Posh table, Mum,' commented Oliver, nicking a handful of peanuts from the coffee table, which had been made ready with bowls of olives, nuts, and Pringles. 'Anyone coming?'

'No, just your dad. He should have been home by now. His plane landed an hour ago. But he called to say he'd got some post or something to fetch from the office first.' Maya loved getting the post. It all went to Rich's office and receiving it was another reason she was glad when he was in town. Her mother had taken to writing a letter to her every week, using those flimsy blue airmail envelopes. She wrote a lot of drivel about the flower-arranging club and the lady in the library, but Maya loved receiving them. It made her feel in touch.

Oliver looked at the dining table and then back to the nibbles. 'Why all the fuss? You're not going to tell us we're moving again, are you? Have we got any Coke?' He slumped into the corner of the newly acquired cream linen sofa, the remote control for the television in one hand, and a thick wodge of crisps in the other. The old sofa had been relegated to the boys' den upstairs.

'Oh Oli, do you have to eat on the new sofa? How many times… ' Rich was only a bit late and the traffic was always murder getting out of the airport, even at three in the morning, he'd said.

'Mmm?' answered Oli through a mouthful that sent shards of sour cream and onion over the cushion next to him. 'You didn't pay for it. Dad's company did. And anyway, mess doesn't matter. Annie will clear it up. She hoovers in here at six every morning, I know, the racket wakes me up.'

Maya walked back to the French windows to stare at the drive that led into the compound. Still no sign of Rich's car. She tried his mobile number again. He still hadn't remembered to switch it back on. 'That's not the point. You never used to be allowed to eat on the sofa in Stamford.'

'Well we are not "in Stamford" now, are we? You wrenched me from my school and all my best mates, remember? We live here. Eating on the sofa should be part of my compensation package, like we get a free flight home and the school fees paid.' Oli reached for some nuts. 'I'm starving. When's dinner?'

'When Dad's home.'

'What's for dinner?'

'Yellow fin tuna. I went to the fish souk this morning. It was fresh today.' Maya waited for a response from her eldest son.

Oliver grabbed another handful of crisps.

'And salad.'

Nothing.

'And garlic bread?'

'Great!' He flicked on the telly.

'And pudding. Annie made an apple pie.'

'What time again?'

'When Dad's home.'

'When's that?'

'Any minute. Stop eating rubbish… '

'… You'll spoil your dinner. You put it here, so I eat it. Oh great. It's *Cribs*.' He settled back into this corner of sofa and increased the volume.

She went upstairs to the computer and switched it back on. She had never found herself addicted to email before. But then she'd never been lonely before, either. Rich being away had never bothered her so much, not even when the kids were small. But maybe she was missing him more because they had more fun when he was home, eating out, driving in the desert, exploring the souks. In a way, when he was home it felt like a holiday. When he wasn't she did a lot of waiting and didn't like that side of herself, the needy side. The blog was a godsend, but she was in danger of spending more time in cyberspace than reality. The computer beeped and a window popped up that said 'Welcome Mum' accompanied by a picture of a butterfly. She sat down. Maybe someone would have seen her blog and left a comment? Or maybe she'd got an email from someone? She clicked on the Send and Receive icon. Silence. No beep of an incoming message. Nothing. She walked to the window. The drive was quiet. Just one more check and she really would turn off for the night. She returned to the blog. She had a comment.

Dear Maya

I am very happy to see your first blog. I stay late at the shop to use computer after work, Jan says that is okay. I can check every day now and print a copy for Jan and Avril. I like recipe. I order limes and will make some marinade ready to sell in glass jars. How are you? Everybody send their love. I make beetroot soup today. Janet says very good.

Bye
Danuta

Danuta was turning out to be a bit of a find. She could use a computer and cook. Perhaps that was because she was so much younger than Jan and Av? She felt a bit deflated. It would have been much nicer for Av or Jan to have been the first ones to respond to the blog. She really looked forward to hearing from them both soon.

Maya stole another glance out of the window and went back to the sitting room. It felt so empty here, just her and the boys, and Annie of course. She had so little to do that she seemed to be shrinking, too. And now, here Maya was, standing at the window killing time again, staring out and waiting. She really must get her act together and find a job. Earn her own money again. It was no fun being reliant on Rich for everything. No, she'd get a job. Just as soon as she got her residence permit.

'Mum!' Matthew shrieked down from the top floor of the villa, where he was supposedly doing his homework on his new laptop. 'When's Dad home?'

'Soon!' Maya shrieked back, knowing that she would normally have told him not to shout but to come and find her and ask her properly.

'I'm starving! What's for supper?'

She moved to the stairwell so that she didn't have to yell at the top of her voice. 'Fish. And salad. And garlic bread!' And with that she heard the Audi draw up outside. 'And pie.'

Feeling calmer now her family was together again, Maya went to sit on the other sofa, twin to the one on which her elder son now lounged surrounded by a confetti of crisps. She tuned her ears into the sound of her husband's return. First there was the rustle of the key in the lock. Then the swish of his briefcase as he kicked it under the hall table, followed by the clink of the keys in the little copper bowl they had bought in the old covered antique market in neighbouring Sharjah. Next he would shuck off his shoes, then climb two flights of marble stairs silently in his stockinged feet to place his case in the bedroom. A few minutes silence while he changed from his work clothes into his shorts and tee shirt and back down to the sitting room. Maya knew every step. He never announced his arrival until his mind was in 'home' mode, and he was never in 'home' mode until he was dressed for the mood.

'Is that Dad?' Oli said from his corner of the sofa. 'Can we eat now?'

Rich stood in the doorway.

Maya looked up. 'Oh, hello!' She smiled, hoping she looked surprised and unable to resist skimming her eyes from the top of his floppy hair to the faintly bronzed tops of his bare feet. At least he got to sunbathe when he was away on a trip. He looked more like an adorable Labrador than ever and she felt that familiar tingle of anticipation that came each time her husband was home from another trip. She crossed her legs quickly and sat up straighter. Maybe she could hang onto this feeling until bedtime?

'How was Bangkok?'

Rich walked over to her and stooped to kiss her mouth. 'Fine,' he said. 'Everything okay back at the ranch?' He stretched out his arm to do a high-five with Oli.

'Mmm,' said Oli.

'Bit bored, Barb's bamboozled me into going to one of her coffee morning things, which got me out of the house. Oh and I did my first blog,' said Maya, instantly regretting sounding negative. 'Any letters?'

'Nope.' Rich was wandering off towards the kitchen. 'First blog, eh? How did it go? Barb's that Texan with a husband in oil, right? Drink?'

'Coke please, Dad,' called Oli.

'Lovely, please,' replied Maya. 'Glasses are already on the table.'

'Red?'

'It's fish. Tell me about Bangkok. Did you visit any temples this time? Ride in any tuk-tuks? Burn your tongue on any more glass noodles?' She followed him into the kitchen, wanting to be near to him, to feel the heat from his body, share in his adventures.

'White, then?' There was a pause. 'Oh hello, Annie, How are you? Something smells nice. Have you been cooking again?'

Maya went back to the sofa. He tried so hard to listen to everyone, include them all in conversation that he could not keep them all going at once.

'Yes, boss,' Annie replied with pride.

Rich returned with two glasses of wine and sat down beside Maya.

'Where's my Coke?' said Oli.

'Get it yourself, you lazy oaf!'

Oli grunted, stood up, and shuffled out of the room.

Rich grinned. 'Cheers!' He lifted his glass to his lips.

'I asked if you had a good trip,' Maya said, raising her own glass.

'Yeah, great. Met some nice people, had a few beers in some dodgy bars near the hotel. The new route's getting popular with the locals. Would you believe that they change into civvies in the loo half way through the flight? The route's taking off big time and I may have to be away a little bit more. You really should come with me now and again. Now we have Annie to mind the boys. Then you can see the temples and tuk-tuks for yourself.' He gave her a hug. 'I'd love to show you the Grand Palace, the floating markets, take you shopping for jade or silk.'

'No jet lag, then?' She hoped he could keep awake until bedtime. Well, past bedtime, actually.

'Not really, only three hours' difference. This wine'll probably floor me though. What have you been doing?'

'Nothing much. I bought a nice little vase, picked some bougainvillea for it from the garden. It's on the table. I've been for coffee with Barb. Been for lunch. To the mall, the tailor's, the fish souk. The usual.' She put her hand up to her hair and ran it slowly through her fingers.

'Have you done something to your hair? Had it cut?'

'Yesterday. And coloured.'

'Oh yes. I thought it looked different. Not a bad life is it, eh? I go away and earn the money and you stay home and spend it! I tell you, when I come back, I'm going to be an expat wife.' He cleared his throat. 'You can thank me later, if you like,' he whispered, and gave her knee a little pat.

'It's not all wonderful, you know.' Maya took another sip of her wine.

'It's early days, love. It won't be long until you recognise this place for the paradise it really is.'

'But it's a fake paradise, don't you think? Some of the palm trees are fibreglass and they even import the grass.'

'The beach isn't fake. You love it on the beach.' He lifted his forefinger and gently touched her hair. 'Hair looks nice, too.'

She stood up. 'I can smell the garlic bread, so that must mean dinner's almost ready. Why don't you go and tell Matt you're home and get him and Oli rounded up at the table?'

Rich walked to the doorway and there he stopped. Maya braced herself. He was going to do it the lazy way.

'Oli! Matthew! Supper!' he bellowed.

Matthew burst into the room. 'Hey, Dad! You're back. Did you get me that new game like you said?'

Rich ruffled his son's hair. 'Sorry, chum.'

Matthew's face fell. 'Well, what did you get me then?'

'Come on, mate. I can't buy you something every time I go away ... Unlike your mum, I don't have time to go shopping.' He grinned at Maya.

'How's school going?' Rich asked his younger son.

'Fine,' he shrugged.

'Enjoying it, then?'

'Not as good as Stamford. No sports matches at all, so far,' moaned Matthew. 'But Dev's got a Wii, so I've been playing tennis and stuff on that. I'm best at skateboarding. Hey, can I have a Wii?'

'I'm not made of money, guys,' said Rich with a smile. 'Put it on your Christmas list.'

'Who's Dev?' asked Maya.

'Some random guy,' Matt shoved a piece of garlic bread in his mouth, then wiping his hand on his shorts. 'Devendra.'

'Is he Indian, then?'

'Doh, Mum!'

'Use the napkin, not your shorts, please.'

'Since when did we use napkins?' asked Oli. 'What's happened to kitchen roll? And aren't you going to ask me how school is?' Maya looked to Rich then back to Oli, wondering what he had to say. So far, since they arrived, he had done nothing but complain about all that he had lost. She knew how he felt, but didn't want to bring attention to it by discussing it. It would be like picking at a scab.

'I've made a friend!' he said as nonchalantly as he could muster. 'Alv.' He looked at his mother. 'Short for Alvaro, he's Spanish, in case you were wondering. It's his second time here in Dubai, so he can show me the ropes and he plays drums.'

Could she start to relax now? Once the boys had friends, she could stop worrying about them and feeling guilty for what they'd done by dragging them away from their home.

'That Bangkok idea, Rich? I'd like that,' she said. 'After Christmas, eh, once we've all found our feet.'

'Cool. I'll start checking out the most romantic restaurants. Actually, folks, I do have something for you. I almost forgot.' He rose from the table, padded down the stairs, clicked open his briefcase, and returned, handing each of them an envelope.

'What's this?' asked Matt, ripping at the seal. 'Oh! My passport. What's so cool about that?'

'Look inside,' said Rich, sitting down and leaning back in his chair with his hands clasped behind his head.

'A residence visa?' He pulled a sour face. 'I thought it would be something exciting.'

'It is exciting,' said Maya, using one of her new acrylic nails to slice open the envelope. She grinned at Rich.

'Yep! We've all got them now. We are legal at last.'

'Whoopeedoo,' mumbled Oliver, not even bothering to open his envelope.

'At last!' said Maya. She took out her passport and flicked through it for the right page. She looked up at Rich. The moment she had been waiting for. Her eyes widened. 'I don't believe,' she whispered. 'There must be a mistake – look!' She passed it to him.

Rich looked down at the page and his hand flew to his mouth. 'Oh, my God!' he said. 'I had no idea!'

'What is it, Mum?' Oliver asked, his face creased with worry.

Maya took a deep breath and stared at the pink label that covered a whole page of her passport. 'It says, boys,' she paused. 'House Wife – not allowed to work.'

That night Maya went up to bed first, leaving Rich behind nursing the end of the bottle of Sauvignon Blanc and the remote control. She took out her book and began to read, but her eyes were not on the words and after the third attempt at the same page, she gave up and turned out the light. Her eyes were wide open, fixed on the crack of light that showed under the bedroom door and came from the landing; her ears fine-tuned to pick up every change in timbre as her husband switched channels yet again. She closed her eyes, but her mind stayed on full alert as she unpicked every sentence, every glance, every inch of body language that had accompanied their fresh tuna in lime after the fateful passport moment. Surely, he knew her well enough to realise that she was not the type who was born to shop and spend time in beauty parlours? That she only had her hair highlighted and coloured because, a, it took up more time, and b, she wanted to look her best for him, now they could afford it? Not allowed to work? What the blazes was she going to do all day now? If he wanted sex tonight, he had another think coming.

She opened her eyes again in an attempt to change the subject. The shapes of the room loomed out at her. The new clothes that she had flung over the back of her chair had taken on the shape of a monster with a long thin finger, beckoning her over as if trying to lure her to a life of wide white shopping malls with clean, bright window displays, lit by crystal chandeliers. Writing a blog was never going to plug the hole in her life. Nor was spending money. She'd rather earn it. But how?

Silence. He had turned the television off at last. Rich's routine was always the same. Telly off. Check the doors are locked. Fetch a glass of water. Five minutes in the loo. Then the door would be flung open flooding the room with light from the landing. She turned over and thrust her head deep into the pillow.

'Aw, don't go to sleep.' He shut the door again and considerately turned on the light in the ensuite bathroom instead. 'I've been away four days and you never know, I may be worth staying awake for,' he growled.

If Maya had been able to see him now, she was pretty sure he would have been raising one eyebrow and winking at his reflection in the mirror. The slop of water in the basin was a sure indication that he was having a shave. Next the rigorous sound of tooth brushing. He cleared his throat. Should she pretend to be asleep or admit she was awake?

'I am awake. Hard not to be, with all the racket coming from the bathroom.' That was below the belt, Maya. Rich's ablutions were not the reason she was not asleep. 'Anyway, I'm too upset.'

With that, Rich slid from the bathroom to the bed in one swift move and there he was, naked and expectant beside her. He nuzzled her neck. His smooth cheek rubbed against her own. Skin to skin never failed to be sexy, but she ignored it.

'I know how to cheer you up,' he said, sliding one hand down the front of her nightie and the other up from the bottom. 'Maya, Maya, you set my heart on fire,' he said softly.

She couldn't bring herself to do him the honour of a response. Not even his favourite lines could put her in the right frame of mind. However much she loved him and had missed him. He removed his hands and within seconds Maya could hear his breath whistle slightly as he fell asleep.

Chapter nine

Barb waited anxiously for her team to appear at her Coffee with a Twist. She had to be sure to get there before the first guests arrived but after the night she'd had, she was not going to take her dark glasses off until the very last minute. It was bound to be busy today. Always was, in Ramadan. She was almost sorry the Eid holiday that signified the end of the fasting was around the corner. The first person to arrive was bound to be a newbie. She'd noticed how newcomers always entered the room in a snakelike movement. First, their heads would appear around the door. They always checked that they had the right room before allowing the rest of their bodies to cross the threshold. Then, they'd enter slowly, looking left and right, head bowed and shoulders raised until they caught sight of the Welcome Table or a familiar face and relaxed at last. The old hands were quite different. Then she spotted the legs first. Bodies would follow, turned back from being deep in conversation with those they had bumped into on the way in. Old faces. They hardly needed to come to the meetings. They could have had just as much fun in the car park.

Ah, here was Maya. Her new hairdo looked tremendous.

'Hey, girlfriend!' called Barb, removing her shades. 'Nice to know I can rely on someone to be on time. Your hair looks great, by the way.'

Maya walked hurriedly towards the table. Her aqua linen A-line dress was a little too long and narrow, and made her walk oddly, as if she were stuck together at the knees. Barb would have advised her to take it for shortening. But it did match her shoes. She liked Maya; with a bit of direction and a decent tailor she'd be an asset to the team. You could tell she was a doer. Just a little bit lost at the moment. Finding her feet.

'Hi, Barb!' Maya seemed really pleased to see her and swooped straight in with a hug at the ready, a little awkward, like a fledgling bird trying to get its wings straight, but not bad, not bad. She was learning.

'Now, Maya, I'm so glad you're here. Alathia never did drop off the attendance register, so I need you to make one fast. Here.' She grabbed a sheet of plain white paper from her purse and a black marker pen.

'Do you have *everything* in that bag?' Maya laughed. 'I wouldn't be surprised to see you pulling a flipchart out of there next. And a white rabbit!'

'Yeah, well, you know me. I like to be prepared. I was a girl scout for years. Now. You need to make three columns and take a note of name, email address, and cell phone number. Right? And make them a label, of course.'

Maya bent her head and began work right away. Her straight hair swung down low, obscuring her face and she poked it back behind her ear, revealing those neat pearl earrings they had bought together in the Ibn Battuta Mall the other week. You never could go wrong with pearls.

Barb looked at her watch. It was 9 o'clock already and people surely should have been arriving by now. She had worked so hard on the agenda and a copy already lay on every chair. They had a lot to get through. And where were the coffee and cookies? They should have been here by now. Barb tutted and Maya raised her head.

'Sorry. I'm trying to make this as neat as I can.'

'No worries. It's fine. I'm just wondering about the refreshments. Looks like they're not here again.' She gave a brittle chuckle. 'Would you mind the fort for me for a moment while I go and find the guy in charge and chase it up?'

Maya was only too happy to help, of course. Her old theory was working again, that people would rather be busy than lonely or bored.

When she returned after giving the food and beverage guy a piece of her mind, she saw Maya had settled in beautifully and her face was flushed with the thrill of doing her job well and efficiently. It didn't take much to make someone feel fulfilled and useful, Barb thought. And the club certainly offered plenty of opportunities to expat women who were looking for purpose in their otherwise superficial lives.

It was her second meeting and Maya still felt like a stranger. Everyone clustered in tight groups and Maya didn't feel she could interrupt or ask to join their conversations. Being on the Welcome Table had been good. It had given her something to do and stopped her from acting like a spare part. But, apart from Barb, she didn't know a soul. Maybe it would take time. Or maybe Maya was just rubbish at networking. She moved to the horseshoe of seats in front of the stage and picked herself a seat near the back, on the edge, content to watch the people coming in, listen to their conversations, and look at their clothes, make up, and hair.

Maya felt sorry for Barb today. Not only had Alathia let her down about the Welcome Table, but also the coffee had arrived late. Now, Barb was looking calm as anything as she took to the stage. She looked at home up there, if a little red around the eyes. Maya reckoned all Americans were cheerleaders at heart. So passionate about their team, their charity, their club, that they could wave their pompoms and grin at people on demand. Barb tapped her pencil against an empty glass.

'Good morning, everybody,' she said, beaming. 'It is my absolute pleasure to see so many of you here. You are all busy women so let's cut to the chase and let me introduce you to our guest speaker this morning, Leila al Farooq.' She paused and stretched out her arm towards a woman in a long dark blue dress, her hair was covered by an embroidered navy *lahaaf*. Maya had signed her in at the Welcome Table and was prepared for her thick Irish accent.

Leila got to her feet. Everyone turned to look at her.

'Come here, Leila. Come and join me.'

Leila was surprisingly tall and very slim, like a model. She glided to the stage and climbed the stairs quickly, the elegant toes of her undoubtedly designer shoes peeping from beneath her skirt.

Barb cleared her throat, giving those who were still whispering hellos at each other the chance to be quiet. 'Leila is something of a pioneer.' She paused for effect. Barb was a mistress of suspense. Her face changed to one of sadness. The curve of her lips inverted and her head tipped to one side. She was a bit of an actress too. Everyone in the room was silent, waiting for the next stage of the mystery to enfold. 'Last year, Leila's sister-in-law died tragically.' Barb paused for a moment.

'Here, in Dubai.' Another pause.

'She was French, came from the Alps. Her name was

originally Mireille, but like Leila, she changed her name when she married a Muslim and became Maryam. But in many ways Maryam was just like you, like all of us,' she paused and opened her arms widely, 'she was an expatriate here. Maryam was married to Leila's husband's brother, Hatim.'

Maya's skin crawled with goose pimples and she straightened her spine against the wooden back of the blue dralon dining chair. Barb took a look at the index card she had been holding, then stepped back and let Leila pick up the story.

'Maryam was my good friend. She'd been here ten years, like me but unlike me she was not a city girl, she had grown up in the mountains, in the snow and the fresh air. Poor Maryam found it tough here. She had a hard time settling in. They had a wonderful home here in the city and another by the sea in Fujeirah. She had everything she could have dreamed of. Lots of staff. Amazing cars. Tons of holidays. But she missed the outdoor life. She missed being a ski instructor. She missed the snow. She missed her brothers and sisters. She struggled to learn Arabic and, unable to have children, became lonely and depressed. She took the Ferrari and drove it into a lamppost on the Abu Dhabi Road. No one else was involved. There was no doubt that it was suicide. She even left a note that explained that she couldn't handle it any more.'

Sharp intakes of breath rang out throughout the room. Maya knew where Maryam was coming from. But suicide?

'I know. It's a terrible story,' Leila continued. 'Tragic.' Her parchment coloured skin, every inch dusted with freckles, was pale. Maya longed to see her hair. She wondered what her name had been before she became Leila. Clasping her hands in front of her, Leila went on. 'And that is why I don't want it to happen again.' She stopped and swallowed hard. Straightening her shoulders, she began again. 'I don't know about you, but I think many of us live a good life here. Better than it would be back home.' She paused. 'Right? But money and servants and sunshine and cars are not everything. When you take away our professional identity, and the things we most love to do, we can become empty, disempowered. Maryam loved to ski. She loved the mountains and log fires and the crunch of snow underfoot. She loved teaching. It made her feel useful, fulfilled. When we lose our jobs and hobbies, some of us feel empty, lost. Like a kind of non-person.' She paused for a moment. 'Am I making any sense?'

Several people were nodding.

'Sure,' said Barb.

'Too bloody right,' muttered Maya under her breath and thought she noticed the slim blonde a few chairs further down her row twitch the corner of her mouth upwards in agreement.

'May I ask you something?'

Everyone raised their eyes in assent.

'How many of you had to give up your jobs to follow your husbands here?'

A sea of hands was raised.

'And who had a hobby back home that they just can't continue here?'

A new selection of hands went up.

'How many of you feel a bit sad, even depressed?'

Though many hands now went back down, a startling number of hands were raised, though tentatively.

'And who feels lonely? Bored? Unfulfilled? Maybe not every day, but sometimes?'

More hands went up as their owners looked at their knees.

'Don't you think that is tragic? I know I do. Living here is a charmed existence, we are very lucky, but sometimes it can feel like a prison sentence and I want to change that. If I can prevent one woman from ending up like lovely Maryam then I will.' Her voice grew stronger as she spoke and she began to clench her fists. Leila looked at the assembled women, seemingly picking some out at random, straight into their eyes. Maya squirmed slightly and wiped her palms on her dress. She knew this pale blue was a mistake.

'My husband, Ali, has a very close, loving family. We used to spend lots of time with his brother, Hatim and Maryam. They had a wonderful marriage. Hatim was kind and doting. He hated watching her suffer. She knew she could have got involved in the ski slope here or sand-skiing in the dunes, but they wouldn't have been the same. Maryam thought that if she could just have had a baby she would have been okay. They had every test there was but it just wasn't to be and so, instead, they would spend as much time as they could with our children, Mohammed and baby Yasmin. Maryam knew how lucky she was and did her best to hide her pain from us all. When she died it was a real bolt from the blue. I had to find a way to come to terms with our tragedy. And then I had an idea. I could take our loss and try to turn it into something positive. I could start a centre for foreign women in Dubai. A place where they could share their pain, and explore other ways to find fulfilment. We could teach new skills, offer therapies to counter stress and depression and, above all, help all those women who want to work to find a way back into the workplace. Even if I only help a handful of people it will have been worth it.' She bowed her head. She had finished.

Barb stood on the edge of the stage, clutching her pile of papers to her chest. Maya watched Barb and Leila exchange a glance, at which Barb moved forward to the centre of the stage once more.

'And ladies, this is where you come in. Leila's centre is to be our next charity. I know this is a cause close to all our hearts. She has only just begun her work here and has a long way to go. So.' She extracted a piece of paper from the bundle in her arms and waved it at the audience. 'I have this sign-up sheet here, which I will leave on the Welcome Table. All those of you who want to help in some way with this important idea, just add your details here and Leila will be in touch.' She turned to Leila. 'Thank you, Leila, for coming to talk to us.' She put her hands together and in seconds everyone began to clap.

All over the room, women moved their heads closer together and mumbled in low tones. Maya heard their murmurs of 'How terrible,' and 'You know, it could almost have been me,' and wished she had someone beside her to agree with. That petite, serene young woman with spiky straw-coloured hair that looked like it took a while to gel up every morning, sat a few seats away, also alone. Maya smiled at her and she smiled back. Her badge read 'Hello my name is Liv.' Funny, Maya didn't remember signing her in. Maybe she'd arrived late?

'Ladies, ladies!' Barb was off again. Now she was looking directly at Maya. 'Maya,' she called out.

Maya blanched. What on earth was she going to have to do now? First the Welcome Table, now this. The penny dropped. She should have realised what was happening from previous meetings.

'Maya is one of our newest members and she comes from a place called Stam Ford, UK.' Barb beamed. Maya blushed. Now they were all looking at her. 'Now, y'alls make Maya real welcome won't you. Maya, would you like to stand up and introduce yourself to everyone?'

Hell, she had no idea what to say. She stood up as slowly as she possibly could to give herself time to think. Her hands were stone cold and clammy. She wiped them on the skirt of her dress. Swallowing hard, she began.

'Hello, everyone.' She paused. Now what? Her mind raced like a desperate housewife in a supermarket five minutes before closing time, supper to cook and no idea what she was doing. She could tell them about who she used to be, who she hoped to become or who she was right now. She didn't want to let Barb down.

'Okay.' She cleared her throat. 'Um. My name is Maya Winter, like the season.' We've got two boys, Oliver, 14, Matthew, 12, they go to Emirates British School, and my husband, Rich, is a pilot with Arabian Airlines.' Everyone was smiling. She was doing all right. 'I've, er, we've been here just over a month and live at Mimosa Gardens.' She'd noticed how this was how most women defined themselves here. 'I used to run a delicatessen back in England.' She stopped again. Was she really going to say this? Then the words shot out of her mouth without warning. 'But I'm starting to feel like I left my identity behind at Heathrow. Leila's speech really resonated with me. Since I got here, I've been a bit lost and bored. Sad even. I haven't done anything at all. Nothing important, anyway. I'm just a wife and mother. And yesterday something happened that knocked me for six, made me feel like a second-class citizen. I got a stamp in my passport that said I was a housewife and not allowed to work. Is this normal? Or was I singled out for some reason?'

Barb answered for them. 'No, Maya, it isn't you. We all get one. Does wonders for the ego, doesn't it?' She laughed in an attempt to lift the atmosphere.

Around the room, the others murmured about the passport stamp and shook their heads. They all knew about it. Why hadn't anyone told her? But other women were working here, like Elske, for example.

'Oh, God, sorry. I shouldn't have said that. It just kind of came out. Not very positive, was it?' She looked up at Barb apologetically. She hadn't wanted to be a party pooper. Now she felt a little faint; saying the words out loud had made that stamp more real than ever.

Liv moved closer and rested her hand lightly on Maya's wrist yet with unexpected warmth.

'Take a deep breath,' she whispered, and she took one herself to show Maya how. So Maya did, obediently. 'Don't worry. There's always a way to fix things. You can fix anything, *ja*.' Then she made a weird sort of um-er-um sound, that seemed to be the equivalent of uhuh or eh. Maya wondered where she came from with that singsong accent.

Barb tapped her glass again. 'A big hand to Maya,' she said and everybody clapped on cue. 'Of course. Here at The Twist we always need volunteers, and joining the board is a great way to get involved with something, put some purpose into your life.'

Maya smiled broadly and did her best to show everyone she had regained her composure before sitting down. Something didn't add up. If they all got the same stamp in their passports, how come some of them still worked? She'd ask Elske later. A cool draught of air ran over her bare calf as the folds of Leila's dress swished past on her way out of the room. Maya looked up. Maybe she should get involved with Leila's centre. She didn't know a thing about women's empowerment, but she shared a passion for the cause. But the Irish girl was gone.

'That was very brave,' said Liv, fixing her with her cool blue eyes.

Maya shrugged apologetically. 'You think?'

'I think most women in this room feel the same. But they don't want to say it in public. Many expat wives choose to be secret drinkers, instead.'

'You think? Stupid more like.' Maya lifted her bag onto her shoulder. 'It's not like me at all. I'm just a bit over-emotional today. I couldn't sleep all night.' She cleared her throat. It was time to focus on someone else. 'So, Liv, where do you come from? I'm not sure I recognise the accent.'

'I'm from Norway.'

'Is this your first posting?' Maya knew she sounded like all the other women who met her for the first time, asking the same old questions. But she had to admit that they did elicit some interesting responses.

'Posting? Ha! I have lived in England and Turkey too.'

'Husband's job, I suppose? Are you what they call a trailing spouse too, like me?'

'That's a terrible phrase! Makes women sound like a suitcase on wheels.'

Maya laughed and waited for more information.

Liv shook her head. 'No. I am alone.'

Maya was shocked. 'You have a job, then?'

'Kind of.' She reached for her shoulder bag.

'Go on.' Maya was intrigued.

'Long story,' she said. 'Must go, I have a client. Good to meet you, Maya. Remember to breathe.' She put her flattened hand to her chest and breathed in and out, slowly, showing that she wore bright blue nail varnish. 'Bye bye.'

Maya sat for a moment watching Liv slide out of the room, nodding her head in recognition to lots of people and handing small business cards to others. And she was gone.

A petite oriental woman approached Maya, putting out her right hand in welcome. 'We haven't met, Maya,' she said. 'I'm Jim's wife, Suchanatta. HR bloke? He took you on the grand tour on your first day, remember?'

'Oh, yes. Hello!' Maya smiled as the penny dropped. 'So you're Sue?'

'Yes, most people call me Sue.' She touched the emerald green silk scarf she wore at her throat. 'You know, Jim should have told your husband about the work permit thing when he had his interview.' She tilted her head on one side and looked concerned. 'I'm sorry, if he forgot.'

Maya clenched her fists. 'Or Rich forgot to tell me, more like.'

'Or he didn't want to tell you, maybe. He probably didn't want you to change your mind. He doesn't want to spend all that money getting people over here and then they say no, right? Men don't always tell you everything,' said Suchanatta.

'Too true,' said Maya. 'By the way, that really is a beautiful scarf you're wearing.'

'It's from Thailand. My country. I have my contacts and get them cheap as chips.'

Maya laughed. Jim's speech had well and truly rubbed off on her. 'You know, you should import them. Get a stand here at The Twist. Ask Barb. You'd go down a bomb.'

Sue winked and tapped the side of her nose. 'Top plan, Maya.'

'Gee, that was a successful morning,' said Barb out loud. She looked around for Maya to give her the reassurance she was bound to need after making her heartfelt speech. She should have reminded Maya that she would have to say a few words. Her fellow Americans were rarely fazed by having to stand up spontaneously, but other nationalities often were. Still her comment had been the perfect cue to plug working for the club. The Welcome Table had been tidied up and the various forms put in a pile with the attendance register on top. Boy, when you asked that girl to do a job, she did it well. The board needed people like her. Now where was she?

'Barb? Can I have a word?' LaShell was at her shoulder. The tousled tawny hair made her look like a lioness.

'Sure,' she said. 'Be a doll and go back in the room to check no one left their agendas on the chairs, would you?'

'I really must go, Barb,' said LaShell.

'It won't take a moment, puhlease,' she said, as sweetly as she could manage. Today, she really was short of hands; surely LaShell could do one teeny job.

As LaShell slid off back through the double doors that led to the meeting room, Barb surveyed the scene. Everyone else had gone. The fun, the noise, and the bustle were over for another week and now all she could hear was the piped background music played over the hotel's sound system. Wherever she lived in the world, it was always the same.

'Here.' LaShell thrust a handful of papers into the box. 'Look, Barb, I'm sorry, but I'm going to have to let you down.'

'If you can't come back with me for lunch, I'm cool with that. I have plenty of other stuff to be getting on with.' Barb shut the lid of the box and placed it in a much larger box filled with club paperwork and lifted it up, ready to leave.

'Well, actually no, I can't.' That told Barb she had actually forgotten all about their arrangement. 'I have something else to tell you.'

Barb set the box back down on the table. 'Go on,' she said.

'I know I said I'd help you out with publicity when Joni leaves, but I've just signed up to an advanced painting class with a professional and it clashes with The Twist.'

She didn't pull any punches, thought Barb. Cut straight to the chase.

'I'm sorry, but painting is really important to me and I don't feel I can help at the club and then not come to the meetings. Even Leila said how important hobbies are, right?'

Barb's heart sank. Soon she would have to run the club single-handedly, and it wouldn't be the first time. 'Really? That's too bad. Are you sure? You'd be so great at it.' She tipped her head on one side.

LaShell didn't meet her eyes. It was always easier to let people down if you didn't look at them. Barb knew the body language.

'I'll still come to book club. And you can rely on me to make cupcakes once in a while, okay? I can't pass up the chance of having such an expert teacher.'

'Sure, LaShell, I understand.' She smiled broadly and laid her hand on LaShell's arm.

'I knew you'd be great about it. And I'm sorry I can't do lunch either. I'm meeting my husband at our club. See you around.' And she whisked out of the door, leaving Barb on her own in the empty lobby.

Stop being active and she'd stop being who she was. Where would the club be without her? Or the school parent teacher committee? Barb was the one who organised the laundry for the whole baseball team when Brandon had an away game. If anyone needed someone to stand in for them or get something organised, they knew they could count on Barb. Barb was a 'brick'. Barb was 'amazing'. Everyone's saviour. She lifted a fingernail to her mouth and absent-mindedly used her neat white teeth to gnaw on her cuticle. Then she stopped herself. She shouldn't wreck her French polish. Now, standing in the empty hall, she delved into her purse for her cell phone and flipped open the lid.

'Megan? Hi… are you feeling better? Saw you weren't at The Twist today… fantastic… yes, it's Barb… yeah, I'm fine… Hey, how do you fancy lunch at my place? Oh. Okay. No worries. You have a great time now. Bye.' She returned her fingers to her mouth for just a moment, then scanned back up through her cell phone's contact list for inspiration. Her eyes landed on Bill's number. He hadn't come home for lunch in years. And the two of them hadn't been out for dinner, either. He was probably busy. Too busy for her anyway. She didn't want to face another disappointment. She snapped her cell phone shut and tossed it into her purse before heaving the laden box up into her arms and walking out of the room backwards.

Chapter ten

Maya's fingers drummed the steering wheel to the rhythm of the song playing in her head. Her blog was a great way to keep in touch with Seasons. That morning she had given a recipe for mango and passionfruit smoothie, inspired by one she had enjoyed with Barb the day before. The sun was shining, of course. It was eight am and she was waiting in the string of cars lined up in the outside lane to do a 'youee' on her way to The Orange Tree for coffee with Barb. Jim had been right. It was becoming her local. The Parking Space Fairy seemed to be on her side. A big truck was reversing from a slot just inside the entrance. She grabbed her chance and nabbed it before anyone else spotted it.

'Ta dah,' she said, pleased with a few seconds of assertive driving.

She switched off the engine. With her keys in her fist, she reached for the new green Gucci handbag that lay on the passenger seat and jumped out of the car in one sliding movement, using the scarf she had tied to the handle of her bag to touch the baking hot door. The high-pitched throb of cicadas replaced the hum of the airconditioner in seconds. Despite being newly paved, the car park sported a sprinkling of pale sand, particularly round the edges. Feeling it crunch beneath the smooth soles of her new pea-green loafers, she looked down. Clouded by dust they would be wrecked in no time. Bunches of flowers on the pavement caught her attention. There had been another fatal accident. The blooms, drained of colour beneath their cellophane wrappings, were masked with a layer of sand. The messages on the condolence cards had already been bleached away by the unrelenting sunshine. She thought of poor Maryam and wondered if there were still flowers beside the lamppost where she had died. Thank goodness Rich had bought her such a big car. He wanted her to be safe.

Straightening her back and feeling the early morning sun on her hair, she headed for the café. It was becoming a bit cooler. Still forty degrees centigrade by noon, but getting there. In a few weeks, the weather would be perfect. She walked towards the café. It was a beautiful building. The white windtower, which somehow reminded Maya of the tower of a Norman church, looked original, but in keeping with recent tradition was probably fake. The food was varied, fresh and organic too and they did normal cafetières of coffee instead of piling a vat of froth onto a tasteless black coffee like most places. Barb was already in their usual spot in front of the Orange Tree mural. As always, she looked immaculate. Her dark hair was perfectly complemented by yet another outfit Maya had not seen before, this time a bright red, waisted jacket worn with a little white camisole beneath and teamed with matching Capri pants.

'Hey girl!' her friend called out, patting the seat to her left. 'I ordered you a papaya and passion fruit smoothie today, and a piece of that apricot and date slice you were hanging your nose over yesterday. How you doin'? Nice purse.'

'Purse?' Maya looked down to check that her bag had not come unclipped again.

'Handbag, sorry!' Barb leaned across and gave her friend a hug. Maya stiffened slightly.

'Oh, right. Thanks for ordering for me. Good choice.' Maya sat down, placed her bag on the floor and started fiddling with the tablemat.

'What wiped the smile off your face? Couldn't park that truck of yours close enough? Say, what's up?'

'I'm not quite used to hugging yet.' She was never sure what each person wanted. Should you do what they expected? Shake hands with a German, kiss the French? Or should you do what you usually did yourself, which in her case, being British, was probably nothing?

Barb turned her face away for a moment to watch the dark-skinned waiter bringing over their smoothies. By now Barb seemed to have learned that Maya wanted a different one every time, whereas she always went for the same old orange and banana.

'Thanks,' said Maya, making sure she looked into the waiter's eyes while she said it. 'Look, I'm sorry, Barb. I'm a bit up and down, you know.'

'Enjoy what you can when you can, that's my motto. 'Cause you never know when it's going to be taken away.' Her eyes lost focus for a moment before she looked down at her nails.

'It's no good. I need a purpose, like you said. Anyway, did I tell you about the blog I'm doing for my old business?'

'Need a purpose you say?' Barb scooted around the blog comment.

'It's time I got off what you would call my 'butt' and did something. Don't you agree?'

Maya put her oversized straw to her lips. Her drink was so thick and creamy that Maya felt her eyes close slightly as she gave a tiny sigh of pleasure. She tried the apricot and date slice. Also delicious. She'd have a go at making it herself some day.

Barb had her 'purse' open and was rummaging around for something. 'Got 'em!' she shrieked. After tipping the contents of her bag onto the orange-lolly coloured sofa, she pulled out a wad of flyers held together with a bulldog clip. 'Right, now. As you were so rightly saying… '

But Maya's attention had been caught by the arrival of the Norwegian who had sat near her at the meeting the other day. Liv. She'd found her intriguing. Barb spotted her too, waved over towards the back of the café where Liv was looking for a seat, and beckoned to her to join them. Liv shook her head and indicated towards the door. She must have been waiting for someone.

'Have you met Liv, yet? She's quite a girl. Into what she calls by the generic term 'therapy' – massages for the body and soul. At least that's what I'm told to tell people. I'm the only one she trusts to give out her cards, you know.' She paused. 'Hey, I have them here. I hear she's excellent. Worth every cent.' She fished a card out of the pile of papers on the table. 'She's very picky about her clients. Doesn't want just any old body booking her in for a Swedish massage, if you know what I mean. You can never be too careful. She says she doesn't list her services on her cards because she would prefer her clients to tell her what they need. All a bit "woo–woo" for me… It's a shame she won't join the club. Says she doesn't want to be on the members' register when that's just the thing she needs to boost her business. Says it's 'cause she has to keep changing her address. Shame. The club's such a good networking tool. Elske joined, you know?' She glanced up at Maya to check she was listening. 'And she booked to have a table in the run up to Christmas so she can sell her cards.'

'Yeah, well if I had a business I'd be the first one to promote it at the club and have a table too,' said Maya, looking at Liv's card. It was rather lacking in detail. Just one word, *Alive*, and a mobile phone number. 'What do you think she could do for me, then? I've already spent a ton of money on beauty treatments.' She laid the card back on the table and sighed. 'I don't like having to ask Rich for every dirham. It's hard after having my independence, you know, what with my job in the deli?'

'Blogging won't solve your problems, Maya, if you ask me. Spending all your time at the computer is not good for you, my girl, especially when it means you can only talk to your friends through a keyboard, eh?' If Barb wore glasses she would probably have put them on the end of her nose at this point and peered at Maya over the top of them. 'I hear Liv's really good with things like stress and, you know, feeling down.' Barb bit her bottom lip as if she thought she may have said too much and waited for Maya to respond.

'Ah! After one U-turn too many, I have that all right! But seriously, I've got too little to do to be stressed out, haven't I? All I need is a bit of exercise to get the endorphins flowing and I'll be right as rain.' The moment the words left her mouth, Maya knew getting moving was just what she needed. She was putting on weight. 'Clever card,' she said, changing the subject. 'Hiding her name, Liv, in the company name like that.' She placed the card down on the table. 'Secretive isn't she?'

Barb looked slightly confused. Word play was probably not her thing.

'What I really want is a job. Preferably a paid one. I could get a real job, apparently. You know, work for a company. Elske says I can get round the work visa thing by getting a local to give me a work permit. I thought maybe Leila... '

'Oh, you don't want to do that, Maya!' Barb butted in. 'I'm not a big fan of finding a local sponsor. They don't give you anything apart from the permit, though they rob you of half your profit. Don't be so sure that you can trust the locals. They're not like us. I'm getting a bit cynical in my old age.' She gave a sharp laugh.

'I need to work, Barb.'

'Nar, you'd be too tied down. You'd never be able to take long vacations. Have you thought of helping me out at The Twist? I've just lost LaShell...'

'Mmm, actually I have been wondering about voluntary work. At least it would keep me occupied and out of the shopping malls.'

Barb sat up straight and looked attentive.

'I was thinking about maybe going to see Leila about it.' She paused and watched Barb's face for a reaction. She seemed to be going slightly pale, but then it was hard to tell with all that make up on.

'We-ell,' Barb began, and her eyes glazed over for a moment.

Maya placed her hands on her knees. 'What do you think?'

'You should have seen the number of names on the sign-up sheet after the meeting. Sorry, Maya, you may have missed the boat there.'

'Oh, so there was a lot of interest?'

'Oh, yes. Heaps.' Barb seemed to relax. 'She used to be called Linda, you know, married Ali, embraced Islam and all that and is now called Leila, as you know. She covers her head and everything, like you saw – mind you, I can see the attraction of that when my roots need doing.' She patted the top of her head. 'Leila has heaps of passion and enthusiasm and the backing of a good local family. In construction, they are. Al Farooq Restoration. She knows what she wants to achieve, but hasn't a clue about how to get there. She's a bit short on creative ideas. To be honest, she's a bit scatty.' She sucked at the tail end of her smoothie. 'Must be her Irishness. Say, shall we get another drink? Coffee this time?'

'Thanks.' Maya smiled at the waiter and mentally kicked herself for not putting her name on that list there and then at The Twist.

'Say, have you had a treatment from Liv?'

'Me? No.' Barb shook her head and swept the heap of cards and flyers back in her bag. 'Nothing with me that needs fixing, girl! Too busy anyways. I can do anything, I just can't do everything.' She let out a little giggle.

Maya leaned back into the squishy sofa and looked across at Liv. She still had the same blue nail varnish, on her toes too, where she also wore a silver ring. A waiter placed a bowl of fresh fruit and homemade granola and a glass of water in front of her, but she seemed engrossed in her book and didn't even look up.

Barb shot a glance at Liv. 'She's into healthy food, like you.'

Maya chewed her inner cheek.

She was not going to give in and help at The Twist until all other avenues had been explored.

Barb's face lit up. 'I've had an idea! I know just what you need! You need to lighten up. I know just the thing. A girls' night!' She grinned. 'Wait there.' And she grabbed her diary from her bag, left the table, elbows out ready for battle, and walked straight over to Liv, who was eating her breakfast slowly and daintily with a teaspoon. Barb crouched down beside her, one hand on the table, the other on Liv's knee. They spoke for a few moments. Barb clapped her hand over her mouth and Liv scowled at her as if begging her to keep a secret. Then they bowed their heads over their diaries, jotted something down, hugged, and Barb returned to the orange sofa.

'Sorted! Liv says that what you need, in fact what we all need, is to find our inner goddess.' She looked triumphant.

'What?' exclaimed Maya.

'We-ell, it'll be next week. There'll be food and drink.' She paused and did a mock cough into her fist. 'And bellydancing! You see, Liv once worked in a bar in Istanbul. Has all the props. Says she'll show us how to love our bodies, curves, lumpy bits an' all!'

Maya leaned forward. Now this was interesting. 'Go on!'

'Anyway, she'll lead an evening for a bunch of what she called 'goddesses in training' at my place. Everyone needs to wear something they can move about in that's comfy and sexy and that will match the belly belts – those are the jingly scarfy things you wear round your waist – she'll bring along for us. Liv says we need to dress in the colours of precious jewels, too. It's time for you to have some fun. And to move that luscious body of yours!'

Luscious? Goddess in training? Had she really put on that much weight? Barb had read her mind. It might be just what she needed to boost her flagging libido. Barb was right again.

'Okay. You're on!' she said.

'Week on Thursday. 7.30. My place.'

It wasn't a question. Not only could Barb read Maya's mind, but she seemed to know intuitively that her diary was a complete blank on that evening.

'Sure. Sounds great,' said Maya.

'Let's get the show on the road, then!' Barb leapt to her feet, took her phone out of her bag and went over to a quiet corner to make some calls while Maya saved her place on the sofa.

The Orange Tree was buzzing – mostly with other ladies, still in their gym clothes fresh from Bums and Tums, undoing the good they may have done in the exercise studio with a latte and an almond croissant. Not that the café was a female stronghold. There was always a smattering of local men too, sitting in small groups, their arms outstretched on the backs of the sofas and with massive bunches of car keys on the tables in front of them. She never tired of watching the way their bodies moved in their sparkling white *dishdashas*. Not that she had ever met one properly or had a conversation, but in her brief encounters in the shops or restaurants she had always found them courteous, yet sporting a slight twinkle in their eyes. They appeared to have worked out how not to be chained to a desk six days a week.

'It's all set!' Barb flopped back onto the sofa with a thump and then sucked up the dregs of her cappuccino.

'Great! I think. I have no idea what I'm in for!'

'Elske will give you a lift to my place. Though I think taxis may be a better idea.'

'You think of everything, Barb!' Maya glanced at her watch then her hand shot to her mouth. 'Hell, I'm going to have to go, I have to pick up something from the tailor and then I'm meeting one of the mums from school at Dominico's. '

'You're learning. Come on, you have to admit, it's not that bad here, is it? You've even learned how to be a 'lady who lunches'.

'And breakfasts.'

'And cocktailses.'

'See you next week for bellydancing, then. '

'Oh, by the way, it's a hundred dirhams each. And she wants cash.' She took some notes out of her wallet and left them on the table. 'I'll get this. Gotta run.'

'Isn't it my turn?' Maya reached for her bag, but by the time she had found the correct money in her purse and raised her head Barb had disappeared.

'Er, bye, Barb,' she whispered.

She looked across to Liv to give her a wave, but she was deep in conversation with a young Emirati, their faces close together, though Liv didn't look too pleased about it. She watched him pocket the keys Liv took out of her bag.

Maya shook her head in well-humoured exasperation at her friend. You had to take your hat off to her. Barb knew how to make things happen. Such generosity of spirit was a breath of fresh air in a place like this where everyone seemed to be striving for more and more and bigger and better and more expensive. She walked back to the car and slapped her hand to her forehead. Blast it, she should have asked Barb for Leila's number.

Chapter eleven

Maya switched on the computer again and thought about Barb while it warmed up. Could becoming a lady of leisure really fulfil her? Could it plug the gaping hole that had appeared in her life when she had left her job behind back home? She was certainly busier now. Her diary was filling up with appointments to collect things from the tailor, coffee mornings and lunches. A routine was emerging.

Oliver was upstairs playing his guitar and Matthew was in the water, as usual, collecting heavy objects from the bottom of the pool. Annie was cooking supper, Rich was away. Maya missed his easy company. She recognised that identity was being reduced to that of mother-of and wife-of rather than manager-of but when Rich was around she felt able to be more like her old self. But she missed her old label and her old identity. As her fingers moved over the keyboard and she entered her password she noticed how tanned her skin was now and how the French polish on her nails made her look elegant but that the false tips made it damn difficult to type.

She had an email. Maya smiled. You could always count on a counter girl.

Hiya Maya

It was Avril.

Love the recipe for the smoothie and by the way, meant to tell you, the lime and chilli marinade is going down a storm. Danuta advertises it as perfect for salmon or tuna though, which was a great idea – broadens the market. The clever girl has also started cutting and pasting from your blog and turning it into a newsletter, which we print and keep on the counter. She's also set up a mailing list of customers. She sorted it so your blogs get sent to something called Twitter and Facebook. And she is going to optimise you too, she says, whatever that means! I hope she optimises Jan and me at the same time! Jan's having a difficult time financially at the moment but can't work out where the money's going. I blame that space cadet of a husband of hers! I hope you don't mind but we gave D your login details so she could set all this up. Don't know how we managed without her.

Hey, that goddess evening sounds great. Bellydancing would give me something to do with my muffin top. I'm sure shimmying will put some fire in your nether regions and take your mind off not having a job. Did I tell you that Mum's into line dancing these days? She's asked for boots with spurs on for Christmas.

I can't wait to find out what goddesses eat. Do share the recipes on the blog. Danuta is going to show us how to add comments to it tomorrow. That should get you some more traffic, apparently.

We really miss you, Maya.

Keep cooking!

Maya had been wondering when she would start to get some comments from strangers rather than from her mates and her mother on her blogs. They would show that her words weren't falling into a black hole and that someone was reading it. Boy, that Danuta knew how to make herself indispensable, but letting her get into the blog felt like Maya was having another piece of her power taken away. She'd not say anything yet, though. It was early days and anyway she was probably overreacting.

   She clicked the mouse on another email. It was Rich.

NB leaving do Thurs. Rx

Sent from my Blackberry

A man of few words. He got his message across though. Loyal as can be, he presumably didn't feel the need to go overboard. That wasn't his style.

She clicked Reply.

Dear Rich

Sorry, but I've something else planned. A girls' night I can't cancel. Are you happy to go alone?

Lots of love
Maya

She wasn't going to tell him about the bellydancing yet. She'd surprise him.

With so much time on her hands, Maya was whiling away more hours than ever at her computer. If Danuta could do it, so could she. There was no doubt that she preferred human company, but for now, the computer filled the gap nicely. Taking a peek at her blog every morning and evening, just to see if anyone had commented yet, gave her day structure and purpose.

She refreshed the page. There was a comment!

This is Danuta. Hello. Thank you for the smoothie recipe. I made some fresh yesterday and it sold well. I may turn some into ice cream soon. Thank you for your ideas. Keep them coming. I think we should do takeaway now and Janet and Avril agree.

Danuta

Employing Danuta had clearly been another of Maya's great ideas. With recession apparently on its way, the shop needed more ways to keep its profits up and Danuta seemed to be coming to the rescue. There was a knock on the door.

'Madam, I bring coffee,' said Annie. This was part of the routine too. Annie now knew to make the coffee nice and strong, with not too much milk and to use one of the mugs Avril had given Maya.

'Thank you, Annie.'

'Madam need anything?' Annie hovered.

'No, I don't think so. I'm fine.' And she was definitely doing better this week. Thanks in part to the blog, but also credit had to be due to Barb. The prospect of showing people her midriff at the bellydance evening later in the week had spurred her into action and she had added a morning swim to the routine. Just twenty lengths before the pool filled up with toddlers gave her the time to plan what she would write about and was making her body stronger. She could feel the difference in her arms already. There was no doubt that Barb had her best interests at heart. She wanted her to be happy. That woman wanted everyone to be happy. And her madcap goddess idea had done the trick and got her moving. In fact, she felt more positive every day. She took a sip of the coffee. It was perfect. Today, she would write about how to make coffee ice cream flavoured with cardamom like the locals did. She would call it Arabic coffee ice cream.

The Stamford calendar on the wall above the computer reminded her that it was Avril's birthday in a few weeks. She knew just the present and if she didn't get it today, it might arrive late and that would never do. Avril deserved a treat.

Maya turned off the computer and rose from her chair. Yes, her back was definitely feeling stronger and she felt taller too. It was amazing what a bit of swimming could do. And by following the early-morning swim with ten minutes on a lounger, she was getting a bit of colour. Swinging her bag over her shoulder, she took the stairs two at a time and went to the door.

'I go shopping,' she called out to Annie, whom she could hear was emptying the dishwasher. 'Okay?'

'No problem, Madam,' said Annie, 'I do iron.'

'Thank you, Annie.' Ironing was something Maya most definitely did not miss.

In half an hour Maya was in the souk that Jim had told them about on their first day. He had been right; this was as close as you could get to the real Dubai. Between the trading on the Creek and the shops that opened onto the street, you could feel the energy of money changing hands. She parked in the cool of the multi-storey and bought herself a fresh coconut juice. It came in its own green shell, the top sliced off and chiselled to a volcano shaped peak, from which a blue straw protruded.

'Hello, madam. You want pashmina?' called the first retailer she passed. 'I have sunglass. Come and try. I give you good price. Come. Come.'

'No, thanks. Not today.' She was getting used to the constant hustling and could ignore it easily now. First she would buy some rosewater for the polenta cake with rosewater and pistachios she was going to experiment later and then she would buy Avril's present.

The sunlight caught the rippling gold discs of the bellydancing outfits that hung outside one of the stalls. The jewel colours were bright as bunting. Maya stopped for a second to take a look.

'Madam, you want bellydance costume?'

'Yes, please. Pink.'

The man stooped to pull a baby red triangle of nylon cloth from a teetering pile and stood to wrap it round her hips.

'No. Sorry. Pink,' she said, moving away from his hands.

'This pink colour,' he said, moving his head from side to side. 'Nice.'

Maya spotted the perfect one low down in the pile and pointed.

'Aha, *acha, acha.* Yes, yes,' he said and yanked it out.

She nodded and he reached to tie it round her hips. 'No. No, that's fine. You have DVD?'

'Yes, yes.' He disappeared into the back of the shop to emerge with a pile of DVDs. Their covers looked like photocopies.

Maya picked one called *Bellydance for Beginners* that showed a comfortingly fattish lady on the cover. 'This one.'

'Only one?' he asked, disappointment in his voice.

Maya hesitated. Would she really watch the DVD or would it lurk in a drawer like her other exercise tapes? Would she even like bellydancing? 'No. No thank you, just the one.'

'I make you special price?' His voice rose to a plea.

She raised an eyebrow. The shopkeeper had a living to make too. She gave in. 'Oh, all right then. Two!' 'You want blouse? Trousers?' he continued, presumably thinking that he was now onto a good thing.

'No, thanks, this is enough. How much?'

'One hundred dirhams.' He grinned.

'Oh no, come on, that's far too much.' She laughed. That was about twenty pounds. 'I'll give you fifty.'

'Sixty?' he asked. 'Best quality.'

'Okay,' she said, delighted at how her haggling had improved. For a belt and two DVDs she had a bargain. Maybe she'd try them both out when she was back home. Alone. After she'd made her cake.

Chapter twelve

She nibbled absent-mindedly at a freshly tipped nail. Darn! She'd no time to get it fixed before the party. After all the parties and coffees and clubs and events and potlucks she'd organised in her time, this one was freaking her out, not because of the organisation or the food, but because she wasn't going to be in charge for once. Merry had laid the table with the ruby velvet cloth they usually saved for Christmas and, decorated with fake pearl necklaces, it looked splendid. She tweaked one of the bunches of grapes that were draped on her silver candelabra and popped one into her mouth. They'd done a great job. Liv had told them they needed more mirrors and so Merry had swapped some of the photographs on the walls for the ones from the bedrooms and bathrooms. It made Barb feel like she was being watched. Liv had been round earlier with the food and now, with Merry's help doing the final tweaks, the table groaned under a Gargantuan feast. Sexy too. Some things were positively phallic. The asparagus tips, the flesh pink shrimps and those thick cut strips of red bell pepper that ringed the bowl of some neat pink dip. Little spicy red wieners. Barb had provided pink champagne and an open bottle sat in an ice bucket on the buffet, ready, beside a silver tray of crystal glasses. She deserved a drink.

The froth rose in the glass and Barb held her breath, willing it to stop before it spilled over the edge. She tipped back her head and raised the glass to her lips, tonight painted a rather whoreish pink, it had to be said. The drapes were drawn and the candles lit. The light flickered from the twenty or thirty tealights Merry had placed on every high surface, safe from the swish of passing scarves. Her most precious ornaments had been moved away. It looked very different by candlelight and the mirrors made the flames repeat into infinity. A real change. She thought of Senator McCain's campaign, 'Change we Need'. See, even he was on her case. Her own outfit was a case in point. She'd been too embarrassed to buy an outfit down in the souk. The thought of a stranger running his hands over her as he held up the silky fabric made her flesh crawl, so she had asked her tailor to make it. She'd picked a full skirt and an extra long bodice in the baby pink she knew suited her so well, even though it wasn't exactly jewel-colored. But it did count. She'd decided against harem pants, though she could have had the neatest, cutest silver bells around the hems. In this colour, she'd have looked like a bag of sausages. To complete her outfit, she'd found the perfect tourmaline and silver necklace and drop earrings; only she had strung the necklace over her forehead rather than round her neck. And she'd had a manicure and pedicure to match. The thought of the red lipstick Liv had insisted on had made her shudder so she'd cheated slightly with the bright pink.

What on earth was she in for? She was nervous on two counts. First because a lot hinged on this evening. She wanted to give the girls, especially poor Maya, a boost. Give them a fun time. Barb would never normally have described herself as fun. Effective. Efficient. Active. Friendly. Chatty. Charismatic.

Caring. Interested. Passionate. But not fun, exactly. She'd left her inner child somewhere back in grade school. She never played a team sport, preferring to wash the kit, serve the tea, or drive the minibus. They went to Disneyland, for sure. She had the photos to prove it. But Bill went on the rides with Brandon. She stood and watched and waved and took video. Her heart fluttered a little. She didn't just deserve that drink, she needed it, and she topped up her glass, waiting again for the bubbles to subside before taking another sip to calm her nerves. She really hoped she wasn't going to have to expose her belly. Then they'd find that her fake tan only covered her extremities.

The doorbell rang and Barb turned, placing her hands behind her as she leaned against the table. She heard the sound of greetings from Merry and the guests, of shoes being taken off and left in the lobby.

'Barb! Hi there!' Suchanatta, wearing emerald green loose trousers and a low cut top and a glorious navy silk scarf at her neck, was the first to enter. She had piled her hair into a cute bun and stuck two glittery chopsticks into the centre. Two of the largest and most bejewelled earrings swung above her shoulders.

'Look at you! That outfit is stunning. Give me a twirl! Is the scarf from your new collection?'

'I'll twirl if you twirl,' laughed Sue and so they twirled for each other, Sue, dainty and slim, like a ballerina on top of a jewellery box. Barb twirled. Her skirt had been made with several metres of silk.

Suchanatta was impressed. 'I'll bet you have a matching G-string under there too, eh?' She lifted her elbow and cocked her head at Barb.

Barb gave a nervous little giggle. Being married to a Londoner certainly rubbed off on that one, she thought.

'Great idea for an evening. Am I first? I did as you told me, see. I wore jewel colours, loose clothes and a sexy new lipstick!' She pursed her lips into a moue and airkissed Barb on either cheek. 'Sorry, forgot to say hello properly!'

Next came Megan, a Twist regular since the start, and Val, who helped her with the boys' baseball, and Alathia, who usually did the Welcome Table, when she turned up, and Jeanie, newly arrived from Jakarta and also needing to meet some new people. They looked great, giggling like schoolgirls as they showed each other their outfits and discussed the difficulty they'd had deciding what to wear. You'd have thought they had conferred, with one in ruby red, another sapphire blue, Val, of course in her favourite amethyst and Jeanie in a stunning shade of aquamarine.

'There's a dish in the hall where you can put the money for Liv, girls,' said Barb. 'Is that cool with you? Maybe you can put it there on the way out? Or right away. In case you forget.'

'Sure.' They all reached for their purses.

'Hey beautiful! What gemstone are you?' asked Jeanie. 'Pale pink is one I'm not familiar with. Is there a pink diamond? I'm aquamarine. My birthstone.'

'It's tourmaline!' Barb replied, pronouncing the word as exotically as she could, hopefully with a hint of a French accent. She waggled her fingers behind her earrings to make the glint of the stone sparkle. 'See!'

'Looks like you pulled out all the stops as usual,' commented Val, looking round and round at the room and up and down Barb's outfit. 'Impressive!'

Barb smiled broadly. 'Do help yourselves to pink champagne.' She wondered when Liv would arrive. 'Food's for later, apparently. We drink first, then find our inner goddess, and only then we get to eat.' She felt quite light-headed already, after two glasses on an empty stomach. She wondered if they would notice that the champagne matched her outfit perfectly too.

'Mmm, bubbly! That's bound to get the party started!' Megan poured herself a drink. 'Anyone else?' she asked, handing over the first glass.

Oh good, the doorbell again. Barb moved towards the door, her anxiety about the evening soothed slightly now she could see how excited everyone was. Merry had got there first. She saw Elske, Maya and Liv all bent over in the hallway, removing their shoes – Elske in cream, which she guessed to be pearl, Maya in what looked like a pair of black track pants, and Liv in a deep purple skirt. Whatever gem it was, it looked superb with her skin tone. She really was tiny. The body of a Barbie doll.

'Welcome.' Barb beamed. Composed at last. Her flock was here. And they had all done as they were told. Almost. She resisted asking Maya if her outfit was supposed to be jet. Surely, she could have made more of an effort?

Elske, Maya and Liv all stood up, turned and grinned through bright red slashes of lipstick. Liv held a huge box out in front of her and carried it into the sitting room. It rattled.

'Wow!' said Maya, entering the room. 'It is stunning. You went to so much trouble. And the food! Oh Barb, it looks wonderful.'

'Why thank you, ma'am!' she said, dropping a curtsey. Important events required a bit more effort. 'Good! Everyone has drinks. Liv, have you been introduced?

Liv nodded. She poured herself a glass of sparkling water and settled herself in the black recliner. Barb's chair. The couches had already been pushed towards the walls so that there was plenty of space to move about when the dancing began.

'Do take a seat, everyone,' continued Barb, moving to sit rather lumpily on the bean bag she had borrowed from Brandon's bedroom. She landed in it with a whoomph of expelled air and looked at Liv. It was over to her now.

'Before we start, you'll need to put down your drinks, stand up and close your eyes,' Liv began, leaping out of Barb's chair like a young gazelle. Her singsong voice was calm, as if designed to put all the guests into the right frame of mind to listen and learn Barb heaved herself to her feet and waited until the last person closed her eyes and then reluctantly closed her own.

'Put your feet flat on the floor. Feel the earth under your feet. Feel grounded. Now put one hand on your tummy, just below the navel, and the other on your upper chest. Take a deep breath, *ja*.' Liv took a deep noisy breath in through her nose. Everyone did the same. 'Fill your lungs, then your abdomen, all the way, down until you can feel your belly push out into your lower hand.' She paused. Her voice was soothing and commanding and it rose and fell in exactly that hurdy-gurdy way Bill said all Norwegians spoke. 'That's it. Right down. Then exhale.' She breathed out loudly again, through her nose. 'Nice and slowly. Visualise the breath coming in from the top of your head. That's it. Just breathe. In and out. Now, I am going to take you on a journey. Imagine in your mind's eye that you are walking in your favourite place in the world. The air is soft on your skin, the ground, or sand, or whatever you choose... '

Oh no, thought Barb. A meditation. I hate meditation. Can never find a picture. Can never see anything or feel anything. Her mind spun. Would they be able to tell that she was cheating? Not doing it? Probably not. She opened one eye and looked around the room. Everyone had a soft smile on her red lips. Everyone looked fully absorbed. Not one other eye was open too. Not even Liv's. Barb made a mental list of all the arrangements for the evening. Food? Check. Drink? Check. More in the refrigerator? Check. Enough soft drinks for drivers, heaven forbid any of them was thinking of driving home? Check. Number for taxi service by the phone? Check.

'Now open your eyes,' said Liv. 'How was that for you?' She looked around the room.

Everyone seemed to be smiling and nodding. It's going fine, Barbra. Stop panicking, girl. Barb tried to match her face to the others' and added her nod and smile to theirs.

'This evening we will explore the goddess inside us. We will go on a journey to find our true feminine nature.' She smiled. 'The one you left behind at the hospital when you had your first baby, right?'

Murmurs of assent filled the room, peppered with a few laughs.

'But I thought we were bellydancing?' interrupted Elske.

'We are,' replied Liv calmly. 'But first we need to get in touch with our core. Only then can we be real goddesses. That's okay, *ja*?' She often made a funny breathy *ja* noise at the end of her sentences, like all Norwegians, but Barb could not stop herself from waiting for it instead of listening to the instructions.

'Everyone sit on the floor!' Liv commanded. They obeyed and watched Liv cross her legs and collapse like a concertina onto the Persian carpet. Next she grabbed her big toes and lifted her legs up and out to the sides like a big V. 'Can you do this?'

The room filled with laughter as everyone collapsed in a heap – everyone except Suchanatta.

'That's it, mmm!' Liv sounded delighted. 'Goddesses should know how to laugh and have fun, *ja*? I was joking. Just sit however you feel comfortable. Barb pulled her skirt over her knees. Everyone fell silent.

'When you focus on your vagina, you can let the goddess energy of kundalini enter your body. She is a coiled snake and lies at the base of your spine. She represents sexual energy.' She paused while everyone tried to make sense of what she had just said. Barb thought that was way too woo-woo for her and decided to pop out to the refrigerator for more bottles of champagne.

'What is a real goddess like?' Liv was asking as Barb returned to the room.

'She's sexy!' called Suchanatta.

Liv nodded.

'Voluptuous!' said Megan, who was so tall and wiry that this clearly didn't resonate with her personally. Barb could check that one, at least. Beneath her folds of pink satin she had proof by the handful.

'With long flowing hair!' Elske tossed back her short, neat bob.

'Like us, eh Barb?' LaShell used her fingers to lift her tousled mane. Barb gave her hair a little shake along with the teeniest shoulder-shimmy that no one appeared to notice – apart from Liv, who shot her a smile.

'She eats the most delicious food, popping it sexily into her mouth,' said Val, opening her mouth, licking her lips, and closing her eyes seductively.

'No, she doesn't, Val,' said Alathia. 'She has a bronze Adonis who pops it into her mouth for her!'

'Yeah, right,' many agreed.

'Where are we going to find an Adonis at this time of

night?' asked Suchanatta. 'My Jim's out at a leaving do, or I'd have called him.'

'So,' continued Liv. 'Goddesses are all about what? Work?'

'No way!' called Val.

'Pleasure?' suggested Maya a little coyly.

'Looking after their body?' added Elske.

'Multiple orgasms!' called Suchanatta.

'Food?' said Barb, aware that she was getting very hungry and more than a little drunk. 'What kind of food?' asked Liv.

'The finest and scrummiest and plumpest and yummiest and fed to them as they recline on a couch made of gold,' said Alathia, triumphant.

'Exactly!' said Liv. 'So that is just what we are going to do.'

'Hurray!' blurted Maya.

'But not until we've danced and got in touch with those snakes I was telling you about!'

Barb was not the only one to groan audibly.

'You can't bellydance on a full stomach can you?' She looked grave as she rose to her feet in one single movement, without needing to steady herself with her hands. 'Now can everyone help to move back the chairs? We need more space'

Barb was a little upset that she had failed to prepare the room adequately and she didn't like the thought of everyone shoving her possessions aside without due care. She refilled her glass and watched helplessly as her increasingly amused guests rearranged her beautiful furniture.

'Give us a hand, will you?' asked Maya, dragging that black recliner closer to the sideboard.

'Sure,' said Elske.

Liv clapped her hands. 'Get into a circle,' she commanded and everyone faced her, ready for the moment they had been waiting for. 'Choose one of these.' She delved into her box and like a magician pulled out one scarf after another, passing it behind her. Triangles of silk and velvet, fringed with beads, silver or gold coins, emerged from the box and each person chose her favourite.

'Tie it on the hips. Low down. Not up by your navel.' She tied a bright orange scarf with golden coins around her own hips. 'Orange is the colour of sexuality,' she said and winked.

'Now.' She lifted her skirt to just above her slim, tanned knees. 'This is how you do the hip shimmy.' She waggled her knees back and forth. It was a surprisingly gentle movement but that made her jingle prettily. She dropped her skirt back down. 'You try.'

Barb had a glazed expression and kept looking over to a collection of photographs low down on that huge sideboard.

'Ready girls? Let's have some music!' Liv pressed a button on the remote control and as Arabic music filled the room, she began to twitch one hip as if a puppeteer had her hip bone on a string and was tweaking it.

'Should we copy you?' asked Suchanatta, whose enviably narrow hip was already lifting up and down in time to the music.

Liv nodded and proceeded to lift her right hip over and over again, then her left. Her arms were slim, her fingers poised as she lifted them up and down, elbows and wrists leading, palms and fingers following. A navel ring twinkled with a diamond and what looked like the tip of the tail of a snake tattoo peeked sensuously out of the top of her low slung waistband.

'These are called snake arms,' she said.

'Think the snake bit me!' muttered Barb.

Everyone was silent with effort. Maya felt an unfamiliar femininity flood through her limbs as she continued to let her arms float up and down as she mastered doing figures of eight with her hips.

Barb refilled her glass.

'Imagine you are dancing for your own Adonis, now,' said Liv, her voice barely audible over the drums. 'Picture someone you know already, your favourite film star, or create your own.'

'George Clooney'll do me!' called Suchanatta.

Maya wondered who her Adonis might be. She tried dressing Rich in a toga, but the thought of it made her laugh. Then, unexpectedly, Mick appeared in her mind's eye, wearing that terrible leopard skin G-string she had once bought him as a joke. He was lean and muscled from working out, weathered from being outside so much, strong from lifting window frames and climbing ladders. His chest was a delicious mixture of freckles and gently curling hair that moved softly and strokably down towards that ridiculous thong. Liv's voice interrupted her fantasy.

'Now we can eat!' she said. 'I need you to get into pairs.'

'Now you've poured it all over my luscious breast!' said Elske, shaking with laughter, more at the fact that her chest was more boyish than goddesslike than the fact that she had a sticky pink river running from her chin to her navel. 'I may have to make you lick it off!'

'God, sorry. You'll have to sit up for drinks, I think!' Maya dabbed at Elske's chest and poked a bit of napkin down the front of her blouse. 'You are not allowed to use your own hands remember!' They were both laughing so hard that Maya was doubled over in hysterics. 'It's no good, you'll have to help. Oh sod it, now I've knocked the glass over.' She winced in the direction of Barb. 'Sorry Barb. Nothing broken.' She wiped a splash off a baby photograph on the bottom shelf of the sideboard with her belly belt, trying to make sure she didn't scratch the glass with one of the gold coins. Then she dabbed at the Persian carpet with the hem of her trousers. Barb rose immediately from where she was crouched beside Liv peeling a prawn, wiped her fingers on her napkin and rushed off to the kitchen for a cloth.

Maya stood up to refill the glass with more champagne. She couldn't remember when she had last let her hair down like this. It had to be the first time she had really laughed, right down deep in her belly, since they arrived.

Barb returned from the kitchen, raced over to pick up that little baby photograph and held it against her chest while Merry mopped up the spill on the carpet. Then she switched off the music.

'Seems we're clean out of champagne.'

Everyone stopped and the room fell silent. Barb stood there, holding her arms out to the side helplessly, the photograph in one hand, and swaying slightly. She looked out of her depth, as if she had lost herself somewhere in this evening of alien events. The mood dropped like a stone.

'I guess that's the end of the evening, then?' Maya said quietly, crunching on a last asparagus spear.

Barb sat down on a hardwood dining chair at the edge of the room. Liv beckoned to everyone to start clearing the table. Merry blew out the candles and switched on the lights. One by one the guests removed their shimmering scarves and dropped them into the cardboard box.

'Feel a bit dizzy from all the dancing. Can y'all see yourselves out?' Barb called without getting to her feet again. 'Hey, didn't we have a ball?'

'Thanks for a wonderful evening, Barb, Liv,' they said trying to keep their voices bright. Maya and Elske linked arms as they left the room.

'We'll call our own taxi outside shall we?'

Chapter thirteen

Calling all gods and goddesses

If you want to spice up your life, or even your sex life...

Did I just write that?

... then the following ideas make the perfect buffet meal. Last night, I attended an amazing party that opened my eyes to the perfect food for seduction. They say music is the food of love, but I believe that food is the food of love. All the best chefs recommend simple but fresh ingredients, in season of course, so the following ideas all rely on good-quality ingredients, preferably organic. And, as a general rule, if you can dip it or dunk it, then it is perfect for romance.

I know that garlic mayonnaise, often called aioli, is not always the perfect partner if kissing is on the menu, so I've substituted it for a pink spicy dip instead, that marries beautifully with the fattest prawns you can find. I love tiger prawns, but here in Dubai I buy four-inch long Gulf prawns. Peeling them is part of the fun. This hot pink dip just loves to be dunked by baby ears of corn, mange touts, or strips of raw courgette. For a change, I would like to introduce you to a bright green dip made from tender raw beans, and finally, because the best things come in threes, a lemony anchovy dip to sit on the tip of a spear of asparagus, which I know is not in season, but can still be bought all year round. I know I'm cheating, but believe me that one is worth it.

Maya's mouth watered as she wrote the morning after Barb's party. Her hair, still wet from her morning swim, dripped onto her keyboard and while a corner of her mind worried about poor old Barb, she recognised that she had not felt so inspired or so creative in a long time. And she had never felt quite so good about herself, either. Her hips seemed to have a mind of their own and still felt as if they were rotating gently – like when you return to dry land after a boat trip and continue to bob up and down for hours. She wasn't sure which had been more of a turn–on, the food, the dancing or all that talk of coiled snakes. Rich had actually arrived home before her last night and had been delighted – no, ecstatic – to hear what she had been doing all evening. He was full of questions. But when he had asked her if she had learned to make her nipples twirl in opposite directions, she had forced his head between her thighs to stop him talking. She squirmed in her seat, cleared her throat, finished the post, and hoped they could forgive her innuendos over in Stamford. The comments would let her know for sure.

No emails from Avril today. That made it a week now. Just one from Rich that, in his usual loquacious style, showed simply a winking smiley face. She leaned back in her chair and lifted her damp hair away from her neck. The bright pink of the belly belt shawl she had bought Avril caught her eye. She picked it up, tied it around her hips, raised her arms above her head, and began to dance. She closed her eyes. She didn't hear the door open.

'Madam? I bring coffee,' whispered Annie, placing a mug on the glass desktop. Maya's eyes snapped open to see Annie tiptoeing out of the room, trying to make herself invisible.

'Thanks, Annie,' she called down the stairs.

Annie looked back, nodded, and scurried off.

Maya picked up her coffee, slid the French doors aside, and stepped out. She would drink it slowly, savouring every mouthful. She rested her arms on the low balcony wall and looked out. Green parrots flitted between the palms and she heard their rough squawks as they dipped and rose. Inspired, her shoulders followed their lead. She raised each in turn coquettishly up towards her ears. Samir, the gardener, hunkered beside a squat palm, slicing away the lower fronds, now dry and pale, to reveal more of the emerging trunk. The blue water in the pool was smooth and glassy as the shadows shrank and the sun lifted towards what would undoubtedly be another beautiful day. Maya stood and watched the shared garden that was now familiar and a place where she now felt safe, belonged. She knew the names of every member of every family there, too. Barb was right. Culture shock did pass. Six weeks into her new life and already some things were beginning to feel familiar. She gave her hips a sneaky little shimmy and the gold coins tinkled like when she poured beans into a bowl. Samir looked up and she smiled then, after one last draught of her coffee, went back inside.

She would press Send and Receive just one more time, just in case. It burbled cheerily as an email entered her inbox. Someone called MileEndMick had made a comment on her latest blog. What kind of a username was that?

'Remember me?' it began. Her heart fluttered as she speedread the entire email, hungry to get to the end, and then had to go back and start again and read it properly. He'd found her.

It's Mick. Bit of a sexy blog post that, Maya. I am well impressed. Coz there I was minding my own business, going through a bit of a dry patch with the missus and thought I'd Google 'spice up sex life' and up popped your blog! You could have knocked me down with a fevver I can tell you! Gordon Bennett, I said. I know you was always the adventurous type, but I never thought I'd find your name in a list of porn sites.

Wow Maya. You're in Dubai I see. Married? Kids? Probably, right? I run my own company these days. Got a few blokes working for me. Branching out. Getting a few big contracts. Don't just do windows these days. Burglar alarms, air conditioning, electric garages, that kind of malarkey. I saw your picture on the blog. You haven't changed a bit, apart from the tan! If you want to see what I look like now take a look at my website www. MileEndServices.co.uk. It's a photo from the last Chrimbo party. Don't take any notice of the Tarzan outfit!

I'm a bit of a cook these days and will be trying out the anchovy dip tonight on 'er indoors to see if it does the trick, like you promise. Her name's Glenda. She loves seafood. We have a place in Spain and we're always down the fish market. Been hitched 10 years by the way.

No kids. But not for want of trying, if you get my drift. You married that RAF bloke didn't you?

Let me know how you're doing.

Warm regards
Mick Mason

After the initial thrill died down, her heart sank. She had never given the words of her blog a second thought, never thought about search engines picking it up. Mick's email was probably the first comment of many she would receive from other people and they were unlikely to be as polite as this one. Mick? Married? He goes abroad? He cooks? Who'd have thought it? Gawd Luvver Duck, he'd probably say. His voice barged back into her mind, jumping the gap of nigh-on twenty years to sound as clear as if she'd seen him yesterday. She checked out his website.

His hair was still sandy, though a little paler, and the tight curls she had loved to wrap round her fingers were cut very short. He still looked pretty trim, but perhaps he was sucking his stomach in? He'd bound to be, wearing an outfit like that. Leopard skin! Typical! He looked good, though she was not quite sure about the gold bracelet and the rings. His hazel eyes still had that twinkle.There was no way she could leave his comment up there for all the world to see. So she deleted it and decided to reply by emailing via the contact form on his website. Her fingers itched to reply straight away, but what if someone else read his emails? What if his wife worked for him and was his secretary or something?

She would edit her post. Dealing with lewd comments from a load of perverts was not what she had in mind. That done, she took a deep breath and switched off the computer. She needed to think about her reply.

The screen went dark. She stood up, untied Avril's scarf, folded it, and placed it with one of the DVD's in a jiffy bag ready for the post.

Chapter fourteen

Now Maya's routine made a slight shift. Checking the computer now came after the school run and before her swim. Then she stood in her bikini in front of the DVD player and bellydanced herself dry, rewarding herself with another stint on the computer straight after her shower. Then another quick one before bed. At least it took her mind off not having a real job. Now she knew that Mick's wife did not have access to the computer they had begun sending each other private messages via Facebook. If they both were online together they could almost have a real conversation. Long messages, packed with 'remember whens' flew back and forth between them. He remembered so much detail, that even small events seemed to have taken on a new significance for him. Flirting in cyberspace felt safe though intoxicating.

There was an email.

Hiya Maya

Thank you for remembering my birthday. I love the sexy scarf. Mum grabbed it and tried it on straight away and has begged to be allowed to try the DVD out today while

I'm at work. She has some life in her that one. Did I tell you she has a new boyfriend she met at line dancing? He's 80.

Jan's pretty sure Andy's having an affair and all these conferences are just a front. He's racking up a fortune on their joint credit card. She says she's sorry she does not have time to email you herself. Danuta's moved in with her to help with the kids so Jan can cook more stuff to sell in the shop and earn some extra cash. So your new recipes are keeping her focused. Keep 'em coming.

Sounds like the bellydancing evening was a hoot. Danuta has big ideas for a special Valentine's Day promotion next year. I don't know why she rejected my idea of calling it Phallic Phood?

Hope you and Rich are enjoying some bedroom bellydance action. Paul wants to know if one should wear anything under the jingly scarf or not? He's getting quite enthusiastic at the prospect. Good present, Maya. Fun for all the family!

Lots of love
Av

Avril was always such a tonic but Maya was worried about Jan. Now, it was time to check what was happening on Facebook. He was already online.

Me again. Tried that recipe for posh prawn cocktail last night in the hope that it would do the trick on the missus, but got the chilli on me fingers and well, you can guess the rest! Your recipes need a health warnin'!

Hey, you'll never believe it but there's an ad in the paper for five nights in a posh hotel in your neck of the woods. What do you reckon? Mick

Posh, hotel, eh? Far cry from our first holiday in that poky little, tent, eh? Maya

Oh God, rained cats and dogs, didn't it? Micky

We ended up almost setting the tent on fire because we tried to cook bangers and beans inside the tent on that cranky Primus? Maya

Remember when you tried to cook that fish in a bag and the bag burst? You always were an exotic eater, Maya!

Yeah, Micky, But remember how you always put vinegar but no salt on your chips?

And how you nicked my floppy chips and gave me all those dry crispy ones?

And how you always had a saveloy and the cod?

And how you hated eating in bed, Minx. But then you always were posh. Too posh for me, I reckon.

Oh, I don't know. I liked 'em rough in those days, Micky.

So, what about that hotel, then? Shall I book it?

Now things were getting out of hand.

'Fuck you, Mick,' she muttered, angry at him for messing with her mind. She couldn't resist a little giggle at his joke. Answering his question would take a bit of reflection. It was time to head back to reality and the day she had planned in the kitchen. Cooking had always been her salve and saviour.

Gotta run, sorry. Talk later. Bye.

It was just a bit of harmless fun, she told herself and did not change the way she felt about Rich, if anything things were starting to get better than ever between them. He always would be her best friend. And after seventeen years of marriage they still fancied each other. Having Annie to feed the kids some evenings meant they could spend more time than ever just the two of them. Maya's favourite was to sit beside him on the beach, watching the sun slip down behind the horizon, then drive to Karama where they would order fresh lime soda, falafel, hummus and aubergine dips, and eat with their fingers, sitting at a formica table outside a pavement café. The way his hot, tanned skin smelled baked and biscuity after a day on the beach, was quite an aphrodisiac. Knowing Mick was back in her life, albeit virtually, was cleverly putting her in the mood for Rich, so clearly the cyberflirting was a good thing.

But right now she needed to return to reality and get dressed.

She considered the salmon-pink and cream dress that hung on the outside of her wardrobe door. The white hand-printed label still lolled out of its scoop neckline, like a flat tongue tempting her to change her mind. But this new outfit was not for today. She couldn't bring herself to wear it yet. Today, it was tee-shirt and shorts for her, just as soon as she had changed out of her swimming costume.

Inspired by writing a tamer version of the goddess food blog and anticipating the deluge of comments that would ensue, she was on a mission to invent indulgent recipes that no one could resist. Av and Jan were telling all the regulars to check out the blog or pick up the newsletter and word was spreading. Danuta was getting really involved. Her idea of spicing up cold winters with a range of fireside soulfoods was inspiring. Now it was up to Maya to get cooking and get writing.

Annie knocked on the bedroom door. 'I vacuum, Madam?' she said, her pretty face peeping into the room.

'Sure,' said Maya, moving into the bathroom to re-apply the lipstick and mascara she now felt undressed without. Silly really, she wasn't going anywhere today. Annie tugged the big red sphere of the hoover into the room behind her and when Maya left she was cleaning inside the wardrobe. Inside it. No wonder the house sparkled. Maya would never be able to compete when they left Dubai. She skipped down the cool marble stairs, tapping the tips of her red nails on the polished banister on the way to the kitchen. Maya was all prepared. Yesterday she had done the shopping; today, she would commence operation Domestic Goddess. All set for a blissful morning creating. Chocolate, she knew, was the answer to anything.

So, date and walnut ice cream first, served with an easy chocolate sauce. The combination of fire and ice would be a winner. Putting the kettle on to boil, her heart lifted as she recalled how her flatmates had always taken the mickey out of her, making proper coffee back at university. She had even ground her own beans. Maya had appreciated the finer things in life even then. It was her father's fault. On one of their long caravan holidays, he had taken them to Florence. The first thing they had done, once they had arrived and found a good spot for the caravan, was to go into Florence.

'I'm going to show you what real coffee tastes like,' he had said, marching ahead of them, like he always did. 'Come along. It's just round the next corner, I remember. I've been here before.' He always had been a great navigator, her dad. A natural geographer, really.

'The kids can't keep up, Graham,' her mother had called after him, as usual. 'Their legs aren't as long as yours... ' but Dad had disappeared around the corner. Mum had grabbed Maya's hand in one of hers and her younger brother Phin's in the other, and ran after him. Dad had never slowed down. He was always caught up in the thrill of rediscovering old haunts.

'There's the Uffizi!' Dad called over his shoulder, waving his arm vaguely to the left. 'Botticellis are in there.'

'I'd like to see those,' Mum said, her voice so small it was as if she knew she had no hope of being heard.

'I hate art galleries,' Phin whined. 'And coffee.'

Maya wanted to go to the art gallery and try the coffee, though. She broke away from her mother and chased after her father, catching his hand instead.

'Good,' he said. 'Here we are, chaps!' And there they stood, outside a dingy little café, the kind you would normally walk straight past without noticing. 'Best espresso in Firenze. Joy, you sit here, I'll go in and order at the counter. They won't come out to the table.' He loved being in the know.

'But I don't like coffee,' whined Phin again. 'What's expresso anyway?'

'Just leave it to me, guys.' Dad disappeared inside. When he reappeared, he held a tiny cup and saucer with an espresso for himself, a larger cup with a mound of white foam raised an inch above its rim for Mum, and some ice cream, so dark it looked almost black, for Maya and her brother.

That was her first taste of Italian ice cream. 'Is – a – *gelato*,' Dad said with a flourish as he placed the sundae dishes, piled high with chocolate ice cream, in front of his children.

Now, standing in her Dubai kitchen, Maya found she could remember that day clearly. It was the day her taste buds had awoken, and after that day she had been keen to try anything new. She licked her lips. Hell, her homemade ice cream may have been responsible for Rich's proposal to her all those years ago. Mick had never been interested in her foodiness, and when they broke up that was one large aspect of his personality she had been glad to say goodbye to. Rich had been a breath of fresh air. And just as clearly as she could still see that seminal moment in Gelato Giovanni, she could see Rich sitting on the floor of his quarters at RAF Marham, his legs stuck out in front of him, surrounded by plates and dishes as she plied him with tempting sweetmeats. Rich's heart and stomach had always been firm friends. She wondered whether all boarding school kids were the same, eternally grateful for any meal that had not been cooked on a large scale.

Coffee made, Maya forced the silver plunger down to the base of the cafetière and poured herself a mug, leaving a little behind in the base of the pot for the ice cream.

Taking her coffee with her, she slid open the vast glass pane of the balcony door, flipped her sunglasses down from the top of her head, stepped outside, and shut the door behind her. The hum of the cicadas filled the early morning air, which was already thick with the smell of the waxy cream frangipani flowers on the tree standing alone in the centre of their little garden below. Her family and friends imagined she could see desert, dunes, and palm trees, maybe the odd oasis. Instead, if she looked beyond the compound, past the greying flat sand that surrounded the newest buildings, she saw a forest of cranes and the busy multi-lane carriageway of the Sheikh Zayed road packed with gridlocked traffic. Now that she had noticed it, the clunks, drilling, and banging of building work and the sound of car horns beeping joined the buzz of the cicadas, slowly drowning them out. And soon, who knew, Mick might just be out there. In the same city. A bead of sweat started its journey from her temple towards her ear and Maya agreed that if she couldn't stand the heat she should go back to the kitchen.

'Pinny on,' she reminded herself, tucking her hair behind her ears.

'Hair tied up,' she reminded herself, fishing an elastic band out of the little dish of bits that she never quite managed to wean herself off, placed, as always, on the windowsill. She'd had that Cloisonné bowl for years. Ever since Dad had taken them there when she was 16.

'Recipe,' she said, opening her ring bound file of old favourites.

'Ready, go!' she finished and at last allowed herself the pleasure of cracking the first egg.

A happy half-hour later and Maya's hips circled in time to the figure of eights she made with her wooden spoon, folding date purée into glistening custard. Brilliant. She removed and licked the spoon, running her tongue into every corner. Delish. The trouble with cooking was that it was too damn sensual. She tried to wrench thoughts of Mick out of her mind, but like a tug of war, the more she pulled one way, the more they pulled the other.

She poured the mixture into a plastic container and put it into the freezer. A couple of hours and it would need its first stir. Now what could she cook? She might as well keep on going while she waited. She looked into the fridge for inspiration: carrots, tomatoes, fresh mint, cream cheese, minced meat. She turned to the food cupboard and peered in at the rows of Tupperware containers, all neatly labelled: oats, currants, three kinds of flour, four kinds of sugar. All sorts, she always liked to be prepared. These days, the lids were not covered in flour, sugar, and smeared evidence of the contents. Did flapjack count as a Fireside Indulgence? she wondered. Of course it did! Nothing would ever taste more like home than her mother's recipe. That was it. She even knew the recipe by heart; she had made it so often. Damn. No Golden Syrup. Then, she remembered she had date syrup. She'd use that instead. Inspired, she set to work and put the oven on to warm up.

When the butter, syrup, and sugar had melted nicely, she stirred in the oats. Flour now. She tipped the tub of plain flour towards the scales, showering herself in white powder. She always had been rubbish at tidiness. When she was in the zone, enjoying herself, filled with energy, like now, happy as Larry in the kitchen, an uncluttered work surface went to the bottom of her agenda. It was creation she liked best, starting things. Stirring the ingredients together in the saucepan, the smell of butter and sugar made her mouth water. Glossy now, the mix was perfect and ready for the tin. Maya was on a mission. Into the warmed oven it went. She picked up the wooden spoon that had stirred the mixture a moment earlier, turned it upside down, and used her bottom teeth to scrape it clean. Yum. She was buzzing. Looking around her, the sea of debris scattered onto every surface was way out of proportion to the simplicity of the dish she had prepared. You could work out from the trails of oats, flour, and sugar on the floor which cupboard each ingredient had come from. A Spirograph pattern of dark brown ring marks showed that she must have picked up and put down the jar of date syrup an unnecessary number of times. A sticky stream, thick as mercury, now dripped down the side of the jar. Somehow, the lid had been left on the opposite side of the kitchen. Sod it. Tidying up was what she had a maid for. She pushed everything to one side, gave the surface a cursory wipe, and flicked on the kettle. Another injection of caffeine would be the perfect way to prolong her mood. She felt good. Damn good. Liv was responsible for awakening several parts of her lower body, while thoughts of Mick inflamed her imagination, making her feel nineteen again.

Now what would she cook? Something savoury. Something that made you lick your fingers one at a time, slowly. Mick had sucked her fingers and her toes, she remembered. She leaned back against the counter and gingerly placed two fingers into her mouth. Her lips felt moist and sensuous and as her tongue circled their tips, she closed her eyes for a moment. Any moment she'd be snogging the back of her hand. Now, where was she? Something savoury. She fancied a bit of Gordon Ramsey. Who didn't? She rubbed her chin and walked over to the bookcase in the sitting room to fetch her well-thumbed copy of The F Word then thought better of it. She didn't need Gordon or any other chef, naked, galloping, or otherwise. She'd make something up. Lamb burgers flavoured with mint and then a dip made of that yummy local yoghurt called labneh with garlic and more mint. Something that a goddess would definitely approve of.

'Ready, steady, cook!' she commanded and returned to the

kitchen where she noticed the faint outlines of powdery white footprints on the floor to and from the bookcase. 'Whoops,' she whispered. 'Sorry Annie.'

After her second cup of coffee, Maya was flying. Her hands were deep in a Pyrex bowl of lamb, which she was mixing with finely chopped shallots, and fresh mint, when the front door bell went.

'Hello Madam,' she heard Annie say to whoever stood on the doorstep. 'My madam upstairs.'

Maya heard the click of heels coming up the stairs. 'Hiya!' she called out. 'I'm in the kitchen.' There, dressed in black, unusually for her, was Barb. A distinct line of grey hair showed deep in her parting. A badge advertising McCain had been pinned to her tee-shirt. No secret who she was supporting, then?

'Hey girl, look at you!' said Barb, picking her way across the floor towards her friend.

Maya left her hips facing the counter and her hands in the bowl as she turned her face towards her visitor. 'Hi, Barb! Wonderful evening last week. I haven't let my hair down like that in years. Thank you. Sorry for the mess, I'm cooking.' She wondered whether she should bring up the rather flat way the party had ended. 'Is everything okay with you?'

'For sure.'

'You said you felt dizzy.'

'All better now. Nothing a good sleep can't fix, eh? My oh my, Maya, you sure do love cooking don't you? It is written all over your face. I shan't hug you today, I have no idea what I might pick up.' She studied her friend from the top of her head down to her bare feet. 'Now, let me guess. You have been making something with chocolate, right? That's up by your nose. Hum. Let me see. And something with yeast extract, that's by your left hip.'

'It's date syrup, actually.'

'And something smells good.' She wrinkled her nose. 'That tray bake looks fabulous. And I can smell another of my favourite smells. Coffee.'

Maya wiped her hands on her apron. 'Shall I make you one?' she said, switching off her music. Barb looked relieved.

'Hell, yes. After the morning I've had, I need a double.'

'Is it okay if I keep on going with this? I'm kind of on a roll. D'you mind? I'm sorry.'

'Hey, get outta here. You keep on doing what you're doing. I'll just – I'll just…' Maya watched Barb look around for somewhere to lean against while she waited. Embarrassingly, nothing really looked clean enough.

'I'll get you a bar stool. You can sit and watch me. Or would you like a pinny to join in?'

'No, that's fine. I'll watch.' Barb looked down at Maya's hands, probably to see whether they looked clean enough to touch the stool on which she was to sit. 'I'll get the stool myself, you carry on.'

'I think my flapjack is probably cool enough, now. Would you like some with your coffee?' Maya placed a one-person cafetière filled with coffee beside her friend and a mug. 'D'you mind doing it yourself?'

'Would you quit apologising?' she said good-humouredly. 'And tell me what on earth you are doing in the kitchen when your maid is a perfectly good cook?'

Maya rinsed her hands and got out a mezzaluna so she could chop the mint. 'Barb,' she said. 'I am having the best fun.' She crossed the kitchen to fetch another wooden spoon from a drawer. 'You know what? I think I've settled in!'

Barb looked over at the CD player. 'Sounds like that bellydancing got you going, girlfriend.'

'I think I'm addicted actually. My hips have not kept still since. I've got a DVD too and do it every morning after my swim. What about you? Don't you love it?'

'It's a bit disturbing.' Barb hid her face in her coffee cup.

Maya winked. 'Oh, that kind of disturbing! I know it certainly got rid of a few cobwebs down below for me too! Does Bill have a grin on his face too?'

Barb swallowed audibly and forced her lips into a smile.

Maya blanched. 'Oh, hell, sorry. I think I misunderstood you.' Operate brain before engaging mouth, Maya, she told herself. She shouldn't go round expecting other people wanted to share the intimate details.

Barb reached for the flapjack, blew on it, broke off a corner and popped it into her mouth.

Maya held her breath.

'Boy, this flappyjack is good, though, Maya. You must give Merry the recipe.'

'Oh get away! It's really easy. Takes minutes to make.'

'Your kitchen is a disgrace girl! Have you looked in the mirror?'

Maya laughed. 'Don't you cook?'

'Not much anymore,' she replied shaking her head. 'Not now I have Merry. I used to love it though, in the old days. I was quite a dab hand at a pot roast and my Thanksgiving dinner was the talk of Amarillo.'

'The food was great the other day.'

'Thanks.' Barb stared out into space towards the window.

'Delicious.'

'You reckon?'

God, the conversation was stilted this morning. Barb seemed a bit out of sorts.

'Say, can I have another coffee? And why aren't you having one?'

'I've already had two. That's more than enough for me. Why? How many do you have a day?'

'I lose count. Ten? More? I dunno. Lots. I guess it doesn't affect me.'

Maya looked at her friend carefully. Barb's eyes looked more than a little bloodshot. Who knew what her skin looked like without that make-up? She could swear her hands were trembling slightly, too. 'Shall I get you a glass of water to have with that coffee?'

'No, thanks. Water is for animals. Do you have any Coke?'

'With coffee?' Maya couldn't help herself, her eyes were wide with amazement.

'Sure.'

Maya wondered why Barb had dropped in. It still didn't make sense. She was mixing the garlic and mint sauce into the yoghurt dip when an insistent beep beep beep broke into her thoughts.

'That's my timer,'' she said unnecessarily. 'That means it's ice cream time.'

'You really have had a morning of it, haven't you?'

'I'm having a ball, Barb, I tell you.'

'Gee it's good to see that smile back on your face. To see you alive again. For weeks I've seen you going through the motions. Meeting me at The Orange Tree, going to the mall, The Twist, but you never seemed quite there, you know?'

Maya nodded.

'I have to be honest, I was wondering if you and Rich, were, you know, all right? Many couples can't handle this living abroad game. Lots of our friends have split up over the years. Bill carries the business cards of a divorce lawyer friend of ours with him in his wallet all the time these days, so many of his colleagues ask him if he knows anyone. He reckons he gives out five cards per posting. Are you sure you're alright?'

'No, we're okay, Rich and me. Up and down, you know. Mostly up.' She began beating the crystals out of her ice cream. 'He thinks I've never had it so good.'

'Yeah. It's a good life, eh? Bill lets me do anything I want and never comments on how much money I spend nor that I do so much volunteering. He just lets me get on with it without so much as a murmur. I guess he feels guilty I had to give up my apology for a career to follow him.'

'I didn't know you had a career, Barb.' Maya's interest was pricked.

'Bill got his first posting and I followed. It wasn't long before I lay down, turned on my back and gave up without a fight. He no longer saw a need for me to work so I didn't.'

'A financial need? What about you and your needs?' Maya put the beater in the sink.

'My needs? Ha! I think they got lost in transit.' She smiled at the image. 'Probably somewhere over the Atlantic. Sunk without trace in a battered old packing case with fragile on the side.' She raised her arms out helplessly to the sides though her voice trembled with something resembling a chuckle.

'It's not funny, Barb. At least I don't think so.' Maya walked closer to Barb and reached out her hand to lay it on her shoulder.

'It's goddamn hilarious.' Her body froze under Maya's

touch. 'What about you?'

Maya moved to place the ice cream back in the freezer. 'I loved my job. Really loved it. Great colleagues, great customers, and I loved being around food all day.'

'Figures.'

'I earned my own money, never needed to ask Rich for anything. It gave me lots to think about and talk about.'

'Why d'you think I do The Twist? It gives me a purpose.'

'Sure. But the novelty of Rich being the sole breadwinner seems to be wearing off. I'd like to find a way to pay for my own lunch at The Orange Tree.' She leaned back on the counter. 'But he's busier than ever these days. Claims he doesn't suffer from jetlag but I don't believe him. Actually, he gets back from Bangkok this afternoon.'

Barb looked at the floor. 'Look on the bright side – it's easier to get on with someone when you hardly see 'em! Bill's home right now and without any golf matches lined up, so there's a chance he may find a space for me in his agenda.'

'You know,' Maya mused. 'I've never met Bill. Amazing. I've seen you almost every week, but I've never met him.'

'And I've never met Rich, though I hear he is gorgeous.' Barb's eyes twinkled.

Maya clapped her hands together like an excited child. She had an idea. 'I've had a great idea. I've done all this cooking and I have to celebrate the fact that we're settling in at last, so how about you come for dinner tonight and we share it?'

'Oh no. We couldn't. I wasn't hinting that we had nothing on so we were bored. Honest!' Barb stood up to leave. 'Look, I have to go. School will be out in a minute. It is short notice and all. But thanks for the offer. Really appreciate it.' Her smile did not seem to reach her eyes.

'No. I insist, Barb. That is – if you would like to. I used to love giving dinner parties. And with all this free time on my hands, I can't think of a better way to spend it. You've been telling me about expat spontaneity, after all. You will bring Brandon, won't you?'

Barb reached her sunglasses down from the top of her head and put them on her nose. 'Oh, I'm not sure. You see, we may have moved a lot, but he is a real American kid in the food department. I'm not sure he'd go for all these herbs and vegetables I can see you have put in your burgers. I don't mean to be rude, but... '

Maya was not to be deterred. 'No problem. I have the whole afternoon ahead of me and the burgers won't stretch to seven of us anyway, so how about I do a proper homemade lasagne for the kids, with garlic bread? And he will like ice cream I expect?'

Barb was smiling. 'Sounds great. Just not too many vegetables in the lasagne eh?'

'Perfect. Then we can have a proper drink! None of this coffee and Coke lark. Such a nice surprise to have you pop in.'

'Wonderful. I'll look forward to it. We all will.' Barb stood in the kitchen doorway and Maya watched her make an effort to lift her chest and push her shoulders back as if ready for battle. 'I'll see myself out.' She paused. 'Oh, by the way, I almost forgot. Not like me to forget what I came for.' She reached into her huge bag, black today to match her outfit, and brought out a little pink bag, like the ones you buy in card shops to put presents in. 'I prepared these for everyone to take home after the other evening, you know, a kinda goddess goodie bag. Filled it with some stuff I thought you might like. Do me a favour and sit yourself down and go through it carefully. Silly me forgot to hand them out afterwards. I don't know why.'

Maya wiped her hand on her pinny and took the bag. 'Thanks, Barb, ' she said. 'You're too generous as ever.'

Barb shook her head, smiling. 'No ways. Look, here's one for Elske too. Would you drop it round for me? I don't like to disturb her while she's working.'

'Sure. Of course I will. About seven-thirty tonight, okay?'

'See y'all later!' and she was gone.

Maya pushed the goodie bag behind the kitchen scales and went to get some mince out of the freezer.

Chapter fifteen

'But Brandon, I'm sure you'll enjoy yourself. Maya has two boys, Oliver's a bit older than you and Matthew a bit younger, I think. Likes sport I guess, Maya is always taking him to some practice or other. I haven't met either of them before either, but I'm sure you'll get on great,' said Barb, desperately trying to persuade her thirteen-year-old to stop looking at his Nintendo thing and get freshened up ready to go out to dinner at the Winters. She really hoped he wouldn't wear that nylon Astros outfit, the pants reached his calves and the tee shirt was far too baggy. Then those massive shoes, all unlaced and gaping. They must be baking hot in this weather. Still, it was the fashion, she supposed. And she didn't want to get into an argument. Not tonight.

Her son ignored her. Elbows splayed to the side, thumbs darting around the keypad, his eyes never left the screen.

'Are you listening to me? Brandon?' She reached her hand out and made a play to wrench the noisy horrible gadget out of his grasp. Its beeping was really getting on her nerves. Brandon turned his back, shrugged one shoulder and kept playing.

'Are you listening?'

'Uh huh,' he said. Or was it just a grunt? Newly teenage, he was rapidly changing from her little boy into a monosyllabic monster, and a big one at that. Even though he had just entered high school, he was taller than her already. His feet were bigger than Bill's and he was already wearing men's clothes.

'Oliver and Matthew go to Emirates British School,' she continued, keen to prolong the conversation, however one sided.

'Do they play baseball?' Hey, that was a four-word sentence. Something of a record. She wished she knew the answer, but she and Maya never really talked about their kids. Barb did her best not to start such conversations, because people would inevitably ask her how many she had and she wanted to answer truthfully, to say 'Two', because she did have two, only one of them was not around anymore. It was impossible to answer in such a way that both of them felt comfortable, so instead, she just said. 'Brandon, thirteen,' because at least that was true. But her mind screamed out, 'And Angelina. I have baby Angelina, but she's with God.'

'I don't know. Maybe. You'll have to ask them.' She heard Bill's key turn in the lock. Late again.

'Bet he doesn't play baseball.' Five words this time. 'Bet he doesn't support the Astros.' Six.

'Well, I'm sure you'll have lots to talk about. Now come on, big guy, you need to wash up. We are out of here in twenty minutes.'

All this time, Brandon kept on playing his Nintendo. Still, he seemed to have been listening, so now she could move on and break the news to Bill.

'Bill?' she called out.

'Coming, honey!' he replied, his deep Texan drawl as rich as chocolate fudge cake. Surprisingly, Barb had discovered she could tire of chocolate cake.

Her husband stood in the doorway, one hand on either side of the frame like a six-foot-four crucifix. She wished he wouldn't tuck in his shirt. Big guys like Bill looked all squeezed in the middle like an apple core when they did their belts up so tight.

'Had good days, you two?' he asked, as if he almost meant it.

'Fine, thanks,' said Barb.

'Gnn,' said Brandon.

Barb walked over to her husband and gave him a big hug, wrapping her arms round his belly. Her hands didn't quite meet at the back these days, though with the added length of her French polished, square-tipped false nails, it did add a few inches, but the effect was the same. A bear hug. She liked Brandon to see them being loving towards each other.

Bill laughed. 'OK, honey, what is it that you want? Let me guess... You have seen this really cute silk carpet or rosewood chest? Or is it shoes?' He always was good-humoured about giving her stuff. Barb laid her cheek against his chest.

'Jeez, Barb, it must be something big you want today, girl. All this attention the moment I walk inside the door!' His words were gentle, but his body was stiff beneath her touch. She guessed his eyes were fixed somewhere else, out the window, perhaps.

Barb steeled herself. When Maya had first suggested they go around for dinner, it had seemed an okay idea, and besides, the food would be great. But for someone whose entire working life had been all about change, meeting and mixing with new people and moving on, Bill didn't much like formal dinner parties with complete strangers being sprung on him. She had never met Rich, nor Oliver and Matthew, and the chances were that they were nothing at all like Maya. Barb liked Maya enormously, loved her quirks, her enthusiasm, and had really enjoyed playing the role of protector. But inviting the whole family around for dinner when none of them knew each other, Bill was tired, and it wasn't certain that Brandon would like the food, was a bit of a risk. Bill was more of a barbecue kind of guy. He hated wearing a tie. Felt it strangled his personality as well as his throat. Being in the oil industry, he was still able to dress like a redneck for work, in checked shirt and jeans – if anything, it was expected of him. When they'd been in London, they'd been to their fair share of candlelit dinners with the locals. There had always been rather refined gins and tonics beforehand, dainty nibbly things, several courses, and changes of wine. Bill had put his foot in it a few times, asking for ketchup or Dr Pepper, but had always laughed it off. She chose her words carefully.

'Guess what?' she began.

'What?'

'You know how you moan that Merry's food is boring?' she continued.

'Ye es,' he replied. 'Why do I feel that you are not about to tell me that we are getting a take-out from Taco Bell?'

'Well, you know my friend Maya?'

'Not sure I do, honey.'

'Yes you do, Bill, she's the one who moved into Mimosa Gardens, remember? I told you? Her husband is with Arabian Airlines. They're British. Been here since August. Their first posting.'

Bill rubbed his chin. Clearly he didn't remember at all. She had not expected him to. He stood there silently.

'Well, I was around there today and she was cooking all

this cool stuff and… ' She paused to see what reaction she was getting. Nothing, so she pressed on. 'And anyway, I let slip that we had a clear agenda and, well, she invited us for dinner.' There she had said it.

Bill nodded. 'Okaaay,' he said slowly.

'Tonight.'

'Oh.'

'We need to leave in twenty minutes.'

'Fabulous,' he said sarcastically. 'Just what I need after a hard day in meetings and traffic jams. Perfect. Now I have to listen to a million questions about Texas and the oil industry and discuss Dallas and ranching. That's the trouble with first timers, they generalise about every goddamn nationality and think we're all the same. I don't think I can stand another evening of that wretched Obama fellow. Roll on November fourth.'

'Let's hope McCain makes it, then.'

'Whatever. I sure am sick of socialising with strangers right now.' He wrenched at his tie and began to loosen it.

'Hey, Brandon, how do you feel about this then, buddy? About as thrilled as me, eh? We had a date with those reruns of the Simpsons.'

Brandon looked up from his Nintendo at last. 'Aw, Mom. It's not fair.'

Barb kept her tone bright. 'Well, I said yes, I am sorry, but we are going and we will enjoy ourselves. Come on, guys, it might be fun. Expat life is all about spontaneity.'

'Only if they like baseball and eat pizza,' grumbled Brandon.

Barb clapped her hands together. 'Come on guys, you have precisely seventeen minutes to wash up and then we're off.'

Bill was rubbing his neck thoughtfully.

'And no, I don't think you need to wear a tie. Just a polo shirt will be fine. Merry's laid your navy one on the bed ready.' She looked at her son. 'And you can wear whatever you like. Come on, if she's invited the whole family it can't possibly be top hat and tails. It'll be casual, I'm sure of it.' Barb had to get the family on her side somehow, and besides, she really wanted to meet Rich, it sounded like he'd be pretty sexy. As a pilot, he had to be.

Bill walked over to his son and cuffed him playfully around the ear. 'Come on, bud,' he said good-naturedly. 'If they have boys, they're bound to have pizza. And hey, if it gets real impossible you and me can always talk to each other. Now that would make a change!'

Barb watched her son glare at her husband before his shoulders heaved forwards ever so slowly, as he forced his over-sized teenage body into a standing position before lumbering off in the direction of his bathroom, his face still bowed towards his game console. She looked up towards Bill, who turned on his heel and moved off towards their bedroom. She sat down on the couch, took her compact mirror out of her purse and reapplied her lipstick carefully, painting on her smile ready to counteract the glum faces of the men in her life when they reappeared in the doorway.

She chattered all the way there in the car, filling them in with all the useful information she could think of about the Winter family. Forewarned was forearmed.

'And Maya is a bit of an English eccentric. Boy, you should have seen the mess her kitchen was in today, but she sure is passionate about food. You know, when we go out to lunch, she always has the thing on the menu she has never tried before.

Oh yes, and it's usually vegetarian.' She shut her mouth swiftly. That was a stupid thing to say. Now they would think there would be no meat tonight.

'Is it left here?' asked Bill.

'Yep, you turn here. Number 7,' Barb answered. Her speech was quickening as she became more and more nervous about inflicting more of her friends on her family. Bill's job was to go to the office and earn the money and be the life and soul of the party. It was Barb's job to organise the party.

It took a while for the door to be answered. A blessing, really, as Brandon was determined to sit and wait in the car with the air conditioning on for as long as possible. 'Finishing his level,' he called it. When a shadowy shape loomed behind the glass pane of the front door, Barb waved frantically at the car to her son. He could be such an embarrassment at times.

A skinny blonde child opened the door. 'Come in,' he said, clearly as excited about the evening's entertainment as her own son. 'Mum!' he screamed up the stairs towards the kitchen. He had to scream, to be heard over the loud Arabic music. The music stopped abruptly. 'They're here.' The boy stood on tiptoe, jumping from foot to foot as if desperate to race off.

Barb led her family into the hallway. She put out her hand towards the boy. 'I'm Barb Schneider,' she said. 'Pleased to meet you.'

'Hi,' said the boy, who shook her hand limply. It appeared he was not used to this.

'And you are?' asked Barb, moving past the boy to allow Bill and Brandon to take their turns at handshaking.

'Matt,' he said. 'Muuuu-um!' he called again, with desperation in his voice.

The Schneider family trooped up the stairs towards the sitting room and stood there looking around. Lost. Matthew had disappeared.

Then there she was. Maya. In the doorway, wiping her hands on her apron and looking flustered. She hadn't changed since Barb had seen her earlier that day. Her hair was still tied up and damp fronds clung to her rosy cheeks. Barb looked at her friend as if for the first time, as if through the eyes of her husband and son. She looked so, well, English. But charming. Ungroomed. Hot and bothered, too.

'I'm terribly sorry,' she began, her opening line an apology. 'I've been dancing along to the music, hence the flush. You really started something, Barb, I think I'm hooked!' She laughed. 'Rich has only just got in. Traffic, you know. He's um, in the shower. Look, let me get you a drink. Kids. Kids? Where are my boys? Teenagers, eh? Like husbands. Never there when you need them! Ha! Always there when you don't, eh?' She paused to take a breath. 'Goodness, what am I thinking?' She stretched out her hand. 'Maya. I'm Maya. You must be Bill... and Brandon. How lovely. Lovely.' My, she was flustered. 'You take a seat while I whizz off and get changed, will you. Rich will be down to do drinks in a jiffy.'

Bill sat. Brandon sat. Barb sat between them.

'See, she can be a bit eccentric,' whispered Barb, patting them on the knees. It was plain as day to her that Rich and Maya were indeed having problems. One thing you could say about Bill was that when they had a party, he was the perfect host, full of smiles and wonderful at keeping glasses topped up. And it was a bit rude of Maya's boys not to be there at least. She could count on Brandon to have been reliable in that area too. 'Have a chip,' she said, pointing to the bowl on the coffee table. 'I wonder where her maid has got to?' If this had been her party, Merry would have been able to see to the drinks too.

Fifteen minutes later, things were starting to happen. Barb and Bill were in the kitchen helping Maya to fix the drinks – though there was no ice dispenser and they did like lots of ice. The three boys now sat in mutual silence on the couch, making sure their bodies didn't touch as they took it in turns to cram their mouths with potato chips. Brandon still stared at his games console.

'Mum?' shrieked Oliver in the direction of the kitchen. 'Can I get my Nintendo, then? Brandon is allowed his.'

Maya ignored him and led her guests back to the sitting room and the second couch, where they too were forced to sit in a row, with Barb in the middle again. She really could have done with more than two in a room this size.

'You've got this room real nice, Maya!' said Barb, looking about her at the hotchpotch of furniture and the clip-framed posters on the walls. 'I love that Turner painting of the Thames. Did you get it from the Tate? We loved the galleries when we lived in London, didn't we Bill?'

Bill was looking out of the window. 'Bill?'

'Yes, honey. I guess we did,' he replied absently, reaching his arm over the back of the sofa behind his wife and rubbing the back of her shoulder with his thumb.

Desperate to escape the grey cloud that hung over the room and the obvious tension Maya felt with her husband still absent, Barb looked for something to say to alleviate the situation.

'Hey, Maya. May we have a look at your balcony? I'd love to see the view.'

'Sure, help yourself. I'm sure Rich will be here in a moment.' She looked agitated. Mind you, Barb would be less than happy if her guests had been there half an hour and her husband was still in the shower too. 'I do apologise. You must be starving.'

'It's okay,' Barb replied. 'We're fine for a moment.'

'Boys?' Maya said, the desperation in her voice making it rise an octave. 'Can you get Brandon a drink, please, while I fetch your father?'

Barb nodded towards her husband, then the balcony door, and they made their exit. Together, they leaned against the balustrade and stared out into the night and the city lights.

'That new tower block is going up fast,' she said.

Bill slapped at an insect that buzzed somewhere near his right ear.

'Still so many trucks on the highway,' she said.

Bill fished in his pocket for a while, pulled out his car key and used it to poke inside his ear.

Barb glared at him. She hated this dreadful habit he had of poking things into his ears when he thought no one was watching. 'Don't,' she whispered.

Bill kept on poking.

'Say something, Bill?' said Barb. 'Please.'

'This is almost as much fun as you said it would be. That do? And my beer was warm.'

'Come on. I'm sure it will be fine as soon as Rich gets here.'

'Well, I know I'm not best pleased when you tell me we have guests for dinner the moment I get home from the office,' said Bill. 'I expect the elusive Rich feels just the same. All he wanted was a quiet night in with the TV and his wife tells him he has to make small talk with a bunch of strangers.' He put his key back in his pocket. 'Boy am I hungry though. I could murder a steak.'

Then the balcony doors slid aside and Maya joined them. Ah! There was the elusive Rich, his dark blonde hair still damp from the shower. He was wearing a tee shirt with the name of a rock band on the front, a pair of faded board shorts, and flip-flops. He hadn't shaved and he rubbed his forehead hard with the flat of his palm. Barb looked at Maya and wordlessly they communicated with shrugs of the shoulder, tilts of the head, and raised eyebrows. No, Maya had not wanted him to dress like this, but it was this or he'd have been in an even worse mood all evening.

Once Rich had sorted the drinks and they'd left the humid balcony for the cool interior, Maya calculated that her guests had now been there for forty-five minutes, the burgers were drying out, the lasagne was a bit too brown for her liking, and Rich was not himself at all. If wine hadn't loosened him up, maybe the food would. It was time to take them to the table. Perhaps he really was just tired, like he said? Or maybe this was part of his own culture shock.'This your first posting?' asked Bill, looking at Rich. Barb's husband really was a big guy, thought Maya. They all were. Friendly, though, which was more than could be said of her own husband, who had his hands over his mouth while he stifled a yawn.

'What's that mark on your arm?' Maya asked, noticing something that looked like a burn on his forearm.

'Really?' He didn't even look at it. 'Doesn't hurt. Must've trapped it in something and didn't even notice! Two long hauls back to back with jet lag and I'm done in. Not slept for twenty-four hours,' he said. 'Bit of a headache.'

'Shall I get you some Paracetamol?' Maya glared at him.

'I'll get it.' He didn't move but then he did look completely shattered.

Maya went out to fetch the food from the kitchen and put it in front of her place at table, ready to serve her guests. She shot a look at Rich, whose face was furrowed in pain, and left the room again. She returned and placed two pills and a glass of water in front of him without a word, then bent down towards Oliver and quietly suggested he tried talking to Brandon.

'Are you from New York?' he asked.

'Nar, Amarillo,' he replied, shrugging. 'Never lived there though.'

Oliver and Matthew looked blankly at each other.

'It's in Texas. I was born in London. You from London?'

'Stamford,' they said. Now it was Brandon's turn to look blank. 'It's in Lincolnshire,' added Matthew. 'Where they filmed Pride and Prejudice?' Still no response. 'What team do you support?'

Rich took his pills. Maya began to relax.

'Astros. Houston Astros,' replied Brandon, pulling at his shirt and rolling his eyes, to indicate that it should have been obvious. 'Baseball?' he continued, putting that annoying upwards inflection at the end of the word, implying that he doubted they had ever heard of the sport, let alone heard of the Astros.

Matthew nodded. 'Yeah, I've seen them on TV.'

At least her sporty son was not letting her down. Now all that remained was for her grumpy husband to make her proud, though at the rate he was going, Barb would be less than impressed with him. At least Bill knew how to behave. And dress. Unlike Rich, it looked as if he had brushed his hair and had a shave. She didn't usually like a moustache, but Bill's was thick and dark and beautifully trimmed.

'This looks lovely, Maya,' said Barb, looking down at her neat rectangle of lasagne accompanied by a line of kebab and circle of yoghurt sauce. 'Doesn't it, Brandon?' she said to her son.

'Help yourselves to salad and garlic bread,' said Maya, noticing how Brandon's mouth was set in a taut line. It looked zipped shut.

'How do you like it in Dubai, Rich?' Barb had decided to do battle with Rich.

'Fine,' he said. 'Thanks. Though of course I am away from the place more than I'm here.'

Come on, come on, thought Maya, This conversation needs warming up. 'I think everyone needs more wine,' she said. 'I'll put on some music while Rich gets another bottle.'

'Oh yes, getting the wine is a man's job, right?' he said. Ouch, that was unnecessarily barbed. She was glad to have an excuse to go off and choose the music. What was eating him?

'Say, Rich? You bin affected by this old credit crunch, then?' Bill asked, cutting his burger into bite-sized pieces before laying down his knife and eating it with his fork. 'We've only been here a few weeks, no chance to start saving yet, not the way the wives spend, eh? Nothing much to lose, anyway.' Maya flinched. 'I'll get the wine, shall I?' she stood up, glad to have an opportunity to avoid seeing the way he was fiddling with his knife, standing it first on one end then the other.

'You weren't with Lehmann, were you?' asked Rich.

'No, thank God. But I've been busy moving money around our accounts, trying to save our skins, haven't I, honey?' He laid a hand on his wife's arm. 'Gotta make sure my girl has enough money to keep her out of mischief!'

Barb wriggled in her seat then smiled indulgently. 'Seeing as I don't have a job, maybe I should look after our money for us?' Maya said brightly, though the thought terrified her. She'd get the wine in a moment. Rich's hand flew to his throat. He started to cough, thumping at his chest. He reached for his glass of water.

Maya began to hit him on the back. 'Are you okay?' she asked, determined not to show how hurt his comment made her feel.

Rich shook his head, more as a request for her to leave him alone than in response to her question.

This was a good time to go over to the sideboard for that bottle. She laid the Cabernet Sauvignon on the table and unscrewed the cap.

'Stuck,' he said. 'Bit of meat.' His eyes began to water. 'Okay now.' He took another sip of water. 'Sorry, guys. Now where were we?'

'I guess talking about money wasn't a wise move, eh?' chuckled Bill. 'A subject that gets stuck in your throat, is it?' His huge chest heaved with laughter at his own joke.

'Not really, Bill. But I guess that is why we came here. We'd no savings to speak of. Just a house, which fortunately we've rented out – we'd never cover the mortgage without it. Hope we can save a bit while we are here or I'll still be flying when I'm seventy!' He took a sip of his wine.

'Lining the pockets, eh?'

'It's a bit of a slow start, Bill. Right now mine are filled with sand!' Rich turned his inside out and watched the contents trickle to the floor.

'Dad!' said Oliver. 'Clear that up this minute. You can't expect Annie to do everything!'

Maya glared at him, then relented and smiled. It was disconcerting when you heard your own words coming out the mouths of your children.

'Kids, eh? Who'd have them!' said Bill, ruffling Brandon's hair fondly.

Fortified by a second drink and the lasagne, the ice began to melt, and everyone chatted comfortably as they ate. Well, most of them ate. Brandon still stared down at a plate full of food. Maya watched his mother mouth something in his direction. The next minute he was lifting the top layer of pasta from the square of lasagne in front of him, and picking out every single carrot and piece of celery. He left them in a neat pile at the side of his plate then reluctantly began on the rest of the food, eating one ingredient at a time, starting with the pasta. Maya had tried hard to disguise the vegetables, cutting them extra small. It seemed she'd failed.

'Would you like me to heat that up for you?' Maya asked in her perkiest voice. 'It must be rather cold now.' She felt rotten. This evening had been supposed to bring them close together, not throw up bones of contention.

'No thank you,' said Brandon.

'I don't mind if you don't eat it,' she said. 'Really, it's fine. I think I may have a pizza in the freezer you could microwave if you prefer.'

Brandon's face brightened and he looked towards Barb for approval, who looked embarrassed.

'What did I tell you?' Barb said apologetically.

'I like it, Mum. Can I have some more?' asked Oliver, who had refused to brush his hair this evening, get changed, or shower. His mobile phone had beeped several times since they'd sat down and Maya had watched him replying to the text messages under the table.

'Tell you what, Oli, why don't you take Brandon to choose a pizza and sort that out for him, while I do second helpings?' She paused. Oliver didn't move. 'Or, better idea, why don't you boys have your pizza and seconds in the playroom and then you can come back for your ice cream and eat that there too, in front of a DVD or something? 'Who's on for badminton?' Matthew offered, racing to the stairs.

'Brandon might prefer to watch a film,' Maya said carefully.

'That's cool,' said Oliver, who unfolded his rather ungainly, growing body from the dining chair, and moved off towards the kitchen, grabbing a piece of garlic bread from the wooden bowl in the centre of the table on his way. As the children left the company of adults, it seemed they had more to talk about.

'Hey, do you guys have any Family Guy DVDs?' Brandon was asking.

'Yeah.'

'Do you have series three?'

'Yeah!'

'Great! I love that show!'

'Kids, eh?' said Maya rather predictably.

'Yeah, too right!' said Bill, his eyes twinkling in her direction. 'Great lasagne by the way. May I have a little more?' He patted his ample stomach.

Maya sighed. With any luck, soon peace, happiness, and full stomachs would reign in the dining room and the playroom. 'Rich, would you do the honours?' she asked.

'Sure,' he said, reached for the serving spoon, and stood up. It seemed he had mellowed at last.

Maya slipped out to the kitchen to see the boys leaning in the doorway drinking Coke out of individual bottles and Annie placing a mini pizza into the microwave.

'Oh thanks,' said Maya, looking about the room. 'Wow! You've washed up everything! That's terrific.'

'I bring ice cream?' she asked.

'That would be wonderful. In five minutes. Thanks.' At last things were getting under control. She returned to the table and poured herself another glass of wine. 'You can guess what the First Officer said,' he was saying, 'They really had moved the runway!'

Bill was rocking with laughter.

'I got my flying licence when we lived in Stavanger,' said Bill. 'The view was fabulous, flying over the fjords. I must get behind the joystick here some day too. Mind you, there's so much air traffic here, eh? Must be as busy as down on the street!'

'Almost!' Rich was softening at last. 'Security's pretty tight, but I reckon I could get you up in the triple seven some time, if you like.'

'For real? That would be great!' Bill took another mouthful of wine. 'Hey, do you play golf?'

'Not yet. It's a bit too pricey for me.' Rich and Bill faced each other, both with one elbow on the table and the opposite arm dangling over the back of the dining chair.

'If you're around this Friday, I could take you along to mine. They're having a guest day. In fact, bring the whole family. They've laid on free taster lessons for all ages.'

'Matt would like that. Sounds good. What time?'

They had planned to go out for brunch on Friday, as a family, but Maya knew better than to remind him. He was getting on with Bill and that was all that mattered.

'The ice cream really was terrific, you know,' said Barb. 'I'd never thought of making a sauce with dates.'

'I can give you the recipe.' 'You mean you can give Merry the recipe!' laughed Barb.

Maya smiled to herself.

'Gee, is that the time? We've had such fun!' said Barb, laying her napkin down on the table. It was a weeknight and they did all have early starts.

'Shall we go and see what those kids are up to, Barb? Leave the menfolk discussing whatever it is menfolk discuss?' Barb picked up her handbag and followed Maya out of the room.

The sound of canned laughter met them before they had even entered the playroom. They poked their heads around the door. There was Brandon, sitting alone on a beanbag, legs splayed out in front of him and a tub of ice cream on his lap, which he was shovelling into his mouth without letting his eyes leave the screen.

'Hey, Mom!' he called. 'You gotta watch this. It is tooo funny!'

'Where are Oliver and Matthew?' Maya asked, concerned that her children were turning out to be as antisocial as their father could be.

Brandon shrugged.

'Did they watch the telly with you?' Maya asked. 'At all?'

'Nope.' He spooned more ice cream into his mouth.

'Oh Barb, I am sorry,' said Maya. 'This is not on. They are not normally so bad-mannered.'

'That's okay,' said Barb, who didn't sound like she meant what she said. 'Maybe they're in the yard. Matthew said he liked the idea of playing badminton didn't he?'

But Maya was on a mission to find her children and reprimand them. Drag an apology from them. How were they ever going to integrate if not one of her family members could be trusted to be sociable?

Barb followed Maya outside. There was Matthew, sitting beneath the badminton net with a racquet in either hand, hitting the shuttlecock in a short steep arc in an attempt to play a game on his own.

'Where...?' Maya began, about to ask if he knew where Oliver had disappeared to. At that moment she saw him, lurking near the edge of the lawn underneath a lamppost, his head bowed over his mobile phone, fingers going like crazy.

'Texting Frog Legs, aka Chantal,' Matthew answered before she could even bring herself to ask the question. 'Been at it all the time. Never played for one second.'

'We'll talk about this in the morning,' she said. 'Right now, it is school tomorrow and high time you were in bed.' She turned towards her elder son, who now had his back to her. 'Oi! bed!' she called to him.

'It seems they're all as bad as each other,' said Barb. 'Let me drag my husband away from yours and my son from the big wide screen. Thank you so much for a lovely evening.'

Chapter sixteen

But it hadn't been a lovely evening at all. Clearly she had misjudged things big time.

'They're nice, aren't they? Bill and Barb,' she said brightly as she removed her eye make up with a ball of cotton wool.

'All right,' said Rich, picking up his book.

Maya's face fell. 'You are not going to read are you? It's really late.'

'It's not my fault we had a late night. Inviting strangers to supper was your idea, remember?' His voice was barbed. He removed the bookmark and laid it on his bedside table. 'The jet lag plays havoc with my body clock, remember? You try flying back-to-back long haul and see if you like it.'

'But you had quite a bit in common with Bill in the end. And he invited you to play golf. And you invited him to see the plane.'

'I was being friendly, Maya. Like you wanted me to be.' His eyes never left the page while he spoke.

'Thank you, Rich. I appreciate it.' She placed her hand on his arm.

'Whatever.'

He closed his eyes, turned on his side with his back to Maya, and placed his book on the bedside table. Her mind went into overdrive as a terrible thought struck her. If she could do it, so could he.

'Is everything okay?' she asked gingerly. 'You've been really weird this evening.'

'I told you, Maya. I had a headache.'

'Is everything all right at work, though? Are the new air hostesses nice?' she tried to be subtle.

'God, you're transparent! No, I am not having an affair with a stewardess. I'm too busy and too damn tired to have an affair, if that's what you're getting at.' He switched out the light.

Maya was glad she didn't have to look at him any more.

'Night.'

'Night.'

The next morning she felt compelled to get out of the villa. She needed time to digest the events of the previous twenty-four hours. Rich was still asleep. Annie followed her round like an annoying overfriendly puppy, asking if she could help. There had been no email, blog or Facebook action to deal with and she still hadn't decided how to respond to Mick's hotel question. She decided that she needed to get away from the villa and have a think on the beach alone. The fresh air would perk her up. Help her to think straight.

She parked by a low concrete wall beside the strip of pale sand on which she was now walking barefoot, her gold flip-flops swinging from her right hand. Ambling along the dark damp shoreline, skinny tongues of clear water licked her toes quickly and then retreated. It was cooler here. She walked the length of the beach, first with the sun on her right cheek, then with it warming her left. Despite the caress of the early morning sun it felt dissatisfying, like her damn dinner party. It only took five minutes to move from one modern breakwater to the next. Then back again. Her glance was drawn to a group of orange-bellied blue-legged crabs danced among the barnacles and limpets on the glossy surface of the rocks. She sat down on a smooth stone by the shore, lifted her summer skirt to just above the knee then tilted her full face towards the sun. The water breathed out and dragged itself up to submerge her feet and ankles then breathed in again, retreating to the horizon. It was so different down here. You could hardly believe that the clanging, chaotic city zipped along on just the other side of the Beach Road. Maya matched her breathing to the sea and mentally threw all the negative thoughts that had plagued her during the recent months out into the Persian Gulf, like jetsam.

She looked down the full length of the beach, the sea shimmering beside her, pale as aquamarine. It actually was pretty perfect here. She reminded herself that it was because of Rich that she was in a position to live her dream. Fate had brought Mick back into her life, and fate would decide what on earth she would do about it.

Over at the far end of the beach a big black four-wheel drive appeared on the sand, drove at a pace towards her, stopped suddenly, and turned 90 degrees to park facing the ocean. Maya screwed her forehead up into a frown. Her peace was about to be shattered by mad local kids with more money than sense. Any minute now, the windows would be lowered and the sound of heavy bass music would blare out at her. She stood up and smoothed down her skirt. Squaring her shoulders, she prepared to walk past the car without catching the eyes of the occupants. She did a good line in nonchalance. Only there was no music.

Instead the silhouette of a woman, swathed in black, walked down towards the shore. She walked awkwardly, a child on one hip. Maya could hear her singing softly to the toddler. The little boy, dressed in a tiny cream *dishdasha*, overtook the mother, pulling his clothes over his head to reveal a pair of Bob the Builder shorts as he ran into the sea.

'Look at me!' he called.

Maya stood transfixed. She had not expected English to come from people who looked like that.

'Ali! Hurry up!' the woman called back towards the car and Maya watched as a bearded young local man, dressed in sparkling white from headdress to toe and wearing designer sunglasses, stepped out of the driver's door. He ran down the sand towards his family, scooped up his son and threw him in the air before exchanging a glance with his wife.

Back at the car, a Filipina woman was busily erecting a sunshade and laying out woven mats and a large cool box beneath it. Once it was finished, she moved down towards the shore, picked up the discarded *dishdasha* with one hand, and took the baby from the mother with the other, before returning to the shade where she knelt down, talking gently all the time.

As Maya got closer to them she realised that it was the woman who had spoken at The Twist event about the car safety campaign. The one who she had promised herself she would telephone, only she never had. It was Leila.

Maya had never approached a local couple before, but knowing that Leila was Irish gave her confidence.

'Hello,' she said towards Leila. 'I saw you at The Twist. My name's Maya. You probably don't remember me. Is this your family? Do you live near here?' She was talking too much. Why did she feel nervous talking to them? Just being married to a local and wearing local dress didn't make Leila suddenly foreign, did it?

'Hello Maya,' Leila replied. 'You were on the front desk, weren't you? You spoke about how you felt when you got that horrible stamp in your passport. Yes, this is my family.' She called to her husband, who now stood ankle deep in the sea, hand in hand with the little boy. 'Ali. I want you to come and meet someone.'

Ali lifted his son up by the armpits and perched him on his shoulders before walking back up the gentle slope towards Maya. He pushed his sunglasses up onto his head, where the little boy immediately placed his sandy hands over the lenses. He thrust out his hand towards her.

'Ali al Farooq,' he said. 'Pleased to meet you.' He reached up to touch his son's right arm that now clutched his right ear as if it were a bicycle handlebar.

Maya looked up. 'And you are?' she asked.

'Mohammed,' he replied, as he was lifted down and crouched on the sand to poke at a piece of flaccid green seaweed. 'Can we eat this, Daddy?'

Maya was surprised to hear father and son spoke perfect English, no hint of an accent. If anything, Mohammed had a trace of a Southern Irish accent, while Ali sounded like he had been educated at a British public school. For a moment, she was too surprised to speak and hid her embarrassment by continuing to gaze at Mohammed in the way that only adults who are parents too can do, slightly patronisingly. Ali's fine boned face was clear and unlined, his beard so neat that a faint pink line ran round its perimeter, making it look as if it had been thinned and trimmed that very morning. He smelled of freshly applied aftershave and his brown eyes shone. She was glad her sunglasses hid the pink that ringed her tired morning eyes.

'Daddy!' called Mohammed, who was racing off towards the breakwater. 'Come and see my baby crabs, over here!'

'Do excuse me, Maya,' he said apologetically, kicked off his sandals and chased after his son, nimble as a cat.

Leila was sitting on the sand, her thin black robes curled round her bent knees and tucked carefully under her. She was smiling up at Maya, her pale face clear of make-up, seemingly not remotely perturbed by the effect her husband and family were having. She patted the sand beside her and Maya sat down too. In a flash the Filipina maid was at their side, baby on hip and offering drinks. Soon they were both sipping ice-cold mango juice.

'And your little girl? What's her name?' Maya looked back towards where they had set up camp on the beach.

'Oh that's Yasmin; she's thirteen months. Mohammed is three.'

Maya found it difficult to look at Leila; she was too confused by the whole set-up. An Irish woman, wearing an *abaya* and *lahaaf*, married to a local, and children with Arabic names. She fully expected Leila to have assumed an Arabic accent. It was all too incongruous.

'I've not been here long,' Maya began. Surely her newcomer status would absolve her of all faux pas. 'How long have you been here?'

'Six years,' said Leila. 'But I married Ali back in Dublin a couple of years before that. We met at university. He was doing civil engineering. I did English.'

'Gosh,' said Maya, immediately feeling stupid for showing surprise at something so, well, normal. People met at university all the time. A host of questions started to battle for supremacy in her mind. How had she felt meeting a Muslim? How did she feel about moving to the UAE? And had she minded converting to Islam? Covering her head, wearing black? Did she speak Arabic? But for now, they would have to wait. Another question won the battle. She took a deep breath, picked up a handful of sand and ran it slowly through her fingers.

'How's your women's project going?'

Leila hugged her knees and rocked gently as she too stared out to sea. 'OK, I suppose. Things are a bit slow.'

'But I thought things would be easier for you, I mean less bureaucracy and language issues, what with being married to a local and everything.' Maya looked at Leila's eyes at last and discovered they were the colour of jade.

'In some ways, you're right,' she explained. 'Ali and his family have been brilliant, got my charity registered at the Ministry of Information, provided me with an office, sourced me a government grant, and of course I have help with the house and the kids, so bits of it have gone brilliantly.' She picked up a tiny white shell, as smooth and perfect as a baby's fingernail, and laid it on her black lap before idly finding another and adding it to the collection.

'That sounds terrific!' said Maya brightly. 'You've achieved more than I have in the last few months. All I seem to have done is shop and cook, when I am allowed in the kitchen, that is. Oh, and bellydance! I really love Arabic music.'

But Leila continued to look a little dejected. 'Sounds cool. The bellydancing, I mean.' She grinned. 'I don't do much shopping myself, either. The babbies only spew up or plaster jam all over any new clothes I buy. It's not worth it. Mind you, now I've got my figure back, there are some sparkly outfits in Zara I really fancy. Though to be honest, I'm not sure how you get sick out of sequins!'

Maya laughed.

'For sure, I have a good life here. Really I do.' She picked at the shells, turning over her hand and resting one tiny shell over the plump tip of every finger.

'You don't sound as if you quite mean that.' Perhaps that was a bit bold. 'I'm sorry. Maybe I shouldn't have said that?'

'No, you're all right, Maya. And I shouldn't burden you.' She paused. Maya waited. 'No, it's not all exactly ticketyboo. Well, not the charity part of it.' She stared out to sea for a moment. 'Ali is fantastic, they all are. Really supportive. Glad I've found something to do. You see.' She paused again. 'I had really bad post-natal depression after Yasmin was born and they're just delighted I've found something to be passionate about again. I have it all. Great life. Great house. Great husband. Great family. Great kids. Great everything. I felt really guilty being depressed. Ali has an older brother, called Hatim. He went to school in England, too. Studied business. Hatim was Maryam's husband. You know, who killed herself? I guess I didn't grieve for her til after Yas was born. It's taking a while to get back to normal.' She stopped. 'Oh Maya, you don't want to hear any of this.'

'Go on,' said Maya, gingerly putting her arm onto Leila's shoulder, unsure whether this demonstration of affection was permitted. 'It's fine.' Leila needed to talk and right now, Maya felt more useful than she had in a long time, just listening.

'Well, if you're sure,' she said. 'It's a bit of a long story, but Barb told me about that Norwegian called Liv, you know, the one with the blue nails and toe rings?'

'She does bellydance too!' added Maya.

Leila raised her eyebrows. 'Well, wouldn't you know! That woman is a mystery to me. What doesn't she do?'

Maya nodded. Liv never ceased to intrigue her, too.

'Well, Liv gave me a few massages with some lovely oils, she let me talk, and that helped a lot. But the thing with Liv is... God I don't know why I'm telling you all this, Maya.'

'Go on.'

'Well, she seems to be a bit of a Gypsy Rose Lee, you know, she's really wise. It's as if she can see into your soul. Each time I saw her she would leave me with one word or phrase that was just so apt, it was uncanny. Weird. Once she just said, "Breathe", and another time she said, "Count your blessings", and then she told me I needed to do things for other people and it was like a lightbulb went on above my head. I thought, doh, yeah, of course, Leila you eejit. That's just what you should do, for Maryam. I should start a foundation or something to try to stop it happening again. And it was as if Liv could read my mind. She just stood there smiling at me, nodding.' She cleared her throat. 'So that was when I had the idea for the charity. And here I am. Sorry, bit of a long story, that!' She laughed softly and tipped the white shells back into the sand.

'Fascinating.' Maya was intrigued. 'But what has this got to do with your campaign not going well?'

Leila clapped her hand to her forehead. 'Here I go again, telling a long story when a short one would have done. I'm always doing this. Must be in my blood, rambling away. Storytelling and all that. I studied English because I wanted to be a writer one day, but then I met Ali and came here so never did a day's work in my life. That's my trouble, no experience, but lots of enthusiasm!' She dug her toes into the sand.

Maya stopped and wiped her forehead on the back of her arm and eyed the sunshade up by the car. 'I'm getting a little hot. Could we move up there, do you think?'

'Sure, only... ' She hesitated. 'Maids have ears.'

'Oh, right. Then I'm just fine here. You go on.'

'Well, like I said, everything should be going swimmingly. I got well, I got something to do, I got all the paperwork sorted, with help, of course, and now, well, I'm a bit stuck. You know I went to The Twist meeting?'

'Yes.'

'Well, I went there because I knew I needed more help. I needed people to really join in properly. Be serious about it.'

'Go on,' said Maya. 'Barb said tons of people signed up at The Twist.'

'Well, yes and no. None of them worked out.' Leila shrugged.

'Oh dear. Why?'

'I think it's because people came forward just because they were curious about me. Because they wanted to know if I always covered my hair, if I only ate halal meat, if Ali had any other wives and why I had agreed to give up my Catholic faith. They weren't really interested in the project at all.'

'Gosh,' said Maya inanely.

'Gosh, eh? Admit it, Maya, even you were thinking all those thoughts weren't you?' Leila looked at Maya determinedly then threw a few more handfuls of sand over her toes and patted it down with her palms.

Maya could not bring herself to respond with words, so instead she just bit her lips together and nodded feebly.

'So, Maya, would you be interested in my campaign? Or are you just interested in weird old me? In the girl who was Linda?' Leila's eyes started to mist over as she turned away and stared far out towards the horizon. 'They told you that I expect?'

Maya nodded, blew her hair out of her eyes where it was clinging damply to her forehead, and thought hard.

'Actually, I need a challenge right now, Leila. And I am truly interested in your project. This charmed life here can be pretty disempowering and I know just where you are coming from. But tell you what, I'm hot, so how about we meet for coffee or a drink later, somewhere cooler, and you can tell me the whole story?'

Leila grinned broadly and leapt to her feet. She looked like a young girl as she clapped her hands together excitedly. 'Will you come for tea tomorrow? I mean a cup of tea? Real tea made in a pot? So thick you can stand a spoon up in it? Come to my house. Here.' She fumbled under her *abaya*; Maya got a glimpse of grey silk Capri pants and a soft leather shoulder bag. 'Here's my card. My address is on it and there's a map on the other side.' Leila turned to run over to join Ali and Mohammed over by the rocks, looking back at Maya over her shoulder now and again and smiling broadly.

'Thanks, Fate, mate,' she said.

Chapter seventeen

The row seemed to have come out of nowhere. When the alarm went off to get Rich up in time to go to the golf club, he slammed on the snooze button and rammed the pillow over his head.

'Don't go back to sleep,' she said.

'Why the hell not?'

'Because you told Bill...'

'If I go out with your friend's husband, I will go because it is my choice, not yours.'

'But, I thought...'

'Well you thought wrong, Maya. At least let me make some of my own decisions. I won't have you controlling me. I'm not your performing monkey.'

'I never said you were.'

'Yes, well you don't have to.'

'But Rich... ' Her voice became smaller by the minute.

'But nothing. Just let me choose my own friends, will you? And choose how I spend my time.'

Maya lay on her side, staring into space through a veil of tears.

'And, if only you didn't spend every last cent of it, how I spend my money.'

'That's not fair,' she said, placing her hand on his shoulder.

'You're not sitting where I'm sitting.' Then the alarm had burst back into life. He flung back the duvet and stepped out of bed. 'See? I'm getting up. I'm going out. It's what you want, isn't it?'

'You don't have to go.'

'Too late. Mustn't let him down. Christ knows why I agreed to go anyway, there is no way on earth I'll join the place. Costs a bloody fortune.'

As soon as Maya heard the shower running, she slipped out of bed, made herself a very strong coffee, and went to the office to get out of his way. She checked her emails. Nothing. Then moved to the blog. Danuta had commented on her recipe for lamb burgers with yoghurt mint dip.

I cannot buy labneh in Stamford. I used Greek yoghurt instead. Maybe you should add this option to your recipes, Maya? Jan made the burgers yesterday with my sauce. It was delicious.

Danuta was right. Of course she should have suggested Greek yoghurt. All this communication with Mick was making her take her eye off the ball. She took a sip of her coffee and shuddered at the bitterness. Annie's coffee was never bitter. She pushed her shoulders back and down to relieve the tension and decided to have a quick look on Facebook.

Dear Minx

Love the photo of your house you put up here on Facebook. A far cry from that council flat in Bethnal Green, eh? Still, we had some fun, didn't we? Listening to Spandau Ballet's Gold and feeding each other chips on the balcony. You'll be able to see the Olympic Stadium from up there soon. Things change. Remember how you used to listen to that Edith Piaf bird on that old Dansette record player? I used to josh with you, saying it made her voice even cracklier! Non regret something, wasn't it? Do you have any regrets, Minx?

What did you think of my idea of coming to see you? I don't want to miss out on those last minute deals in five star hotels. Would I have a good time? Or would Glen just spend all my dosh on jewellery?

Love Mickey

Just a few lines and she tried to read between every single one. Did he have regrets? Was he inferring that he had treated her like a goddess all those years ago, only using greasy chips not Gulf prawns? Was his mention of the Olympic Stadium a metaphor for how far she could have gone if she had stayed with him and how the world would have come to her doorstep in the end? And he'd signed it with 'love'. What did that mean?

She ignored her quickening pulse and opted for a quirky reply.
Mickey
Mick
Too many questions.

Yes.
Yes.
Yes.
Yes.
Only one.
Not sure.
Probably.
Yes.

Love
Minx

That would keep him busy! And she did only have one regret. She wished he'd left her the recipe for pepper sauce. Which reminded her. She had a blog to do.

Fire and ice

When you can't stand the heat they say you should get out of the kitchen. Here in Dubai, thanks to the air-conditioning, the kitchen is often a cool place to be. At least for me. This week, I experimented with one of my favourites – ice cream. So that's the ice part of today's recipe. The fire comes from the sauce. There is nothing better than cold ice cream with hot chocolate sauce. The recipe below takes about a minute to make and works every time. Better still it uses store cupboard ingredients.

Enjoy!

Maya

She clicked Publish and her weekly message was posted. Job done, she took her coffee out to the swing seat in the garden. It was the weekend. Rich was out with Bill and the kids were still asleep. The compound pool was crammed with younger children and every now and again an extra large splash would send a shower of water over the fence.

By three, Rich was back from the golf club and holed up in his office. He didn't mention his morning and Maya didn't deign to ask. She'd let him stew. Oliver and Matthew were happy doing what they called 'chilling', Oliver playing his guitar outside under an umbrella, doubtless in the hope that Chantal would hear him and be impressed. To be fair, he was pretty good at it and today she had heard his attempts at singing along to his music in a hushed voice. She was gratified that his song of choice was *Wish You Were Here* by Pink Floyd, from her own era, and not one of the modern songs filled with obscene lyrics. 'Two lost souls swimming in a fish bowl' had been one of her favourite lines too. There were probably countless lost souls in the fish bowl of Dubai, she mused. People said that most people came here because of a D word – debt, divorce, depression, drink. You'd have thought they could be more romantic and think of desert, *dishdashas*, dancing, or even the Middle Eastern delicacies Avril had reminded her of all those weeks before. And talking of fish, Matthew was in the pool again. Trying to beat the world breathhold diving record, apparently. So far he had managed forty-two seconds. He had a long way to go, but was determined. Annie had been instructed to keep an eye on both the kids while Maya was out. Sometimes the expat life and the privileges it brought with it were pretty special. She no longer felt like a fish out of water.

She dressed with care that afternoon, not sure if it would embarrass Leila if she turned up in a knee-length skirt and short-sleeved tee shirt. Instead, she chose a rather bohemian kaftan in her favourite dark sea blue over pale blue cargo pants. Silly really, she thought, to worry so much about her outfit when she was only going to see another woman. But what if Ali were there? It was Friday after all. The weekend. Or did they live separately? She stopped herself thinking about just the stuff that drove Leila crazy and gave herself stern instructions to treat her hostess normally, just as she would her own next-door neighbour, Elske.

Generalising about nationalities and situations you knew nothing about was easy to do, but dangerous. Look at Barb and Bill and Brandon. She had half expected them to arrive for dinner wearing matching Stetsons, to do a lot of backslapping and yee-haahing, but actually their accents were faint and Brandon sounded the least Texan of them all. For sure, he had worn the kind of baseball gear she had expected, and he had been rather on the chubby side, but then so many kids were these days. Nope, no more would she leap to conclusions about people based on their passport.

She fished around in a drawer for a cream headscarf and draped it round her neck. Maybe she would need it.

'Mum!' called Matthew, who was dripping his way up the stairs towards her. 'Where are you, Mum? I've been calling you for ages. Guess how long I did?'

'I don't know,' Maya said. 'Please don't come into the house all wet, you'll turn the place into a skating rink. Marble floors are lethal. Couldn't you at least dry your feet?'

'Right. Guess how many?' Matthew stood in front of her, his tanned, skinny body covered with goosepimples from the shock of the air conditioning. He put his hands under his armpits and started to jog up and down on the spot. 'Mu-um!' he growled. 'Show an interest. And anyway, what are you wearing? Are you going to be Mary in a nativity play or something?'

'I'm going to meet a new friend of mine, called Leila, at her home. She's married to a local and, well, you never know if I might need it.'

'Cool!' Matthew perked up, still jogging. 'Will she have camels and stuff?'

Here we go again, Maya thought. 'Really, I have no idea, but I will tell you later.'

'What about my dive? Guess what? I did forty-two last time, right?'

'Fifty-five?' Maya asked.

Matthew tutted loudly. 'Come on, Mum, I'm not likely to improve that fast, am I?'

'Forty-four?'

'Better than that. You're rubbish. I did forty-six. Can you believe it? Forty-six?'

'Well done, darling, that sounds lovely. Now go and get a towel or something. I have to go out now.'

But Matthew was already skipping back down the stairs, nimbly avoiding the wet puddles he had left on his way up. Maya was careful to hold the banister.

Holding the card with the address on it, Maya drove carefully around streets that were close to where she lived herself but had never explored. Instead, she had just mechanically driven up and down the main roads along with all the other traffic and joined the race to get wherever she needed to go as fast as possible. Here, on the other hand, just a couple of streets from the mayhem of the Al Wasl Road, hardly another vehicle shared her space. Here, pavements were scarce, sometimes just a rim of pale kerb filled with sand and scrubby low-growing plants. Big silver skips had been dotted about for local rubbish. Black bin bags, pale blue plastic shopping bags, and garden waste protruded from them. Scraggy cats patrolled the area, tails held high. Fat bushes of bright pink, dusky apricot, or white bougainvillea spilled over the high white stucco walls that enclosed every villa, their lower leaves turned brown from drought and sand storms. As she passed a driveway, the wrought-iron decorations on the large gate opened back to reveal a black-windowed Toyota Landcruiser, swarming with boys in *dishdashas* and girls in silky dresses worn over long trousers. A pair of dark-skinned maids heaved cool boxes into the open boot. At another house, a houseboy slipped into a side gate. He wore an open-necked white shirt over a vest with a checked sarong knotted round his lower half like a skirt and carried a blue bag of shopping in either hand.

Leila's house was at the end of this particular street. Palm trees poked their heads over the crenulated wall, making it look like a Moorish castle from the outside. But Maya had learned her lesson: she wouldn't pre-judge. She would not. Pulling her Range Rover alongside the wall, she stepped out into the warm afternoon. It was remarkably quiet here. A light breeze moved a crushed tin can in the gutter, crickets sang, and pigeons hooted. Their song was almost the same as the call they made in England. 'My toe bleeds Betty,' her mother had said they were saying. But here their song was more staccato, higher-pitched. Here they sang, 'Haha hoho haha.' Were they laughing at the fool she was about to make of herself?

Maya pushed at the gate. It was shut firmly. She looked around and found an intercom device fixed to the wall. She pressed the button and heard a click on the other end, then nothing else.

'My name is Maya, I have come to see Leila,' she said, knowing she was taking extra care to enunciate and that she sounded impossibly British.

'Mammy!' A small voice could be heard through the crackle of the intercom, then she heard a buzz and the gates eased open as if by magic.

Peering around the gatepost, Maya saw a bright green square of lawn framed by a ruddy jigsaw of paving. In the middle were a brightly coloured plastic playhouse, a paddling pool, and a slide, as well as a jumble of ride-along and push-along vehicles prostrate on their sides. It was silent. Ahead of her stood the polished teak of a carved front door, studded with brass fittings. It looked rather grand. She skirted the perfect lawn and followed the paving down towards a carport wide enough for three vehicles but which now housed only the black Wrangler Jeep she'd seen on the beach. To the right, under the shade of the awning, was another door, more modest this time and decorated with a line of flip-flops in varying sizes and colours, neatly paired. What if this led to the kitchen or the maid's quarters? No, she would have to brave the front door, after all. She retraced her steps, admonishing herself for not being bold enough to march straight up to it the first time. It was not so hot, but damp patches were forming under her arms. She widened them and wheeled them slightly in the hope that the pathetic breeze that caused would rectify the problem.

The door opened and a young Filipina woman, not the one

she had seen on the beach, opened it wide for her, standing back against the wooden frame to let her pass. The woman nodded and looked behind her. Maya climbed the steps.

'There you are!' Leila stood in the hallway, baby Yasmin clinging to the side of her mother like a koala. She was no longer wearing her black *abaya*. The loose leggings skimmed her trim thighs and slim hips. Her matching sleeveless top was cropped to reveal a centimetre of stomach beside the clutching baby's chubby knee. But it was her hair that took Maya's breath away. The colour of conkers and burgundy wine, it flowed in gentle waves down her back, fanning to her waist.

'Hello,' said Maya, unsure how long she had been staring. 'I'm sorry. I wasn't sure which door... '

Leila, rocking the baby back and forth on her hip. 'Won't you come in?'

Maya stood there. 'Your hair!' she said inanely.

Leila grinned. 'Well, yes, it does exist under my scarf, you know. Were you surprised?'

Maya nodded. 'I suppose I had wondered, but nothing had prepared me for this. It's beautiful.'

'It's the henna. Oh, that and keeping it out of the sun. The sun is dreadful for hair you know. My sister's is the same colour as mine, but you know, it goes all frazzly, in fact it looks burnt, when she spends all day in the baking heat, sunbathing. But look at me, I'm covered in freckles. I don't really tan anyway. My freckles just seem to join up closer together. She's the same, but it doesn't stop her sunning herself the whole time she's here. Daft eejit. Now, where do you want to sit, Maya? Sitting room, in the garden, or by the pool in the shade?'

Maya had no idea which to choose. She wanted to see it all. Despite her good intentions, she wanted to know everything about this transplanted Irish beauty and her life in this alien landscape. The white doors that led off the large white hallway were all closed and gave no clues of what might be behind them. The staircase swept up and away in two cream-carpeted wings towards what had to be the bedrooms. Apart from a couple of red Persian carpets, a gold-framed mirror, a piece of art made from a mosaic of blue tiles, and some potted plants, the hall was empty.

'The pool, please.'

'Good choice!' and Leila led the way through one of the white doors, down a white corridor decorated with black and white photographs of Parisian scenes towards the sound of laughter and splashing. If the corridor had been white, then the pool area seemed even whiter, dazzling and dotted with skinny olive trees in turquoise pots. Blue and white. Blue sky. Blue water. White stucco walls, white tiles around the edge, blue tiles to line the pool. And there was the brown body of Mohammed, still wearing his Bob the Builder shorts, running and jumping in, clambering out, water glittering like dew on his slippery skin the colour of melted milk chocolate.

'Mammy! Look at me!' he called out.

At the edge of the pool, seated at a white table beneath a wide white umbrella and with a white towel over her lap, sat the Filipina nanny from the beach. They exchanged smiles.

'Hello, madam,' she said, her eyes returning quickly to settle on her charge.

But Maya just smiled. The maid sat, slightly hunched, focusing on the boy. She wore a shapeless white tee shirt decorated with the sun, a palm tree, and the words: The best summer I ever had was a winter in Dubai. Her hair was scrunched behind her head into a scraggy knot. She wore no sunglasses, so her eyes were scrunched up too.

The maid extended a smile and her open arms towards Yasmin, who tottered to her feet and wobbled for a second or two before she was picked up and seated on the fluffy white towel and the lap that was intended for her brother.

'You watch,' said Leila. 'In half a second, Mohammed will be desperate to get out of the pool, shivering like a frozen wraith and with his teeth chattering like nobody's business.'

Leila led Maya to a secluded area, rather like a bower, its white trellis walls and roof intertwined with the pale blue flowers and lacy caps of climbing plumbago. Beneath the bower were two wooden, reclining steamer chairs, covered with plump cushions. They sat down and in seconds the Filipina woman who had let Maya in earlier appeared.

'Oh thank you, Baby,' Leila said, squinting up at her from beneath her flattened palm to shield her eyes from the afternoon sun. 'What would you like to drink, Maya?'

'A glass of water?' she asked, her weak voice inflecting annoyingly at the end. Oh God, she was sounding like a teenager.

'Still or sparkling?' asked Baby, her face serious.

'Er still, please.' How ridiculous that she was panicking over something as simple as this. She took a deep breath and told herself not to be ridiculous.

Leila ordered a cup of Typhoo tea. Maya wished she had asked for the same and must have looked transparently wistful. 'Make that two, please, Baby. And some Ginger Nuts.'

There was another loud splash, followed by a splutter from the direction of the pool. Maya turned to watch as the maid set Yasmin back down on the ground and hoisted Mohammed from the deep end and wrapped him in a towel.

'Your children seem very happy with your housemaid,

don't they?' said Maya, slightly incredulous. Oliver and Matthew seemed to treat Annie with an indifference that was occasionally rather too close to contempt.

'Oh yes, Lily is like a second mother to them. She left her own children behind in Manila, so mine are very special. It makes me feel really guilty, though. Wouldn't it you?' Leila's constant chatter was the perfect mask for Maya's reticence. She ably smoothed over every gap in the conversation like soft putty between panes of glass.

The tea was good and hot and strong. Together they sat and dunked their biscuits a sliver at time, quickly racing them to their mouths before the crescent of soggy succulence collapsed into the tea.

'Old habits die hard, eh?' said Leila. 'I am so glad we can get Ginger Nuts now.'

'And McVitie's Chocolate Digestives,' added Maya, confident of this topic of conversation.

'To be sure, only they melt too soon in this heat!' Leila laughed.

Maya watched as Lily scooped up Yasmin and silently ushered Mohammed back inside without so much as a murmur. She took it as her cue to change the subject to the one that she really wanted to discuss.

'You're looking for help with your project, aren't you?'

Leila's green eyes lit up in a flash and she moved up onto her knees. She put her hands behind her neck, gathered up that impressive maroon skein of hair and gave it a twist before pulling it forwards over one shoulder. Then she looked straight at Maya.

'You are serious! I didn't dare start the conversation in case you'd changed your mind and only agreed to come round here, you know, because you were nosy about how I lived. Jesus, because you only wanted to see my hair.' Absently, she flicked her hair back over her shoulder to hide it again. 'You do know that there is no money involved. Sorry.'

'I realised that. I'm serious. Only a few hours a week, mind. I've not got any experience in this kind of thing and know nothing about psychology or women's empowerment or anything. But I need to get my teeth into something and having been on the receiving end of that bloody passport stamp, it really appeals to me.' Maya wasn't exactly selling herself, was she? 'But why don't you tell me a bit about what you have set up so far?'

'Farooq's family have been in construction for years, you know. And they have recently restored the most gorgeous old building by the sea. It's a windtower house. You know what that is?'

Maya nodded.

'So we have a beautiful place with an inner courtyard, some rooms round the edge, a kitchen and a lovely big meeting room that overlooks a wide terrace and the sea. You'd love it.'

'Sounds amazing. Really peaceful.'

'It is. So we have the venue.'

'And?'

'That's it! That's all so far. Of course being Emirati Ali and Hatim have done all the boring bureaucracy stuff and it's all set up and legal.'

'Does it have a name?'

'I thought The Sunshine Centre?' she sounded hesitant. 'Is it okay?'

'I love it!'

'Hatim suggested the Sunshine bit and I like alliteration so

I went for Centre. He used to say that Maryam really loved the sun. But you know, in the end, even the endless sunshine of Dubai was not enough to make her happy.'

'I'm sorry.'

'But enough about me. Now it's your turn. I want you to tell me about you.' Leila's brow furrowed in concentration.

'I set up my own business in England. A deli, with two of the mums from the boys' school. It was really successful and I loved it,' she paused and watched Leila raise her eyebrows encouragingly. 'I know how important it is to be fulfilled and, having just moved here, the memory of the agony of not knowing anyone and not knowing what to do is still raw. I'm not sure I'm even out of the woods yet, to be honest. Barb says it takes anything from three months to a year to get over this culture shock.'

'That Barb is a one, isn't she?' Leila shook her head and took another sip of tea and Maya began to relax.

'To be honest, I need an excuse to wriggle out of helping her at The Twist. She's been dropping hints for weeks.' She laughed.

Leila raised a forefinger as an idea emerged. 'So, you used to run a delicatessen, didn't you?'

'Ye-es,' said Maya slowly. 'I'm not sure where food fits in.'

Leila scratched her chin. 'Oh, I don't know. There has to be a way to link food with this, isn't there. I mean, everybody has to eat.'

'And food makes lots of people happy.'

'Food can taste of home but it can also make you homesick. Food can bring back memories. It can make you feel safe.'

Maya rubbed her chin. 'And food is for sharing. I can cook too by the way. In fact, I love to cook. I write a cooking blog for Seasons, that's the deli.' She stopped talking for a moment so she could think.

'Go on.'

'Well, I guess I could cook something and the profits could go towards funds?'

'Like cakes at a coffee morning?'

'No, There's got to be something better than that. Not just a one-off.'

Leila looked confused.

'We can do better than that, Leila. Perhaps something we could sell to a number of places, so that we don't have to keep holding events.'

'You've lost me.'

'No, not cakes. They need preservatives. Perhaps I should make things with a longer shelf-life, things people would give as gifts too. I know! Pickles, jellies, chutneys, jams. Now they are a real taste of home.' Maya's voice rose in pitch as the words tumbled out of her mouth.

'Go on.' Leila clapped her hands.

'We could sell them at The Twist meetings and Barb's blessed Christmas fayre, too.'

'Good old Barb, eh?' Leila roared with laughter. She stuffed another biscuit in her mouth. 'Love it! Love it!

'Not only can we raise funds for the project but the labels on the jars can advertise it and that will raise awareness.' Maya felt rather pleased with herself and took a sip of tea, raising her eyebrows at Leila expectantly for more affirmation.

But Leila just kept on nodding and finished her biscuit, then wiped the crumbs off her lap.

'You know, you could ask those ladies who said they wanted to help but only wanted to look at your hair to man the stalls for you.'

'Brilliant!'

Maya was on a roll. The ideas came out of her mouth faster than her brain could invent them. 'What about we make a three fruit marmalade with limes, lemons and oranges? To me, that is the real taste of home.'

'Me too.'

'In fact, that could be the perfect Sunshine Preserve; they grow all three here, don't they?'

'Grand!'

'Maybe we should make sure all our food has a local twist?' Maya began to mentally leaf through her favourite recipes. 'Date chutney of course.'

'Of course.'

'And we could do a special fundraiser event. A big first PR thing? Like a launch of the charity. Selling lots of homemade stuff and of course, we could run some taster workshops and discussion groups.'

'Cool idea.'

'And a barbecue.'

'Maya, you are amazing!'

Maya ran her fingers through her hair coyly, shrugging slightly. She was having a ball. 'And the press could be invited. We had an open day at Seasons once, had some promotions, got some publicity, and it did wonders for the business. Doing this would put The Sunshine Centre on the map.'

'Holy Mary, Mother of God, Maya you are a marvel. And here's me not even able to boil an egg!' Leila unwound her legs and sat on the edge of the steamer chair, facing her.

'Oh glory. You really are just what I needed!' said Leila. 'I can't wait to tell Ali.'

Maya was grinning. 'Hang on. I did just say I'd a few hours to spare a week, not a few days!'

'But you do have a maid, right?' Leila was very persuasive.

'Well, yes, but Rich, my husband, is away a lot and I have the boys to look after, and they have a busy social life, and I'm their taxi service most of the time. Don't get your hopes up too high.' She could feel her smile subsiding as reality set in.

'Look. Anything you can offer will be better than what I've had so far. I'd welcome the company, the brainstorming, someone to dunk biccies with. Someone with a bit of enthusiasm and who wants to know me, not whether I eat bacon any more. Which, incidentally, I do. It's my only vice!'

'That and saying Holy Mary Mother of God, Jesus and Christ, I suppose.' Maya felt more at ease than ever now.

'To be sure. You got me there. It's a habit I just can't break. It's in me blood, like Liffey water! I'd best say six hail Mohammeds and ask forgiveness.'

Tea spluttered out of Maya's mouth as a bubble of laughter erupted. She liked Leila.

Leila leapt up. 'Look, I'll leave you for a sec. Better check Lily's coping with the kids and I'll fix us a celebratory drink in the sitting room.' She winked. 'Not that there's any pressure or anything! I'm going to call Ali, so he can join us.'

A celebratory drink? Now that could be interesting. No, she only said she had one vice.

Chapter eighteen

Leila's sitting room stretched the full length of the villa, with three sets of French doors down the longest wall. Like the rest of the downstairs, it had a white marble floor with a selection of rugs, only in here, they were pale cream and pink, woven from silk not wool. Maya had been to the carpet souk. She'd seen the backs of carpets like these – and the price tag. There had to be a thousand knots per square inch. The room was clearly made for entertaining. That had to be why Leila had suggested they take their 'celebratory drink' in here and asked Maya to go ahead and wait for her, while she gave instructions to Baby in the kitchen. Sofas and low occasional tables stood everywhere. She spotted a deep, curved alcove, lined with thick jewel-coloured floor cushions, some upright like chair backs, some lain flat like seats. It was a real Middle Eastern *majlis*, a meeting area. Maya was thrilled and made a beeline for the *majlis*, to admire the pen and wash sketches of the mosques, alleys, and windtowers of old Dubai on the walls above. She heard the door close and turned quickly. There stood a man: not Ali, but similar, the same dark hair and neat beard, though his was flecked with grey. The same chocolate-coloured eyes. A delicate fringed tassel hung from the embroidered neck of his crisp white *dishdasha* and his headcovering was so fine it looked as if it were made of lawn. His feet were lean, brown, and bare. He flicked his head to flip the ends of his headdress behind his shoulders, held out his hand, and smiled.

'*Ma'a salamaa*. I am Hatim,' he said, his Arabic accent thick as syrup when he pronounced the open sounds like a and h. He put the emphasis on the second half of his name. 'Ali's brother.'

Maya was deeply grateful that he had introduced himself so completely, answering her unspoken questions. 'Maya Winter, Leila's friend,' she replied, putting her emphasis and a touch of inflection on the word friend. She hoped that was the right word to use. She touched the scarf around her neck, should she place it over her hair? Hatim's English was impeccable. She wondered whether he too had attended school in England.

'You like the *majlis*?' he asked. 'You like the paintings?'

'Oh yes!' She gazed round at the circular space. 'I love it.'

Hatim indicated that she should sit down. 'Please?' he said and waited for her to precede him.

She was glad she'd worn trousers, though she was unsure of the correct way to sit down without looking ungainly and, more importantly, without showing the soles of her feet, which she had been warned was taboo. In the end she opted for a sideways kneel, which was likely to only be comfortable for about five minutes. Hatim fell into a cross-legged position without using his arms for support and without flashing an inch of leg. A *dishdasha* was designed for this kind of sitting, keeping cool and dignity intact at all times. He placed his hands behind his head and leaned back against the cushions. She could feel the space between her upper lip and nose start to moisten, and raised her face to the white fan that circled above them, realising as she did that the move elongated her neck. Now what? she thought. Was Hatim joining them for the drink? Had he just popped round? Did he live here too in one big extended family? It was a large house, after all.

'Hatim?' she said eventually, but her question dried on her lips for she was saved at that moment by Baby entering the room, carrying a huge tray laden with glassware in front of her. She too squatted down expertly with a straight back to lay the tray on the floor between them.

'Thank you Baby,' said Maya, noticing that Hatim merely nodded at the maid, wordless and straight-faced. Baby bobbed upright and left the room. On the tray before them a sea-blue jug appeared to contain some kind of cocktail decorated with sliced star fruit, lemon segments, mint leaves and lots of ice. The bowl held nuts, dates, and cubes of the sweet sticky almond flavoured nougat called halwa, which Maya had not yet got round to trying.

'Shall I do the honours?' Maya offered.

He merely raised one eyebrow and sucked in one corner of his mouth as he raised one hand in assent.

Like a Geisha, she knelt forwards and poured them each a glass.

'*Shukran*,' he said. 'I mean, thank you.' He leaned forwards to cradle his glass in his lap. 'Maya. Do you speak Arabic?' His eyes twinkled as if he knew her answer would be no.

Maya shook her head. 'Sorry,' she said, beginning to long for Leila to return to the room. She sipped her drink. It had a definite tang, as if it contained alcohol. It burned her throat. 'Mmm,' she said. 'That's nice.'

Hatim smiled and allowed his dark eyes to land on Maya's blue ones for a split second longer than she felt comfortable with. Then the door opened and in burst Leila, swathed in black now, like a billowing sand devil, followed just a step behind by Ali.

They both flopped down onto the cushions, pouring themselves a drink and raising them to chink in toast with Hatim and Maya.

Leila reached into her own glass to pick out a slice of lemon and nibble at it. 'Yummy, isn't it? Fools all our guests it's alcoholic, but we're a dry house here. I'm afraid that if you come for dinner, you can't even bring a bottle of your own wine. It's the ginger beer that gives it the tang.'

'You must give me the recipe. I'd like to put it on my blog.'

'Sure, I'll get Baby to write it down for you. I call it Punch with a Punch.' She placed the peel back in her glass. 'Well then?' asked Leila, excitement in her voice. 'You haven't changed your mind have you?' She turned to Hatim. 'Maya cooks. She is just what we need.'

'A cook?' Hatim looked confused.

Leila fluttered her fingers and frowned at her brother-in-law. 'She's going to cook Sunshine Preserves to raise funds and awareness for the Centre. Cool, yeah?'

Hatim and Ali nodded and exchanged a glance.

'But let me introduce you properly, Maya.' She looked at Hatim, with sadness in her eyes. 'Hatim is Ali's brother, Maryam's husband. He is very much part of the project.'

'I'm so sorry,' Maya said a little awkwardly. 'I can't imagine how you must feel. A tragedy. Awful.'

Suddenly, in Maya's eyes, Hatim switched from being a self-assured local into a victim, bereaved. It was a clever move on Leila's part, to let her meet Hatim: there was no way she could refuse to help with the project now.

'Allah has the right to give life and take it away,' said Hatim. 'It was Allah's will.'

He pronounced Allah 'ah lah', breathy gutteral sounds rising from low in his throat. Leila and Ali remained solemn and nodded their heads.

'I knew Hatim was coming round this afternoon.' Leila touched her headscarf to show that this was the reason she had changed her clothes. 'Families are very close here. And ours is even closer now, after the accident. So, Maya, will you join us? Say you will, please?'

'My wife always gets what she wants,' said Ali. He smiled at her adoringly.

Leila grinned. 'Not that I'm begging or anything!'

Maya liked this effusive, enthusiastic Irish girl. She was funny. She had balls. This was her chance to really get to know Dubai and, more importantly, to make a difference. She reached out for a cashew nut and popped it into her mouth.

'You're on!' she said. 'I'll do it.'

Leila flung her arms around Maya. 'Oh, Maya, that's splendid news.' She grinned at Hatim and Ali. 'Isn't it splendid news?'

And they raised their glasses again.

Just at that moment Maya's mobile phone rang.

'It can wait,' she said, then glanced at the display panel. 'Oh hell, Rich!' she exclaimed. 'My husband,' she added. 'Excuse me.' She flipped open her phone and turned her face towards the cushion behind her.

'Right. Right. Okay. I'm out. I forgot the time. I'm sorry. Give me ten minutes.' She flipped the phone shut. 'I have to go. Supper to get. It's the weekend. I like to do a roast, you know,' she said unnecessarily. She stood up, unsure whether to put out her hand to them all. Instead she waved her fingers rather stupidly. Leila jumped up.

'I'll see you out,' she said.

'*Ma'a salamaa*,' said Hatim. '*Shukran*.'

'Bye bye,' said Ali. 'We're really glad you're going to help with the project. Thank you.'

At the door, Leila hugged Maya. 'Thanks. I hope you don't feel forced into anything. I didn't arrange for Hatim to come round, honest. He hates going home. Sorry we kept you so long.'

Maya looked over at the burnished disc of the sun slipping out of view behind the rooftops. 'It's fine. I was having such fun I forgot about my family duties.'

'And you want to do your Sunday-Friday dinner. I understand. Tell you what, I'll give you a couple of days to get used to the idea, then let's meet, say, in The Orange Tree for coffee, Monday, 9 o'clock? I can take you to the office and we can make a plan? A plan that works for you and your family. Okay?'

Chapter nineteen

The Orange Tree was deserted when Barb arrived and quickly spread the contents of her capacious purse onto the orange couch. She shuffled the papers into piles. One set of flyers for the next meeting at the club. Her checklist of places where she would distribute them throughout the day. Four sets of minutes from the last board meeting of Brandon's baseball team, neatly stapled in the top left hand corner – she would put those through the doors on the way home. The receipt for Bill's drycleaning – she would collect that en route too. Mentally, she planned the route she would take to avoid any backtracking, U turns, or wasted time. Boy, she had a full schedule this morning. It was all going to go wrong if Maya turned up late for their breakfast meeting. She looked at her watch and shook the two gold bracelets that she wore beside it further up her arm so she could get a better look at the face. Five past. She caught the waiter's eye. Maya was bound to want a weird smoothie, so she made the order. That would save a bit of time.

'Double espresso for you, madam?' The waiter guessed at her own order.

She nodded, straightened her papers and her skirt, and went through her to-do list, of which the first item was probably the most important: persuade Maya to join the board once and for all. She was just tapping the tips of her square-cut French-polished acrylic nails on the brass-topped table in front of her as the waiter brought over their drinks and Maya entered, her eyes downcast.

'Hey girl! Good to see you. You sit right here,' Barb patted the arm of the chair beside her; there was no room for anyone else to sit on the couch with all those papers spread about. 'What's eating you?'

Maya reached over to plant a dryish kiss on each of Barb's cheeks and flopped down in the chair, sinking so deep into its linen-covered folds that her bare knees almost touched her chin. 'Ugh!' she said. 'Don't ask.'

'It's a bit early to be having a bad day already, isn't it? What is it? Kids? Husband? Housemaid? Traffic?'

Maya shook her head, 'All of the above, but not necessarily in that order.'

Barb knew it was her job to delve further into the cause of her friend's black mood, but shooting another glance at her watch, there simply wasn't the time. Not today. Instead, she chose to change the subject. 'Got you a smoothie with bits in it. That'll cheer you up. Just think of all those vitamins coursing through your veins!'

'I need coffee, Barb. Today, passionfruit is not on my list of must-haves.' She called to the waiter, 'Double shot cappuccino please. Large,' and pushed the smoothie to one side. 'I'll have that later. I'm meeting someone else after you.'

'Elske?'

Maya shook her head. 'Nar, she's permanently holed up in that studio of hers.' She paused and looked awkward, almost guilty. 'Leila, actually.'

Barb tilted her head kindly. 'Oh,' she said. That was her own stupid fault then. She always had been good at connecting the right people. 'You'll like her,' she said helpfully, thinking that no one would get her converting to Islam and covering herself from head to toe in black in this heat, however much she might love a man. Following her husband around the world for nigh on quarter of a century was enough of a sacrifice. But there was no time for thinking. To business.

'Did you get a chance to look in the goddess goodie bag I left with you the other day?'

'No, sorry. Clean forgot.'

'So, you didn't see the list of positions that were open at The Twist then?'

'No, sorry.'

Barb scowled slightly. 'Look I'll cut to the chase. I'm in a bit of a jam at the club. LaShell's let me down over the PR role, now Joni's off to Sakhalin and I kinda thought... '

'Sakhalin?'

'Some island near Russia. Lots of oily folk go there.'

'Oh no,' Maya leaned back in her chair. 'No way, Barb. I'm sorry. It's impossible now. Not that I'm not flattered or anything, but...'

'Now come on, Maya. It's not so much work. You've met the board, right? And they're fun, right? Had a ball at the goddess evening, didn't we?'

Maya blew at the froth on her coffee cup before taking a sip, keeping her eyes down.

'Joni has it all set up, really, it's just a matter of attending a few meetings, which you do anyway, coming to a few board meetings, and they're pretty fun, and advertising meetings in the local magazines and websites. Nothing to it really. Please?

We're supporting Leila this year, as you know. We mention our chosen charity in the ads an' all.'

Maya remained silent.

Barb decided to play the flattery card. 'I'm sure you'd be awesome at it.' The only thing left for her now was to beg.

'Look. I know I could do the job and I'm very keen to do something that helps The Twist, it's a great organisation, and I'd love to help Leila's centre. I just don't think I can. I'd better tell you why I'm in such a bad mood and then you may understand. I bumped into Leila on the beach. I'd been thinking about her project for a while, but never plucked up the courage to pick up the phone. Stupid of me really, as if I thought she'd have two heads or something hidden under her *abaya*.' She paused for another sip of coffee. Barb just wished she would get to the point and drained her own coffee in one gulp.

'Anyway, one thing led to another and I went round there for tea.'

'You did? You went to her house?'

'I did. Anyway, we talked about the project and, to cut a long story short, I agreed to work with her.'

Barb was desperate to find out more about Leila's life and home, but she was on a mission to replace Joni so this had to wait. 'Wonderful!' She filled her face with relief.

'Wonderful?'

'Sure. It's a perfect fit. You can kill two birds with one stone.' Barb reached for her diary, checking the date of the next board meeting. Maya was bound to agree.

'I'm capable of doing what you suggest, Barb, but the trouble is I am not sure I can.'

'Of course you can, dummy. Leila believes in you. I believe in you. Of course you can!' Keep perky, Barb. Keep positive.

'It's not me. It's Rich.'

Curiosity now got the better of Barb, she had to know about this. She sat forward in her seat and called the waiter over for more coffees. Maya looked as though she hadn't slept well; her eyes were distinctly pink today.

'First of all… ' Maya held out her thumb, ready to count the straws that had broken this particular camel's back. 'Rich rang me up when I was having a celebratory drink with Leila, Hatim, and Ali and told me to go home and cook the supper. He's never done that before.'

Barb was agog. She made a mental note of questions to ask later about the identities of the men and the contents of the drink, but for now she wanted the lowdown on Rich.

She held up her second finger. 'I was excited about having found a really interesting project to do with Leila, told him all about the villa, they have a *majlis*, lots of staff, original art, a beautiful pool, but when I told him he shot me down in flames.' She shook her head. 'Told me I shouldn't have been so impulsive. That I had to start putting the family first and that just because we had a maid I could not expect to relinquish all my responsibilities. Then he went on about me expecting I'd want him to hire a driver next to take the boys to school. Said that if I was going to commit myself to something it could at least have had a salary attached, oh and that I could not expect to trust everyone.'

'Never!'

'Oh Barb, it was dreadful. Totally out of character. He is usually my biggest fan.'

'So then what happened?' Barb was on the edge of her seat.

'He stormed off to the sailing club bar, and I was asleep by the time he got back. Oh, Barb, I hate it when I piss him off. I should have talked to him first, I suppose. I'm sure something else is eating him and he's not telling me.'

'D'you think it could be all about money?' Barb asked, her face filled with concern.

'He does think that money's being spent like water, which is true, we had lots to buy when we got here and I do spend a lot on clothes and beauty these days. But you know, we have more disposable income now than we did before. Our house is rented out so we don't even have a mortgage.'

'Has he started playing the stock market yet? Maybe he's made a bad investment?'

'Maybe. He didn't say. Like you saw, I don't do the money in our house.' Maya looked thoughtful. 'He is spending a lot of time on the computer in the evenings though. And he's always got his nose in the paper. Maybe that's what he's doing?'

Barb tapped the side of her nose. 'Once they have the taste for money, they can get a bit obsessed by it.'

'I suppose. He did say that if I'd found a job then I should at least have got one that paid some 'bloody' money. God, Barb, I thought he would have been pleased for me. You know, moving on from the passport stamp moment.'

Barb's mood was picking up, aided by the extra buzz of her third coffee that morning. 'Look at you! You've really blossomed lately. The hair, the clothes, the make-up. And now your body is getting trimmer by the minute and you have a tan. I bet he's jealous that you get the time to enjoy his money and he doesn't.'

'I guess you're right. I know he had high hopes about starting to save but so far we've not managed to put anything by. I think he rather hoped I'd contribute something to the retirement pot.'

'Surely Rich wouldn't have a problem if you helped out at the club though, would he?' she continued. 'Do you not think you might be overreacting?'

'You're like a dog with a bone.' Maya was laughing now. 'I'll think about it, okay? Give me a couple of days. Rich's on such a short fuse I don't want to piss him off again. Look, Leila will be here in a moment.' She looked over her shoulder in the direction of the door.

'Before you go...' Barb started gathering her papers, taking a few from the top of each pile.

'Ye-es!' Maya was already holding out her hand.

Barb picked up a bundle of papers from beside her on the couch. 'Any chance you could post some of these flyers on the noticeboards at your compound, at your kids' school, and your local supermarket?'

Maya smiled warmly. 'You are incorrigible!' She reached for her purse.

'No worries. I'll pay it on my way out.' Barb gathered up the rest of her papers and stood up to leave. 'It looks like Leila's just walking in now, and she has a rather handsome man in tow. See ya'll later.'

Maya leapt to her feet, glad of the opportunity to get out of that awful chair, move to the sofa, and straighten her skirt. During her conversation with Barb the café had filled up and Hatim was greeting a group of men seated by the door. She watched him grip the hand of each man in turn and touch his cheeks to theirs, first one and then the other. Leila stood by and watched from a slight distance, saying her greetings rather than joining in with all the hugging. Maya rearranged herself on the sofa and reached for the smoothie that she had rejected earlier, placing the straw between her lips and looking towards the group at the door. At least this gave her a few moments to think about Leila and her centre, rather than the fact that Mick had not replied yet and Rich wasn't talking to her.

'*As-salam alaykum*, Maya,' said Hatim, infusing her name with aitches as he extracted his mobile phone, prayer beads and car keys from the pocket of his *dishdasha* and deposited them on the table with a clatter. 'How are you today?' The outer edges of his dark brown eyes crinkled into a smile.

'Never better!' she replied, bolstered by twice her normal caffeine intake. No wonder her heart was racing.

'Mint tea everyone?' Leila suggested, nodding towards the waiter and tucking her scarf closer to her chin.

'Great idea!' Maya needed to dilute the stimulant in her veins and mint sounded just the salve she needed.

'So, how are you, this fine morning?' she asked. 'I am so excited I can't begin to tell you. I've had Sunshine Preserve going round my brain all day long. Can we make strawberry jam too, do you think? Now that really makes me think of home? And there is a strawberry farm in Dhaid, so that gives you your 'local twist'.'

Three glasses of tea were placed on the table, each crammed with fresh mint leaves. A tiny beehive shaped pot of honey, the colour of molten gold, was set in the middle.

'That's grand,' said Leila. 'Thanks.'

Hatim took a tiny silver spoon out of the beehive and twirled it gently, coating it with a thick teardrop of honey, before holding it over his tea until every skein of sweetness had coiled like a sleeping snake inside his cup.

'You take honey, Maya?' Hatim asked, offering her the spoon, which she noticed had a little golden bee on its tip.

'No thanks,' she said. Honeyspoons had always been her weakness. From the side, Hatim's nose was a dominant feature. It would probably be called aquiline. He slapped his hands on his parted knees and looked at Maya expectantly. His nails looked manicured. The local men knew how to look after themselves. When he reached for his mint tea the scent of something spicy rose with his arm. Was it sandalwood?

'So, Maya,' he said. 'How do you like our country?'

'Wonderful,' she said. Actually she had seen very little of it so far. She wracked her brains to think of what else she'd seen since they arrived, but to be honest most of the time they just moved from one marble-floored villa to another, from one poolside barbecue to another, and through a variety of restaurants, malls and coffee shops. Come on, Maya! What else had she seen? What had she noticed? 'I love the creek, of course, and the beach. Your sunsets are spectacular.' Was that a good enough answer?

Hatim rubbed his neat beard carefully. 'Hmm,' he said. 'Have you been into the desert? Have you seen the dunes in the night, when all the stars are out and the sky is huge?' He widened his arms and looked up at the ceiling.

She began to relax. 'Oh yes, we tried our car out in the sand when we first arrived and had a barbecue at sunset. That was something else.'

He shook his head. 'No. No. I mean the real desert. Where there are tiny villages, ruins, farms, and beautiful oases?'

No, she had not seen the real desert, she supposed. In fact, if truth be told, she had not seen anything real at all.

'Have you seen the wadis, the aflaj, the camel farms, the fishermen trawling the long nets on the East coast, filled with tiny sardines? I will take you. Let me show you my home and my people. Let me show you Arabic hospitality.'

It was not a question; it was a statement.

'Thank you,' she said, keen to know what these wadis and aflaj were. 'But I am sure you must be far too busy to do that for me,' she said.

'But it would be my pleasure. You and your family will be my guests.'

Leila cleared her throat and glowered playfully at her brother-in-law. 'I do apologise for him. He should work for the tourist board! Hatim is determined to show people that there is as much richness, variety and culture here as there is in Europe. He gets really angry when all the expats who come and stay a while in his country never bother to find out about the reality of the place. I guess I can see his point. But Maya, we need to talk business. Hatim's pleasure trip can be for later, okay? Now, let's finish our tea. I want to show you the office. And then, after you've seen that, we can see if we can't find a way to move things forward, eh Hatim?' With that, she called a waiter, paid the bill, drained her tea, and rose to her feet. Like a mother penguin, in black from head to toe, she led the way out of The Orange Tree. 'Hatim will drive.' So far, Maya had not found a moment to explain that maybe her joining the team was not cut and dried after all.

Chapter twenty

The car turned hard right, mounted the kerb and drove straight over a patch of sand, past the large wooden hoardings that masked the edge of what seemed to be yet another building site. There was a kind of sentry box beside a wide carved wooden gate. Hatim tooted his horn and a wiry old man with a long white beard shuffled out of the sentry box and opened the gate manually.

'*Shukran*, Omar. *As-salam alaykum*,' Hatim called out of the car window.

Omar smiled broadly, showing his teeth, one at the top and one at the bottom. '*Wa alaykum e-salam*,' he replied.

'Omar is from Northern Pakistan, he's been with the business for years. He used to be the driver, and should be retired by now, but he adores the family and so they created this job for him and he lives in that tiddly little box by the gate with his family. Amazing, eh? We offered to build them a bigger house, but they refused.'

Behind the gates everything was immaculate. White, bright and beautifully renovated. The low, white one-storey dwelling had a few high windows, a flat roof, and a square windtower, just like the one at The Orange Tree. A garden surrounded it, with flower beds crammed with bright red hibiscus, their thin tongues lolling thirstily. On flame tree acacias, frothy, burnt orange flowers, each shaped like an individual bouquet, turned their faces to the sun. Behind the building paving stones sparkled before abutting a pale stucco wall over which a thick aquamarine strip of the sea was just visible. Leila jumped down from the car. 'Come on, slowcoach!'

'But,' Maya began.

'But nothing, come on in, you ain't seen nothin' yet.'

The hallway struck her immediately by its cool, dusky tranquillity beyond which the courtyard flashed as brightly as if struck by lightning. In the centre stood a gnarled old olive tree.

'All thanks to Al Farooq Restoration. As you noticed, Hatim's passionate about our heritage – though maybe obsessed would be more accurate.' Leila led the way.

Maya followed them into a long cool room on the right-hand side. Two fans whirled quietly beneath slender wooden beams. A heavy teak desk stood at each end and a row of cupboards ran along the length of the wall. There were no bookshelves but the wall was peppered with useful cubbyholes carved out of the thick stone.

'It's stunning. I've never seen inside a real windtower before.'

Hatim sat down and rested his sandaled feet up on the desk as he lounged back in the deep leather chair. He picked up a pen and began tapping it between his teeth as he spun gently to left and right surveying the beautiful room that was far too gorgeous to be an office.

'You see, Maya, we have so much hidden beauty in our country,' Hatim said.

'Do you work here all the time?' she asked.

'No, no. We have a big office with many staff at The Emirates Towers. This place is for your centre.'

Maya smiled weakly. It was not 'her' centre and was not likely to be if Rich had his way.

'Right. Now that you've seen our place of work, let's go onto the terrace for a cold drink and a chat.' Leila seemed determined to return the conversation to the subject of business.

It was surprisingly cool outside. A canopy of palm leaves made the terrace into a veranda. Fans circled beneath it, slowly and rhythmically. They sat on rough, wooden pew-like benches, softened by silk cushions the same colour as the sea. A low coffee table made out of an old door stood before them and on it a jug of lime soda, the ice still rattling. Maya thought she saw the bare brown legs of a young boy disappear around the side of the house, just as she sat down.

'Omar's grandson,' explained Leila. 'Hari. He's ten.'

Maya sat and admired the scene.

'You look pensive,' Leila said, handing her a tall glass wrapped in a white napkin to absorb the damp chill of condensation that clung to it.

'It's perfect, Leila. The perfect place for a fundraiser.' She deliberately kept her voice flat. 'You can serve drinks out here, have stalls of food for sale inside and, oh, I don't know, do something for the kids in the safety of the courtyard.' She deliberately avoided using the word 'we'.

'You think so?' Leila appeared to have picked up on the doubt in Maya's voice.

'People are nosy, and, like you say, Hatim, they rarely get to see the real Dubai. I think using this fabulous place would guarantee the crowds.'

Hatim was rubbing his chin.

'It will be a good publicity for Al Farooq Restoration too,' said Maya, who simply could not help herself from being as drawn to the project as she was to these people and the place.

'Good idea,' said Leila. 'But there's a but, isn't there? I can sense it.'

Maya went quiet. She really needed to have a good idea. Looking out across the sea, Maya saw the pale azure of the water darken as it deepened towards the horizon, which then stretched beyond her vision to east and west. Drawn by the soft swell and fall of the Persian Gulf, she decided to say what was on her mind.

Dragging her gaze away from the sea, she squared her shoulders and went for it. 'I don't want to mislead you, so I need to say something, well a couple of things, now, at the outset.'

Leila nodded. Hatim took his sunglasses off the top of his head and put the end of one arm between his teeth.

Maya took a deep breath. 'Firstly, I can only really work during school hours, and then maybe just four days a week, say Monday –Thursday.' She felt between a rock and a hard place unable to keep herself, Rich and the family all happy at the same time.

'No problem,' said Leila. 'I can't do full time either.'

'No problem,' echoed Hatim. They smiled.

Maya cleared her throat. 'This is a long shot. And very cheeky I know, but this is the first time in five years I've not had my own income. I'd really like to find a way to earn something, you know so I'm not always having to ask my husband for money?' She laughed awkwardly and looked at Leila. 'So, if there is any way I could do something that might earn me a bit of money too, that would be wonderful.' She paused to scan their faces for shock and seeing none, she continued. 'It would be a real help.' There. She'd said it. Hatim scratched his beard. 'I am sure we can think of something you could do to earn some money,' he said.

Leila glared at him. 'Well, that's easy to solve,' she said. 'Is it?'

'To be sure, it is. Just keep some of the money from the jam and stuff for yourself. Keep a bit of the profit.' She turned to Hatim. 'She can do that can't she?'

Hatim nodded.

'What about the legal side of things? I don't want to get into any trouble. I'm not really supposed to work, you know.' Maya wasn't at all sure that this particular problem was easy to solve.

'No problem,' said Hatim. 'Al Farooq Restoration can get you a work permit.'

'Really?' said Leila. 'That would be so cool!' Then her face fell. 'Oh, but that costs money. The charity can't afford it. It's several thousand dirhams.'

'Oh well, never mind. It was just a thought,' said Maya.

Hatim placed his hands behind his head. 'I will pay. No problem. Maybe you can do some other work for me? You have run a business before, yes?'

'I guess so, but a delicatessen is not much like a construction company, Hatim. What do you suggest?' For once the ideas deserted her.

He flipped over his hands and lifted his palms. 'No problem. For now, the Sunshine Centre is the most important. I'm happy to give you a visa so that you earn some money. And that will make your husband happy, right?' He smiled. 'Start with the jam. We can worry about what else you can do for us later.'

Maya could not quite take all this in. It seemed too magnanimous.

'And then you can make Leila happy. And me happy. And the centre happy. And anyway, if the centre is to be successful I need to invest in it. And Leila cannot do everything alone.' He shrugged his shoulders. 'Really, no problem.'

'Thank you,' said Leila, lifting her glass to chink her brother-in-law's.

'Thank you, Hatim.' Maya lifted her glass too.

Hatim raised his glass, but simply inclined his head.

'Do we have a deal, then?' Leila asked. 'Do you think you could bear to work with me? With us?'

Maya broke into a smile. She'd found solutions to Rich's every objection, but something else niggled at her. She was pretty sure that money wasn't the only thing that was eating her husband.

Chapter twenty-one

Barb looked at her watch for the second time in a minute. It was still only just after eight. Brandon had a ride to school that morning with a friend and for Barb, that meant she had no reason to shower and dress. For once, her diary was clear for an entire day and that scared her, particularly today of all days. Not that she'd left it clear. She'd planned a mall trip with Suchanatta and LaShell to pick out some new tableware at the department store that had just opened up. They were to follow that with lunch outside the Parisian café, right on the sidewalk. It had such a cool atmosphere there, authentic, dark-green wrought-iron tables and chairs and you got your coffee in those cute green cups with the gold rims. They even had an accordionist playing at peak times. Who'd believe it? Only in Dubai would they recreate a French street in a mall. Complete with fake cherry trees in full blossom all year round. But Suchanatta had had to dash to Thailand on business to do with those scarves and LaShell wanted to finish a painting, so the day out had been cancelled and time dragged its feet like a teenager getting up and ready for school on the first day of the new semester. Being alone and idle was like Chinese water torture.

She wandered aimlessly into the lounge and sat down on her 'throne'. Her purse sat on the coffee table in front of her.

She picked it up and tipped out the contents. A clatter of papers and loose change fell out in heap and Barb set about separating it into piles. The business cards, the flyers, the coins, branded pens and brochures on one side, and the lost lipsticks, her diary, cell phone and stray tissues on the other. When she had finished only a sprinkling of desert sand remained in the centre of the glass table. She'd discard the things that were no longer current and force order on what was left. Elastic bands for the cards, clear plastic wallets for the flyers and a separate bag for her make-up. She brightened up at the prospect of a shopping expedition to purchase the necessary stationery items and maybe a new purse in which to arrange them. But as she surveyed the piles of items before her, she had a sudden thought. It was as if these things personified her. Like some kind of party game, you could look at the contents of a woman's purse and guess what she was like and what she did all day. Anyone looking at Barb's stuff would put her down as an active, promoting type, who was always busy, always involved. A woman who looked after herself. The only sign that she had a family was the photograph of Brandon that she kept tucked inside her credit card wallet. No one would have a clue what she felt like inside, deep down in the pit of her stomach. No one would guess that if you took away the contents of her purse there would be nothing left. No remaining shred of personality. Take away her diary and that busy schedule and there would be no Barb. Remove the lipstick and there may even be no smile. Come on, girl, she said to herself. You're getting too deep. What are we going to do with you today? She looked over at the tiny framed photograph of her baby girl.

'What sort of a mommy do you have, Angelina?' She whispered, not wanting Merry to hear her talking to herself.

She blinked and swallowed rapidly. Merry could come in at any moment and the last thing she wanted was for anyone to catch a glimpse of her like this, not even her maid. As the mist cleared, one particular card seemed to wink at her. It read: ALIVE.

A massage was never top of Barb's agenda. Alternative therapists always tried to get inside your mind as well as the knots in your muscles. It scared her, to be honest. Liv scared her. She'd watched Liv sizing her up during that excruciating goddess evening. When she thought about it, her back ached from top to bottom and she had been over-emotional lately. Fall did that to her, even in a place like this. Angelina was born on October 29. Leaves fell at the end of October. Life ended in October. Maybe a massage was just what her back needed. She reached over for her cell phone then stopped, placing it in her lap as she leaned back in the chair and closed her eyes. Ask Barb to make a call to ask for support for one of her causes or to promote one of her friends' businesses and she was dialling in a heartbeat. Ask her to pick up the phone to do something for herself and it was a different story. Manicures, pedicures, and hairdressing were fine; after all the effect of the treatment was visible to others afterwards. Was there really any point in having a massage? There would be nothing to show for it afterwards. No one would be able to tell she had had it done. She picked up the phone. Liv was thrilled to hear from her – there had been a cancellation in an hour's time.

'It's okay, I know where you are, remember! I found it for you' she said. 'Oh, really?' she continued and carefully wrote the new details down in her address book. Fancy Liv moving without telling her? Then she sprang into action, swept the contents of the coffee table back into her purse, and climbed the stairs towards the shower.

She drove to a sandy parking lot and walked gingerly in her high heels over the scrubby land to a surprisingly old and grubby block of flats. Barb would never have normally known people who lived in apartments like this. Liv should have asked her for help with accommodation again, silly girl. The disappointing lobby contained an empty reception desk and a rubber plant in a plastic pot. The lift was clean but the corridor smelled faintly of curry. She took the lift to the ninth floor. Outside Liv's apartment, a pair of sandy-coloured pottery urns, each containing an olive tree, flanked a red doormat. Inside, the décor was minimalist. In fact, there was scarcely any furniture to speak of. That would never suit Barb but it was the Scandinavian way. White muslin floated at the windows and a neat row of candles and healthy looking plants stood on the single shelf that ran along one wall.

'Well, this is a surprise!' said Liv, opening the door.

'Not as much of a surprise as it was to find you living in this part of town. It's not your usual style?'

'You mean it's not your usual style?' she said, her mouth twisting at one corner. 'Come. Let's sit down and have a little chat.'

Barb looked startled.

'It's okay, Barb. I just want to talk about your medical history.'

It was all very systematic and that made her feel safe. Normally Barb was the one who asked all the questions. After fifteen minutes, Liv stood up.

'You can remove your clothes now,' said Liv.

Barb's jaw dropped.

'You can keep your underwear on. I have a robe.' She was very matter-of-fact about it all.

Barb nodded, relieved about the robe, even though her underwear did match. It always did.

'And take off your make-up. I am going to treat your face too, *ja*?'

Barb was not so happy at the prospect of removing the make-up she had just spent twenty minutes applying. 'What. All of it?"

'*Ja.*' Liv stood there and smiled. 'I have cleanser. It's okay.' She pointed to the door in the corner of the room. There would be no room for negotiation.

Barb went to the restroom, wishing she had thought to bring her own brand of toiletries. As she opened the door, a wind chime tinkled softly from the draught of air. White towels were piled in the corner on a white rattan shelf unit, a fresh vase of white gerbera sat on the washstand, and a scented candle, smelling of summer roses, burned beside them. Some music played, or was it? More like the sounds of the ocean, seagulls calling and the waves lapping on some invisible shore. Fortunately for Barb, the lighting was muted and reduced the trauma of removing her foundation, powder, blusher, mascara, eye-liner, lip-liner and lipstick. Two hooks on the back of the door held an empty clothes hanger and a pink-and-white striped towelling robe. A pair of matching slippers had been tucked into one of the pockets. It took just a few minutes to strip herself of personality and protection for the second time that day.

'Lie down,' instructed Liv, pointing at a massage table covered with white towels.

Barb did as she was told and realised how alien this experience felt to her. Shameful really, she had been telling everyone about Liv for almost two years but had never tried it for herself. She lay down, placing her head on a ring-shaped pillow at one end.

'Now, I am going to give you my gold level treatment today, *ja*?' She paused. 'This takes one hour and a half and begins with Reiki. Do you want me to tell you what I'm doing as I work? Sometimes it is better if I work in silence, then I can feel more.'

Silence was not Barb's favourite sound, but at least it would stop too many probing questions. 'Fine,' she said. 'I'll try not to talk, either.' she said. She had heard about this Reiki business, but had no idea what it entailed.

Liv smiled, turned down the lights, and disappeared into the restroom to wash her hands. Barb closed her eyes and noticed how much louder the music became and how strong the scent of the candles. Maybe this would be all right after all? She didn't hear Liv return.

Her treatment began when Liv placed her hands on Barb's temples and held them there for what felt like several minutes. Then she moved them slightly closer to Barb's ears and left them there again. Next they moved to cover her eyes and Barb found the warmth and gentle pressure soothed and quieted her mind. She had no idea how Liv had the patience to hold her hands so still for quite so long. It was as if her body let out a large and long-awaited sigh as Barb finally surrendered to the experience. A natural smile twitched at the corners of her mouth. This really was good. Very good. So good it made her want to cry. Liv's hands moved down to Barb's throat, then her upper chest, always with a pressure so gentle she could hardly feel it, yet with a surprising warmth and weight. Barb listened to the dolphins whistling, the slap of the tide on wet rocks, and the distant laughter of children. The smell of roses drifted towards her and every now and again, as Liv shifted position, the windchimes sang for just a second or two. This was bliss. Yet Barb felt as if she were on a precipice. Above and beyond a beautiful view, but with danger too close for comfort. After a few more minutes, Liv's hands hovered carefully in the area just below her heart, not touching her body, but Barb could still feel their presence glowing close by. All of a sudden, she felt a bubble of emotion pop somewhere inside her while tears pricked her eyes behind closed lids. She raised her left hand to shield them and her right to cover her mouth, which now quivered with a sob. This was so embarrassing. She would have to sit up. She lowered her elbows in readiness. What was Liv doing to her?

'It's okay, Barb,' Liv whispered. 'It's normal. I was working on your solar plexus. It's the seat of emotions.'

As Barb pushed herself into a sitting position, Liv removed her hands and stepped away from the massage bed.

For once in her life, Barb couldn't get the words out. She tried to form them, but her lips wouldn't be controlled. 'I. I can't,' she said.

Liv stood there, the epitome of calm, her blue eyes fixed and firm as she waited for Barb to continue.

'I. I. Can't,' she repeated.

Liv moved back towards her and leaned against the bed, in her white tee-shirt and skinny jeans she was as tiny as a child. She put her hand onto Barb's, gently.

Barb wasn't used to this. Liv was so calm and moved so slowly that she never made too much noise, moved too much air, or caused a stir. Yet there was something powerful about this wraithlike blonde.

'What can't you, Barb?' she said at last.

Barb just shook her head. 'This,' she said eventually, shrugging her shoulders. 'It's too hard. Too hard for me, I guess.'

'What's too hard?'

So Barb thought. 'Someone being really nice to me?' she said, as her mind hissed with the belief that her full schedule was superficial and that despite knowing more people than anyone else in Dubai, probably, all her friendships were based on action, on doing things, and never just being. Let's face it, she thought. No one knew who she really was. No one knew about Angelina. All those people she had entertained in her own lounge and not one had ever asked who the baby girl in the silver frame was.

'Someone touching me in a loving way. Don't get me wrong. I don't mean in a romantic way. It's just that we Americans are great at all those hugs and stuff, but I'm not sure we really put our hearts into it. Bill never touches me when we're behind closed doors. When we're out, sure, he puts on a show. But we don't even make love anymore.' She clapped her hand over her mouth. That was too much of a confidence. Now she had started talking, she was in danger of never stopping. 'I'm sorry,' she said.

Liv was unperturbed. She kept her focus on Barb. 'It's okay. I think it's not just Reiki you need. You need a massage; your back is all hunched over. And today you need to talk, *ja*?'

'I'm not sure.'

'Okay. I know. We continue the treatment a bit longer. I think I need to do more work on your solar plexus and your back. And then we will talk. In confidence.' It was not a question. 'I have no more clients for three hours. It will be my pleasure. You can stay for lunch. As my friend.' There was no room for discussion.

The music changed from sounds of the sea to some kind of Indian drumming that made Barb's body sway inwardly as she lay back down and succumbed once more.

'Just focus on the breath,' she said. 'If you have a thought, just take it and then blow it away, like a cloud.'

The windchimes were silent. The music off. Barb kept her eyes closed and focused on her breathing but could feel it quicken as she began to feel uncomfortable. She opened one eye very slowly. She was alone. Liv had gone. It felt as if she had been in a deep, drugged sleep. She raised her head and the room swam. Her limbs felt like lead as she moved into a sitting position and she took a break before swinging her legs over the side of the bed.

Liv appeared with a tray of food and two plain white mugs of some kind of green tea and set it down on the floor beside two huge scatter cushions by the French window that opened onto the narrow balcony. A buttery stripe of sunlight lay across one cushion. Liv sat down. 'You can get dressed now,' she said.

On her way to the bathroom, Barb noticed the door to the bedroom was ajar. Here too, there was hardly any furniture. Open suitcases lay on the bed. Liv was on the move again and Barb knew she would ask for help if she needed it.

Lunch was far removed from the toasted cheese and ham sandwich Barb had been destined to order, again, at the Parisian café at the mall. Instead, Liv presented her with a large oval platter covered with nuts, pumpkin seeds, dried dates, sliced avocado, bean sprouts, and fresh strawberries. There was a basket of dark, sliced rye bread but no butter. Neither were there any plates. Liv gave Barb a fork and a napkin and suggested she help herself.

'This is very healthy,' Barb said.

Liv moved her cushion to one side and sat in the lotus position directly on the wooden floor. 'Of course,' she said. 'If you want a healthy body and a healthy mind, you need healthy food. This is all organic. I sprout the beans myself. Very nutritious. And I make the bread.' She poured some weak-looking tea into two mugs and handed one to Barb without adding cream or sugar.

The food was delicious and Barb was surprised by how light her stomach felt when at the same time she was nicely sated. The bread was not as dry as she would have imagined. But she would have liked some butter. She took a sip of her tea and tried hard not to pull a face.

'Do you like the tea?' Liv asked.

'You know, I could murder a coffee.'

'Coffee is bad for you,' Liv said sternly.

'Please?'

'Redha may have left some instant coffee in the cupboard.'

Barb thought hard whether she knew any Redha and decided she didn't. 'Redha?' she asked.

'Oh, no one important,' said Liv. 'Do you know that coffee dehydrates you? You need to drink four cups of water to replenish the water you lose drinking one cup of coffee.'

'I still want one though. Please?'

'I only have soya milk,' said Liv, as if trying to put her off.

'I'll take it black,' said Barb, who hated black coffee, but not as much as she hated this funny green tea. 'Moving on again?'

'Uh huh.'

Dragging facts out of this woman was like getting blood out of a stone. 'What is your reason this time?'

'The usual.'

'I see.'

'But did you know they are changing the law.'

'Really?' Barb was agog.

'For the last two years I have lived on a tourist visa, as you know.'

Barb nodded. 'And you went to Hatta every three months on a visa hop... right?'

'Well, they are putting a stop to it.'

'Darn it.' At last Barb had a turn at being kind and caring.

'And soon we will all need an ID card too.'

She really should read the papers as well as the club magazines. 'I am so sorry.' She laid her hand on Liv's arm. 'And you are not sure how long you can keep going, right? You know, if you need a place to stay, you only have to say.'

Liv shrugged as if she really wasn't terribly concerned. 'Everything happens for a reason Barb. So, we'll see. But today you are the client, remember?' She laughed. That was the end of the matter and Barb was forced to change the subject.

'So, did you discover anything while you were massaging me? Leila told me that you can read all sorts of things from touching a foot.'

'You need to drink more water, Barb. Your kidneys are hard. That is one reason why your back hurts.'

'I can sense that you are going to tell me the other reason!' Barb laughed.

'And you do too much for other people. You have too much on your shoulders and not enough support.'

'That's right, for sure.'

'And your solar plexus is stucked.'

'What?'

'Stucked. It is stuck. Fixed. Letting nothing out.'

'Do you mean blocked?'

Liv ignored the language lesson. 'You do not speak your emotions... ' She took a sip of her tea. 'The body is a mirror of the soul. It tells me many secrets,' she said. 'But right now, I think you have a secret you need to share. It is stopping you from being happy. Do you know what I am talking about?'

Barb's shuffled uncomfortably on her floor cushion. She knew it would do her good to talk to someone about the thing that broke her heart, but it had stayed locked away for so long that she wasn't sure where to begin. She should have gone into therapy years ago, but what with moving again and again, she never really got around to it. Bill never talked about it and couldn't handle her talking about it either. It was as if the story stayed in a packing case in the basement, moved from place to place and never opened.

'You don't have to share. Not if you don't want to. But you can talk to me. I am your friend. Look.' She handed her a piece of blue lapis lazuli. 'Hold this. Blue is the colour of communication. It will help.'

Barb took the stone and felt its grooves and contours with the tips of her fingers before cradling it deep in her palm. Come on girl, this is your chance, she said to herself. 'This is really tough for me,' she began.

'I know,' said Liv softly, as if she really did.

'Seven years ago today I had a baby girl,' she began, her throat constricting painfully with the agony of words unspoken for so long. 'Her name was Angelina. We were living in Kuala Lumpur back then and we wanted to make sure that our baby had a US passport, so I decided to go back to my folks in

Amarillo, Texas, for the birth. Brandon had turned six. I took him out of school. It was such an adventure. We took the trip when I was thirty-five weeks pregnant and Bill stayed behind. He had to work, of course. But that was fine, we were used to it. Brandon and I had often taken long holidays back home on our own.' Barb took a sip of her coffee. It tasted strong and bitter.

Liv nodded and stayed silent. When Barb realised she was not going to comment, she filled the silence with more of the story.

'Anyway, before I left, the girls at the club in KL gave me a baby shower. We knew we were having a girl and it was a very happy time, what with having a boy already, and we were very excited. Back in Amarillo, Brandon and I had a great time together just the two of us. There was no maid around and we really bonded. About a week before I was due, things started to feel different in my belly. There was a kind of silence there. A stillness. I didn't feel her move and I was sure I'd been feeling her move a lot before then. You know, her little elbow would suddenly poke me in the ribs, or I'd see a kind of bump sticking out of the middle, like a broken bone. I went to the doctor and they did a scan.' Barb's breathing sped up and she could feel the same panic return that she had felt when in the doctor's surgery all those years earlier. Liv put an arm out towards her and clasped the hand that was clutching the lapis lazuli as if she were trying to give her the strength to continue.

'My baby was not moving for a reason. My baby was dead.' The pain in her throat rose like a geyser of boiling water. Any moment it would blow and spill like a flaming waterfall down her cheeks. There it went. She was glad of the tissues in her purse and blew her nose loudly.

'It's okay. Stay with the pain. Face it. Feel it. Be with it.'

Barb blew out long and slow through pursed lips. It wasn't okay, making a fool of herself like that. But letting go sure was something she had needed to do for a long, long time. Eventually, the wracking sobs that made her chest heave calmed down.

'How terrible, Barb. I am so sorry,' said Liv, shaking her head in sorrow. 'Breathe.'

'They booked an appointment for me to be induced and have the baby,' Barb took a deep breath. She tried to keep her voice steady despite the agony of describing what came next. The injustice of it. 'They couldn't fit me in for a few days and I had to carry on with life, with Brandon, knowing the little sister he wanted so badly was still inside me, but was not going to join our family alive.'

'And Bill?' prompted Liv.

'Oh, he came as soon as he could, but he missed the birth. A full twelve-hour labour I had. Can you imagine? At least my sister, Angela, was with me.'

Liv just shook her head and clasped Barb's hand, which was now starting to shake as her body prepared itself for another uncontrollable string of convulsive sobs. It took several minutes for her to recover, during which time Liv continued to sit there, holding her hand.

'So, our baby, Angelina Barbara was born on the twenty-ninth of October and I had her baptised in the hospital. Bill arrived soon after. The next day we had her funeral. A teeny white coffin made of pinewood, drowned by a cross of pink roses. Brandon stayed home. Bill went back to KL, but I wanted to stay near to Angelina for a while longer. I didn't feel ready to return and face them.'

'Face who?' asked Liv gently.

'Them. Everyone. The girls. It would be so hard for them.'

'Hard for you,' Liv corrected. 'But you went back, *ja*?'

'I went back in mid-December, just as everyone was about to leave or had already left on vacation. It was like walking onto a ghost ship. I felt invisible. If there were any people around who knew me, they made as if they hadn't seen me. And if they did end up talking to me, they had no idea what to say.' She paused. 'Do you have another tissue?' Liv stretched out one leg and reached for a box of tissues with her toe, then handed it to her.

'Of course not. No one ever knows what to say.'

'When I got back to KL I felt as if I had had my limb chopped off and no one even noticed.'

'And Bill?'

'Bill?' Barb raised her eyes to the ceiling. 'He was a typical man. He said "there there" a couple of times, patted me on the arm, realised he had no idea how to fix this particular problem, and went out to play golf. If he ever caught me crying, he simply walked out of the room. He didn't mean to be cruel, he just had no idea what to say.'

'He hurt too.'

'Sure. I guess,' said Barb, blowing into another tissue and using it to wipe her eyes. 'He never said. I thought he just didn't care.'

'Some men are not good at expressing their emotions,' said Liv. 'Mind you, it seems you are not that good at letting yours out either, *ja*?'

'It just became easier to pretend everything was okay and not to talk about it, after a time. Boy, have I resented that. Then, thank God, we were moved from KL to Miri and no one there knew about Angelina and so they didn't cross the street to avoid me. I just never told anyone about it. I got really involved in the club and suddenly everyone did want to know me again. For a long time, that's kept me going. Oh, and Brandon.'

'Brandon? How has this affected him?'

'Well, I guess I have overcompensated. He never got the sister, so I make sure he has lots of sleepovers, and we spoil him too. It's hard not to.'

'So, why no more children? Or shouldn't I ask?' Liv said, withdrawing her hand at last.

'I guess you could say that our bedroom activity hasn't been the same since Angelina. I can't bear to face the pain of a stillbirth again. Sex is off the menu. Bill's never commented. He works away so much and does such long hours, it would be easy for him to hide having a mistress from me, and to be honest I wouldn't blame him. I've chosen not to ask him and to ignore the receipts I find for dinners for two in his pockets when I take his pants to the dry cleaners.'

'Maybe he wants you to find those receipts, Barb? That's why he leaves them there. Maybe it's his way of showing you that everything is not alright between you and he wants to fix it.'

Barb knew her eyes were red and puffy from crying. She must have looked a sight, but Liv was willing her to continue her story. Maybe Liv was right? Maybe Bill was trying to communicate with her, maybe the till receipts screwed into tight balls left in the corners of his pants were the closest he could get to love notes. Some love notes! To be honest, she had no idea how Bill really felt about her. She couldn't imagine what he saw in her these days, she was so far removed from that keen little housewife he'd left behind in Amarillo, on the porch with the picket fence.

'Bill is a great guy,' she said. 'He can be so fun when we're out with company. Everyone loves him. He becomes the best father and the ideal husband. You wouldn't believe how many of my friends say they'll have him after I've finished with him.' She laughed. He lets me do what I please, never criticises all the stuff I do for the club, lets me have anything I want, takes us on great holidays. He's away on trips so much. And if he is here, he's playing golf. But money can't buy you love, eh?' She sniffed and smiled wryly.

Liv nodded patiently, as if waiting for more.

But Barb had shared more than enough for one afternoon. Telling her story to someone who wouldn't judge her was a relief. She stood up and handed the blue gemstone back to Liv. Her shoulders felt lighter. She squared them and reached for her purse, taking out several red hundred-dirham notes.

'Maybe you should talk to someone?' suggested Liv, folding the money in half and tucking it into her back pocket.

'A shrink?' Barb squeaked.

'I think it will help you. You need someone to share with.'

'Come on, Liv. I have the girls. You know that.'

Liv tipped her head on one side 'Really?'

So, Barb didn't express her emotions, was destroying her kidneys, and didn't love herself either? The session had been just as she expected, Liv had messed with her mind, and as new, unwelcome thoughts began to line up for attention, she felt the start of a headache and lifted her hand to her temple.

Chapter twenty-two

Maya stood beside the sink, sniffing loudly as tears poured down her face.

'I can help?' Annie appeared in the doorway.

'Onions!' she said with a laugh.

Annie turned on the cold tap. 'Come, madam. Put hands here and paining will stop.' She smiled.

Maya did as she was told and placed her fingers under the running water. In seconds her tears had dried. 'That's clever,' she said and when she looked back saw her maid had taken over her knife and stood at the chopping board in her place.

'I will doing.'

'Thank you,' she said. 'Today I am making chutney. You know? Pickle.'

Annie nodded.

'Date chutney.'

Annie wiped her eyes on the corner of her scarf and furrowed her brow. 'You need adding chilli, madam.'

'You think?'

'And garlic.'

Maya was impressed. Garlic she had expected but the chilli was a surprise that she liked, as was getting out of onion-duty. She headed for the packs of pre-pitted dates she had bought the day before and put them into a heavy saucepan with the spices and vinegar leaving Annie to deal with the garlic and chilli and soon the house was filled with a sharp smell that she was glad to leave behind while she went back to the computer to write the recipe for the blog.

Minx

Flight's booked. Be there next week! Staying at the Intercon in town. Send me your numbers and I'll give you a bell. We can share a wine and have a catch up under a moonlit sky, eh?

Can't wait.

Mickey
0776 655 2210

Maya stared at the screen. Hell, it was happening. A shiver ran up her arms as her palms became increasingly damp. She didn't know what to think. One minute he was talking about his wife, the next he was definitely giving her the come-on. She didn't want to give him her home phone number and in seconds raced off a reply that she hoped didn't make her look too keen but did include her mobile number. Then she looked at the time on his email to her and felt slightly sick. He'd sent his email at three in the morning. Maybe he couldn't sleep for thinking of her?

Annie appeared in the doorway with Maya's coffee, in her favourite mug.

'Thank you, Annie,' said Maya. 'Sorry, did you need some jars for the chutney?'

'No, madam. I am having.'

'Okay.' Maya turned back to the keyboard but when she heard no slap of retreating flip-flops she swivelled her chair round to see Annie still standing there, winding the ends of her scarf round her fingers.

'I have problem.'

'Oh dear.'

'My daughter, Matilda, have problem.'

'Ye-es.'

'She need getting married.'

Maya stopped typing for a moment and faced her maid.

'My sister Margaret found her nice boy with good job.'

'Super!' Maya wondered where the problem lay.

'I need money for dowry, wedding, everything.'

'Ah!' Now she knew where this was going.

'Maybe I can get another job?'

Maya's face fell. 'You mean leave us?' Were they not paying her enough already? Was Annie not happy? Was Maya so crap at being a boss that she wanted to leave for somewhere better?

'Oh no, madam,' Annie looked coy. 'I happy here. I need more work. I need earn more money. Maybe I can babysit for other family sometime? Do their iron? It's okay?'

Maya knew that it was illegal for a maid under her sponsorship to work for a third party, but she also knew that lots of people borrowed other people's maids for babysitting and didn't get caught. She had a better idea. 'Maybe you can cook for other people too? You are a good cook!'

Annie's face lit up. 'You think?'

'Yes, I think.'

'You can help?'

Maya checked herself and put on her most serious face. 'Give me one two days to think,' she said. 'I ask boss.'

Annie tipped her head on one side.

'Okay?'

Annie tipped her head from side to side repeatedly in the way that meant kind of yes and kind of no at the same time but could still count as a conclusion. Then her flip-flops slapped against the cold marble stairs as she returned to the kitchen.

Right now, Maya had other things to think about, but she would keep a compartment of her mind open to think about a solution for Annie's plight while she got on with other matters. Like today's blog.

That night at supper, Rich spooned half a jar of the chutney onto his plate. She hoped it might put her back in his good books.

'Do you like my chutney?' she asked.

'Better than Branston,' he replied, pressing a sizeable dollop onto his fork along with a square of spinach quiche.

'It's date,' she said.

Rich kept on chewing.

'With chilli,' she continued, hoping for a response that resembled approval not only of her cooking but of her, Maya, his wife, too.

'Nice,' he said.

The kids stood up to leave the table.

'Plates!' she reminded them and Oliver rolled his eyes before taking his to the kitchen.

Maya screwed the lid back onto the jar of chutney. Rich poured the end of the bottle of wine into his own wineglass.

'I heard from Av today.'

'Oh yes.' He raised his glass to his lips and stared out the window towards a sky that was darkening with the dusk.

'She said her neighbours have just put their house on the market. You know, the one you always wished we could buy?'

'How much?'

'Only 400 grand. Good, eh?' she said, keeping her voice bright.

'Probably means ours is worth less than we paid for it too.' He took a slug of wine. 'Typical!'

'Well, I think she said 400, it could have been 395. I may have got it wrong.' She reached for the empty bottle and realised that more wine was not going to lift the atmosphere tonight. What was eating him? He'd always been so easy come easy go about money before.

'I'm going up to the computer, then I'm having an early night. I'm on the red eye to bloody Bangkok again,' he called out and left.

'I was only making conversation,' she said, too quietly for him to hear and stayed at the table for a moment, trying to absorb her husband's odd behaviour. He was working hard, for sure. He was tired, true. They had been unable to save since they got here, which was a disappointment, but it was early days. And he was drinking more than was necessary. She'd countered all his objections to her working at The Sunshine Centre and she'd cooked one of his favourite meals. She wished he'd tell her what the matter was. But each time she tried, he'd close up even more or leave the room. He hadn't even wished her luck for her first day at work.

Chapter twenty-three

Wish me luck, then,' said Maya, tipping the boys out of the car at the school gate.

'Uh?' said Oliver.

'My first day at work!' She twisted around. 'Don't forget your games kit. I can still see it on the back seat.'

'Oh yeah. Good luck, Mum!' said Matthew. At least one of her family sounded genuinely enthusiastic.

'Now you'll know how it feels to be the new kid,' said Oliver. 'Trust me, it sucks. Bye.'

She'd have no problem being the new kid. Not with Leila as her boss.

'Bye boys!' she called out. But they had already disappeared into a swarm of uniformed teenagers, dragging games bags and rucksacks behind them.

She felt buoyed up, light and free as she drove to the windtower, all thoughts of the previous day's argument shoved to the back of her mind like the wellingtons that were now shoved to the back of the wardrobe. The roads were not too congested, she wove between the cars, skirted the bends and dodgemed around the roundabouts like an ice skater. How she loved the mornings. The light was clear, fresh, and not yet thickened by humidity. When the sentry box came into sight, her heart lifted.

She was here. Omar was at her side in an instant. She lowered the window.

'Hello,' she said.

'*As-salam alaykum*,' he replied, his expression blank as he waited for her to explain who she was and what on earth she was doing there.

She had not considered for a moment that he might not speak English.

'*Wa alaykum e-salam*, Omar,' she said, using one of the handful of greeting phrases she'd learned so far. She hoped that if he realised she knew his name, he might feel no need to question her. 'I'm Maya. I come to see Leila,' she said as simply as she could. Omar nodded gravely, walked to the gate, and opened it, before standing back and allowing her to pass. She drove in and parked next to the black Mercedes she knew belonged to Leila and began to relax. This was such a magical spot. For a while, she drank in the sights, the sounds, the smells of the place: the lawn, as immaculate as ever; the birds singing their familiar ha-ha ho-ho ha–ha; and the distant salty tang of the sea. A green parrot swooped in front of her before rising to settle in the leafy branch of the Indian bean tree. She was so lucky. Now she had to make sure she didn't blow it.

Suddenly, the gates swept open again and in swooped a bright yellow Ferrari. Its occupant was invisible behind the smoked glass windows as it swung in to park beside Maya. One sandaled foot emerged from the driver's door, soon followed by a crisp white *dishdasha*.

'Good morning, Maya!' said Hatim, holding out his hand to her. 'Welcome.' He reached into the pocket of his *dishdasha* and pulled out two keys. 'One for you, one for me. Here, I'll let you in.'

Maya walked slowly, enjoying the warmth of the morning sun on her hair and the beauty of the building. Hatim let her enter the office first. It was dark – little light entered through the high windows.

'No Leila?' she said, surprised. 'Where's the light?' She didn't think it was appropriate to be alone in a darkened room with him and ran her hands along the whitewashed walls in search of a switch.

'Leila will be here soon,' he said, rotating a dimmer switch so that the room lit up.

'But her car?' Maya began. She was sure the black Mercedes was Leila's.

'I know. She left it here last night. We had a dinner here beside the sea, all of us, children and all. Three brothers and families.' Hatim lowered his eyes.

'That must have been very difficult for you,' she said softly, hoping she was not being over-familiar. She put out her hand to touch his arm but thought better of it and used her hand, instead, to tuck her hair behind one ear.

'Yes.' He moved over to his desk and perched on the front of it, pulling a necklace of black prayer beads out of one pocket and his car keys out of the other. He placed the keys on the desk and laced the beads through the fingers of both hands, flicking through them slowly, one at a time, so that the loop of beads shivered like a millipede. 'Allah's will.'

'Do you really believe that?' She bit her bottom lip.

'I don't know,' he said sadly, tapping first one foot and then the other against the desk. 'But we believe that everything is Allah's will. Allah has the right to give life and take it away.'

'But sometimes it's cruel.'

'God is merciful. *Allah kareem.*'

Maya looked unconvinced.

'Allah gives us all the brains we need. It is up to us how we use them. Maryam was so bright, so clever but she could not find a way to be happy. Maybe it was because she, we, could not have children?' He shook his head. 'She had many miscarriages. Many.'

'I'm sorry. You must miss her very much.' She looked down at her hands.

Hatim folded his beads up in his palm, got down from the desk and moved to sit behind it, leaning back in his chair and putting his hands behind his head. The subject appeared to be closed. 'So, you like the office?'

'I love it. It's very beautiful.'

There was a tap on the door and Hari stood silently in the open doorway with a newspaper under his arm.

'Hari is our houseboy. He will come and offer drinks throughout the day. Coffee. Tea. Cold drinks. If you want something special, he will get it in for you. So, Maya, what would you like?'

'Water, I think. Thank you.'

Hatim said something hurried in Arabic and Hari dropped the paper on Hatim's desk then slipped away, returning in record time with a brass tray carrying a tiny eggcup-shaped cup filled with black coffee for Hatim and a bottle of water. Hatim nodded at him and he moved shyly towards Maya's desk, cracked open the water bottle and poured it into a glass. Every couple of seconds he looked over to Hatim for approval. Eventually Hatim said something else in Arabic and Hari left the room.

Maya adjusted the height of the chair. Now what? She had no idea what she could do until Leila got there. However nice he was, being in Hatim's company was unnerving. She looked over at him and smiled. He was now leaning so far back in his chair that he was almost horizontal and had his sandaled feet up on the desk in front of him as he leafed through the local paper. It was in Arabic, so she couldn't even read the side that was exposed to her for something to do.

'Maya?' said Hatim from behind the paper, so she couldn't see his face.

'Yes.' She cleared her throat and waited.

'When are you going to allow me to show you my beautiful country?' He looked over the top of the open pages.

'Oh, thank you. But my husband's away this weekend and the kids have activities they need me to drive them to.'

'Your family is welcome. But it's okay for you to come alone if you want.' His eyes returned to the paper.

Maya pushed her hair behind her ears.

'Soon?'

'Soon,' she replied.

He raised his paper once more. She watched his toes twitch for a while in his sandals and then settle down.

She cleared her throat once more. 'Hatim?'

Laying down the paper, he smiled at her warmly. 'Yes, Maya.'

'What shall I do?' she said.

'Oh, Leila will tell you what to do when she gets here. For now, you can relax. Take it easy.'

She took a sip of water. 'Would it be okay if I just looked around the place?'

Hatim nodded and Maya left the room to wander from room to room, lacing her way through the inner courtyard between the doors. She ran her fingers over the rough white walls, touched the woodwork and looked up at the beamed ceilings. She walked through the two empty rooms and thought it a terrible waste that no one was enjoying their beauty. She opened the door to the kitchen and found it already occupied. Hari stood at the sink, rinsing glasses. When he saw her, he nodded at her and scuttled off, keeping his eyes lowered. What a kitchen! Modern stand-alone units in bleached pine, a huge stainless-steel range, and a vast fridge with an icemaker. She peeked inside: nothing but soft drinks. Every surface sparkled, which proved that either it was desperately under-used, or Hari was an expert cleaner. She bent down to open a cupboard and found it filled with brand new saucepans. At that moment, the door burst open. Maya straightened up fast, hoping to God that Hatim hadn't just caught her with her bum in the air.

'God, I'm sorry I'm late Maya, and on your first day too. Rotten of me. I'm sorry. I had to get a lift in from Ali and he had a meeting first and was late home. Oh, you know the story. Anyway, I'm here now and you look like you're making yourself well and truly at home. Has Hatim been looking after you?'

Maya grinned and followed Leila back to the office, where she flopped down onto her chair, thrusting the bundle of papers she had been clutching to her chest onto the desk in front of her. Her mobile phone skittered across the surface and landed on the floor.

Hatim tutted softly before walking over and picking it up for her, rather like a grandmother would hand a dropped rattle back to her first grandchild, indulgently.

'Yes, thanks,' said Maya. 'And Hari of course.'

Maya looked around to see if there were a third chair available and when there wasn't, leant rather awkwardly against Leila's desk.

Hatim raised his eyes to hold Maya's for a second. 'I have to go now Maya. My job was to be here to welcome you.'

'That was kind,' said Maya.

'I think we need to buy another chair!' He laughed and stood up, picking up his car keys and indicating that Maya take his seat. She sat down obediently, feeling the warmth he had left behind in the soft leather.

'Hey!' said Leila, opening the drawer in her desk and pulling out her own laptop. 'You're actually here, Maya. I can't believe it.'

'And I can't tell you how happy I am to be here. Really.'

'Hatim seems to like you.' Leila flipped open the lid of her laptop and looked at the screen.

Maya felt herself blush. 'Rubbish!' she said. 'He's just being polite and friendly, but he does not need to invite me to go into the desert with him.'

'He's so passionate about his country. Maryam used to love going into the wadis with him and the farms at first, but in the end they just weren't enough for her any more. But our Hatim is a Bedouin at heart. He grabs anyone he can to give him an excuse to go.'

'I'll look forward to it then. But for now, Leila, I am here to work, remember, so come on. Shall we start? I've been having some ideas, based on some of the things we needed to do at the deli. Do you have a website yet?' she asked.

'Er nope,' said Leila.

'And a logo.'

'We could ask Elske to do that.'

'Great idea.'

'The only thing I know is how to read books!'

'And you love to write, yeah? So you can write the blog and the website copy and stuff.'

Leila's green eyes flashed. 'Do you think I could? I've no experience.'

'Neither have I, but I managed it all right.'

'I'm such a scatterbrain, Maya. I needed someone like you to tell me what to do.'

Maya was on a high. She shared every big idea, every small one and even the scraps of thoughts that she had come up with since she first met Leila at The Twist.

Leila slid her chair over towards Maya's and flung her arm around her shoulder. 'I do believe this project has a chance of working,' she said and began to unwind her headscarf.

'Actually, I've had another idea,' began Maya. 'Well, just a thought.'

'Go on.'

'I was wandering around this morning and saw the kitchen here.'

'Fabulous, isn't it?'

'I thought that maybe we could have one day a week here when we are a kind of open house and serve food. What do you think?'

'You mean like a soup kitchen?'

'Hey, that's a great idea!'

'Really?'

'Sure. Soup is a bit of a cure-all. It's a brilliant idea.'

'You could make, er, Sunshine Soup?' Leila clapped her hands together like an excited child.

'I think I might manage that,' she replied ironically. Soup was a cinch and already her mind started to work on the precise ingredients she would include in Sunshine Soup.

'Now, I think we need to start making a list of who we will invite to the fundraiser. We need to be a showcase for the centre, right?' Leila reached into a drawer and extracted a notepad and a biro, the end of which she planted between her teeth.

'Right,' began Maya, excited to be getting started. 'We'll have a food stall for Sunshine Preserves – marmalade, strawberry jam and spicy date chutney.'

'And then the kitchen selling Sunshine Soup.'

'And then some Taster Workshops. Right?'

'Hey, I like this food theme! You're a genius!'

'We could ask Liv to do some mini-massages, perhaps?'

'You mean Taster Massages!' Leila wrote that down.

'And we could ask Elske to teach painting, perhaps and sell her cards? How about we ask stallholders to pay us a percentage of their takings?'

'Absolutely.'

'Maybe LaShell could bring some of her art too?'

Leila wrote that down. 'But what about Barb? What can we ask her to do?'

Maya rubbed her chin. What could they ask Barb to do? 'Dunno. Does she have anything to sell?'

Leila shook her head.

'Can she teach anything?'

Leila sucked the biro for a moment. 'Poster-sticking and flyer distribution?' She giggled.

'Ouch. Poor Barb. She always does so much for other people, but nothing for herself. I can't think of anything.'

'We could ask her to put up posters about our fundraiser?' Leila sounded reticent.

'I'm sure we could. But really I would like to help her to get something out of it too. I'll keep thinking. Now, who else?'

'So,' continued Leila, scooping up her long hair and flinging it behind her. 'What about setting a date? I think we need to set a date!'

'I think soon, yeah?'

'But not too soon, we need time to plan... and book the speakers... and make the preserves.'

'Early December? Then we can have a bit of a Christmas theme too. If that's okay in a Muslim country?'

Leila put her arm round Maya's shoulder and squeezed. 'Of course it's okay. Jesus is one of our prophets too, you know. Deal!'

'Then, we need to start making some phone calls,' said Maya picking up her mobile phone, which beeped the moment she picked it up.

Can't wait. Mick x

Her heart raced. Shit. The virtual flirting lost its innocence. Now what?

Chapter twenty-four

Around one, Barb returned from another solo trip to the mall to an empty house. Out of habit, she checked her reflection in the hall mirror, on her way through the kitchen.

I look older than dirt, thought Barb, checking she had no lipstick on her teeth and shaping her hair with her fingers. She pursed her lips and breathed out, a long slow breath like Liv told her to. It wouldn't be too long before she succumbed to Botox.

She was tired and needed company. The shock of the Democrats getting in had shaken her to the core. She didn't trust that man, Obama. She and Bill had stayed up all night watching the television in stunned silence. When the Republicans lost Virginia, that was the moment they knew they'd lose the whole darn thing. Bill had stormed into the kitchen, grabbing yet another cold beer and a huge bag of chips, and gone back to his place in front of the screen, every time another seat was lost he yelped in agony. And when it was over he'd just got up from his chair, had a shower, and gone to work without a word. It made Barb's stomach turn to see all those expats, who didn't understand what a disaster that man was going to be, rejoicing about the new president like he was the Messiah.

Taking an oversized glass decorated with Marge Simpson, blue hair and all, from the cupboard, she held it under the ice dispenser of the refrigerator and listened to the cubes crashing down into it. When it was up to the brim, she filled the remaining space with Coke, full strength, then went over to her recliner and leaned back to enjoy the cool, refreshing sweetness. According to habit, her gaze fell on the family photos, starting with the living on the right, and then ending, so she could linger, on the one no longer here, on the left.

'Oh Angelina, my angel,' she said softly. 'What is the world coming to? Daddy just doesn't seem to want to talk about anything that matters anymore.'

It wasn't fair of Bill not to talk about stuff like this. Liv had got her talking and it was as if the cap she had placed on seven years of bottled-up grief had popped off and the sorrow just bubbled on out like cola from a bottle. She took another sip of her Coke. It would taste better with Bacardi. She rose and crossed to the drinks cabinet, looked around for a moment just to check no one was looking, and filled the space at the top of her glass with rum.

'I know you're watching me, angel,' she said. 'But you won't tell on Mommy, will you?'

She wandered back to the sideboard and picked up the framed photograph of her wedding day. Bill was such a handsome man. So kind. He had always wanted her to be happy. Always let her do anything she wanted. Her Bill was a good man. Let her spend as much as she liked with no need to account for it. Let her go on trips with the girls, let her bury herself in the club. Never complained if she wasn't home and certainly never expected her to have cooked a meal from scratch. Sure thing, he treated her like a lady. He remembered her birthday, brought her perfume when he had been on a trip; he even helped with Brandon's baseball. Hell, he attended every match, never expected Barb to go too. He left her to get on with whatever she wanted. Never even asked what she was doing. He must trust her. What did she have to complain about? No, she should count her lucky stars.

Barb drained her drink quickly, leaning back against the sideboard and straightening her back. It was Liv who had messed with her head. It was the first time she'd tried something, so – well – unusual, and it would be the last. Did her no good at all. That was it. Look at her. She was still a wreck though her session had been a few days ago. The Bacardi was simply replenishing her energy. She took her glass, still half full of ice, back to the kitchen and emptied it into the sink before running the faucet for a few moments just in case the smell of alcohol lingered. Then she rinsed the glass, dried it and replaced it in the cupboard. If she was quick she just had time to have a shower and reapply her make-up before she fetched Brandon from his marching-band practice.

She drew up at the school just a minute late and found a parking space close by. Brandon would find her easily, no need to get out and face the throng of mothers that stood chatting by the gate. Normally, she was keen to join the group, catch up on the gossip, and discuss the day's play, but not today. Despite her freshly lipsticked smile, she was still feeling less than her normal self. Aircon up high, she tuned into the local radio station to keep her mind occupied while she waited.

Suddenly there was a tap on the window. It was Joni Summers. She looked tired. Probably from all the packing and the trauma of all those goodbye parties.

'Can I have a word?' she mouthed.

Barb smiled broadly and pressed the button to lower the window. 'Hey, Joni!' she said brightly.

'Not getting out today? Brandon played real well, you know. Jeez that drum is loud! He's doing great. You should be proud. I'm real scared Kyle won't be able to keep up with Marching Band in Sakhalin.'

'Sure,' said Barb, thinking quickly. 'I was engrossed in the radio. Wanted to listen to the end of the show.' Please don't let her ask what it was about. Best tack might be to change the subject. 'So, what can I do for you?'

'I'm in a bit of a fix. My dad's sick and I have to go and give Mom a hand. So it means I have to leave even sooner. I'll have no chance of a handover to Maya. She did agree to take over, didn't she?'

With the window open, the car was hot and steamy in no time. Barb flushed. Holy guacamole, she had failed to get a final commitment from Maya and now she'd got herself all hooked up with Leila. 'Oh your poor mom, your poor dad,' she said instead. 'Of course you must go. Don't you worry. You've written it all down, haven't you, in your job manual, you know what you do and all the contact details? I'm sure we'll manage. When do you go exactly?' she said, her stoic expression hiding the panic inside.

Joni's face fell. 'Job manual?' she said softly. 'Look, I'm sorry Barb, I have no time to do that.' She looked back towards the schoolyard and raised her hand to wave. 'There's Kyle. I'm sorry, but there's nothing I can do.'

'Now you take good care, won't you?' said Barb, hoping her smile still looked genuine while she raised the window.

Barb had not heard a word of the radio show. But she had

heard Joni's news. She was not sure she could stand this. She'd given up without a fight again. What was happening to her? Where was her spirit? Maybe this had been one move too many? Maybe she was starting to wear out?

The trunk clunked open and was thrust upwards as Brandon threw his bass drum and sticks inside. Out of the corner of her eye, Barb could see he was not alone.

'Hi Mom!' he called through the trunk to the front seat. 'Can Cory come home with us? He really wants to play on Death Rally. You know, the one Dad just bought me. Can he? Oh, and Jake said he wanted to come by and watch the game later. And stay for pizza. I know it's not the weekend but can they sleep over too?'

'Sure,' said Barb, feeling the fight drain from her with every second. The last thing she wanted was to take care of three hulking teenage boys or to have her couch taken over by them for the whole evening. 'If their moms don't mind.'

'Cool!' A flurry of additional instruments landed in the trunk, which was banged shut so loudly that it made Barb shudder. In seconds her rear view mirror was filled with three suntanned faces topped with hair spiked with sweat. She doubted they heard her sigh or even noticed her face, filled with resignation, as she drove them home.

'Hi honey, good day?' Barb called out from her 'throne' towards the hallway when she heard the front door click shut.

'Fine,' said Bill.

'You want some pizza? It's pepperoni.'

'Nar. I'll grab something back at the club. There's a quiz night. I told Layton I'd make up a team. You didn't want to come, did you?'

'Guess that means I'll be alone again, then.' Bill was always so tolerant of her hectic social life that she didn't like to complain when he went out too. But she did resent it a little. He dragged her around the world, went out to work, went off on trips, and then when he was home, he was always playing golf or at the bar. She didn't want to whine. Bill hated it when she got upset.

'Just taking a shower...' he called. Their conversation might as well have been carried out on the phone or by text message; they still hadn't actually set eyes on each other. Barb felt ragged at the edges. Frayed. As if parts of her had been torn away. Tonight, she needed to be with the big, strong bear of a man she had married. She needed to feel his arms around her, but right now the only sign that she had a husband was the sound of running water. Topping up her glass of white wine and soda, she followed him into the bedroom and sat on the bed, leaning back against the pillows as she listened to the sounds of Bill whistling as he showered.

He emerged, naked, rubbing his thick, dark hair roughly with a towel. 'Hey! What you doin' in here, honey?'

Barb looked down from his head to his toes, enjoying the sight of his wide shoulders, the black hairs that coiled on his chest, spreading out as far as his shoulders but then, mercifully, stopping. His belly was no longer the washboard it had been when they married and billowed softly from his breastbone to his groin. She watched him tuck it neatly into his underwear and then pull up his new golf pants. He still had good legs, shapely. And a nice butt. She smiled to herself.

'You admirin' what you see?' he said. 'It's been a while. It's been a while. But I don't like, you know, to make you do anything, you know.'

Yes, she knew all right. He didn't like to even consider she might want to be close to him, with or without making love.

He turned to the dresser, took out a red polo shirt and pulled it over his head before tucking it into his pants and tightening his belt. Then he put his wristwatch back on his wrist. He'd received that for twenty-five years' service with the company. You couldn't say Bill wasn't loyal.

Barb took another sip of her spritzer and curled her legs beneath her. 'Do you really know how long it's been?'

'Honey, I don't count. You know that. And I don't complain. But it's been a long while since you looked at me like that, that's for sure.' He stooped to look in the mirror and smoothed back his hair with his fingers.

'Do you have to go out quite yet?' she said, desperate to keep the whine out of her voice. She hoped she sounded more, well, seductive.

'Why, darlin'. You offering? You pick your timing, don't you? Just after I've been in the shower and just before I'm going out.' He lowered himself down onto the bed beside her and lifted first one leg than the other to pull on his socks.

Barb reached out her hand and touched his knee. 'I know. I'm sorry. But I've had a bit of a bad week and I could have done with talking to you this evening.' She paused. 'About Angelina,' she said so quietly that he may not even have heard. She took another sip of her wine.

'Honey. Girl. This isn't the time and you know it. I promised to meet the guys down at the bar. We have to talk quiz tactics. We can talk another time.' Bill shoehorned on his black and white shoes. He reached into his pocket and pulled out his wallet before pulling out a bunch of notes. 'Hey, take this. Buy yourself something nice tomorrow.'

Barb watched Bill leave the bedroom and listened as he went into the sitting room to have a few words with the boys about the game before the front door closed and he was gone. She unzipped her dress and threw it to the floor, undid her bra, and slipped under the covers wearing only her panties. Lying there, her eyes wide open, she stared at the ceiling and tried to make her mind go blank. She was still lying there like that when Bill eventually returned home.

Chapter twenty-five

'Will you at least let me bring a pudding?' asked Maya, shielding her eyes from the glare of the afternoon sun as she helped Elske to rearrange the tables and chairs.

'No. It's fine. Thank you. I have some ice cream in the freezer,' answered Elske. 'You have only just got back from work. You must be tired.'

But Maya wanted to contribute. Elske had little enough help as it was and she knew Rich would appreciate a proper pudding. 'Look. It's no trouble. I'll ask Annie to make one. She's always on at me to teach her how to cook new things and that means I make her happy while I don't have to do it. How's that?'

'OK. Thank you. That would be lovely. Nico loves homemade cooking too. He's always on at me to make Dutch buttercake. It's the easiest thing in the world but it is still easier to buy yoghurts.' Elske picked up a table and walked across the grass with it to place it beside the rather grubby-looking gas barbecue she had dragged over earlier.

'No problem,' said Maya, knowing that Rich would be pleased not to be the only man at tonight's poolside supper. However much he was confusing her right now, she longed for a glimmer of a smile to appear on his worried face.

'Afraid Nico's flight's delayed in Tokyo. He'll be late,' Elske said matter-of-factly.

Maya's heart sank. 'I'll leave you to it. See you at seven, yes?' Dutch buttercake, eh? She'd have to look that one up on the Internet.

'Yes,' she said, piling four chairs on top of each other. 'See you.'

Maya went back inside. By the time they all met outside later, the humidity would have dropped with the dusk. There was no point checking her email. Mick was on his way. Apart from the spectre of the past that loomed over her, she was feeling pretty pleased with herself. Not only had Elske agreed to do the poster for the fundraiser free of charge, but she had also agreed to take one of the stalls at the fundraiser and then there was Suchanatta with those gorgeous scarves and LaShell with her watercolours. She'd had a good day. In fact, this evening was a cause for celebration and not just because America had elected its first black president. Rich was home after a week away and she had successfully completed her first week at work.

She walked over to the fridge and opened the door, staring at its contents for inspiration. Next, she looked in the freezer, then the fruit bowl, and finally the food cupboards. What could she teach Annie to do in a short space of time that would appease her husband, please the kids, and that used only the ingredients she had already to hand? Her job was making a difference, she had to admit. She simply didn't have the time to go shopping every day and didn't fancy battling the rush-hour traffic to go to the supermarket again. It was the perfect time to have a go at the apricot and date slice she so loved at The

Orange Tree and Nico's buttercake. Both would be perfect for a barbecue because you could eat them with your fingers.

'Annie!' she called.

'Yes, madam!' came the reply as her protégée hurried up the stairs to serve her.

Maya took her apron down from the hook behind the door.

'We cook?' asked Annie.

'Apricot and date slice!' Maya replied.

'No recipe book?'

Maya tapped the top of her head with a forefinger and the two women grinned from ear to ear.

Discovering that he was to be the only man that evening until Nico came was the first thing to turn Rich's good-mood dial down a notch. Their estate agent's email, saying their tenant had lost his job and was moving out in just a month, turned it down a few more.

'And you made me cancel a squash match tonight to come to this,' he moaned, pulling his Rolling Stones tee-shirt out of his shorts like the boys were always reminding him to do.

'Elske is expecting you. I won't lie and pretend your flight was delayed too. I'm sorry.' She turned away, avoiding his eye.

Rich pulled a cold beer out of the fridge and snapped back the ring-pull. 'Beer time,' he said. 'The best time of day.' He took a long drink. 'Want one?'

'Not yet, thanks.' She paused. He had forgotten. She managed to wait about a minute before continuing. 'Aren't you going to ask me about my day at work?'

'God, sorry,' he said, moving over to sit on a bar stool and patting the one next to him. 'I forgot. How was it, then?'

He pulled a face, then stood up again, took his phone out of his pocket and laid it on the counter.

Maya tried hard to stay looking disgruntled but the joy inside her was like a young puppy on the lead for the first time, desperate to escape. Her eyes lit up. 'It was heaven, Rich. I loved it. And d'you know, I felt worth something again. Leila loved every single one of my ideas.

'Good ideas? You?' said Rich, his eyebrows raised ironically. He was trying to be nice for once.

'Yeah! Of course!' She grinned at him and punched him playfully on the shoulder. Maybe things were getting better after all. 'Good trip today? Doha wasn't it?'

Rich set down his beer and focused on it. 'Fine.'

'Right.'

'Whatever.' He closed his lips into a thin line and ran his hand through his hair. 'At least it wasn't bloody Bangkok again.'

As the atmosphere thickened Maya decided she might as well broach the subject that had burned at her all day and get it over with. 'Bummer about the tenants, eh?'

'It's more than a bummer, Maya. It's a total disaster.' He stood up and fetched himself another beer. 'Want that wine now?'

Maya nodded. 'Please.'

There was a knock on the back door, soon followed by the tap of bare feet running up the stairs towards them.

'Hi there! I wanted to tell you that I invited Jim and Sue along tonight too, Maya. Did you make enough dessert? I don't want to embarrass you,' Elske asked, getting straight to the point.

'Maya always makes enough dessert,' Rich responded for her.

'All under control!' said Maya, aware that her comment did not apply to every area of her life. 'Bye!' And Elske, job done, was already on her way out, back down the stairs. 'See you later!'

Rich opened his mouth wide and poured beer into it hungrily as he stepped down from his stool. 'I'll go back to the PC, then.' And he was gone too, leaving Maya alone. She looked at his Blackberry. He had left it on the counter. It was tempting to grab it and retreat into a corner and look at his messages to see if a clue to his erratic behaviour lurked in his inbox. She reached out to touch it but then she heard footsteps. Rich was back.

'Oops,' he said, putting his phone back in his pocket quickly and disappearing upstairs again in seconds.

Why 'oops', Maya thought.

'Sausage?' asked Sacha, Elske's youngest, who may have only been eleven years old but was happily in charge of the barbecue this evening. 'They're ready now.'

'Yeah, me,' said Matthew. 'How many am I allowed?'

Maya glowered at him. 'Just take one for now, eh?' she said. 'Boys!' She rolled her eyes at Elske.

'It's fine,' said Elske. 'We can always defrost some more if we run out. When will the kebabs be done?' She turned to her daughter.

'Ma-ma!' she replied, clearly disgruntled that her mother had the audacity to ask and wanting to be left alone.

'Kids!' Elske said, turning to Maya. 'Too grown-up too soon these days!'

'You're so lucky,' responded Maya, busy studying her husband's face in an attempt to judge his mood, which, at this moment, didn't look promising again. 'Wish my kids were interested in domestic things. You're fortunate to have girls, Elske. Rich can do all the boys' stuff with Oli and Matt, you know, things like sports and boats and cars, but they don't really want to go shopping or cook with me.'

Elske laughed. 'I hate to cook! I'm sure my girls would love some lessons from you, wouldn't you, girls?' She looked over at Sacha, who certainly seemed to be happy with her role.

Sacha nodded, her tongue sticking out the corner of her mouth as she used over-sized tongs to turn over a piece of meat. 'Can you show me how to make a cake, Maya?' she asked. 'Or cookies?'

'I'd like you to learn to cook the supper, Sacha! Not cakes and sweet things!'

'Sure!' said Maya happily. 'Any time. Even supper!' She shot a grin over to Oliver, who was hunched over his hot dog.

'No, Mum!' he said with his mouth full. 'No ways. I've better things to do with my time.'

'Like snog Chantal,' added Matthew, who was listening to the conversation after all.

'Shu-up.' Oli grunted, glowering in his direction.

Rich, meanwhile, was miles away, a fake smile on his lips, his eyes glazed, seeing into the distance.

'What about you Rich?' asked Elske.

'Uh?' he said. 'Sorry? I was wondering about the match tonight, hoping they found a new number two to play for me. I thought Jim and Sue were coming.'

'They are,' she said. 'Come on, go up and get some food. You don't have to wait for them to arrive.'

Rich stared over in the direction of Jim's villa, or was it into space? Maya was not sure. And when the sight of Jim and Sue hove into view, his face remained blank.

Jim put his hand in the small of Sue's back and let her approach the party first. He wore a brightly coloured Hawaiian shirt and board shorts. Suchanatta had wrapped a white sarong round her slim hips and wore a cropped top that showed her flat stomach.

'Hello there me old mate!' he said, slapping Rich on the back. 'Still enjoying the delights of Arabian Airline's newest route?'

Rich had just taken a large gulp of beer and was unable to speak for a moment. Instead he did a kind of nod and shrug.

'Been to the Lucky Cowboy, yet?' He grinned.

Rich went pale.

Sue hit Jim playfully on the shoulder. 'Come on, it's not that bad there! After all, it is where we met?'

'What's the Lucky Cowboy?' asked Maya glad of a lighter topic to discuss.

'It's a bar. In Pat Pong.'

'The sex area? Where they do things with bananas and ping pong balls?' Maya was beginning to enjoy this conversation. She had always suspected Sue was a dark horse.'That's the place!' Sue looked rather proud of herself. Rich walked away from the table and over to the cool box.

'What's your poison, Sue?' he called out.

'Just a lager, please! Now, Maya. How did you meet the gorgeous Rich?' Sue leaned closer conspiratorially.

'We-ell, I had a boyfriend, called Mick. He fitted double-glazing and one week he got a big job at some air force barracks in Norfolk. I was between jobs and so I went along with him for the ride. I met Rich in the NAAFI, you know, the shop on camp. I went in to buy a packet of Polos and came out with my future husband's phone number.' There, she'd done it. She'd mentioned Mick's name. Made him real.

Rich approached with Sue's drink.

'Elske? What about you?'

'Short story. We were at school together. Went to university together and bought a house in the same street I grew up in. We'll go back there after Dubai, I expect. Get the kids into Dutch school again.'

'Cheers!' said Maya, keen to change the subject.

'To our lucky cowboys!' said Sue.

Maya took a bite of her sausage. 'Elske,' she began, slowly, carefully.

'Mm-hmm,' she said, her mouth full of coleslaw that Maya had already identified as shop-bought.

Maya was not quite sure how to play what she was going to say next. 'Sometimes I don't want to cook either,' she began. 'And that's when I'm really pleased to have Annie. Rich and the boys may not cook for me, but Annie is fantastic. Really fantastic!'

'But I thought you didn't like her taking over in your kitchen,' Elske said, correctly, as it happened. But Maya was on a mission.

'Well, sometimes, yes, but on balance I'm glad to have her.' She turned to Rich. 'She made a fabulous tuna lasagne the other day, didn't she?'

'Did she?' said Rich unhelpfully. 'I must have been away, again.'

'I prefer meat ones,' said Matthew, who, unbelievably, was still listening to the conversation. Food was keeping him in one place for once.

'Annie makes good meat lasagne too,' added Maya.

'Oh, and that butter chicken was yum the other day,' said Matthew. 'You know, when we came back from the beach and she had left it for us in the oven. She even made those flat bread things, chapattis. Not sure about the yoghurt stuff though.'

'My Malee is a good cook, too,' said Sue. Her Tom Yam Kung is as good as my mother used to make.'

'What's that?' asked Matthew.

'A kind of spicy soup. Come round when the girls are back from boarding school and we can all eat Thai food.'

Matthew didn't look impressed, but Oli pricked up his ears.

'When I've had a long day in the studio, sometimes the last thing I want to do is cook,' said Elske. 'And right now I'm in the middle of packing up hundreds of Christmas cards. I'm so busy. I sometimes wish I had a Malee or an Annie, but I need to use the maid's room as a studio. It's okay. I manage.'

'Yeah and we end up having a toasted sandwich,' said Sacha.

'Or baked potato with cheese,' said Hanneke, Elske's older daughter, who was her sister's polar opposite – as indoorsy and Sacha was outdoorsy.'You like baked potato with cheese,' said Elske. 'You could cook instead.'

'I have homework, Mama,' said Hanneke.

Maya took a deep breath. 'Annie's having a tough time at the moment, actually,' she continued, determined to stick to her guns. 'She needs money for her daughter's dowry.'

'Oh dear,' said Elske, squirting mayonnaise from a squeezable bottle onto her plate.

Elske, Sue and Rich all looked at Maya. It put her on the spot. Come on, woman, she thought. Get to the point. 'So, I thought,' she began. 'I thought maybe, as Annie is a good cook, that I could find some people who would use her like a kind of takeaway service. You know, they order a lasagne or a curry and she makes it.' There she had done it. Now she had to just let her idea sink in for a moment. But someone else had arrived and changed the subject.

'Papa!'

Nico walked over to the poolside, pulled a blonde ponytailed daughter into either side and kissed Elske firmly on the lips. Then he released his daughters, stooped down to kiss Maya and Sue on either cheek, and reached to shake first Rich's then Jim's hands, all without taking a step in any direction. He had to be about seven feet tall with arms to match.

'Great news about Obama, right!' he said. 'Air Traffic Control told us the news, so we announced it over the tannoy and a huge cheer went up. It was something, I can tell you!'

'Absolutely,' said Rich. 'The world needs some good news. I only hope he can sort out the global financial situation, don't you?'

'Give him time!' laughed Nico, going off to the coolbox for a beer.

'Talking of money,' said Elske. 'Do you think Annie's food will be expensive? I don't want to pay too much. Food has gone up in price so much since we came here, I can't believe it.'

'No. No it won't,' said Maya, thinking on her feet again. 'It'll cost less than the local takeaways. And it will taste an awful lot better.'

'But I hate cooking things that come in those tin takeaway dishes,' said Elske. 'You can't put them in the microwave.'

'Then you can provide your own dishes. Just bring them around earlier in the day.'

Elske nodded. Hanneke and Sacha stared at her. 'Can we, Mama?' said Hanneke. 'I don't like baked potatoes.'

Rich was frowning. 'So, when does Annie do this cooking? In the time we're paying her to work for us?'

'She has four hours off in the middle of the day, Rich,' Maya said.

'And she will use our electricity, too, I suppose?'

Maya kicked him under the picnic table and shot him a look that meant, We will talk about this later. She should have discussed it with him first, but in his current mood she hadn't dared.

'Actually, the company pays the utility bills, Maya,' interjected Elske.

'Too bloody right, Elske!' Jim said, hands on hips in mock indignation. But let's not talk about money.' 'Has the global financial meltdown hit you too? I'm sorry, mate. What was it, Lehmann?' Rich was being pally.

'Icesave.'

'Shit,' said Rich. 'Puts our situation into perspective.' He looked pensive.

'Our house is without tenants at the moment,' Maya explained. 'Or it will be in a few weeks.'

'So the house will be empty during the winter, which is always a nightmare, what with frozen pipes and all that,' Rich muttered.

'And there are rumours that you're going to be laying people off, right?' asked Nico.

Jim puffed out his cheeks and nodded gravely. 'Too soon to say, mate. Too soon to say.'

'Look, let's not talk about jobs and money. Let's all have another drink!' said Nico brightly.

'Drown the old sorrows,' said Jim.

'Too right!' said Rich, raising his beer can. 'Cheers!'

'You know, I'd love Annie to cook for me sometimes,' Elske joined the conversation again. 'Maybe once a week or so. Can you give me a menu to look at?'

'And me?' said Sue. 'Malee can only cook Thai and I fancy a bit of a change now and again.'

'Sure,' said Maya wondering when she would have time to tell Annie about her idea. She hadn't discussed it with her first either, but Annie was someone she could always rely on. 'Tomorrow?' she said, crossing her fingers.

'Can we go, now?' said Oliver, his plate clean.

'That's fine,' said Elske. 'Off you go, kids. Just take your plates back inside.' When the children had disappeared the remaining adults all settled back into a contemplative silence. Rich went to help himself to another sausage.

Suddenly the tinny sound of *Seasons in the Sun* broke into the atmosphere.

'Mum! Your mobile!' shrieked Oliver.

'Bring it out to her, please!' called Rich.

But Maya leapt up. 'No, it's fine, I'll go,' she said and walked swiftly towards the back gate. Oliver met her there.

'Some guy,' he said, handing the phone over.

Her heart skipped a beat. 'Hello?' she said quietly, with hesitation in her voice.

'Guess who?' said a gravely voice on the other end that was as familiar as if she'd only heard it the day before.'Oh!' she said, trying to sound surprised and moved into the house to finish the conversation.

A few minutes later she approached Rich slowly and put her hand on his shoulder. 'You'll never believe who that was!' she said brightly, while in another part of her mind she was trying to absorb the fact that she had just discovered that Mick had not brought Glenda with him and had never intended to.Rich looked at her and waited. 'Leila? Hatim? Barb? That bellydancer?'

'Mick,' she said.

'Oh.' He turned to his sausage and cut a slice off the end.

'At the Intercon.'

'Oh. And?'

'He wondered if we'd like to meet up on Saturday.'

Rich didn't look up from his sausage. 'I'll be in Thailand, remember? Back late.'

'Oh yes. That's a shame.'

He pushed himself back in his chair, rubbed the stubble on his chin, which she normally loved to see him do, and then crossed his arms across his chest, which she didn't like at all. 'Whatever.' He rocked back and forth in his chair.

'Maya?' Elske was listening. 'Can you get your dessert please?'

'Oh, sorry,' she said, glad of an excuse to run away from the situation. It would give her a few moments to think. For once, she was glad that Rich was off on yet another long haul the following morning and was missing the weekend. When she was inside, she sent Mick a quick text:

See you Saturday.

With Rich away, she escaped her need to tell the truth and there was no need to lie either.

Chapter twenty-six

Maya didn't fall asleep until after she had heard the morning call to prayer. Rich's mood, his apparent obsession with money and her impending meeting with Mick in the flesh kept her mind fizzing hour after hour. And what did Mick expect of her? He'd come alone. Thinking about something did not class as adultery did it? She felt unfaithful already. Maybe it was her fault that Rich was so weird? Maybe she was the one behaving oddly? And she had gone over the top about him not asking her about her first week at work. She had been snappy too. Rich had always been so loyal and supportive. He would never think to even check her mobile phone for messages, yet she had almost done that with his Blackberry. It was as if her own guilt made her suspect him too. Now was she really considering jeopardising her marriage? And for what? Mick was gorgeous to look at, knew all the lines and had the moves, but he had lied to her and probably to his wife. Fuck. What had she done?

The sound of her mobile phone ringing broke into her half-sleep. She reached for it, said 'Hello' sleepily, and then hoped liked hell that it wasn't Mick.

'*As-salam alaykum, Maya.*' It was Hatim. 'Hatim al Farooq, good morning. It is a beautiful day.'

'Yes, isn't it.' She cleared her throat to clear the sleepiness from her voice and reached to lift the corner of the curtains. It was a stunning day.

'Perfect for our little trip to the hidden Emirates.'

'Lovely,' she said, her voice flat as the city landscape. He was her boss and she didn't want to disappoint him, not till she had her work permit anyway.

'I come to your house in one hour. I have picnic, drinks, everything, okay?'

'Lovely,' she said.

'Er, Hatim...' she began. But Hatim had already hung up. Maybe if he had known that the boys and Rich would not be joining them he would have let her off the hook.

The dark lines under her eyes would probably look like she had enjoyed a night of fun, Maya decided, as she applied blue eyeliner over the concealer she had rubbed under her lower lids. A pale pink smile for today.

A white shape could be seen on the other side of the glass panes of the front door.

'Bye, boys!' she called up the stairs. 'Sure you don't want to come?'

But there was no reply.

'I brought us some cake!' she said cheerily, collecting the Tupperware box Annie had packed for her from the hall table.

'*Shukran*, Maya,' said Hatim. 'Thank you.'

As soon as she was settled beside Hatim in the front of his brand new Range Rover Vogue, her mobile rang again. She reached down to her bag on the floor in front of her and pressed a button. Mick

Sure, you can't make it today? Mx
Sorry, no. Mx

And she was sorry. However charming Hatim seemed to be, and however chivalrous, the thought of a day on her own with him, far from home, made her uneasy.

She wondered what Avril would do in such a situation. She was bound to see the funny side. Jan would have been more serious about things. She'd have come up with a practical solution, found a way to keep everyone happy. As for her new friends, Barb, Elske, Liv, and Suchanatta, what would they do? Elske would be brutally honest and tell Hatim she didn't want to go. Barb would never find a 'window' for the trip. Liv would simply shrug her shoulders and get on with it calmly. Sue? Well, she'd probably go along anyway and have a great day. What was she, Maya, going to do?

She settled back in her seat and looked at the area she now knew so well. The spike of the slow-growing spindly Burj Tower seemed to be permanently in sight. Her mobile rang again. It was Barb, at a bit of a loose end and wondering if she would like to meet for coffee. She knew it was late notice and a bit of a long shot an' all – but Maya had a suggestion that was much more exciting than coffee. Thank you Barb! And soon she and Hatim pulled into the car park at Park 'n' Shop and Barb stepped out of her car and into theirs and sat herself down on the back seat.

'Pleased to meet you, Hatim,' she said offering him her hand between the two front seats.

'Hey girlfriend!' she said to Maya, laying her hand on her shoulder.

Maya turned and smiled. Christ, that poor woman looked like death warmed up.

'How are you?' asked Maya, and she meant it. She turned back and continued to look at her friend through the large wing mirror.

'Hey ho, you know, so so.' Barb put on her dark glasses.

'That bad?'

'Uhuh. But you know me, we battle on. We battle on. People to see. Places to go. Yadda yadda.'

'Not at Bible study today, Barb?' Maya asked.

'The Lord knows my country needs our prayers, but no, I couldn't face it today.' Barb took her lipstick and a small mirror out of her handbag and reapplied her bright pink smile.

'How many times have you visited our beautiful desert, Barb?' asked Hatim.

'I am embarrassed to admit, Hatim, that this is my first time!' she giggled coyly.

'But you've been here ages. You've seen lots of the other cities though, haven't you?' Maya chipped in supportively.

'Nope.' Barb put her makeup bag away. 'Bill's too busy to take me and Brandon would rather see his landscapes on the Discovery channel. I never see the countries I live in.'

'Then, today, you are in luck!' said Hatim, settling back in his seat and moving the dial on the iPod he had plumbed into the car stereo until he had found some jazz.

Great taste, thought Maya.

Was that jazz, he was playing? She used to love that, but Bill preferred Country and Western so she didn't get to listen to it much these days. She was beginning to be glad she succumbed to Maya's persuasiveness again. Spontaneity could have an upside after all, not like the time she'd agreed to go to Maya's for that terrible dinner! Barb had been at such a loose end too. Couldn't face being alone today after the night she'd had. She'd been a bit down lately and needed a boost that would last a little longer than a cup of coffee or a shot of Bacardi. And now here she was, sitting in the back of a car with blacked-out windows and that belonged to a local. At least no one would see her.

'You like Miles Davies, Barb?' asked Hatim.

'Sure,' she said.

She knew she looked a little pale today. Not her normal self. She felt like a kid here in the back, but in a funny kind of way it was liberating and they all talked easily.

'Say, Maya. How's the job going?'

'Great. Thanks. Very exciting.' Maya smiled at her quickly then looked back out of the window.

'Got enough stalls for your fundraiser lined up?'

'Guess so. Thanks.'

'Hey, did you take a look at Suchanatta's scarves?' she asked. 'She taken a stand?'

Maya turned round slightly so she could face her. 'Yes, she's really busy, apparently. And they're selling like hotcakes.'

'Maybe you should take a stall at The Twist sometime? You know, sell that jelly you've been talking about.'

'Jelly?'

'Oh, you mean jam! Oh, I've not even started making it yet. Too busy.'

'And Elske's Christmas cards are going down a storm, she tells me. I hear that the Ministry of Tourism want her to do some posters for them too. Did you know?' Barb loved to be the first to hear things.

'Yes, she has a stand too.'

All this time Barb kept leaning closer, but Maya just kept on staring out of the window.

'You decided about the PR role yet? For The Twist?' Barb just could not keep the question in any longer.

'Um.' She looked at Hatim. 'I'm not sure I'll have time, Barb.'

'Oh.'

'I work four days for The Sunshine Centre, you see. Hatim's getting me a work permit and so I may have to do more work for him too, so I will be very busy.'

'That's nice,' she said, but it wasn't nice at all. She had been relying on Maya.

Hatim turned his head to the right and looked at Maya and smiled. 'But I told you not to worry about that, didn't I?'

Barb wondered whether that meant that she still had a chance. 'Is everything okay? You know, at home?' Often all it took was an acknowledgement that you were taking an interest in their problems to encourage people to change their minds. 'You know, our PR is pretty straightforward. Won't take too much time. Tell you what, I'll let you think about it for a couple more days.' Not that she could afford to leave this hanging much longer.

'Well, there's been quite a lot of stuff going on lately and I have to admit that I haven't given the position much thought.'

'Stuff?'

'Just stuff. You don't want to know, believe me.'

But she did want to know. If Hatim had not been in the car, she was sure to have been able to weedle it out of her. Was it Rich? He had been a bit cool at that dinner party.

'I should have let you know sooner, but I've a lot on my mind.' Through the crack between the seats, Barb watched Maya pluck at her skirt then look at her in the rearview mirror, probably to check she was listening. She was listening, all right.

'I'm sorry to hear that.' Come on girl, come on. Darn that man, this was fascinating.

'Our tenants are moving out, leaving us in a financial hole.'

'Oh dear.' Barb laid her hand on Maya's shoulder as reassuringly as she could. And?

'And Annie wants to earn more money.'

'Bad timing.'

'Too right.'

And?

'Look,' broke in Hatim, pulling over to the side of the road. 'These are our most magnificent dunes. See how red it is? They call that really big mountain of sand Big Red.'

Maya and Barb looked out of the windows obediently.

'Stunning,' said Maya. 'The sand looks all rumpled, like a puppy's wrinkled fur.' She could be very poetic. 'And not a tree in sight. Shame they have fenced it off. Hey, are they charging people to drive up it?'

'Yes, Maya. It is terrible what is happening to my country. They turn everything into gold. No, we are not going to drive there. I know a better place. A special place. Nice and quiet.'

'Neat,' said Barb, settling back for an adventure.

Behind the next petrol station Hatim found a track that no one would have spotted unless they had been looking. He turned hard right onto a rocky track, stopped the car and opened the door.

'If we are going to drive in that beautiful sand we need to let down the tires first. They need to be really soft. Don't worry, okay?'

'You go right ahead,' Barb said. What a lovely chap he was. He clearly adored his country and loved showing it off to folk. There he was grinning up through the windows at them. 'Dune-bashing' was not something she had been exactly bursting to do but hey, maybe it was time she let her hair down?

In moments they were off, up to the top of Big Red like a rat up a drainpipe. Barb bashed her head on the roof.

'Ow!'

Hatim laughed. 'Hold the bars!' he said. He turned sideways and reached his left hand behind him, looping his fingers over the handle above one of the rear windows. Barb would have preferred him to keep both hands on the wheel. Men could be all bravado.

Perched at the top of the dune, they looked at the sandscape below them. It was stunning, Maya was right.

'My camera!' exclaimed Maya.

'You can get out of the car, if you want,' suggested Hatim.

Maya looked incredulous.

'Go on, it's safe.'

Maya got her camera and opened the door. 'Don't leave me,' she said and left her shoes behind as she walked gingerly away in the deep sand.

'Shall I pretend to leave?' asked Hatim, grinning at Barb.

'No. You can't,' she said, but couldn't help a little giggle leaving her lips.

'Oh yes, I can!' he said and they were off. Barb didn't know when she had last gone so fast down a hill. She didn't go on rides at the funfair. She usually hated speed with a passion, but as they bumped down and down the steep dune, she found herself whooping with something resembling joy.

They reached the bottom and kept going. Off to the right

and up another smaller dune, where he stopped, again perched at the top. 'Can't stop in the sand,' he said. 'We'd get stuck. Always stop at the top.'

Barb looked out of the window at Maya, who was sliding down the dune towards them on her bottom, holding her camera high in the air with one hand and attempting to keep her skirt covering her legs with the other. Barb was glad she'd worn pants today, for sure. Then, just as Maya was close to them, stumbling through the deep sand, frustration colouring her face in a most unflattering way, Hatim grinned back at Barb again.

'Watch,' he said, and pushed the car into first gear again. He went left, then right, pausing on the top of each dune as he made a circuit and climbed once more to the top of Big Red,

'Mind my hair!' said Barb through a mix of spluttering laughter and shrieks of fear. Each time the car lurched, she was thrown this way and that, her hair tangling more with every move and sticking to her face that was flushed with excitement.

Hatim turned to look at her. She patted her hair into place as best she could. She must look a fright.

'Put your hand on the wheel,' she yelled, buoyed up by the unexpected thrill of the unusual car ride. Jolted into life.

The car passed Maya, close enough to spray her with sand. She raised her hand to cover her eyes. She didn't look pleased. Hatim drove up the nearest, lowest dune and stopped, flinging the door wide open for Maya. His shoulders rose and fell with laughter.

'You ... you,' she growled, spitting sand out of her mouth.

'Thank you, Maya, I haven't laughed so much in years,' laughed Barb. 'Here.' She handed her a Wet Wipe.

'Here,' said Hatim, handing her a bottle of water.

They calmed down while Maya composed herself, then Hatim winked at Barb. 'I'm sorry,' he said, totally insincerely.

'You have passed the test.'

'What test?' Maya spluttered. 'I may not walk on water, but I can walk on sand?'

'The Al Farooq employee test!' he chortled. 'Now you can be sure of your work permit!'

'I think he just wanted to show off!' said Barb.

'Yeah, right,' agreed Maya. 'Well, he passed that test all right.' What had happened to her sense of humour today? She seemed nervous and more than a little distracted.

'OK, I'm sorry,' he said, wiping his forehead with a handkerchief.

'Yeah, right!' Maya took a drink of water.

'But did you like it?' Hatim asked.

'It is beautiful out there. Perfect temperature. Glorious light. You were right about your country.' But her voice was a little flat.

'Now I show you something even more wonderful!' and off they drove, back to the road.

They passed drab, dusty villages with not a crane in sight, no fake grass, no curbs on the sidewalk. No sidewalks. Shacks that said the businesses did 'painting and denting' or offices that offered 'docoment tping'. Maya spotted every one and Barb laughed politely, but she was in a world of her own, still basking in her earlier five minutes of hedonism. On and on they drove as the winter sun rose high in the pale blue sky.

'Now for something really exciting,' said Hatim, swinging the truck between a gap in the buildings, past a dumpster overflowing with rubbish and crawling with cats and onto a dirt road. In fact, it was hardly a road at all, just a load of rocks squished down by years of heavy vehicles. This was really bumpy.

'Hold on!' he laughed. 'Now you get to see my country. The real United Arab Emirates.' He turned to Maya. 'Just like I promised and not in any guide book.'

The track wound around the side of a dried-up river bed they called a wadi. First dune-bashing and now wadi-bashing. Two things Barb had never expected to do. Bill and she preferred hotels to the idea of camping out here in the wilderness. Coolboxes never really kept the drinks cold. The landscape was grey, with touches of silvery, dusty bushes. Tall, pale grasses waved in the breeze of the truck. White goats with swollen udders clambered sideways up and down the steep slopes and stood there, lower jaws moving sideways as they chewed and raised their heads, chewed and stared at them. Unimpressed.

'This is the old village,' explained Hatim as they passed through the flat base of a dip in the landscape. Piles of smaller, neater stones lay in rudimentary circles, topped with dry, blackened sticks, and beside them the roofless, windowless, and often wallless shells of old houses. At the edge, closer to the wadi bed, a cluster of palm trees teetered, their leaves now dead and faded to the same uniform grey. He stopped the car, switched off the engine, and pointed. 'This was their water supply, an oasis, where they would gather and wash their clothes in a clear pool beside those big white stones. Look!' He pointed deep inside the ring of trees.

'It's all dried up, filled with junk. How sad,' said Maya, opening the window beside her. 'Tragic. You can feel the silence. Listen!'

'Gee, I don't know about silence but they sure need a trash can around here,' commented Barb.

'No water, so they moved on,' he said. 'Even the birds.' They climbed up the track and over the brow of the hill. He perched on the top and came to a stop before stretching his right arm out expansively. 'Now look!'

Before them lay a valley filled with rows of green vegetables and clusters of fruit trees.

'Are they limes?' asked Maya.

'And oranges, peaches, papaya,' he said proudly. 'See where they put the new village?'

'Neat!' said Barb, looking at the bright white one-story dwellings that huddled near a bunch of neatly tended palm trees.

'And they have a brand new oasis too!' said Maya. 'I can even see the water glinting there in the middle.' She turned to Hatim. 'You were right. This is magnificent. I'd never have guessed.'

'When the oasis dried up, the government built a new village, laid pipelines of water and electricity, and helped the people to start farming properly.'

'They even have TV and satellite!' exclaimed Barb as Hatim drove them down into the valley.

From closer, the village became even more impressive. Hatim seemed very pleased with himself and drove slowly for the first time so they could really see what was around them. He drew up beside the oasis and a group of children approached the truck, shouldering each other. The girls, dressed in shiny knee length dresses over matching pants, put their hands over their mouths and lowered their eyes as they giggled. The boys, in grubby *dishdashas* that reached their calves, picked up stones and pretended to throw them at the car. All were barefoot. Hatim jumped down from the driver's seat and went around to the trunk where he took out a large plastic bag and went to talk to them. They grabbed the bag delightedly and immediately began picking out their favourite candy. Next the children raced over to the open trunk and struggled to remove the cool box, a wicker hamper, a foldaway picnic table and a blanket and lugged them awkwardly to the middle of the oasis where they arranged them carefully in the shade of a cluster of pink oleander bushes. Hatim crouched down to child height, said something to the kids, and they scuttled off, still laughing behind their hands. He stood up and beckoned Maya and Barb to join him.

'Wine?' he said, taking a chilled bottle of rosé out of the coolbox and unscrewing the cap. Barb and Maya exchanged glances. 'I don't drink, but I thought maybe you would like one.'

'Well, I don't normally drink in the day,' said Barb coyly.

'I'd love one!' said Maya. 'Thank you.'

'Oh, alright then.' Barb gave in. She couldn't have Maya drinking alone.

'Can I do anything?' asked Maya. This was a lovely spot and beat sitting outside Starbucks at the mall. Hatim began to serve them cold cooked chicken, flat Arabic bread, hummus, and salad. 'Great food,' she said. 'My favourite. Rich would love this.' She turned to Barb. 'Don't you wish Bill were here?'

But Barb didn't wish that at all. He'd rather have been inside with some aircon and a stack of ice cubes in a cold Coke, lying full length on the sofa watching a game. The only time he was happy to be outside was on a golf course or at a Disney park. Barb had to admit that, rare as an occasion like this was to her, it felt real good, despite the heat and the flies and the rocky ground beneath her rickety plastic seat. They ate in thoughtful silence. Drinking gave Barb something to do with her hands.

'Thank you for letting me join you,' she said in an attempt to get the conversation going again.

'Welcome. More wine?' he asked.

'Just a small one,' she replied. 'I think I'll move over to that rock by the stream.' She stood up, easing her squashed behind from the teeny square seat.

'Maya?'

'I think I'll pass, actually, Hatim. I'd like to take my camera and wander about a bit. Is that okay?' He nodded. She got up and moved away. Barb leaned against a rock and sipped her wine and, as she relaxed, the trilling of birds and the hiss of cicadas filled the air and she closed her eyes.

'Barb?' Hatim was at her side.

She opened her eyes.

'You seem sad. Why are you sad?'

'Do I?'

'Do you wish your husband was here?'

She shook her head and took a sip of wine. 'Not really. He wouldn't appreciate it.

'I wish my wife was here.' He sighed and took some prayer beads out of his pocket.

Barb looked across at him and saw the sorrow etched across his forehead. 'It must be very difficult for you. Without Maryam,' she said gently, pleased she had remembered her name. She was good at names.

He nodded. 'You know, in our culture, we believe that we should grieve hard and fast and then move on. I know my Maryam will be waiting for me at the gates of heaven. She will be there with our babies.' He tossed his beads up from his palm and caught them again.

'Babies? But I thought…'

'We wanted a child so much and Maryam got pregnant many times, but each one ended in miscarriage. We believe that children grow older in heaven and will be there at the gates, waiting, when we join them.'

'That is a beautiful image, Hatim. But, you still grieve, right?'

Hatim closed his fingers over his beads and looked away into the distance.

'I lost a child too.' There. She'd said it. Liv would be proud of her.

'I'm sorry.' He moved his beads through his fingers, one at a time, as if he were counting them. 'It is hard, yes?'

Barb nodded then dropped her head.

'Your child will be waiting for you too, Barb.' He looked into her face.

Barb looked into his deep brown eyes and smiled, giving a little snort of hopeless derision.

'It is so hard, Hatim.' 'I know.'

Barb flicked stray crumbs onto the warm stone on which they sat.

'Only a parent who has also lost a child can truly understand this type of pain,' he said softly.

Barb took a deep breath. A knot of grief had lodged itself in her gullet. She felt safe in the company of this complete stranger. 'Angelina was just a baby.' Was she making a huge cultural gaff, sharing such intimate truths? Maybe it was the wine, or the fact that she was already way out of her comfort zone that she felt able to release the words that lived in her head and her heart.

'I'm so sorry,' he said. 'When?'

'Seven years ago. I went back to the US for the delivery. She was stillborn. Bill arrived too late. The nurse took a photograph, though. He won't look at it.'

'But you did, Barb. You saw her.' His body may not have been making contact with hers, but he reached out towards her with his eyes and his heart and the effect was as embracing and soothing as a warm hug. She could have sworn she felt his soul move closer to hers.

'I did, Hatim. But Bill can't understand. Won't understand. And I'm left to mourn alone.'

'I think we all feel alone in our grief, though we may not be. Not really. That is why friends and family are so important to us. I don't know what I would have done without my brothers.'

She set her wine glass down on the flat stone beside her and raised her knees and hugged them to her chest. 'Well, I know how much it would have meant to me if I felt that Bill at least understood, that he would hold me in his arms at night and say he missed her too.' She had said too much. That second glass of wine. She felt the colour rise in her cheeks. 'I'm sorry,' she said. She hoped she had not embarrassed him.

He laid down his Sprite and hugged his knees too. He tilted his head closer to hers and she could sense its warmth. 'Every day I ask Allah to help me heal.'

'It is still very soon, Hatim. I still hurt just as much after all these years. Be patient.'

'It is lonely.' He was frighteningly frank. 'Like this.'

'I know.'

Barb looked out towards the mountains. 'What's that?' she asked, pointing to a man who stood on a high rock. He seemed to have something with him.

'He's training his falcon. Watch!' And together they watched the bird fly up into the air and circle high above their heads.

'Wow!'

'We have much to learn from falcons.'

'Really?'

'Really, yes. We need to know what we want in life and then go for it directly. We must be brave and we must be fast or we miss our chances.'

'Gee.'

Barb did not notice Maya approach them.

'Hi there. I see you saw the falconer too. I got some super photos. Did you see those goats skittering down the slope? It was a picture! Do you mind if I get myself some water, I'm parched?'

'Of course,' said Hatim. 'Help yourself.'

Maya walked over to the coolbox and lifted the lid. 'Anyone else? And hey, we forgot my cake. Does anyone want a slice? I can bring it over.'

The magic was broken.

Chapter twenty-seven

Maya hated being late so she ended up arriving outside Mick's hotel embarrassingly early. It had been a relief to know she would meet him during daylight hours. When Barb had called her that morning to see if she fancied meeting for coffee to thank her for such a super day in the desert, Maya had lied, saying she had to drive the boys here, there, and everywhere all day. She had kept her dark glasses on in the taxi. Now she sat on a blue plastic bag she had laid on a grubby bench beneath a dusty acacia tree, just a few hundred yards from the hotel. Sucking mango juice out of a little box with a straw as slowly as she could manage, she looked up and down the creek she had first seen three months or so earlier with Jim. Another Cockney. She'd dressed carefully, in a low-cut pink camisole trimmed with lace beneath a long-sleeved fine linen shirt, white to show off her tan. Round her neck she wore a leather necklace that bore a pink heart-shaped stone that dropped just inside the start of her cleavage. Oh and pretty, beaded platform sandals that showed off her latest pedicure. She crossed her legs and waggled her top foot nervously.

The water sparkled in the early evening sunlight and the shadows shrank to leave little respite from the heat. Looking away from the relentless trading on the banks, she turned her gaze past the stream of cars to the buildings, which seemed today to be less colourful than she had remembered. Pale, beige and coated with a film of sand. Tipping back her head and shielding her eyes from the glare of the sun, she looked upwards through the tiny leaves of the acacia to the clumps of satellite dishes punctuated by the long necks of swaying cranes and found an unexpected pinkness in the sky, drifting slowly into solid blue the higher it rose. She hoped Mick would appreciate the beauty there was to be found here. The juice slid down her throat, thick as milk. Despite the traffic, the dust and the cracking pace of life it was a good life. A very good life. She glanced at her watch. It was time.

She checked her reflection in the mirror of the lift that took her to the tenth floor and nervously reapplied her lipstick, then thought better of it and pressed her lips into the back of her hand. The last thing Mick would want would be to have his face marked with a pink smile when she greeted him. She rubbed the stains from her hands and wiped any residue of clamminess from her palms on the inside of her camisole. She had no idea how he would greet her, but wanted to be prepared. Her heart thumped. The lift pinged and the doors slid aside. She stepped out and made for the cocktail bar called 'Up on the Tenth'. God, she hoped he was there already. The bar was almost empty. A slim man wearing fine linen trousers and a very fashionable – certainly, very expensive – patterned shirt, stood against the bar, his broad back visible. Could that be him? He always had scrubbed up well. One of those people who looked edible both dressed and naked. She watched a hand move to the right to raise a glass of white wine. His soft cotton shirt cuff had been folded back just enough to expose a flash of muscled forearm and a modern gold watch on a lean wrist. Clearly, he still worked out. She approached the bar. He turned. He grinned.

'Maya Winter!' he said, his voice as cracked as his old leather biking jacket. Suave and smooth until he opened his mouth.

She flinched at the use of her married name. 'Mick Mason.' She found herself grinning. Play it cool, Maya, she told herself. Her eyes settled on the open neck of his shirt where the chest hairs she had so loved to nuzzle with her cheek or curl around her fingers crawled up towards his throat. A gold necklace was just visible beneath his collar. He kissed her twice. Once on each cheek and Maya knew she was blushing. He smelled of cigarettes and aftershave.

'What's your poison, darlin'?' he asked as Maya watched him look her up and down, settling ultimately on her cleavage. He dragged his eyes back up to hers and waited for her reply.

'A glass of dry white wine, please?' she asked.

'Sure! I'm on the Polly Foomay, or however you pronounce it. It's very good. You want to join me?'

Maya reached for his glass and took a sip, rubbing her lipstick off the rim with her thumb before she replaced it on the bar. 'Okay.' Being with him made her feel cheeky. Even after a few seconds in his company, she felt as if she had jumped into a time machine and skipped back a couple of decades, back to when she was reckless, carefree, and earned herself the nickname of Minx. She lifted herself up onto a bar stool at his side, twisted her body sideways so she could face him, and crossed her legs. Impressive. So he not only drank wine these days, but knew the good stuff from the bad too. The rest she approved of. Even the cigarettes, if she were honest with herself, because they were part of Mick. They represented the way he managed to inject a bit of naughtiness into everything he did. She picked up a cocktail stick and helped herself to a stuffed olive, sucking it into her mouth. She uncrossed her legs and leaned a little closer to him.

'Want one?' she said, reaching to skewer a second, but Mick turned to take her wine from the waiter and didn't hear her, so she ate it herself and studied his face from the side. His hair was short and had been styled with some kind of gel that cleverly disguised any signs of age.

'Let's make ourselves comfy over there by the window.' Holding a glass in either hand, he inclined his head towards a table for two. 'And you can bring me up to date.'

He asked about her old job at Seasons and her new job with Leila; he asked after her parents, her brother, about Rich, her villa, her cottage in Stamford. Where she'd been on holiday. If she still smoked pot, drank pints, or owned a crash helmet. She didn't. She mirrored his questions, filling in the missing years with details, mostly about Glenda. Though she had no right to the emotion, she felt a little betrayed. Mick had become hugely successful. He got to travel abroad for work now he was doing air conditioning, even had corporate clients overseas. As she heard about the places he had been, she found herself thinking that if she had, perhaps, stayed with Mick, she would have had a similar life, after all.

'What did you tell Glenda, then?'

'Business trip. No trouble and strife allowed.' He winked.

'But you said...?' Maya's jaw dropped.

'I've been thinking about you ever since I found you on the web, Minx. I needed to come and see a business contact over here so I made it happen. I never thought you'd agree to see me if you knew I was alone.'

'That's a dirty trick, Mick.'

'But you have to admit it was sharp of me!'

'Indeed.' She nodded. Of all the things that had attracted Maya to Mick, his brains had never featured on the list.

Mick tapped the side of his nose. 'I told Glen I needed Friday for work and Saturday to buy her a really nice present before I head home Sunday. So I've seen me client and now we have a luvverly day to ourselves. Better still, your old man's away. Perfect!' He rubbed his hands together.

'Well...' Maya began. She checked her body language. Hell, she had 'come on' written on every limb of her body. She had been sitting with her legs slightly apart and her arms pressing her breasts together, making her cleavage look bigger. She had been leaning in too and tossing her hair – that is, when she wasn't twirling it around her fingers. She altered her pose, crossed her legs, leaned back in her seat, and brought the edges of her blouse closer together. 'Actually, Rich gets back tonight.'

'But are you 'appy?' he asked, draining the last of his wine.

'Very,' she said, nodding furiously and thinking that the conversation was turning into a version of The Truth Game and wondering whether it was okay to lie a little too.

'With Rich?' He fixed her with his hazel eyes. 'I've strayed from Glenda, can't tell a lie. Never meant it to happen. One night stand. Nothing serious.'

'Well, I've never had an affair, if that's what you mean.'

'Have you wanted to?'

'No.' Her voice wavered.

'But could you? Would you?' His eyes twinkled.

'I don't think so,' she said, knowing as the words left her

mouth that she very probably could, right now, at this moment. He might be a bit of rough, but he was a sexy bit of rough and her pheromones were on a mission. Maya laughed awkwardly.

'So, you couldn't do it then? Is that what you're getting at?'

'Maybe.' She looked out of the window at the beautiful windtowers of the old town on the other side of the creek. He'd know she meant maybe with him. 'Oh, I don't know.'

'More vino?'

'I'm not sure.'

'Don't tell me you're driving?'

'Well – er...'

Mick's face fell. 'No worries. I drink too much of the stuff myself anyway.'

'Look, I'm sorry,' she said and she was. Very. Her body and her heart longed to stay, to undo the buttons on that crisp shirt one at a time and see if his stomach was as flat and toned as she remembered, but after a glass of wine she could not trust herself to refrain from doing something she might regret. She laid her hand on Mick's and felt the electricity leap up her arm. Then her phone beeped three times and she felt compelled to take a look. It was a message from Rich. 'Excuse me,' she said and turned her back to read the text.

Problem with plane, staying an extra day. Sent from his Blackberry.

'Everything okay?' Mick asked.

Maya nodded and her mouth opened before she had time to keep her impulses in check. 'He's coming back a day late.'

'Which means we now have twenty-four fabulous hours, right? My plane's not til the evening.'

'Not exactly. I have the school run and work tomorrow. Sorry.' She had to admit she was relieved to have an excuse. The atmosphere between them was too dangerous.

'Shame.'

She smiled and held out her hands palms uppermost.

'I've always known that you and me have something special. No one's ever lit my fire quite like you did, little Minx.'

And no one had quite lit her fire like Mick either. But sex wasn't everything, was it?

'I love Rich,' she said.

'Okay. I get it,' he said. 'But we can still go out and you can help me choose Glenda's present, right?'

'Oh yes, we can certainly do that!' she said, taking Mick's offered hand and stepping down from the bar stool.

Maya knew the quick way and led him through the covered alleyways of the old spice *souk*. She loved to look at the sacks of wrinkled dried limes, the hard dark goats' hooves, the bright orange sunflower petals, crumpled chillies, and knobbly, waxy lumps of frankincense. Today she loved them even more, for the way they spilled out of the shops and onto the narrow streets, forcing her to move closer to Mick as they snaked past.

'D'you mind if I buy a few of these?' she asked. 'I'm doing some experimenting in the kitchen and I'd love to try some of these out. You know, for the blog?'

'Ah, the blog! I have a lot to thank it for, so go and fill your boots. Just don't expect me to eat that mouldy looking stuff!' He stood back so she could enter the shop before him and was there waiting for her when she emerged with a thin blue plastic bag filled with clear cellophane packets of potential excitement.

'Whatever turns you on, Minx,' he said.

The streets widened and they passed shops where brightly coloured clothes hung from the open doorways, swaying gently, just like Maya's hips.

'Take a look at them costumes,' he said looking up at the bright orange bodice, skirt, and scarf of a bellydance outfit. 'I've got a mate sells them down Spitalfields. Like hotcakes, they go.'

'I've done a bit of bellydancing, actually. I love it.'

'I bet that husband of yours thinks all his Christmases have come at once when you do the dance of the seven veils for him in the bedroom, eh?' He winked at her.

'Actually, I haven't even bought an outfit. I just do a DVD by a woman called Pushpa.'

But before she had a chance to object, he'd darted into the shop and Maya stood outside nervously, fingering a length of slippery nylon sari material until he reappeared.

'For you, milady.' Like Prince Charming, he swept a low bow, doffed his imaginary feathered cap, and handed her a plastic bag. She peeked inside and saw he'd chosen a scarf in her favourite shade of azure blue. Just like the sea.

They passed through the thick red pillars at the entrance to the gold souk and ducked away from the navy blue night sky, studded with stars. She pointed out the peachy stripes of sunset, the sliver of moon, the minarets; she paused to marvel at the Mullah's song. But Mick was more interested in the jewellery on display that filled every shop window with yards of yellow gold. Pale-shirted, dark-trousered men leaned against the doorways, their nets baited to ensnare any passerby who paused to look at their display.

'Come inside, I give you good price,' they said. 'No problem. What you want?'

But Mick didn't linger. A few shops down he approached a window, asked Maya's opinion on a plain gold necklace with a diamond pendant and when she approved, went in and bought it swiftly. He haggled first, of course.

'Job done!' he said and put his arm around Maya's shoulder to turn her in the opposite direction, back towards the hotel.

'You can't!' she muttered, peeling his arm off her shoulder. Not in public.

'Oopsy,' he said.

Maya was hungry with nerves. She had no clue what plans Mick had for her but delaying the moment of truth was definitely a good idea. 'Can we eat first?'

'First?' he replied softly, leaning into her face as they walked, faster now, back towards the skinny, dark passageways of the spice souk.

'I didn't mean… 'And she hadn't meant what he thought she meant but in her nervousness the wrong words had formed themselves in her mouth. The reality was that now her fantasy had a chance of becoming reality she had never been less sure in her life, further, she realised that she had chosen Rich over Mick all those years ago for a good reason. Deep down she and Mick were different, while she and Rich were always on the same page. Or at least, they used to be. 'Didn't you?' he said, his voice smaller, softer, and sexier than ever. 'Prince Mick has it all under control. His princess will not be disappointed. She will be fed.' And he bowed again.

With her heart hammering, they stepped into the hotel lift up to the top floor. They were alone and he, at last, took her hand and kissed it.

The bed had already been turned back. Beside the window, in an alcove with two chairs, a trolley had been placed and on it, a bottle of champagne on ice beside two silver domes. Mick walked over and lifted the domes away to the side in one swift move. Maya approached and looked down at a wonderful mixture of green asparagus, cucumber sticks, strips of bright red pepper and plump prawns, fanning out in a circle.

'I don't believe it! You clever thing!' She put out her hand towards a cluster of tiny dishes. 'Homemade mayo, by the looks of it!' Mind you, in Mick's hands, his brilliant ideas were usually carefully crafted and part of his seduction routine.

'They could only do Thousand Island and tartar sauce, not the anchovy job. Sorry. I wanted everything to be perfect. Like you.' He kicked off his sandals.

She stepped out of her pretty new shoes. They had been killing her.

Mick pulled out a chair, held out a crisp white napkin and waited for her to sit down. He kissed her softly on the lips and stroked her cheek for a second. 'That was for starters,' he said. 'Now, let's eat.' He picked up a champagne flute and tilted it sideways as he filled her glass, then his, then chinked. Maya suddenly lost her appetite.

'To us!' he said.

But Maya couldn't reply and instead reached for a prawn and began to peel it, starting with its head.

'Peel one for me,' asked Mick, unbuttoning his shirt.

And so she did, as agonisingly slowly as she could. As the champagne's first fizz took effect and she realised she would have to make that glass last or she would find herself forced to take a taxi home.

Leaving his shirt dangling from the arm of the chair, he fetched two pillows from the bed and moved to the floor, making himself comfortable.

'Would you care to join me?' He patted the thick carpet beside him and lay down the second pillow. There was a swirling black tattoo over his left shoulder. She didn't like tattoos, but on Mick this one was rather beautiful, like a delicate vine. The golden hairs that curled across his chest, spread softly as they became smooth and languid, leading down to tuck inside the words Giorgio Armani, which embraced the band of his underpants, his leather belt, his button-fly jeans. She wrenched her eyes from his torso.

'Don't you want to eat?' she said. 'I'm ravenous.' Once she started eating her hunger would return, she knew. She dipped the peeled prawn into the pink dip sprinkled with paprika and handed it to him. 'Here.'

Mick returned to his seat. Maya poured herself a glass of water and they began to eat until not a scrap remained. 'Hey, weren't you going to do a bellydance for me?' Mick asked, wiping his lips on his napkin.

'Oh, I am sorry, I really must be getting back. Babysitter.'

'Am I supposed to buy that, Maya? Oliver is fourteen and anyway you have a maid, right?'

'Well, yes, but, it is school tomorrow. I have to get up at five-thirty. And I have work to go to.' She was feeling increasingly uncomfortable, and, gorgeous as he was, Maya really had not planned on having an affair. She just wanted to feel attractive and have someone listen to her. In truth, she wanted to resurrect that feeling of being twenty again. But not forever, just for a few hours.

'Really. I must.' She stood up. The sound of Seasons in the Sun blasted out of her closed handbag. Was someone looking out for her?

'Guess that'll be the phone!'

'It might be important. What if one of the boys… ?'

She rummaged in her handbag and fished out her mobile phone. 'Hell! It's Rich. And I've ten missed calls and messages. Guess I never heard it over the noise in the souk. Excuse me.' She listened to her voicemail, concern flooding her face.

'And?' He reached for her hand and pulled her to him.

'He's on his way home after all.' She wriggled out of his grasp and held his hand gently.

'Seems we missed our chance, eh, Minx?'

'I'm sorry, Mick.' She reached up to kiss him on the cheek. 'Thank you for a lovely afternoon and a very thoughtful dinner. Oh, and for the outfit. I will think of you when I wear it, promise.'

'Will you?' he looked downcast.

'Say hi to Glenda from me, will you?' She let go of his hand and waved at him quickly before opening the bedroom door and stepping out leaving Mick slumped in the chair.

In the lift Maya read all the messages on her phone. They all said much the same thing.

They can't fix the plane. On my way back with KLM. We need to talk. Sent from my Blackberry.

Chapter twenty-eight

People of Richard's size were not designed to fit in economy seats. His unscheduled return home had, typically, forced him to take whatever was going, and that meant the back row, middle seat, a place where he knew the legroom was less than usual and it was impossible to lower the backrest. With his arms crossed to avoid jabbing his elbows into the Emirati women on either side of him, and his knees higher than his hips, he closed his eyes and begged sleep to come and soon. The last few weeks had been a nightmare of such outrageous events that he wondered if he had been imagining things, if in fact what he was experiencing was the effect of the drugs. But no. He had been trying in vain to contact Maya and his Blackberry had bleeped at last just before the plane was airborne – but his heart had sunk. It had been her again. The woman who was ruining his life, yet he doubted he even knew her real name. She had turned up at his hotel, apparently, and wanted to know why he had checked out. Serve her right, conniving bitch. If he could sleep, then maybe he could forget. He'd tried everything. Threats, ignoring her relentless texts, deleting her emails the moment they arrived, switching his phone to silent when he was home. Hell, he'd become a slave to the computer. He couldn't risk Maya using his Blackberry or seeing his emails. The stress was destroying him, piece by piece. It robbed him of any pleasure he might have been able to have when he was with his family. It made him live a constant lie. Put him on permanent tenterhooks. Made him ratty with the people he cared for most of all, and what was worse, he couldn't even bring himself to make love to his wife. The thought of what he'd done – if, in fact, he actually had – was eating him alive.

He became aware of an excruciating pain across his shoulders, as if he'd spent a day carrying sacks of rubble. He looked down at his hands, to find he'd balled them into fists. His teeth ached from grinding them in his sleep. This had to stop. Maybe if he told Maya the awful truth, he might find a way to feel just a little better about things. She was always the one with the good ideas. Though God knew this was not a subject he wanted to discuss with her. Not after the way he'd been behaving. He pushed his hands through his hair and straightened his back, moving his lower jaw left and right to try to ease the pain. The lady to his right groaned and moved in her sleep. At least he thought she was asleep; it was hard to tell when she had her black headscarf over her face.

'Sorry,' he whispered. These seats really were impossible. It was a travesty that the airlines charged the same price for them, particularly on a night flight. If Maya had been here, he would have been able to lift the armrest, put his arm around her, and be comforted by the warmth of her head on his chest. He'd breathe in the scent of her hair and drop his face into it. He longed to be safe.

Moving to Dubai was supposed to have been the culmination of their dreams. And here they were, three months in, and they were supposed to be living their dreams. That was a joke! They had a house that was large enough to be tidy for a change. He had the cars he'd longed for, petrol was cheap, and he could afford to buy the boys everything they wanted. Maya had help in the home and he had to admit that he was pretty fond of Annie, though he still preferred Maya's cooking.

He could sail with the boys, bond with them, talk matey talk, and teach them about knots and jibs and mainsails. And then there was the sun. The endless sun. He should have been able to afford for Maya to take it easy for a while. She'd worked her socks off for five years in Seasons and taken the pressure off him financially. She deserved a break, though he knew he'd never managed to explain that to her and that she reckoned he was only interested in her earning potential. It always came out wrong. He tried to say the right things. Women's rhetoric was a problem. He had to read between the lines, know when he was supposed to read her mind. He was crap at that. Always putting his clumping great foot in it. And since Orchid had wrecked everything, he'd got even worse. Countless times he'd wanted to say one thing and another came out of his mouth. And then he'd watch Maya flinch, turn her back and walk away, her shoulders a little lower than before.

He loved Maya so much. He knew how hard she had tried to help them all settle in and how hard she'd worked on sorting herself out, pulling herself together despite feeling lonely. She must have been missing Jan and Av and her mates back home desperately, and yet she had grabbed the chance to make new friends with both hands. She'd got out there, probably made an effort to be nice to people she wouldn't normally have met, people like Elske, Suchanatta, and that Barb woman with the sulky teenager. He should have made more of an effort that night. But he'd just got back from the worst trip to Bangkok in his life. Layover? It had just about laid waste to his life as he had known it. What should have been the best time in their lives was being demolished by a malicious little Thai hooker. It wasn't fair on him and it certainly wasn't fair on Maya and the boys.

'Excuse me, sir,' said the air stewardess, leaning across Rich's row to open the blind. She looked as tired as he felt. 'We're landing shortly.' She was undoubtedly Thai and looked exquisite in her purple suit. The colour of fucking orchids. He closed his eyes and dug blunt fingers into his damp palms. He'd bitten his nails for the first time in years.

Chapter twenty-nine

The house was in darkness when Maya drew up outside the villa. The air felt heavy, like an impending storm. A veil of clouds dragged thin fingers across the moon. There were no stars now. She hoped she'd beaten Rich home, it would save any explanations, not that she had done anything to be guilty about. But the moment she spotted his car in the garage she was engulfed in remorse. She may as well have had 'unfaithful' tattooed on her forehead. If she were honest, her journey towards adultery had begun the moment she had happily become Minx again. Guilt coursed through her veins like hot wax, settling there, solidifying, threatening to stay as a permanent reminder like a melted candle on a carpet.

When she entered the bedroom, the light from the landing sliced through the darkness. There was her husband, slumped in the corner of the room, half-dressed. His hands were clasped around his knees, shirt unbuttoned, socks kicked to the corner and trousers sunk to his ankles.

'Rich?' she asked, unsure whether this broken man really was the man she married.

He looked towards her, but not at her. His eyes looked dull, blank, bloodshot. His hair was lank and lifeless and his cheeks speckled with the stubble of someone who had not shaved for two days. Beside him were several sheets of printed paper; they looked like emails. 'Where were you?' he asked. His voice was weak.

'With Barb, she had a crisis, I'm sorry, I turned my phone off because I didn't want to disturb her' she lied, glad she had at least managed to come up with a plausible excuse during the long ride home.

He looked blankly towards the white marble floor.

She looked down at her own clothes and noticed orange smears on her camisole and skirt, evidence of her illicit meal in a hotel bedroom with a married man. The emails by his side were more evidence of her infidelity. It wasn't rocket science. Anyone could have guessed her password on the computer. He must've found her Facebook messages and emails to Mick. Now she would have to explain herself. For once in her life, Maya had no solution at the ready. No idea how to justify what she'd said and what it must be blatantly obvious she'd done. Rich had known full well that Mick was in town. He could have put two and two together. Fuck. Fuck. Double Fuck. What was she to do? More lies? He could tell when she was lying. She quickly took off her camisole and skirt to hide the evidence and stood there in her bra and knickers for a moment while she reached under the pillow for her nightie.

'Don't,' he said.

She sank to the floor beside him and reached out to touch his rough cheek. The air-conditioning made the floor icy cold.

'I'm so sorry,' she whispered.

He didn't move or look up.

'Rich?'

'Don't be? Barb couldn't help having a crisis.'

So, he'd believed her and she was rubbish at lying. He must

be in a state. Now she was really confused. Sitting in the corner of the room looking like a cross between a tramp and something the cat had sicked up was not Rich's normal behaviour, even if he had been drinking. She lifted her hands out to the side in a sign of helpless misunderstanding. 'You are beautiful, you know.' Now he looked at her, though not so much at her semi-naked body, but at her face. 'Really beautiful. More than ever.' He sounded maudlin.

'Have you been drinking?' He certainly looked as if he had.

'Nope.' He shook his head and looked at the floor.

'Thanks.' She shouldn't have doubted the reason for his compliment. It was just that his compliments were so desperately rare.

His eyes stayed staring at the space of white marble between his bare feet. 'You look lovely, Maya. You know?'

Maya had no idea how to respond. She didn't dare point out that he was repeating himself. There was something vulnerable about him. He seemed in pain. 'Can I put my nightie on, please?' she said. 'The aircon, you know?' She rubbed her hands over the goosepimples on her forearms.

'Right. Sorry.' He rubbed his palms across the floor.

An increasing sense of her betrayal grew in Maya as she removed her underwear, put on her nightie and got into bed as if everything were normal.

'Are you coming?'

'We need to talk.'

'Now? I'm too tired to think straight. Can't it wait?'

He continued rubbing his palms on the floor, around and around in circles as if he were polishing it. He meant what he said.

'Look,' she said. 'I…' There was nothing for it, she'd just have to tell the truth, be honest, say she got carried away, and that she was sorry, really sorry and that it was Rich she loved, but he interrupted her before the words she was forming could spill from her lips.

'I've done something terrible,' he said. 'Or at least I think I have.'

Was this conversation about her, or him? What the hell was going on? Her heart started to beat faster.

'I think I was bunged a Roofie.' He flicked a look at her for just a second, then returned to his study of the plain, white floor.

'What the hell's that?'

'Rophenol, Rohypnol. It doesn't matter what it's called – the date-rape drug.'

'What?' Maya thought that only happened to women. 'Oh my God!' She clapped her hand over her mouth.

'You think?' Her voice trembled. How could he not know? Had he been willing? Was that why he was unsure?

'The day before that infernal supper party.'

Words failed her. She let him continue while she absorbed the facts.

'By a manipulative bitch of a Thai girl who calls herself Orchid.' He ran his hands through his hair. 'I met her in a bar. The Lucky Fucking Cowboy.'

'Shit. You mean, where Jim met Sue?'

'It's notorious, apparently. Anyway, she picked me up, I suppose you could say. Came to chat while I drank an overpriced Singha with Nico. We only went along for a laugh. Bought a second obscenely-priced beer and then Elske called, some crisis with Hanneke being distraught because she had come

314

fourth in a test, and before I knew it I was on my own with a strange hand running up and down my thigh.' He paused.

Maya's pulse was racing. She was both disgusted and furious. Shocked and surprised. Half of her wanted to join him there on the floor and cradle him in her arms and half of her was dumbstruck, numb.

'Anyway, this girl, Orchid, she said her name was, but I know that was more of a kind of stage name, asked if she could have Nico's beer, and of course, I could hardly say no, then she moved her hand towards my crotch and looked into my eyes, told me I was handsome. All bollocks. All patter. I'm not that stupid.' He paused and looked at Maya for a moment. 'I've never been unfaithful, Maya. Never.'

She had always known he was loyal to the core. Never doubted him. Not really. 'I know,' she said.

He looked back at the floor. 'I panicked a bit, said I was hungry and needed to go and eat and before I knew it I had agreed to go with her to some divey 'greasy spoon' that she said belonged to her uncle or something and did a really good Nasi Goreng. I hadn't a leg to stand on, I tell you. Then, quite suddenly, I hadn't.'

This was not happening to them, surely? The whole story got more and more surreal. It was as if this story didn't concern her husband, it was some sordid story she had read about in the papers.

'She'd put something in my drink. She must have done, because I'd only had two beers and suddenly I was legless. I mean blotto, completely rat-arsed. I couldn't string a sensible sentence together. Calling for a taxi or yelling for help was way out of my league. The next thing I knew a Thai bloke with a bald head, big biceps, and a bunch of gold bracelets was closing a car door on me and folding me into a taxi. His grip on my arm was like a vice.'

'Christ almighty!' Maya's heart did a nosedive towards the pit of her stomach. 'That mark on your arm!'

'It gets worse. The last words he said to me before closing the taxi door, were "contact the police and you will be sorry, okay?" and his dark eyes drilled into mine.'

'Oh my God!'

'I got to the hotel somehow and managed to come round a bit on the way. I found my wallet was empty of all my cash and cards. Even the photographs of you and the boys.'

'What?' Her heart flipped. What would they want with their photos?

'Anyway, I cancelled the cards right away. I'd nothing to pay for the ride. I had to beg the hotel to add it to my bill. She'd also taken out all my business cards. Left only my driving licence.'

'How much did she take?'

'Enough to make me fucking furious.'

'So that's why… ' Another penny dropped in Maya's mind.

'Then, the next morning I started to get these calls, tons of them, from Orchid, claiming I'd raped her.'

'So that's why she took your card. To get your number!'

'I don't need you to be Miss Marple, Maya. Just let me get on with the story, okay? It's bad enough as it is.'

'Sorry, she claimed you had raped her. How?' Maya was no longer sleepy.

'Yeah, well, there was no way I had raped her. It turns out, it was she who had raped me of course. Drugged me and raped me. But I had to believe her. I had no memory of what had happened.'

'But? Didn't you, er, couldn't you tell?' Maya was suspicious.

'Well, apparently I did. The drugs don't affect men that way it seems. Evidently, she had the whole thing planned.' He still sat in the floor in the same position, his hands now clutching at his skull in an attempt to remember. He groaned.

'It could all be a lie, though, couldn't it? And anyway, even if she hadn't raped you, you were so drugged up you wouldn't know.'

'I'm just telling you what happened.'

Maya sat upright in bed and folded her arms. 'What you think happened, right? What she told you happened? She's having you on. So, let me guess, she's blackmailing you, is she? Surprise surprise. Says she'll tell your wife and your employers.'

Rich nodded.

'We must go to the police, Rich. Do you have any proof?'

He raised the papers at his side. 'She's emailing me. Got that address from my card, too. I'm only glad my card doesn't have our home address on it. She's got photos, apparently.'

'Of what?'

'Dirty photos,' he said softly, shaking his head incredulously.

'Have you seen them?'

'Some. They're very grainy. Could be any white bloke.'

'Then it can't be proved.'

'Oh, but it can. She says in the latest email that she's pregnant and that she's having the baby and that she'll do a DNA test to prove I'm the father.'

That bitch was a chancer but surely she didn't think they were going to fall for that one? 'She's just having you on, surely?' But Maya was beginning to believe it too.

'How do I know it's not mine? It could be.'

'But there again it may not.'

He waved the sheets of paper again. 'If she had just wanted money for an abortion it would have been bearable. But she says she wants to keep the baby. She's found an apartment.'

'Hoo bloody ray, now that's a relief.' Maya clenched her fists.

'She just wants me to pay for the upkeep of my child.'

'Rubbish, Rich. She's a crook. She probably does it to all the men. The baby could be anyone's. She may not even be pregnant! Hell, you may not even have had sex with her! But if you did, had you thought about AIDS?'

He turned towards her again and looked at her with big scared eyes. 'Only like all the bloody time, Maya. God, I am so so so sorry. I don't know what to do. It's all such a mess.'

'We can go to the police, like I said.' Maya knew she didn't sound hopeful. AIDS was a real possibility. No wonder sex had been the last thing on his mind lately.

'Then I get tried for rape. Besides, the Thai mafia would probably slaughter me before I got to court. I'd lose my job…' 'Rich hit at his forehead with the heel of his hand. 'Aaaggh! Help me Maya. I don't know what to do.' He reached out towards her, searching for her hand to hold and Maya took it willingly.

'Okay, so you change your mobile number, change your email address, and stop staying at that hotel. Ask to be taken off that route. You could disappear, you know.'

'She may be uneducated but she's damn clever. Her English is good too. The only way I can escape is to leave my job. To disappear, really disappear.'

Maya didn't want to leave Dubai. She had to find a solution. Swilling around inside her mind, in between that tart's cunning and the unfairness of his appalling experience the reality of the financial impact of all this came to the surface, but she pushed it back. Money was not the issue here. Rich needed her help. She regretted every sordid second she had just spent with Mick that evening. She regretted every fantasy she had had during the last few weeks and felt guilty as hell that she had doubted her lovely, kind, innocent, husband. If anyone was guilty round here it was Maya. She had known exactly what she was doing exchanging emails and text messages and flirting shamelessly over glasses of wine with her old lover.

'Maybe Jim will have an idea. Pull strings?'

Rich stared at her. 'I can't tell him. I can't tell anyone. I only told you because I couldn't bear the strain of it another second. You're my best friend, Maya, I had to tell you. I'm sorry I had to, but Jim? Never!' He went back to rubbing circles on the floor.

'I'm sure he'd understand. Come on, come to bed. It looks like you haven't slept in days.'

'Weeks.'

'Talk to Jim, yeah?'

But Rich just shook his head, slid his slumped back up the wall and lurched onto the bed, where he shoved his heavy body under the covers, still wearing his shirt. He turned on his side, facing the wall and instinctively Maya curled her body against his back in a spoon. She'd think of something.

Chapter thirty

With the fundraiser a few weeks away, Maya had to make a start on her recipe for Sunshine Soup. Inventing a recipe was like meditation to her and boy she needed a break from mental turmoil. She'd roast tomatoes and peppers and use chilli, garlic and onions to give it a zing. But what else? And in what quantities? But even culinary creation could not stop her thoughts from muscling in. She knew she'd taken the coward's way out, ignoring Mick's texts and calls and avoiding the computer in case he had emailed her but she could not justify spending one more minute thinking about it, not when Rich needed her. She had just reached into the basket for onions and started to peel back their skins when Rich came in.

'Hi, love. I didn't think you needed any more things to cry about!' He stood behind her and put his chin on her shoulder.

Maya sniffed. 'It's the onions. I'm making Sunshine Soup.'

'Now that sounds just like something the doctor ordered! Will it be ready for lunch?'

'Should be. I thought you were off playing golf with Jim this morning?'

'Can't face it.' He reached for a tissue and handed it to her. 'You're being amazing over this Orchid business. I'm surprised you're not scratching my eyes out.'

Maya waved away the tissue. 'Let he who is without sin cast the first stone,' she whispered and turned on the cold tap, holding her fingers under the water. 'This works better,' she said, drying her hands. 'I trust you, Rich. I know you. Even when you were at your grumpiest and lousiest it never crossed my mind that it could have been another woman. Well, not seriously.'

He took a knife out of the drawer and started to peel an onion.

'So. Have you had one of your brilliant ideas yet? On how to get rid of the scheming bitch and save our financial skins and my job?'

'Not yet, but I'm sure I will.' She raised her hand to his cheek. 'You don't need to help me, you know?'

'I want to. Circles, semi-circles or chopped?'

'Chopped, please.'

'Are you going to ask Annie to make it for the centre? I expect soup is something she could make standing on her head. After you have devised a scintillating recipe, that is.'

She turned to face him, aghast. 'But you were dead against her working on our time before.'

He shot a self-mocking breath from his nostrils. 'That was just me panicking about all the money going down a Bangkok drain and hadn't the guts to tell you about it.'

'Really?'

'I don't even mind if she uses our kitchen. Or our electricity. As Jim said, we don't pay the bills anyway. In fact, if she can make that damn chutney for us it would be a blessing. It stinks the place down.'

'You're sure?'

'I'm sure.'

'So you won't mind if I ask her to make the chutney for me this lunchtime? I've got 40 jars to make and with that, the soup and the jam I'm up against it.'

'If it means I can have you all to myself then she most certainly can!' He turned and laid his hand on her cheek. 'It's been a long time, Maya.'

'Only if you wash your hands first – you stink of onions!'

'And you don't?'

'Touché!'

Maya wiped her hands on her apron and paused while her heart missed a beat.

'I'll wear a condom,' he said quietly. Maya smiled bravely. 'Let me just show her what to do then and I'm all yours.' And she ran down the stairs two at a time to fetch Annie. If she agreed to take over the chutney she could give her a percentage of the profits towards her daughter's dowry.

Chapter thirty-one

'Hi, honey. I'm home!' Bill called out, the front door crashing shut behind him and making the whole villa rattle.

'Oh hello,' Barb responded, mostly to herself.

'Who's on for a trip to Taco Bell? The Schneider family is celebrating!' he bellowed, bursting into the sitting room, rubbing his hands together. 'Hey. Where's the big guy?'

'With Kyle, remember?' Barb smiled up her husband and pushed the lever on her chair so that she could lie a little flatter, further away from him. 'Drink?'

'Too right. As we're celebrating... Merry!' he yelled towards the kitchen, just knowing she would be lurking there, waiting. 'Get us some Veuve Cliquot out the chiller and two glasses, please?'

'Yes, boss,' she called out and moments later an opened bottle and two glasses, a dish of olives and another of peanuts, had been laid before them on a silver tray.

'Thank you, Merry,' said Barb, her heart hammering away. What on God's earth were they celebrating? Usually, this behaviour meant one of two things: money or move.

Bill poured the drinks a little too fast and a cascade of fizz whooshed over the side, puddling on Barb's favourite tray. 'Bill?'

'Sorry, hun.' He took a gold-edged cream napkin from the silver box that was kept under the coffee table and mopped the spill. 'Guess, I must be excited.'

She knew what was coming next. She could read him like a book. Usually, at moments like these her mouth would go a little dry while her palms became a little damp and her heart sank. But at moments like these, Barb would always have ensured her eyes were bright and her smile wide. This time, her usual composure was less forthcoming.

'You got some money back from Lehmann?' she tried.

'Nope. But money is kinda involved.' He topped up their glasses and handed one to his wife, inclined his head and his glass to hers. 'Cheers!'

'Cheers.' Unlike the champagne, her voice was flat.

'To us. The three of us!' he chimed.

She sipped. 'You got a raise?'

'Yeah. And…'

'You got a promotion?' Please God let this be all he was about to announce.

'Yeah. And…'

Barb stared at the teeny bubbles dancing in her slender crystal glass. She watched them chase each other round in circles, never quite getting anywhere. She couldn't bring herself to say the words that now screamed silently in her head. 'No, darlin'. You say.' She sipped again.

Bill shuffled in his leather chair. 'Whaddaya think about going to…'

Oh my good Lord, the suspense was killing her. And not a good kind of suspense. More like a criminal would feel in court as he awaited the judge's verdict. Get on with it, Bill. She wanted to put her hands over her ears but instead, she set down her glass on the neat little wooden drinks' rest on the arm of her chair, laid her hands on her knees and waited.

'The Sultanate of Oman!'

'Oman?' she squeaked. Please don't make it down south in Salalah – that was the back of holy beyond.

'They're making me country manager. So that means a way bigger pay check, the biggest house on the beach, a brand new car and a promotion. Gee, I can't believe my luck, can you?'

Barb cleared her throat. 'Guess you deserve it, honey.'

'And I get to travel all over. Australia, England, Paris.' He paused, looking a little concerned for a moment. 'And Houston.'

'Where exactly are we going to live?'

'Muscat no less. Just imagine, honey. There are the coolest hotels, beautiful beaches and lots of new shopping malls. You'll love it, I promise. Good school for Brandon and all.' He put his arm round her shoulder and squeezed. 'Shame the boy's not home, we coulda gone out for enchiladas to celebrate. Say, how about you and me go out instead? Where d'you fancy going? Just name your place!'

'Actually, I don't much feel like going out.' Her mind was whirling. What about The Twist? What about Book Club? What about Brandon's teams and his friends? Now he was almost fourteen his mates were really important. Moving was always a wrench, but this time, this time, things were different. She was different. You know, if Bill had come home and said this just a month earlier, she'd have been okay. Not overjoyed exactly, but okay.

'You don't feel like going out? Hey, girl, what's got into you? You don't need to worry about Merry. I guess we could take her with us – not to the restaurant, to Muscat...' he chuckled. 'It's only four hours away by road you know.'

Barb stopped listening. In her mind she was back in Amarillo, twenty-five years earlier, paintbrush in hand, mentally calculating whether that meant her husband could commute instead and she and Brandon could stay behind. Tears pricked at the back of her throat.

'It's not Merry.' Hell, she was not going to cry was she? She reached for a napkin and crushed it in her hand, ready to dab at the corner of her eyes should the dam burst.

'Is it your friends? Hey, they can all come and visit? You can come back and visit? Like I said, it's only a short drive away. Just a hop, skip and a jump on an airplane.' He stood up. 'Guess, I might just go and take a shower. Come back when you've decided where we'll go eat. I thought we could try that new pizza place in the mall.'

He wasn't listening to her. He never listened to her. Barb lifted her glass to her lips and took a large mouthful that made her splutter when the bubbles went up her nose. She never had really liked champagne. What was happening to her? Could she, would she, stand up to her husband? Did she have the right to say no to a posting? Would he lose his job altogether if he declined? These were tough times. People were losing their jobs left, right and centre. Nobody dared to rock the boat. The company'd never agree to paying for two houses so she could stay in Dubai, so why should Bill? Anyway, what would happen to her visa if she stayed behind? If Bill were not here to sponsor her residence permit, how could she stay? She gritted her teeth and frowned. Was there really no alternative? Those darned golden handcuffs seemed to apply to her marriage as well as Bill's job.

But what if Hatim... what if? No, she stopped herself. That was just silly. Impossible.

She'd start a new Twist in Muscat. Another Book Club. Do what she always did. Find her feet. Make friends. Join a board. Get involved. She'd get Brandon settled first of course. Wasn't that like what they told you to do on a plane? Fit your child's oxygen mask first? No. They didn't. The adult had to first fit theirs. Since when had Barb done that, put herself first?

She set the half-drunk glass of champagne down on the table and stood up from her chair, took their wedding photograph from the surface of the shelf unit and replaced it with the one of little Angelina from the bottom. Then she helped herself to a handful of peanuts and wiped her salty, greasy hand on her skirt. She knew what she needed right now. A walk on the beach to clear her head and to stand and stare at the sea. Fresh air and nature would do her the power of good. As for the rest, it would come. One step at a time, girl. Ha! That was ironic, tasting her own medicine. She didn't even bother to tell Bill she was going.

Chapter thirty-two

She clicked a button and the boot swung open and she stood for a moment proudly surveying the boxes filled with chutney, jam and marmalade. Rich had made the labels for her and Matthew and his friend Dev had stuck them on the jars for a few dirhams. They had all helped to load the car the previous evening. Leila would be delighted.

'Madam?' said the small boy who had appeared at her elbow, already reaching in to take a box.

'Thank you, Hari. *Shukran*,' she said. And in seconds the young boy had taken over and lugged them into one of the empty rooms.

'I see someone's been busy!' called Leila, flushed from running in late again. 'Sorry. Got held up talking to the *Gulf News*. You made all that in double quick time. That's grand.'

'We made forty of each. D'you think that's about right?' asked Maya.

'Well, we'll find out soon enough,' said Leila. 'I told the interviewer all about the amazing food we were going to have for sale, made by a professional.'

'Our stallholders are popping by today, aren't they, to talk logistics?'

Leila looked at her watch. 'Crikey Moses, they'll be here any second.' She tucked her headscarf closer in round her chin and walked into the courtyard, Maya following. 'I hear you went on Hatim's magical mystery tour at the weekend,' she said. 'And what is that supposed to mean, Mrs Farooq?'

'I hear you had a guest with you and it appears that my brother-in-law found her compelling company.'

Was she being sarcastic? 'Really?'

'Oh yes, it seems he was quite taken with her. Said he'd found someone he could talk to. That she was blown away by the trip. Now that's a shocker, I can tell you. I thought her idea of an adventure was to explore the newest mall.' She leaned against the wall of the courtyard and crossed her arms expectantly.

'Poor Barb, she seemed in need of some cheering up, mind you she didn't exactly love the way her hair flew about when we went dune-bashing. I hadn't realised they had hit it off, though. It must have happened when I was taking pictures.'

'Shame. I was in the mood for a bit of gossip.'

Maya nodded. 'Are we using the *majlis* room for the stalls, then?' The view of the sea over the terrace would be amazing from there.

'I rather thought we could have the stalls here, in the courtyard,' said Leila. 'It's not too hot now, is it?'

'I thought the courtyard should be the place for the kids.'

'Oh yes, I forgot. I'll grab a pen and paper and let's go onto the terrace for a brainstorm with a nice cup of coffee, what do you say?'

'Just what I was going to suggest!'

They didn't hear Liv approach the terrace.

'Hello girls! I didn't know the way in, so I came round the

side, through the garden. That was okay, *ja*?'

'Sure thing, Liv. Won't you sit yourself down?' said Leila. 'You are going to offer some Taster Massages aren't you? That's grand.'

Liv perched, straight-backed on the edge of one of the rough wooden chairs.

'And I thought I could maybe lead a discussion group about the reality of living abroad. It would be a place to share. A safe environment.' She tipped her head on one side prettily, waiting for a response.

Maya loved the idea. Leila clapped her hands together to show her agreement, at which Hari appeared beside her and Leila sent him off for some drinks. When he reappeared, he was followed by Elske, Suchanatta, LaShell, and one extra they had not expected.

'Barb!' said Leila, leaping to her feet.

Barb looked embarrassed. 'I thought you could maybe use some help.'

Maya and Leila exchanged a glance.

'You mean you wanted to check out our office!' said Leila.

And its owner, thought Maya.

'Now would I do a thing like that?' She smiled and looked around her. 'Oh my gosh, this is quite a place! Is it for real?'

'Yes, it's real. Authentic old Dubai,' explained Leila. 'Family renovation.'

'May I look around?'

'You won't find Hatim!' said Leila, trying to conceal her amusement.

Barb blanched. 'I didn't mean...'

'I hear you were quite a hit!' said Maya with a chuckle.

Barb patted her hair. 'I have a way with men, you know,' she said, in a way that showed she knew full well that she didn't, and sat down on the nearest chair.

'You're very welcome, Barb. The more the merrier, I say!' Leila indicated that they should all sit down and lifted the jug of lime soda to pour them all a drink.

'Actually, Maya, I brought you a list of Joni's contacts from last year. I though they might help you with the PR here. No pressure or anything to make you accept the role with us too, you know.' Barb reached for the coffee pot then looked at the rest of the group. 'I'm trying to persuade Maya to join The Twist board? Need the club to be in safe hands.'

Maya smiled at Barb in the way a doting grandparent would watch an adored grandchild gleefully pushing the boundaries. 'You've succeeded, Barb. I'll do it!'

'Will you?' Barb clapped her hands together delightedly.

'Of course I will. I'll be happy to.' Now Rich was back on side Maya had run out of objections. Besides, Barb looked like she needed a boost; her eyes seemed a bit puffy and bloodshot.

Elske strode over to the terrace wall and looked out. 'This is lovely, Leila.'

'It's ace,' said Suchanatta, who then turned to Maya. 'You are so lucky to work here.'

'We-ell,' said Leila grinning. 'We do have two spare rooms available to rent if anyone's interested. With colleagues of a guaranteed quality, of course! We thought you could all put your stalls in the *majlis* room with the windtower, so let's take a look, shall we? You can bring your drinks with you.'

Leila led them back inside. Maya held back to have a private word with Barb.

'So?'

'So, what?'

'You and Hatim, eh?'

'He's a nice guy, Maya. We got on well. That's all,' she said, avoiding Maya's eye. 'Now what can I do to help? I don't mind getting my hands dirty.' Yes, she was definitely changing the subject.

'You can help us count, sort and bundle the flyers, if you like?'

'With pleasure.'

If only making everybody happy was that easy. Soon everything was in hand and Barb was issuing instructions as to the prime noticeboards in the city as Elske and LaShell walked off to their cars. Barb did seem a little out of sorts though.

'May I have a word?' Maya said to Suchanatta. 'In private.' The two peeled away into one of the empty rooms. Maya sat down on a box of chutney. Suchanatta did the same.

'What's up?' asked Suchanatta, crossing one slim leg over the other, placing her flyers on the floor and looking at Maya. 'Judging by your face, it seems serious.'

Maya shuffled on her makeshift seat. 'Look, this is going to seem a bit of an odd question, but you know Jim was talking about The Lucky Cowboy?'

'Of course I do. It's where we met. I told you.'

'Rich says he's been there. With Nico.'

'No one can resist Pat Pong!'

'But, do you think it's safe?'

'No way. It's as corrupt as hell! I was one of the lucky ones. Behind the bar.'

'So you were a bar girl? I thought, you had just met him there, you know, because you went out for a drink.'

'Ha! That's a joke. Thai girls don't tend to go to bars in Pat Pong for the lager, you know. All there for one reason. I may have been serving drinks but that didn't mean I was supposed to turn down any, you know, offers. I kept my knickers on as much as I could and was very choosy, I can tell you. But it is expected that all the girls chat up all the customers. And I mean all. Both sexes. Even the married couples! Why, are you worried about him?'

Maya's eyes widened. She nodded. 'Did you get paid well?'

'Salary? No! In tips – yes!' She gave a dirty laugh. 'Why do you want to know? It's not really a career option for a girl like you!'

'So what happened? How did you end up there?' Maya was gathering facts. She never knew what might be helpful. 'I've been thinking about it ever since,' she lied. 'And I'd really like to hear your story.'

'Aren't you too busy today?'

'No, actually. Barb bossing us all about won me a bit of time. Go on.'

'I come from Loei Province, in the north of Thailand. It is very poor, lots of farmers. Most of the girls in Pat Pong come from this area. I was lucky. My father was rich and sent me to a Catholic convent school. The nuns taught me English. But then my mother died, my father remarried, and my stepmother hated me, wouldn't let me stay at that school, wanted all the money for her new baby. I was sixteen years old and one day I ran away. Jumped on a bus to Bangkok.'

'Gosh, how dreadful.'

'Oh, yes. I sat on the kerb at the bus station and cried. I was tired and hungry and frightened.'

'Oh my God. Did a pimp find you?' asked Maya.

Sue shook her head and smiled. 'No, I was lucky again. A hooker found me. I remember she was wearing the most beautiful high red shoes and an expensive black silk skirt. She looked nice. She worked at The Lucky Cowboy.'

'So she got you the job at the bar, then?'

'She found me work doing stuff for the other hookers at first, running errands and things. Let me stay in her room on the floor. Gave me food.'

'You didn't have to be a prostitute then?'

'No. Lucky again. When the bar owner learned I could speak English, he let me work in the bar. And that's where I met my Jim.'

'Lucky Jim!'

'Lucky Suchanatta!' She paused. 'So, is this what you wanted to talk to me about? Somehow I think you are hiding something from your Aunty Sue.'

Maya cleared her throat. 'Well, erm, you see... '

'It's Rich, isn't it? You think he's being unfaithful now he's on that route all the time.' Suchanatta leaned closer to her. 'You wanted the lowdown on the sex clubs.'

'No. I trust him, but Suchanatta – you have to keep this a secret. Something awful has happened and I think you may be the only one who can help.' She told her everything. Every detail. Rich would have been apoplectic if he had known, but Maya knew that if anyone knew how to solve this, it would be someone who understood the scene, the Thai mafia, and the language. Suchanatta sat in silence and listened.

'Blimey, Maya, that's terrible. But I know it happens. You do know she's probably trained by the gang to do this, probably underage as well? Got sold by her family. The lot.'

'No!' This was getting worse.

'Look. She probably isn't pregnant and there's a real chance she never had sex with him either. You do realise that, don't you? Girls like that often string five blokes along, telling them all they're the father of their kids. The money they extort goes back to the gang lords of course. Terrible. Those poor girls.'

Maya nodded, but she hadn't realised that, just hoped like hell. She grabbed Sue's hands in hers and looked into her eyes. 'Please say you can do something. I can't think of any other way. I hate having to ask you such a big favour, but Christ, it's just so awful.' Please God that he never did have sex with her at all. The agony of waiting for the result of his AIDS test coupled with the fact that he may truly have fathered a child was excruciating.

Suchanatta chewed her bottom lip thoughtfully. 'Let me have a think about this. I'll see if I can pull some strings. I still have some contacts. You know what they say about keeping your friends close and your enemies closer!'

'You won't tell Jim, will you?'

'No, you're all right. Not unless things get really sticky. I'll keep it shut.'

Maya flung her arms round Suchanatta. 'Thank you, thank you, oh God, thank you!'

'Tell you what, darlin', if you can get the date Rich met this Orchid I can find out if they have any CCTV footage of the night.'

'Christ, am I glad I talked to you.'

'Even better, I may have to go home again soon to visit the factory. The buggers are trying to overcharge me, but they've got another thing coming, I can tell you! She spat on her palms and wiped them against each other as a sign that this job was as good as done.

Maya burst into tears.

'Leave it out, Maya. Guess you just struck lucky! I like to spread my luck around if I can. My way of saying thanks.'

'You were lucky that girl helped you all those years ago. And I'm so lucky that you are my friend.' Maya was grinning from ear to ear. She put her hands on Sue's shoulders and squeezed.

'I'm telling you, Maya, I owe Malee everything.'

'Malee?' Maya's brow furrowed. 'Your housemaid?'

'Oh yes, Maya, the very same. Malee was the hooker who found me in the bus station.'

'You're kidding me? But I thought she made a lot of money… as a hooker? Why would she want to be a housemaid?'

'Then she married a guy from back home, went back to the north-east, had a couple of kids, and her husband was killed by a truck. Her money soon ran out. I tell you, she thought meeting me was her lucky break. I brought her here with her children. They're grown up now. Have their own jobs. When you need money, I can tell you, pride does not come into it. Doing the best for her children was all that mattered to Malee.'

'Gosh,' said Maya. 'I don't know what to say. But thanks. Thank you so much. You are a gem, Sue.'

'Rubbish! What are mates for?' She made a dismissive tutting noise as she left the room.

Maya stayed where she was, on the box of chutney, thinking. Part of her was itching to tell Rich the good news and part of her dreaded his reaction to her having spilled the beans to someone. She checked her phone for messages.

Missing you, babe. What happened? You haven't explained

and we still have unfinished business, I believe. Or have I been dumped? Mick x

'I guess you have,' she said aloud.

The door opened and in walked Liv.

'Oh!' She looked surprised to find Maya here. 'I was looking for my phone.'

'Let me help!' Maya stood up.

'It's okay, I can see it, here by my chair.' She held it high. 'Don't know what I'd do without this.'

'It's the only way to contact you, isn't it? If you don't mind me saying so, you are rather mysterious. No flyers. No posters and just a business card without your name or even an email address on it. I don't understand.'

Liv shook her head. 'It's impossible. I can't promote my business.' She leaned against the wall.

'Of course you can. You offer great services. I can find some time to help you with flyers, if that's the problem. You don't have a website. And your cards need more detail at the very least. A slogan would help... and an address!'

'I daren't.'

'Don't be silly.' It didn't make sense. In no way could Liv be described as a shrinking violet. She had a personality ten times the size of her tiny frame.

Liv looked around the room, up to the corners, down to the floor, as if sizing up its proportions. 'This would be the most beautiful class room.' She stroked the bare wall with her tiny hands, which fluttered like creamy butterflies against its surface.

'It would. You could put mirrors over there!' Maya could see it now.

'But I can't.'

Maya patted the box of chutney that Suchanatta had just vacated. 'Do you want to tell me what the problem is?'

Liv sat down on the floor in the Lotus position a few inches from the packing case, took a deep breath, and began.

'You promise to keep a secret?'

Maya nodded.

'I'm not registered here, Maya. I have no work permit. I am illegal. I have no rights. I dare not advertise. And now they want everyone to get ID cards by the end of the year, I think my time has run out.'

'Is there nothing you can do? I don't quite understand the rules myself, yet.'

'I'll move on. I've learned to love moving on.' She shook her head sadly.

And now it was Maya's turn to listen to a sorry tale. She heard how Liv had fled her home in Oslo eight years earlier to escape her abusive husband, Knut. How he had beat her and controlled her, consumed with jealousy. He made her run her massage business from their home and installed secret cameras so he could watch her every move, check she was only working with female clients. He had bugged all her phone calls. Never let her go out with her friends. She'd wanted to run away, but had no money. He'd controlled her finances too and even when her clients paid her in cash, he would see the transaction on the tapes later and demand she hand it over. This was not the Liv they all saw in Dubai and Maya was shocked to hear how different life had been for her.

'I was treating an English woman, Ellen, who said I had a special touch. She had a cottage in England that she only used during the school holidays when her family would return home. She said it would be doing her a favour if I looked after the house for her. And so, one time, when she went back for half term, she took me with her in the car on the ferry. I ran away.'

'How did Knut not find all this out then? He had the camera on you?'

'I spoke English. He was too stupid to understand. Too proud to ask someone to translate the tapes.' 'Go on.' Maya was intrigued. 'Anyway, I learned more therapies, ran a cash-only business. I didn't need a visa there, of course, so I was safe. I met a nice guy, who loved me, who let me live my own life, so I left Ellen's cottage and I went to live with him. Then he told me he wanted me to get a divorce and asked me to marry him. I froze with fear. I couldn't do it. Someone was controlling me again. One day, when I was walking on Glastonbury Tor, I met a Turkish tourist called Isil. We had a kind of spiritual connection. She said I could go back with her to Istanbul, so I did.'

'And that's where you learned bellydancing.'

'Sure. Isil introduced me to the expats there, people I could speak English with, and suddenly I had clients again and earned cash again and everything was great again. And then I met this guy... ' Liv stared at the floor. 'And he fell in love with me too.'

'And you ran away again? Here, this time.'

'The moment the guy begged me to stay; I knew I had to leave and was looking for my opportunity. I believe that there is always an opportunity, you just have to pay attention and to notice things.'

Maya nodded. Liv believed in lots of new age stuff.

'Then I met another man. From Dubai this time. He went to the same gym where I was taking bellydance lessons. We got talking, mainly about the weather – it was snowing. He asked me if it made me homesick and I said that if I ever saw a snowflake again it would be too soon. He said it would be warmer in Dubai and that his cousin, Khalid, had a flat that was empty, and so I came here.'

'So how did you end up staying? Without a residence visa, you can't get a work permit. You can't even stay for more than a few months.'

'I was in the supermarket, looking at the noticeboard and saw a lady bending over with her bottom in the air. She was looking in her bag... '

'Don't tell me!' Maya laughed. 'She was putting up flyers.'

'Barb. Yes. And, well, she asked me questions, and then, well, she helped me. Like she does. She's a good woman. She encouraged me to go to The Twist.'

'That sounds like Barb! And then she helped to promote your business?' Of course. That was why Barb was always handing out her card.

'Barb's been terrific. I don't know what I would have done without her.'

'And are you still in that flat?'

'No. You can guess what happened,' she smiled weakly.

'He fell in love with you!'

'Of course, if I had married him I could have stayed, but that wasn't the point. Barb said I could flat-sit for people who were away or who couldn't sell their properties because of the housing crisis. Barb usually found me my next home. Sometimes I found it myself.' She gave Maya a look of wistful irony. 'I've moved so often I've lost count. The moment yet another 'generous guy with an empty flat' fell in love, it was time to hand back the housekeys. It's so stressful. I'm sick of lying.'

'So that's why you don't have an address on your card?'

'And because I don't have a work visa, I have to keep leaving the country and coming back in on a tourist visa.' She sighed. 'All these visa hops cost money. And now they changed the law so I can only stay for a month each time. I think maybe the Universe is trying to tell me something.'

'What a shame. The Sunshine Centre would be perfect for you.'

'I could put up a partition and do treatments over there, by the window.' She waved her arm towards the high window through which light streamed, stamping a long column of sunshine on the rough floor. 'It's gorgeous here, with the sea and everything. Great energy.' She closed her eyes, touched the first finger and thumb of each hand to form a circle and breathed in deeply. 'If only... '

'We can make it happen. I'll ask Hatim to sponsor you.'

The door opened. 'Talk of the devil,' said Maya and Liv opened her eyes.

'*As-salam alaykum*, ladies,' he said. 'It seems you are the last in the building.'

'Hi Hatim.'

'I've come for your passport, Maya. My man will start on your permit tomorrow.'

Maya took her passport out of her handbag, got to her feet and handed it over. Liv began to unfurl her legs.

'I'm sorry. Very rude of me. Hatim, meet Liv. You two need to talk and I need to get off home.' And she walked out of the room to leave them alone. She walked back to the terrace and looked out over the sea. It was calm as glass; impossibly perfect, as if the slightest movement would shatter it. Only four more hours til Rich came home and she could tell him the news.

'You want cup of tea, Madam? I will do,' said Annie, increasingly cheerful by the day.

'Thank you, Annie. Not too much milk.' She stood in the kitchen, leaning back against the counter and watched and waited as her maid prepared it for her. 'Annie. Are you okay?'

'Yes, Madam. Very okay.' Annie took one of Avril's mugs down from the cupboard.

'Not too busy? You know, with the takeaways, the chutney?'

'Oh no, Madam. I am very happy,' and she turned and grinned. 'Thank you, Madam. I like lot of work. Lot of work means lot of money.'

While she still loved the blogging and keeping in touch with Seasons, Maya no longer felt as compelled to keep checking in with the computer. Thankfully, Mick had stopped Facebooking now but today she had an email from Av. She opened it greedily.

Hiya Maya

It was inevitable I suppose. Seasons has got itself in a bit of a pickle. The season of goodwill has turned into the winter of discontent. I'll try to give you the short version. Hold onto your headdress... About a week ago Jan got a call on her mobile from Andy. Only he hadn't called her. It was one of those calls that the phone seems to make accidentally, usually because you are sitting on it. Anyway, she heard him talking to the saintly Danuta. Seems like they were in the car, driving somewhere. Anyway, they were talking about her altering her shifts so she could go with him on his next 'training weekend', only there was no training weekend, just a B&B in Norfolk. You can guess the rest. Danuta has gone, of course, from Seasons. Andy has been kicked out once and for all, presumably taking Darling D with him, so Jan has the house and the kids and – wait for it – all the bills. Of course he's claiming he has no money and can't pay child support. He's even stopped paying the mortgage, which of course is now more than the house is worth. Jan is broke, maxed out on her credit card. She's worried sick. She's facing a 'credit crunch' Christmas that even shopping at Aldi won't be able to solve. I have taken over the reins of course, started making executive decisions, Jan's in no fit state. Profit's down on last year, but I expect that's no surprise to you, so I had to think fast. Deep breath Maya. I've got my mother working in the shop. Just to fill in. Actually, she's quite a hoot and lots of old gentlemen have taken to coming to us to buy two ounces of Cheddar twice a week.

So now we have no one to do the newsletter Danuta started and so we've decided to let it slip. Thank goodness we still have your blog. Jan's made a ton of chutney and mincemeat and we just pray it gets sold. I have to say that Danuta's Sunshine Preserve is going down a storm, damn her! Maybe you should turn your blog recipes into a book? It could make us all some extra cash.

Miss you SO much, Maya. Are you coming back for Christmas? I need a boost.
Av

Oh poor Jan. Poor Avril. If only she were able to go over to England and give them both a hug. It seemed like everyone's lives had become surreal lately. She hated to disappoint Avril, but her immediate family was more important than ever now.

Maya turned to the blog. At least that made a difference, however small. Clever Avril, coming up with that cookbook idea. Leila had always wanted to write, so this could be the answer to several prayers at once.

She put her fingers on the keyboard and waited for inspiration. What was it that Leila had said about food tasting either of home or of homesickness? Here I sit in a land of sunshine and it seems impossible that Christmas is a few weeks away. Sure, there are fairy lights in the palm trees and Jingle Bells playing in the supermarkets but it's not the same. It makes me a bit homesick and longing for food that reminds me of my childhood. When I was little, my mother would make flapjacks for my brother, Phin and me, and to this day, whenever I make or eat them, I am filled with memories of log fires and cups of tea. My mother would always be waiting for me when I got home from school with a cup of tea and a homemade cake or biscuit.

Here is my mother's recipe for flapjack. I have substituted the Golden Syrup for date syrup to give the recipe a modern, Middle Eastern twist. Date syrup can be purchased in Seasons.

She inserted a photograph of the flapjacks she had made on the day of that fateful dinner party and clicked on the Publish icon just as she heard the click of the front door. Rich was home. She walked downstairs to greet him.

'Okay?' she asked.

'Fine.'

'Did you speak to Jim?'

'Not yet. No.'

Maya could not contain herself. 'I spoke to Sue!' She watched Rich blanche. 'But it's okay.'

'Really?'

'Just wait til I tell you this…'

And after she had explained everything she was delighted to add the final layer of icing on the cake. 'Sue leaves for Bangkok tomorrow!'

Chapter thirty-three

Barb waited patiently for Hatim to finish his meeting with Liv and for the last scrunch of car tyres on the gravel to signal that they were now the last two left in the building. The scent of his spicy aftershave told her that he was approaching the terrace where she had been sitting and staring at the sea.

'What do you think?' he asked, his eyes sparkling as if he knew darn well she was blown away by the beauty of the scene.

'Gee,' she said, for once lost for words. 'Real nice.'

'Nice?' He lifted his dark brown eyes to hers.

'Very very nice?' she tried. It was an attempt at humour and it worked. He rocked with laughter.

She felt the warmth of an arm across her lower back and her palms pricked with sweat. They stood there side by side, staring silently out to sea.

It was several minutes before she spoke. 'It's just so perfect,' she said, regretting that it had taken her so long to notice the natural beauty of the city in which she lived. Hoping that it was not now too late. 'I know,' he said. He took her hand, led her to wooden seat with the turquoise cushions, and sat beside her.

She shook her head. 'I'm sorry,' she said, though she was not sure why. Was it because she was over-emotional? Because she was in danger of not being herself? That she could soon be leaving town? Or was she more sorry for herself than for the beautiful man who stood beside her? Whatever it was, it was agony. She felt as though she were teetering on the edge of something that could be either wonderful or disastrous. Something that could change her life, and Bill's, and Brandon's forever. She had no idea what was on Hatim's mind but he had been on hers for days. It had only been a touch on the shoulder, an arm behind her waist to guide her. But was it already a step too far? How she wanted to follow her heart, to listen to her body that was shrieking at her to do something reckless. She was nervous, wondering whether she would be or do what he expected. If he expected anything.

'Drink?' he asked, raising his hands to clap for Hari's attention.

'Yes, please.' She smiled at Hari.

Hatim spoke in Arabic and Hari scuttled off.

'You're welcome,' he said.

Barb smiled nervously and straightened out the skirt of her dress to make sure it covered her knees. The sun now hung like a ball of amber suspended just above the horizon. A ribbon of sunlight stretched towards them, resting gently on the waves that eased towards the shore. Hari returned with a tray of food, covered over with a cloth and a pitcher of what looked like some kind of cocktail accompanied by two glasses filled with ice. He disappeared and returned to light the lanterns along the balustrade, which separated them from the sea. Hatim poured the drinks from the pitcher, taking care to ensure that her glass contained one slice of strawberry, another of orange, and a piece of fresh mint. He used his fingers and then sucked them clean, shrugging his shoulders in apology for his bad manners. He wrapped a white paper serviette around the glass and handed it to her with charm and grace.

'Cheers!' he said, raising his glass and making her laugh. It sounded weird coming from a Muslim. She doubted it would have alcohol in it and for once she was not sure that she wanted alcohol. She needed to keep her wits about her if things went in the wrong direction – and to be sure to remember every second if they didn't. And which was the wrong or the right direction anyway? All she knew was that her heart was thumping so loud she was pretty sure he could hear it.

'Lime soda,' he explained. 'Fresh limes from my farm.'

'Gee,' she said again. 'Cheers!' she said and took a sip. 'Oooh!' she exclaimed as the bubbles went up her nose. She raised the back of her hand to her mouth. Nothing and everything made perfect sense this evening – a rather overweight American woman, sitting here in the candlelight dusk, drinking something that tasted both sweet and sour at the same time, with a tall, slim Arab wearing a long white dress and who had grey in his beard and hazel flecks in his eyes. A man who had just laid his hand on her upper thigh and made her heart do a somersault. Then he reached around, took her drink out of her hand, and laid it on the table, before placing his hand on her shoulder and twisting her around to face him. And that was when he kissed her. Not forcefully and hungrily like Bill used to kiss her, so hard sometimes that it felt like he was biting into an apple. Hatim's lips were soft and yielding, holding hers as gently as you would hold a newborn baby. His hands were light on her shoulders and she could sense his fingers fluttering as if he wanted to keep her there but also wanted her to feel safe to leave at any moment. Barb let out a whimper of pleasure. He pulled away.

'I am sorry,' he said.

'Oh, don't be. It's fine, really.' She brushed imaginary crumbs off her skirt.

'I need time.'

'I know. Really, I do,' she said, and much as she wished things were different, she did actually understand. Grief took a long time to heal. Years.

'You are beautiful, Barb,' he said. Then he gazed at her body, scanning her from top to toe and making her squirm with embarrassment.

'Gee, don't,' she said, placing one hand on her chest and waving him away with the other.

'Why not?' he said. 'Women are beautiful to look at. That is why so many cover themselves, so that only their husband can see their beauty.'

'Oh, no, now I feel naked!' She crossed her legs and arms. 'And I eat too many cookies to be considered beautiful.'

'In Islam we say that our first duty is to our mother, then to our mother, then to our mother. Mothers are to be loved and worshipped. You are a mother, so you are very special.' He turned back to sit upright beside her, facing the table and Barb felt a pang of guilt for refuting something that he genuinely seemed to mean.

'Hatim?' she said, her voice small.

'Yes.'

'What do you want from me?' There she had said it.

'I want to be with you, talk with you, make love with you. One day. Soon perhaps. But now we must eat.' He lifted the cloth off the food to display a silver tray of Arabic mezze; all the kinds of things Maya raved about and that Bill was never keen on. He preferred one large plate with a sensible meal on it, not lots of bitty things you ate with your fingers.

Hatim pushed the platter of mezze closer to her and indicated that she help herself. He reached for a triangle of flatbread, dipped it into the hummus, and then wrapped it round a ball of falafel. That looked like an interesting combination.

'You are so lucky to have this beautiful place.'

'I have a beach house too. On the East Coast. I have a houseboy and cook and car. Lovely garden. Terrace like this. You can stay there when you want. Look at the sea.' He took a bite of his parcel of food. 'You can take your family.'

Boy, this guy was a one off, magnanimous to the last.

When the food was finished and all light drained from the sky, the candles began to flicker, taking their two faces in and out of each other's vision.

'You are like a goddess,' he said. 'Really.'

'Why?' she asked him.

'Because you understand me,' he said, taking his white linen napkin and using it to wipe something from the corner of her mouth.

Barb was suddenly reminded that she had not reapplied her lipstick since she arrived.

'Because you listen. Because you care about everyone. You are a special person, Barb. You do so much for other people. Always other people. You need to be loved too. And you need to love yourself I think.'

'Aw, shucks, come on,' she began coyly. He hardly knew her.

'Leila told me. She says you do so much good work. Maya too. They are pleased you are helping with the fundraiser. Thank you.'

'And you are very kind too. You gave Leila this building

for the Sunshine Centre. You are giving Maya a work visa and now I expect you will help Liv too.'

'Liv has changed her mind.' He shrugged. 'Said she wanted to stay a free spirit.'

'So, what is she going to do? Where will she go?' Barb was intrigued.

'She won't stay here in my country. Not like you,' he said with a twinkle in his eye.

Now was not the time to tell him her terrible news.

Chapter thirty-four

Maya flicked to the CNN website for the umpteenth time that day. There was a siege at Bangkok airport and she knew from Jim that Suchanatta was stuck in it. She was a week late but Maya didn't like to keep pestering him for news. He had his own concerns with the girls due back from school soon, Malee on her annual leave, no one to do his laundry or cook for him in his wife's absence, and tempers frayed at the office thanks to furious stranded passengers and pilots. Apparently Sue was 'going ape' with frustration. So was Maya, who had thrust a fistful of hair into her mouth and was sucking it violently. Rich had endured several sleepless nights waiting for the results of his AIDS test and the results could still take weeks. Every time her phone rang she jumped out of her skin.

'Stop panicking, Maya,' said Leila. 'If Sue can't make the fundraiser, it can't be helped.' She stood up. 'Will I get Hari to bring us a coffee? And then can you get your eyes off the screen long enough to talk about the schedule we need to write. We're running out of time and it needs to be sorted today. Not that I want to nag or anything.' She shoved some of the papers on her desk to one side to make room for her coffee cup.

'Sorry,' replied Maya, who didn't want a coffee at all, but did want to have another go at calling Sue's mobile while Leila was out of the room. 'And yes please to the coffee.' She'd already left two voicemails and a couple of text messages, but it seemed her phone was off or had run out of battery. Leila returned to the room, closely followed by Hari, who silently placed a cup on each desk.

'I got you a Jaffa Cake. You'd better eat it before it melts,' said Leila, opening her notebook and scrabbling around for a pen.

'Thanks. Like I said, sorry.' Maya refreshed the CNN webpage once more for luck.

The siege was finally coming to an end.

'Thank you, God!' she cried out, leaning back in her chair and raising her arms to the ceiling in supplication.

'I can't for the life of me imagine what you are quite so worked up about, Maya,' said Leila. 'If you eat that Jaffa Cake, it might stop you eating your hair!'

Maya crammed it into her mouth just as her phone rang.

Maya pressed it to her ear. 'Hello! Sue?' she chewed and swallowed as fast as she could.

'Yes. What happened?'

Maya stood up and left the room. She'd take the call outside on the terrace.

'Thank God!'

'That's a bit over-dramatic, isn't it?'

'You're okay.'

'Why wouldn't I be?'

'It's over, I hear. When are you getting home?' Maya leaned against the balustrade looking out over the sea. It had never looked so beautiful. 'I mean, are you all right? Safe, you know?'

'I am home.'

'What!' Maya was screaming now. The stress of the last few days had made her over-emotional and she knew it. 'How?'

Sue was as calm as Maya was agitated, as she explained how she'd driven for 'bleeding hours' to get a flight out of Chiang Mai and had been stuck in 'cattle class' in some 'poxy airline' with a million 'sodding changes' in the middle of the night. But she was home.

'So?' The suspense was killing Maya. She couldn't mess around with small talk. She wanted her news.

'I went to the factory. You know, the blighters wanted to screw me for more cash. Well, I wasn't having any of that, I can tell you. Didn't take long for them to realise I wasn't a pushover. Ended up paying less than I did before, tee hee.'

'Great,' said Maya flatly, wishing Sue'd cut to the chase.

'It took me a while and a few bribes to get what I wanted. So, I was almost out of time by the time I got to the Cowboy.'

'Fantastic. So, you went to the Lucky Cowboy, what happened?'

'Before I arrived I'd phoned security to get them to dig out the tape for 21st October. And of course, I went round to look at it when things were quiet. First thing in the morning.'

'And?' Maya dug her nails into her palms.

'Sure enough, I found the part of the tape where Rich, you know, er…'

'He met Orchid.' Maybe if Maya finished her sentences for her, they would get to the denouement more quickly.

'She's not called Orchid, of course, surprise surprise, they usually do take on a stage name. Don't blame her. Her real name is Somporn.'

'So then what happened?' Maya's mouth was dry.

'I bribed the security guard to let me sit in his office that evening and watch Somporn aka Orchid come in. And then I made a call to one of my old mates and bingo, before you could say knife I was having a friendly chat with her over a cup of tea and promising I'd get her sister a job in Dubai if she could quit bugging Rich, pretend he'd disappeared off the face of the earth. She said she'd probably get a beating for it, so I offered her some money, some of your money, paid directly into her bank account and she agreed. Her sister is a trained beautician and massage therapist and sick of all her clients expecting a happy ending. So, I think you could say "job done".'

Maya burst into tears. 'Thank you, Sue, thank you so much. Is there anything I can do for you? To thank you?'

'My pleasure,' said Sue. 'Your job is to help Amani get a job with a visa! And to find me a thousand dollars to pay Somporn off with.'

Maya gulped. 'Fine.' They'd find the money for sure, but surely she could not ask Hatim for another favour?

'All you have to do is persuade Leila she'd be perfect for that spare room at the Centre. Not that I have any idea how you justify hiring both Liv and Amani, that's Somporn's sister's name, by the way. But that's your problem.'

'Sure. I'm sure I'll find a way.' Maya was bound to come up with a solution. She always did. 'So, can I get back to my family now?' Sue chuckled.

'Er, did you, er, find out if they did actually do it?' To Maya that would be the last piece of the puzzle.

'Oh I very much doubt it. And anyway, Somporn assured me she always uses a condom, so you are safe as houses.'

'You're sure?'

'Sure as eggs is eggs.'

Before she went back into the office she had one more call to make. To Rich.

Chapter thirty-five

'Right everybody. I need you behind the stalls, I think,' said the photographer from the Gulf News. Maya, Leila, Elske, Barb, LaShell, Liv, and Suchanatta stood behind their stands in the *majlis* room displaying their burgeoning tables, just before the gates were to open and allow in the public.

'I need the little girl at the front please,' said the photographer. 'I can't see her.'

'Go on, Liv, he means you!' said Elske.

'I wish they thought I was a girl!' laughed Barb, who looked pretty fabulous today in a frilly and floaty red chiffon dress. Liv moved to the front and held out her arms, leaning them back against the table.

'Now, everyone smile and say *Insha'Allah!*' said the photographer.

Everyone grinned and called '*Insha'Allah*', hoping that, indeed, God was willing to make their own private dream come true. 'Good. One more time.' He flipped the ends of his red and white headdress back over his shoulders.

'It'll be a lovely reminder of us all, won't it? Now Liv is going and you too, Barb,' said Maya. 'Can we all get copies?' she asked the photographer.

'Of course,' he said.

'The end of an era,' said LaShell. 'You sure will leave a big hole here when you're gone, Barb.' She put her arm around Barb's waist.

'Oh, get outta here!' laughed Barb, but her voice sounded decidedly wobbly. 'I'll only be a coupla hours down the road. Oman is as good as next door. You won't get rid of me that easy. Besides, I'll need to keep a check on my Twist, wont I?'

'Oman is a beautiful place. You'll have a ball,' said Suchanatta.

'People make the place, Sue, people make the place. And here in Dubai I have met some of the very best.' She cleared her throat and pushed back her shoulders. 'Say, Liv will leave a big hole in our hearts too.' Barb reached out to grasp Liv's hand and it was swallowed up whole by Barb's larger, pudgier one.

'Liv, where are you going? Have you decided?' asked Elske.

Liv turned to look at her friends. 'Wherever I may go, I will still be here with you somehow. My energy will stay here and my good wishes.'

'Answer the sodding question!' joked Suchanatta. 'Don't leave me in suspenders.'

'Suspenders?' queried Elske. 'I don't think I know that one.'

'Suspense,' explained Leila.

'Shall I tell them?' asked Liv, 'Or will you?' She looked at Maya.

'She's going to England. It made sense. Now that we've lost Danuta, who worked in my shop, we need more help. And as you know, our house is empty, so Liv will stay in our house until we find tenants. She'll keep it warm and lived in. Well, as lived-in as you can be with no furniture!'

'That's no problem. I will have all I need, *ja.*'

'And Avril, you know, I've told you about Avril, is delighted to know that bellydance classes are coming to Stamford. And Jan, that's my other partner, says she can move in with her as soon as we get new tenants, as long as she does some babysitting and gives Jan free massages. I'm thrilled for her. For them all.' Maya put her arm around Liv and hugged her. 'Everything is falling into place. I can't believe it.'

'It is such a shame that you won't be able to take advantage of the beautiful room here, Liv. It would have been perfect for your massages,' said Leila.

'Yes, it's a shame, but I understand from Maya that she has ideas for a super oriental new occupant, right?'

'Really?' said Barb. 'Do I know her?'

'A friend of Rich's.' Maya smirked and winked at Suchanatta. It was fun to leave Barb in the dark sometimes.

Elske looked at her watch. 'I guess we should get moving, girls, they will be here in a moment.'

No one moved; they were still enjoying the feel-good moment.

'Well, isn't that marvellous,' said Leila. It's like everything you touch turns to gold beneath your little fingers.' And Leila put her arm round Maya and squeezed her tight. 'And boy oh boy am I glad you came into my life, Maya. I can't tell you how pleased, really I can't.'

'Well, save your thanks for when we count the money up later, okay? You never know, maybe nobody'll come.'

'What rubbish you talk, Maya Winter. They'll be thronging in, so they will!'

And they did.

Later, the embers of Matt and Sacha's barbecue glowed red against the darkness and the last saucepan of Sunshine Soup was empty. The sun was long gone and a sliver of moon now hung halfway up the sky. Lanterns had been lit with candles and only a handful of guests remained. Bill and Brandon had never arrived but Barb was still there somewhere, making herself useful. Taking her mind off things most probably. Despite what she said, this move to Muscat seemed to have knocked her for six. After so many relocations, you'd have thought it would have been water off a duck's back but this time she seemed softer and fluffier about things. Oli and Chantal had gone for a walk along the beach, drifting out of sight hand in hand in the direction of the Burj al Arab hotel. Matt sat alone at Maya's desk in the office playing with his Nintendo DS. Ali and Leila, with Mohammed on Leila's shoulders and Yasmin on Ali's, stood at the shore, scuffing up the phosphorescence with their bare feet. Rich and Maya, side by side, their arms wrapped round each other's waists, leaned against the balustrade.

'Look,' said Rich, reaching into his trouser pocket.

'New trousers?' she laughed.

'Nope, better than that!' He pulled out two miniature bottles of vodka. 'The Punch with a Punch is all very well, but this will improve things mightily!'

Maya leaned into her husband while he tipped the vodka into their glasses. 'Being an airline pilot has its perks!'

'Plenty more in the car. Guess we had better get a taxi home tonight?' He planted a noisy kiss on her cheek.

'Look!' She pointed at the crescent moon that seemed to smile at them as it hung in the deep black sky, strung between two stars. She placed her arm round his waist and hooked her index finger inside the waistband of his trousers.

Rich inched her closer. 'You are my sun, moon and stars, Maya,' he said.

'Pardon?' she was unsure whether to believe her ears.

'I do listen you know. I know that Mick used to say that to you and that you wished I was better at the romantic patter.'

'I don't need you to be romantic,' she said snuggling into him. 'I just need you to be back to normal.'

They looked down the terrace to the cushioned bench where Sue and Jim sat drinking coffee before heading off to the airport to collect their girls. It was hard to believe it was the Christmas holidays already.

'Lying to you was absolute agony.'

Maya nodded and bit her bottom lip, leaned back against the balustrade and reached up and touched her husband's cheeks with both her open palms. Now it was her turn to find the right words. 'I do love you, you know. More than anything. Anyone.'

Rich held her close and they stood in easy silence, each lost in their own thoughts. Maya's attention was attracted to the French doors that led onto the terrace. A breeze lifted the muslin curtains away from the window. Something flashed. A watch face in the moonlight, perhaps? Inside, in the *majlis* room, she could just about make out the bright white of the back of a crisp *dishdasha* against the dark, like a white shirt under disco lights. If Ali was on the beach, then this had to be Hatim. Judging by the sight of a red court shoe standing beside his sandaled foot, he was not alone. The breeze dropped the curtains back into place and the scene disappeared.

'Look,' whispered Maya, turning Rich around to face the window. 'Can you see what I see?' With the next flurry of soft wind, the curtains moved aside once more and for a split second they could see two arms around Hatim's waist – one wearing a Rolex, the other two plain gold bangles.

'Is that… ?' asked Rich, his voice cracking with disbelief.

'Yes, I think it is,' she whispered with a smile.

'Could you have perhaps fixed one thing too many?' asked Rich.

'If anyone deserves real happiness it's Barb. She thought no one could see her pain. But she was wrong.'

Rich took Maya's hand and walked down the steps to the sand.

'I can tell you what's right though,' he said.

'What?'

'You and me here. That's what's right. Look at this place. How could we not be happy with all this beauty on our doorstep? This could have been your best idea yet! I love you Maya Winter.'

SEASONS
IN THE SUN

TWENTY RECIPES

FROM THE KITCHEN OF MAYA WINTER

Contents

Sunshine soup

Serves six to eight

Maya makes this in Chapter 30 for the fundraiser.

Ingredients

1 large red onion, chopped
500g carrots, chopped
1–2 green chillis – halved and seeded (to taste)
2 yellow peppers, halved and seeded
500g tomatoes (yellowish is preferable), chopped
1 green pepper, halved and seeded
2 tblsp olive oil
1 handful of sunflower petals if available, otherwise decorate with chopped herbs such as coriander or tarragon
Salt and pepper
1.5 litres of water
1 dessertspoon of single cream per serving

Preheat oven to 180°C

Method

1. Place the peppers, chilli and tomatoes on a baking tray and toss in one tablespoon of the oil.

2. Roast for 45 mins.

3. *Meanwhile fry the onion in the remaining oil until translucent.*

4. *Add the carrots and stir for a few seconds before adding the water and bringing to the boil.*

5. *Add salt and pepper to taste and simmer for about 20 minutes until soft.*

6. *Add the roasted vegetables to the boiled vegetables and blitz in a liquidizer or hold a handheld soup maker in the saucepan and whizz until smooth.*

7. *Scatter the petals or chopped herbs on the surface just before serving and a spiral of single cream.*

Tabbouleh

Maya makes this in Chapter Six after her first trip to the market. It is the first time she dares to claw back control in her kitchen.

Ingredients

50g bulgur, fine cracked wheat (use medium if you cannot find fine grade bulgur in which case you will need 2 tblsp hot water and a microwave too)
Juice of 1 large lemon (you will need about 100ml)
Large bunch (approx 150g) fresh flat-leaved parsley (stalks removed, washed, dried and finely chopped)
3 sprigs fresh mint, finely sliced (stalks removed)
1 large red tomato, diced
2 spring onions, thinly sliced (with green stems)
1 baby cucumber (about 50g) finely chopped.
3 tblsp extra virgin olive oil
Salt (to taste)
Romaine leaves and chicory leaves, for serving

Method

1. *Place the bulgur in a bowl with the juice of the lemon and leave it to swell. If, by the time you have made the rest of the salad the bulgur is still hard, then add 2 tblsp hot water from the kettle and microwave on full for one minute. That should do it. If not, then add a little more hot water and wait!*

2. *Mix the parsley, mint, tomato, onion, cucumber and oil in a serving bowl.*

3. *Add the softened bulgur with the juice.*

4. *Mix and season to taste.*

Serve with the romaine lettuce and chicory leaves so that you can take a lovely scoop of tabbouleh in a leaf.

Hot pink dip

Serves six to ten as a dip

Barb asks Merry to make this on Liv's instructions for her Goddess Evening (Chapter Twelve). Maya recreates it for the Spice up Your Life blog, found by Mick and then Mick attempts to reproduce it for his seduction dinner in the hotel room.

Ingredients

1 red chilli, deseeded and roughly chopped
1 large garlic clove, peeled and roughly chopped
Salt
100ml plain yoghurt
1 small very red tomato, chopped
100ml mayonnaise

Method

1. *Place chilli, garlic, tomato and one tablespoon of the yoghurt in the blender and whizz til smooth.*

2. *Fold in the rest.*

3. *Add salt to taste.*

Maya likes to serve this with fresh, fat, cooked prawns (Barb calls them shrimp), but you can enjoy this dip with anything dippable.

Anchovy and lemon dip

Serves six to ten as a dip, particularly delicious with asparagus

Barb asks Merry to make this on Liv's instructions for her Goddess Evening (Chapter Twelve). Maya recreates it for the Spice up Your Life blog, found by Mick and then Mick attempts to reproduce it for his seduction dinner in the hotel room but the hotel can only provide tartar sauce.

Ingredients

100ml thick, plain yoghurt, such as Greek or labneh
1x 50g can flat anchovy fillets in oil, rinsed, drained and very finely chopped
2 garlic cloves, finely chopped
2 tblsp mayonnaise
1 to 2 tblsp fresh lemon juice
Pepper

Method

1. *Mix the anchovies, garlic and plain yoghurt in a bowl.*

2. *Fold in the mayonnaise.*

3. *Add the lemon juice to taste.*

4. *Season with pepper to taste.*

Broad bean and mint dip

Serves six to ten as a dip

Barb asks Merry to make this on Liv's instructions for her Goddess Evening (Chapter Twelve). Maya later adds this to the blog.

Ingredients

500g fresh broad beans (shelled) or 100g shelled broad beans (you can also use edamame, the green soya beans)
Juice of ½ a lemon
12 large leaves of fresh mint
Salt
Pepper
1 large clove garlic, crushed

Method

1. *Whizz all the above ingredients together in the blender. Adjust the seasoning and add more lemon or mint to taste.*

Barb serves this with slices of fresh red pepper, carrot and celery, though Liv suggested dipping hot spicy sausages into this delicious dip. Maya has discovered this goes really well with slices of cold cured sausage too, such as chorizo or with skinny, spicy French sausages called merguez.

If you remove the pale outer skins from the broad beans then this dip is even greener and fresher.

Squash Goulash

Serves four to six

This is Maya's recipe but Jan makes this to sell in Seasons. This is the last meal Maya and Rich share before they leave Stamford for Dubai in Chapter One.

Ingredients

Goulash
2 tblsp olive oil
3 large shallots, chopped
2 cloves garlic, minced
1 tblsp paprika
1.5 tsp cumin
2cm piece fresh ginger, grated
1 large tin tomatoes, chopped
1 glass red wine
1 glass water
200g French beans, chopped into 2cm lengths
1 red pepper, deseeded and sliced into nice long lengths
1 large (400g) tin aduki beans, drained
1 jalapeno pepper, diced small
1kg butternut squash, cubed
Salt

Minted yoghurt
100ml Greek or sheep's yoghurt
2 tblsp fresh mint
Salt, pepper and a pinch of sugar

Preheat over to 200°C/400°F

Method

1. Roast the butternut squash in 1 tbsp olive oil in a preheated oven 200° for 40 mins.

2. Fry the onion in the send tbsp oil until translucent.

3. Add the garlic and ginger and stir for approximately 1 minute.

4. Add the cumin and paprika. Stir.

5. Add the tomatoes. Stir and bring to a simmer.

6. Add half of the wine and the water and a twist or three of salt.

7. Add the pepper and French beans and simmer for about 10 minutes.

8. Add the squash, the jalapeno and the aduki beans and simmer for another 10 minutes

9. Stir in the remaining wine and serve with minted yoghurt and brown rice.

Tuna steaks with chilli and lime

Serves four

The dish Maya makes to welcome Rich home, that becomes the day she receives that terrible stamp in her passport in Chapter Eight.

Ingredients

4 tuna steaks (salmon can also be used)

Marinade

Juice and rind of two limes
2 tblsp olive oil
1 tblsp soy sauce
Thumb sized piece of fresh ginger, peeled and chopped
1 fresh red chilli, seeded and chopped
1 clove garlic, peeled and chopped
Salt and pepper

Method

1. Place the chilli, ginger, garlic and oil into a blender and whizz until you have a smoothish sauce. Add the lime juice and rind, salt and pepper.

2. Place the sauce into a baking dish big enough for the fish to lie side by side in.

3. Add the fish and turn it over to coat it on both sides.

4. Leave for at least two hours.

5. Remove the fish from the dish and barbecue or griddle to taste.

6. Serve with salad or green beans and new potatoes.

Lamb and mint burgers

Serves four

A version of this recipe also appears in the second edition of Dates. Maya makes this in Chapter Fourteen on the day when Barb, Bill and Brandon come over for dinner.

Ingredients

500g minced lamb
2 shallots (chopped)
1 level teaspoonful of salt
Freshly ground black pepper
1 clove garlic (finely chopped)
1 heaped tblsp fresh mint (chopped) or 2 tsp mint sauce
Plain flour for coating

To serve

2 rounded tblsp Greek yoghurt or labneh
2 tblsp mint sauce
1 clove garlic (crushed)

Method

1. Place the mince into a bowl and sprinkle over the salt. Knead and mix with your hand until the mince becomes slightly sticky to the touch and the colour is slightly paler.

2. Add the remaining ingredients and mix in thoroughly, kneading the mix.

3. Divide mixture into eight. Roll each section into a ball, and then roll each in the flour to coat. Now firmly press each ball between you hands to flatten a little into a burger shape.

4. Fry, grill or barbeque the lamb burgers until no pink is left in the centre.

5. Serve with salad (include some red capsicum and perhaps some pine nuts and sunflower seeds) in a pocket of Arabic bread or brown pitta bread.

6. Mix the yoghurt, garlic and mint sauce to make a dressing that can be served with the burgers or on the side.

Spinach quiche

Serves four to six

Maya serves this to Rich with her homemade date chutney on the day that she learns Mick has booked his flight and Rich is in a filthy mood in Chapter Twenty-two. This recipe first appeared in *French Tarts*.

Ingredients

Pastry
200g plain flour
salt
100g butter
3 tblsp cold water

Filling
750g cooked spinach, chopped
1 small onion, chopped
Grated nutmeg to taste
1 tsp lemon juice
100g cream cheese
2 eggs, beaten
3 tblsp milk
Freshly ground black pepper
50g Cheddar cheese grated

Preheat oven to 200°C/400°F

Method

1. To make the pastry, sift the flour and a pinch of salt into a bowl. Dice the butter into the flour and rub in (cut in) and mix to a dough with the water. Roll out the dough on a floured surface and line a buttered 22cm/8½ inch flan dish or tart pan. Prick the base lightly with a fork and bake blind in the oven until the pastry has begun to form a slight crust.

2. To make the filling, mix the well-drained spinach in with the onion, a pinch of nutmeg and the lemon juice. Spread evenly in the pastry case.

3. Beat together the cream cheese, eggs, milk, salt and pepper and pour over the spinach. Sprinkle with the grated cheese.

4. Bakethe tart for 30 minutes, then reduce the heat to 180°C/350°F and continue to cook for a further 10 minutes.

5. Serve warm as a starter or with salad and potatoes perhaps as a main course. Don't forget the chutney!

Butter chicken

Serves four

This recipe was given to Jo in Dubai, by her wonderful Indian housemaid, Julie. Here Annie cooks this for customers of her take away service and sometimes leaves it in the oven waiting for Maya, Rich, Oliver and Matthew when they come home from a day out as Matthew comments in Chapter Twenty-five.

Ingredients

1 tsp coriander powder
½ tsp chilli powder
½ tsp turmeric
½ tsp cumin powder
2 tbsp yoghurt
½ tsp salt
1 pinch tandoori colour
2 medium white onions, sliced
1 tsp minced fresh ginger
1 tsp minced fresh garlic
1 chicken
50g cashew nuts
200g fresh tomatoes
50g butter

Preheat oven to 200ºC / 400ºF

Method

1. Make a marinade of the first seven ingredients.

2. Cut the chicken into pieces and coat with marinade.

3. Fry the onions in the butter until golden.

4. Liquidise the tomatoes with the cashew nuts then add to the pan of onions.

5. Simmer until the fat rises.

6. Add the chicken and its marinade, bring to the boil and simmer for 15 minutes.

7. Put into an ovenproof dish and cook, covered, for 30 minutes.

8. Serve with rice, chapattis, raita and dahl.

Maya loves to cook with cast iron cookware so she can use one pan to fry the onions, then cook the chicken and tomatoes and then place straight into the oven.

Julie's raita is made with 500ml plain yoghurt, 1 small spring onion, half a tomato, an inch of cucumber (all chopped) and mixed with 1 tablespoon of fresh coriander, a big pinch of salt and 1 teaspoon of sugar.

Date chutney

Makes about 1.5kg/3 jars

Annie does most of the chopping for this recipe that is used to raise funds for The Sunshine Centre. Maya makes this first in chapter Twenty-two. This recipe also appears in *Dates*.

Ingredients

350g fresh or dried dates (stoned)
350g cooking apples (peeled, cored and diced)
1 medium onion (peeled and finely chopped)
350g raisins
2 tsp salt
2 tsp garam masala
1 garlic clove, peeled and crushed
250g molasses, molasses sugar or date syrup
450ml malt vinegar

Method

1. Place all ingredients into a large pan and bring to the boil, stirring occasionally.

2. Reduce the heat and simmer for two to three hours until the mixture is thick, yet still moist.

3. Let the chutney cool, meanwhile sterilise three jam jars by placing them in the oven for about 10 minutes.

4. Place the chutney into the jars and seal.

5. Serve with cheese or cold meats. Rich loves to eat chutney with quiche. Maya prefers nut cutlets.

Note! You can easily double or triple the quantities for this recipe.

Dutch buttercake

Makes sixteen

Maya makes this for Elske's barbecue in Chapter Twenty-five because Nico appreciates traditional Dutch home cooking and Elske is too busy to cook.

Ingredients

140g plain flour
125g butter
125g caster sugar
Pinch of salt
Half a beaten egg

Preheat the oven to 200ºC/ 400ºF

Method

1. *Put the flour, butter, sugar and salt into a bowl. Cut the butter into the flour using two knives until the mixture resembles chunky breadcrumbs.*

2. *Quickly shape the mixture into a ball with a hand.*

3. *Press the mixture into a round or square cake tin that is about 9"/ 22cm across.*

4. *Brush with the beaten egg.*

5. *Cook for about 15 minutes.*

6. *Let it cool in the tin before slicing into sixteen pieces (or fewer if you have hungry guests).*

Maya prefers to cook this in a round tin and then slice into about 12 triangles.

Flapjack

Makes sixteen

Maya makes this in Chapter Fourteen on the day Barb comes round and watches her cook, while still wearing her sunglasses inside. In Chapter Thirty-two the recipe is added to the blog.

Ingredients

125g brown sugar
1 tblsp Golden Syrup, honey or date syrup
125g butter or margarine
150g porridge oats
100g self-raising flour

Preheat oven to 200°C/ 400°F/gas mark 6

Method

1. Melt the butter, syrup and sugar in a saucepan over a medium heat.

2. Remove from heat and stir in the oats and flour. Mix well.

3. Press into a square cake or slice tin of approximately 9"/22cm diameter and level the top with the back of a metal spoon.

4. Cook for 15 minutes.

5. Mark into squares while still hot.

6. Cool and store in an airtight tin.

Maya loves flapjack. She sometimes adds some sesame seeds or pumpkin seeds to the mix.

Polenta cake with rosewater and pistachios

Serves eight to ten

Maya makes this in Chapter Eleven on the day she buys Avril
a pink bellydance outfit.

Ingredients

200g butter
200g caster sugar
200g ground almonds
3 eggs
Zest of two lemons
Juice of one lemon
2 tsp rosewater
100g chopped pistachio nuts
100g polenta
1 tsp baking powder
Pinch salt

Preheat oven to 160°C/320°F

Method

1. Beat sugar and butter together in a large mixing bowl using an electric beater or a wooden spoon.

2. Stir in almonds and rosewater.

3. Beat in the eggs one at a time.

4. Fold in all remaining ingredients.

5. Grease and line an 8" / 20cm round cake tin.

6. Bake for 35 minutes or until golden.

7. Allow to cool before removing from tin.

8. Delicious served with a dried or fresh fruit purée.

Maya's favourite is apricot. To make this, she soaks unsweetened and colour free apricots in orange juice and then whizzes them up in the blender.

Apricot and date slice

Maya first tastes this at The Orange Tree then makes her own version for Elske's barbecue in Chapter Twenty-five.

 With many grateful thanks to Quirky Lunchroom, Tasmanstraat, The Hague, for the inspiration _www.cafequirky.com_

Ingredients

500g seedless dates, chopped
100g apricots, chopped
500ml water
1 small sachet of baking powder or 1 dessertspoon of baking powder
175g butter
150g dark brown sugar (they call it bastard in Holland ☺)
2 eggs
125g flour
60g self-raising flour

Pre heat the oven at 180ºC

Method

1. Line an A4 baking tin (the size of a piece of printer paper or equivalent) with greaseproof paper.

2. Boil the water then add dates and apricots and simmer for approx. 15 minutes.

3. Beat butter and sugar until it is light and fluffy (can also be done in a kitchen mixer).

4. Add eggs and mix well.

5. Once the dates/apricots have simmered for 15 minutes, take off the fire and add baking powder, stir thoroughly.

6. In a large bowl pour the butter/sugar/egg mix and then add gradually the date/apricot mix and sieve the two flours through and mix it all gradually until all are in one big bowl.

7. Then press into baking tin and cook for 55 minutes.

Date and Walnut Ice Cream with Hot Chocolate Sauce

Serves six to eight

This recipe also appears in *Dates*. Maya serves it with hot chocolate sauce at her dinner party, attended by the reluctant Schneider family in Chapter Fifteen. She makes it in Chapter Fourteen.

Ingredients – ice cream

210g dates (stoned and halved)
150ml water
450ml single cream
3 egg yolks
60g caster sugar
150ml double or whipping cream
60g walnuts (chopped)

Ingredients – chocolate sauce

200g sugar
4 tblsp cocoa
75g butter
¼ tsp salt
100ml water
1 tsp vanilla extract

To make the ice cream:

Method

1. Soak the dates in the water for four hours. Cook in a saucepan over a medium heat until soft (this takes about five minutes).

2. Purée the dates until smooth, or rub them through a sieve. Leave to cool.

3. Meanwhile, heat the single cream in a saucepan to simmering point.

4. Beat the egg yolks and sugar together in a large mixing bowl until pale.

5. Gradually pour the hot cream onto the mixture, stirring all the time. Return the mixture to the saucepan and stir over a gentle heat until the custard will coat the back of a wooden spoon. Do not boil. Cool.

6. Stir the date purée into the custard and add the orange rind.

7. Toast the walnuts briefly under the grill. Cool and stir into the custard mixture.

8. Beat the double or whipping cream until it forms soft peaks, then fold into the date mixture.

9. Pour into a freezer container and freeze. Beat the mixture twice, at hourly intervals, returning to the freezer each time. Alternatively freeze in an ice cream maker.

10. Cover, seal and freeze until required.

To make the sauce:

Method

1. Combine sugar, cocoa and salt in a small saucepan.

2. Add enough water to make a stirrable consistency. Add more water if you want a runnier sauce.

3. Add butter to pan.

4. Allow the butter to melt then bring to the boil and boil for one minute.

5. Remove from the heat and add the vanilla.

6. Poor into a jug and serve with ice cream, banana splits or even with brownies and cream!

Arabic coffee ice cream

Serves six to eight (it is very rich and you only need one large or two small scoops)

Maya decides to make this in Chapter Eleven on the day she buys Avril's bellydance outfit.

Ingredients

100g coffee beans (use decaffeinated if you want to serve this at a dinner party and also get to sleep!)
4 egg yolks
20 cardamom pods
100g caster sugar
200ml single cream
200ml milk (full or half fat)

Method

1. *Either put the coffee beans and cardamom pods in a plastic bag and beat them to submission with a rolling pin, or, whizz them up in a coffee grinder until they are chopped but chunky.*

2. *Place the coffee, cardamom, milk and cream in a saucepan and bring slowly to the moment when it is shuddering nicely. Remove from heat, cover, and leave to infuse for one hour.*

3. *Strain the coffee, cardamom mixture through a sieve into a bowl.*

4. *Whisk the egg yolks and sugar together in a large bowl until pale and thick.*

5. *Rinse the saucepan so you can reuse it. Return the infused milk and cream to the saucepan and bring back to shuddering point.*

6. *Pour the hot milk and cream onto the egg and sugar mix and stir well.*

7. *Return to the saucepan and bring to the boil slowly, stirring all the time until it has thickened to the consistency of a thinnish custard.*

8. *Remove from the heat and cool completely.*

9. *Pour into a freezer container or icecream maker and freeze.*

10. *If you are doing this old-fashioned way (without an ice cream maker) you will need to remove this from the freezer every couple of hours (about three times is enough) and beat it to remove the crystals then return to the freezer. Maya finds this part of the process a bit boring, so she just beats it with a fork inside the container.*

If you want to be really decadent serve this with Tia Maria and cream. For a bit of fun, why not serve it in a coffee cup?

Punch with a punch

Serves lots, but it depends on the size of your glasses

Leila serves this as the celebration drink at her home in Chapter Eighteen and at The Sunshine Centre in Chapter Thirty-five.

Ingredients

2 litres orange juice
1½ litres lemonade, 7-Up or Sprite
1 litre ginger beer
Sliced fruit to decorate. Star fruit, kiwi and strawberries look best

Method

1. *Just mix!*

Mango and passionfruit smoothie

Serves two

Barb thinks this is Maya's favourite smoothie, but Maya likes to ring the changes so she makes it with mango or pineapple too, both of which are easier to obtain than papaya and passionfruit. She has a smoothie at The Orange Tree in Chapters Ten and Nineteen.

Ingredients

3 or 4 dried dates (stone removed)
Flesh of two passionfruit
Flesh of one mango
2 tblsp yoghurt
150ml milk or soya milk or equivalent
150ml orange juice

Method

1. Soak the dates in the orange juice for at least one hour or overnight.

2. Blend all the ingredients together and serve immediately.

Sunshine preserve

Makes about four jars of preserve

Maya has the idea for this in Chapter Seventeen and it is sold at the fundraiser in Chapter Thirty-five.

Ingredients

4 large oranges
2 medium lemons
3 limes
1¼ litres water
1½ kilos sugar (approx)

Method

1. *Cut the unpeeled fruit in half and then into thin slices. Remove the pips and tie them in a muslin bag or an old pop sock.*

2. *Combine the fruit, muslin bag of pips and the water in a large bowl and leave to stand overnight.*

3. *Transfer the mixture to a large saucepan, bring to the boil and then simmer, covered, for about an hour or until the rind is soft. Remove the bag.*

4. *Measure the fruit mixture, return to the pan and add 3 parts sugar to every 4 parts fruit mixture.*

5. Stir with a wooden spoon over a medium heat without boiling until the sugar is dissolved.

6. Bring to the boil and boil uncovered this time, without stirring for about 40 minutes or until the marmalade jells when tested.

7. Testing: First put a china saucer in the freezer. You are going to need this to test when the marmalade is ready. Test by dipping a wooden spoon into the mixture, holding the spoon above the mixture and tilting the bowl of the spoon towards you. As the mixture thickens the drops will fall more heavily from the spoon. When it is ready two or three drops will roll down the spoon together and form a heavy mass. Now, drop a teaspoon of mixture onto your frozen saucer and replace in the freezer for a few minutes. The marmalade is ready and need no longer boil if the surface wrinkles when pushed with your finger.

8. Leave the marmalade to stand in the pan for ten minutes before pouring into hot sterilised jars; seal when cold.

About the author

Jo Parfitt has been a professional writer for over 25 years and has published 27 books on subjects ranging from computers, to careers and cookery. Living overseas in France, Dubai, Oman, Norway and now the Netherlands, she was born and raised in the stone town of Stamford in Lincolnshire. Jo's first foray into publishing came when she was in her twenties and her cookbook, *French Tarts*, was accepted by the first publisher she approached. In 1995, while in Oman, she co-authored a second cookbook, with Sue Valentine, called *Dates*. A writer, writing teacher, journalist and publishing consultant, Jo specialises in helping others to achieve their writing dreams. She has run Summertime Publishing since 1997 and has lived in The Hague since 2005 with her husband and a nest recently emptied of two wonderful sons.

Extra Material for Reading Groups

1.   The book is set in Dubai. To what extent do you think the setting affects the story? Could it happen anywhere?

2.   The book has three points of view, Maya's, Barb's and Rich's. How would it affect the story if the whole book were told through Maya's point of view only?

3.   Identity and personal fulfilment are major themes in the book. To what extent does the place in which you are living, the person to whom you are married and the work you do affect your identity and self-worth?

4.   Over the course of the book Barb and Maya's roles reverse. To what do you attribute this and what would you identify as their turning points?

5.   Seven nationalities feature in this book: British, Irish, Emirati, Dutch, Norwegian, American and Thai. To what extent is each nationality stereotyped and how is this either achieved or avoided?

6.   Choose a character from the novel and discuss what might happen to him or her were they to be given a book of their own.

7.   How would you describe the author's style? Is there a difference between the style employed for Maya and Barb? If so, identify the differences and comment on why the author has chosen to write in this way.

8.   In the plot involving Rich's odd behaviour and its eventual conclusion, what devices does the author use to build and maintain suspense?

9.   How important is food to the story? Could the same plot have been achieved if cooking were exchanged, say, for another career, passion or hobby?

10.   The author has strong opinions about the effect of living abroad on the people who live that life. What do you think those opinions are? How does she show them and state whether you agree or disagree and why.

11.   Maya and Barb both potentially have extra-marital affairs in the novel. How would it have changed the story if the affairs had been more serious and explicit?

12.   Several housemaids feature in the novel to greater and lesser extents. What do their stories contribute to the characters with whom they interact?

Also Published by summertimepublishing

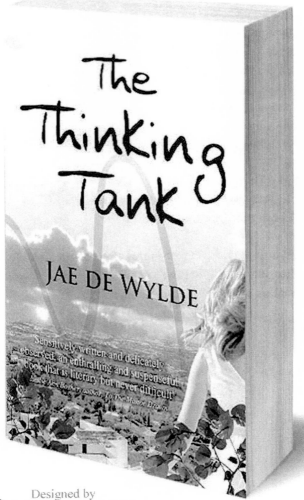

The
Thinking
Tank

JAE DE WYLDE

Sensitively written and delicately observed, an enthralling and suspenseful book that is literary but never difficult

Designed by

CREATIONBOOTH
DOT COM

Anne O'Connell

@home
in
Dubai

GETTING CONNECTED
ONLINE AND ON THE GROUND

Discover what the bedouin have always known about the fruit that symbolises Arabia like no other. Full of energy-giving fruit sugars and fibre, the humble date has been a life source for the people of the Arab world for millennia.

Dates is packed with traditional Middle Eastern flavour along with some quirky, modern twists. With mouth-watering recipes such as Lamb Burgers and Date and Nut Cutlets, and delicious desserts such as Date and Lime Cheesecake, this unique cookery book has something for everyone.

Get cooking! Make a date with your dates today.

CPSIA information can be obtained at www.ICGtesting.com
Printed in the USA
LVOW071640301011

252726LV00003B/1/P